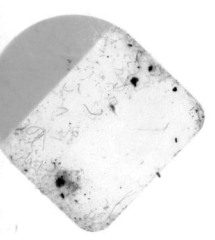

APARTHEID, **SOUTH AFRICA**.

In the spring of 1976 matters of the heart are strictly controlled by racist doctrines. In that toxic mix of segregation and tribal mistrust, an unlikely union between a black man from Malawi and a white woman—an Afrikaner—shocks the nation. All sides across the color divide are represented in the inter-racial couple's painful journey in an unaccepting world. Harried by the brutal Security Branch, the inhumane enforcement apparatus of the intolerant regime, the lovers desperately fight to remain to-gether—as the nation wages a deadly struggle for freedom...and eventual redemption.

≈

THE ZEBRA AFFAIRE

THE ZEBRA AFFAIRE

MARK FINE

A PASSION ▽ PREJUDICE NOVEL

Copyright © 2014 by Mark Fine
Cover design by M.J. Fine
Cover Photograph: Courting Zebras by William Warby
        http://www.flickr.com/photos/wwarby/2405490902/[Cropped image. Replaced background with night sky. Added text and iconography.] This file is licensed under the Creative Commons Attribution 2.0 Generic license.

Library of Congress Catalog Card Number: 2013923461

ISBN-10: 1494762609
ISBN-13: 978-1494762605

CreateSpace Independent Publishing Platform, North Charleston, SC

This book is dedicated to all the members

of my Fine family tribe: everyone, everywhere.

Especially my sons Nico & Derek—you are my proudest legacy.

And to the ILLOVO BOOK CLUB where as a child

I learned to cherish the written word.

≈

ABOUT THE **AUTHOR**

Mark Fine was born in Johannesburg, South Africa. He has made the United States his home since 1978, living in New York, Minneapolis, and Los Angeles. Now he resides in the South Bay, where he lives with his two sons and a neighborhood dog that drops in from time to time.

For a decade Mark headed an award-winning record label that united non-profit organizations with world-class celebrity and music talent to create benefit albums and entertainment events in aid of breast cancer awareness, at-risk children, the blind, freedom of speech, and wildlife conservation. He has also contributed articles to entertainment industry publications, and conducted public speaking engagements at multimedia trade events.

Visit the author's website at
www.finewrites.blogspot.com

≈

NOTA **BENE**

I confess footnotes frustrate me. And I sense they may exasperate others as well. The need to wedge a tidbit of information (when clearly the topic requires deeper analysis) in a sliver of space at a bottom of the page—set in a miniscule font type that's difficult to read—does not make for a satisfying experience.

But, I understand the need not to intrude on the core narrative with scintillating detours and insightful asides; so a remedy was needed. In this book I've implemented a device based purely on personal preference. These tangents are clearly identified with the symbol **, before and after, the margins are wider, and the paragraphs are fully *italicized*.

Of course the reader is welcome to skip these asides in order to stick to the main trail of the tale. However, if you are interested in further historical context, editorial exposition, commentary and opinion, and the odd rant—please take a brief detour, and then kindly continue on with your journey.

**

PART **ONE**

PRELUDE

"No one is born hating another person because of the colour of his skin, or his background, or his religion. People must learn to hate, and if they can learn to hate, they can be taught to love, for love comes more naturally to the human heart than its opposite."

Nelson Mandela

≈

CHAPTER **ONE**

THE WOUNDED *bakkie* limped along. The rear wheels out of step with the front, its gait lame, the chassis's spine twisted from an earlier clash. Its flanks revealed claw marks from many close calls; the once-bright blue upper panels were bleached bone white by the relentless South African sun. With its best years behind, the pickup's outer skin now shed great swaths of paint, unveiling crusts of dried-blood rust beneath.

Like a tormented animal, it found itself uncertain and fearful among the herd of predatory machines as the powerful and the swift approached their prey. The straggler expected to be picked off at any moment now that these pack hunters had its scent. As they probed for weakness, a Mercedes, menacing and large, worked in concert with an Alfa Romeo. The Italian sports car dashed across the pickup's front quarter panel, abruptly checking its forward momentum. The larger car rode aggressively on the *bakkie*'s rear bumper, held in place with two wire hangers, in hopes of forcing a fatal error. The weathered tarpaulin that covered the rear quarters flapped a teasing tail in the wind, as if beckoning prying eyes.

The driver shot a glance over his shoulder, his heart pounding as he willed the Mercedes to move from behind. He turned again, clutching the cracked steering wheel as he stared ahead, resolute. His eyes stung as sweat sluiced into them, the sweltering midday sun unrelenting. He didn't dare move a hand to wipe his forehead as the Mercedes swerved and the Alfa Romeo slowed.

Then, inexplicably, the metal marauders gave up interest and sped off.

He squinted through the grimy windshield. Another street sign and still he was lost. Frustration grew on his dark, clammy face as he traversed the idyllic playground of the "mink and manure" set. He didn't belong here, but he had a job to do. It wouldn't do to disappoint the *Big Baas* (the Big Boss).

The *Big Baas* headed a consortium, the first organization granted a license to manufacture television sets. In the flatbed of the wayward truck sat the first dozen TVs produced in the country. These twenty-seven-inch tellies were destined for the homes of lobbyists responsible for persuading the authorities "to come out of the dark ages." But television still had powerful enemies. It wouldn't do to flaunt these new machines at this critical moment—hence the secrecy of the driver's mission.

**

In 1976 South Africa, after an absurd struggle, a truculent government capitulated and "the devil's own box" was reluctantly introduced to the Republic. The most advanced nation in Africa finally joined the twentieth century and agreed to plug into the rest of the world. An expectant nation was hoping to witness the first test television broadcast by the third week of January.

4

Neil Armstrong's lunar landing seven years prior had proved decisive in the debate—only South Africans never witnessed that singular event. Being deprived of sharing with the rest of the world that seminal moment in mankind's history had hurt, and so the stubborn government was shamed into change. But they had their Luddites, and change was a long time coming.

Many in the ruling party resented the introduction of television. It was a threat to their Afrikaner culture, a Pandora's box of sin, and an unwelcome "window to the world of enlightenment." In fact Afrikanerdom was split into two camps, the slowly emerging Verligte wing ("the enlightened ones") who demonstrated the glimmer of a liberal bent, and the Verkrampte establishment ("the conservatives") who judged any notion of liberalism as weakness.

The latter Afrikaner Christian-Nationalists held sway over the national debate. To them "enlightenment" was a dirty word, almost traitorous, because an informed population could be dangerous and threaten the status quo. By outlawing television they had, until now, effectively controlled the aspirations and expectations of the public; after all, an immature population was a malleable one. But this time the Verligtes had won a rare victory; and things on the ground were about to change.

**

To the north of the gold fields surrounding Johannesburg sat the "richest square mile in all of Africa," Sandton. Formerly a suburb of Jo'burg, Sandton successfully divorced itself from the golden city and became a municipality in its own right. Now free of spreading urban blight, the affluent white community of Sandton safely prospered in its exclusive posh enclave.

The color of the driver's skin disqualified him from living in Sandton (even in the unlikely event he could afford it). The place he called home was bleak and dangerous. It was a bastard—an unloved city within a city. Institutionally named South Western Townships, better known as Soweto, this long-ostracized "black suburb" of Johannesburg was a soulless ghetto. Row upon row of decaying shacks inhabited the featureless landscape. The flotsam and jetsam of lost lives reflected an indescribable waste—carcasses of spent tires, broken glass bottles, rusted oil cans, and dank corrugated cardboard boxes—littered the uneven roads and unkempt alleys.

A pervasive sense of darkness haunted the place despite the cheery brightness of the African sun. No wonder—the place was smothered in a sulfurous gray cloud of wood-fired stoves and gas fumes. And the tramped-down spirit of almost one and a half million souls added to the gloom. Their misery was understandable, being deprived of basic civilizing amenities such as electricity and indoor plumbing.

The overwhelming *vrot* of the place—the stench of an underserved and overcrowded population—was pervasive. It clung to clothes, hair, and bodies of the township's inhabitants. This stench remained with a Soweto resident even when leaving the confines of the ghetto.

Soweto's deprivations made driver Stanwell Marunda's expedition to Sandton all the more disorienting.

The beaten-up pickup wasn't his. It belonged to a coworker at the company warehouse. Normally he got around by "green mamba"—the puce-green painted buses reserved only for blacks. These unkempt monsters were unsafe and unreliable. Suffocating diesel fumes, numerous breakdowns, frequent crashes, and inexplicable delays were cause for concern, but the *tsotsis*—the gangsters—were the greatest threat. They preyed on hardworking commuters, men and women.

Stanwell was terrified each payday. These hoodlums had no compunction about murdering a victim over a meager twenty-rand pay packet. Their killing method was both quiet and bloodless, like the strike of a serpent's fang; a sharpened bicycle spoke was shunted between the victim's ribs.

With the threat of imminent death, it's no wonder these segregated buses were nicknamed after the deadliest venomous snake in Africa, the nine-foot mamba.

◄►►

"*Eish,*" Stanwell muttered. "Where am I?" He slapped himself on the temple in frustration. Frozen by indecision, he slowed to a crawl, only to be rewarded with the blaring horn of the irritated driver behind him. Stanwell quickly accelerated.

The house he was looking for was lost behind the high walls and gates protecting the massive homes that inhabited the well-heeled neighborhood. Here, the homes were personal monuments to the affluent, and playground to the architects who indulged them.

Every magnificent home had the derivative look of a Hollywood film set. Faux foreign styles from different eras strove for attention: a mock Tudor neighbored a Mediterranean revival, a Victorian Queen Anne faced a Frank Lloyd Wright look-alike, and a manor house vied with a Southern plantation for its place in the sun. A pity really, considering South Africa had a beautiful authentic look of its own.

It was as if the Western Cape had a monopoly on colonial architecture and prevented other provinces from using it. These definitive, fine-looking whitewashed Cape Dutch-styled homes were modeled from the late eighteenth century. Their classic distinctive features—the flowing, ornate gable soaring in a curlicue above the centered front entrance, with smaller gables boxing in each end, and tall wooden shutters framing the windows—would have added handsomely to the local Highveld architectural scene.

A more modest structure, the indigenous rondavel was used in Sandton as a tool shed or child's playhouse—although in the countryside and game parks, the humble rondavel was a staple, with its distinctive conical shaped straw-thatched roof, rustic stone wall, and local-content organic floor (sometimes crafted from cow dung).

For Stanwell, owning a humble rondavel would have been splendid. His drab home was a makeshift shanty. The twelve-by-fourteen-foot shack was cobbled together from corrugated zinc panels, discarded shipping pallets, and tin sign hoardings; a large rust-scabbed sign advertising KOO apricot jam served as the focal point of the structure.

Crudely mortared cinder blocks added strength to the corners, and a patchwork of sheeted canvas and plastic, pegged down with bricks and twine, buttressed the leaking roof. As for the windows, they were glassless, with ripped burlap sacks lending scant protection from the elements and nosey neighbors.

This crude structure was built over an uneven floor, with cheap linoleum covering the raw dirt beneath. However, for Stanwell, living in this home was cruder still—it lacked internal plumbing and electricity. For him the niceties of civilization were the communal outdoor pit toilet, a shared garden tap, a wood-burning stove, and kerosene lamps.

▶◀▶

Now desperate, Stanwell reached into the glove box hoping to find a map. Mechanically his eyes followed the motion of his hand as he rummaged below the dashboard.

Big mistake! The impact was sudden, sharp, and shocking.

With eyes off the road and hand off the steering wheel, Stanwell had collided with a delivery van parked by the side of the road. The ill-fitting seatbelt, sized to fit the expansive girth of the pickup truck's owner, conspired with the sudden deceleration to propel Stanwell forward. His upper torso met the steering wheel. It buckled under the stress. With velocity barely spent, Stanwell's face and head shattered the windshield.

The intense violence of the accident overwhelmed Stanwell's ability to process what just happened. His ears were assaulted with a crack of sound, then silence. His vision seared with a bright yellow-white flash, then darkness.

◄►◄

He tried opening his eyes. They hurt. Specifically his eyelids: it was as if a cluster of white hot needles had pierced them. Now determined, the need to survive greater than the pain, Stanwell forced open his eyes. His lap came into view. In the ripples and folds of his gray work trousers were fragments of shattered glass, as if mounds of glittering diamonds were trapped there.

Though dazed, he noted the brilliance of the dangerous shards as they sparkled in the midmorning sun. Blood dripped onto his lap; the scarlet fluid went its way over and between the glass crystals before it seeped through his pants and stained the vinyl seat below. Panic set in. He had to get out. *Quickly!*

◄►◄

CHAPTER **TWO**

ELSA "KAT" MARAIS had been summoned. She had no idea why. She had received an invitation from a Lydia Duncan requesting Elsa's presence for morning tea at her toney Killarney Road home in Sandton. To her knowledge she had never met Lydia, but curiosity had got the better of her.

A maid in a crisp yellow uniform, starched white pinafore apron, and matching white *doek*—the headscarf indicating both respect and her marital status—greeted Elsa at the front door. She was politely ushered through to the *stoep.* This broad paved verandah extended the full length of the house. It overlooked a grand estate, with swimming pool, tennis court, and guesthouse nestled in acres of manicured lawn.

At the Kiaat teakwood table laden with embroidered tablecloth, napkins, and stately silver tea service sat her hostess.

"How are you, my dear?" welcomed Lydia. "Please do sit down."

"*Dankie*, thank you for inviting me," said Elsa, taking in the refined domestic setting that lay before her.

Elsa was not accustomed to wealth, so her senses soaked up her surroundings: first the fragrances as they wafted in the air, a mix of the oil of bergamot (from the Earl Grey tea) and Lydia's Chanel No. 5 perfume; then the flavors promised by the dainty watercress and cucumber finger-sandwiches (with crusts immaculately trimmed), and warm scones (with strawberry jam and clotted cream), all resting on doily-covered platters.

Elsa considered the meticulously groomed, attractive suburbanite seated across from her and felt nervous. Her hostess was of English stock, and she was an Afrikaner, a farmer's daughter—a *boeremeisie*.

"Perhaps you are wondering why I asked you here today," said Lydia, sensing her guest's apprehension. "But first," Lydia prompted. "Please do tell me a bit about yourself."

As Elsa responded, Lydia quickly did an inventory of the young woman: a natural beauty, modest, from the rural *platteland*, new to the big city, presumably single, unadorned (no jewelry except a turquoise-inlaid silver watch), and dressed simply in a blue sundress, the only discordant note being the white *takkies* or sneakers on her feet. Not appropriate attire for a tea party, but probably indicative of Elsa's practical nature.

Elsa collected her thoughts. "I came to Jo'burg eight months ago from Brakpan."

Lydia was familiar with Brakpan. It lay east of Johannesburg and was fatefully fertile in coal, gold, and platinum when its predominantly Afrikaner population consisted of farmers who were contented tilling the soil in the fresh air. Now, however, these farmers were disillusioned miners, having traded their plows for jackhammers to earn a harsh living underground.

"I'm staying in Hillbrow now," Elsa continued. "It's okay, I guess." She shrugged.

The truth was that Elsa detested Hillbrow. Living eighteen stories above the ground in a high-rise tower was alien to her. Add the congested traffic, the honking car-hooters, the relentless flickering neons, and the drone of the masses, and it was too much for her.

These things Elsa didn't like, but it was the fear after dark—the perpetual state of vigilance needed against night crime—that was especially wearisome. Another annoyance was the *dronkies*—the European winos that grifted outside Hillbrow's trendy international hotspots—who constantly accosted her in the crowded streets.

Though upbeat by nature, Elsa found this wasn't the kind of excitement she needed right now and she yearned to return home to the house of her parents, with its rustic brick walls, oxidized-red corrugated iron roof, and the oxblood polished *stoep* out front. Maybe with time I will adjust to big city life, thought Elsa. Putting on a brave face, Elsa said, "I guess I can't complain. I found a two-bedroom flat, a roommate—she's a nurse—and a nice job really quickly."

"That's nice," Lydia said. "Then what happened after you matriculated high school?"

"I got my bookkeeping diploma from Damelin College, a correspondence school."

Elsa gave a shrill squeal of surprise. A tall, sleek, muscular dog had streaked over to her. As way of greeting, it had buried its damp snout in Elsa's crotch. Then quickly the dog pranced away, chastened by the admonitions of its owner. Both women regained their composure, but the hound's shenanigans had dispensed with all sense of decorum.

"Sorry about that!" exclaimed Lydia. "He's so darn forward. Let me formally introduce you to the third member of our family. Meet Leo, our Rhodesian ridgeback. I was quite proud of him—until now!"

The dog's amber eyes locked onto Elsa's. They appeared intelligent, so welcoming, and hinted at a twinge of remorse for his tawdry behavior. The regret was probably an illusion Elsa had read within those canine eyes; she had always romanticized her understanding of animals. But in Leo's intelligent gaze, proud stance, lustrous mahogany-red coat, and strong curved wagging tail, she saw a friend. In this African lion dog, with the distinctive darkened ridge of against-the-grain hair marking the length of his spine, she had found her first true companion since coming to the big city.

"He's very comfortable with you, I see." Lydia looked at the mooning Leo. His muzzle nestled on Elsa's thigh, his left ear enveloped in the soft folds of her percale dress. Lydia was pleased. She needed to trust Elsa, and Leo's unfailing devotion was a most positive testimonial.

"Hey, that's like a coincidence. Leo the dog, and I'm Elsa from *Born Free*...both lions," said Elsa. "You know what I mean?"

Lydia nodded with a somewhat patronizing smile.

Elsa's parents adored the movie *Born Free*, a furry true-life epic about Elsa, an orphaned lioness cub, and her rescue by a game ranger in Kenya. The cub was raised as a domestic pet until the Adamson couple, George and Joy, realized her true home was the bush. With Elsa's human family serving as a guide, the lioness learned to fend for herself, and in a bittersweet farewell returned to the wild.

With Africa in their hearts, the film resonated with *Meneer* and *Mevrou*, Mr. and Mrs. Jannie Marais, and they named their infant daughter after the spirited lioness. In keeping with her feline namesake, the Maraises nicknamed their daughter "Kat."

"Elsa, did you see the movie?" asked Lydia. "I must say I like the film's theme tune very much."

"*Ja*...my folks often took me to the bioscope to see *Born Free*, and we always left with happy tears after the film."

Elsa pronounced "film" with two syllables, as *fi-lem*. Lydia winced at the girl's ungainly expression of the English language. Afrikaans was Elsa's mother tongue. It's such a *grotty* little language, Lydia thought, shaking her head.

Lydia's difficulties with the Afrikaans language were complex. It was more than a matter of taste, though the guttural consonants and swallowed vowels were not to her liking. Her problem was the Afrikaner's cultural insecurity and the long-term impact it had on the country as a result.

Despite English and Afrikaans being the country's official languages, all South Africa's laws were promulgated exclusively in Afrikaans. This was unfortunate.

The Afrikaans language simply lacked the depth of vocabulary required for something as complex and nuanced as the law. And the reason for the language's immaturity was the desperate need by the early settlers to be self-sufficient, and independent of meddlesome administrative supervision from Europe.

Like rebellious adolescents refusing contact with doting parents, these first-generation Afrikaners severed all links with Mother Holland (unlike the English speakers who maintained their relationship with Great Britain) and as free burghers they shunned their Dutch roots. Isolated from Europe, the Afrikaans language failed to mature. And without having the rich panoply of words of matured languages at their disposal, the nation's laws tended to be brittle, absolutist, and unkind.

This is why the government's use of Afrikaans as the nation's official language vexed Lydia so much. For when there wasn't a word, the regime invented one. And the National Party's ability to invent the worst words possible to define components of their ideology was uncanny—with "apartheid" being the greatest travesty of all. Just the ominous grate of the word (it sounds like "apart-*hate*") should have disqualified it from the lexicon. But to the detriment of all, the government persisted with both word and policy.

However, Lydia admitted to some moments of inventive charm in the Afrikaans language, and she had a personal favorite: the description of a cul-de-sac being *Straat Loop Dood* (literally, "street walks dead").

**

Tension between black and white in South Africa is well documented. Less well known is the schism between the two white "tribes"—the English and Afrikaners. Originally of Dutch descent, the Afrikaner ruled the roost from 1652. They were joined by the Huguenots in 1685 who had escaped France to gain their freedom from anti-Protestant legislation. These early settlers were content to be left alone. That was until 1795, when the British seized the Cape to prevent it falling into French hands. The British briefly returned the colony to the Dutch in 1803, only to take it back in 1806. However, when the 1820 settlers landed at the Cape, full of pomp and circumstance, the full brunt of British imperialism was felt by the locals and hostility flared.

British rule and Afrikaner resentment of this domination led to two Anglo-Boer Wars, culminating in cessation of hostilities in 1902 with a British victory. Regrettably the Boers' hatred for the British never ceased, making any prospect of genuine peace impossible. And this antipathy from the Boers ran far deeper than the mere petulance of being poor losers—rather, it was an inflamed wound encouraged to fester further so as to unite the volk in their drawn-out campaign for eventual independence.

Major anti-British feelings remained in the Afrikaner community for generations. During World War II, flagrant pro-Nazi sentiments were apparent among influential Afrikaner leaders, including future prime ministers—all in the name of nationalism. This passion reached a crescendo in 1948.

By beating the drum of anti-British imperialism, the Afrikaners' National Party ousted the pro-British statesman and genteel Afrikaner, Field Marshal Jan Smuts. In a fashion similar to the unseemly dismissal by the British people of Winston Churchill at war's end, Smuts, another heroic wartime leader, was discarded by his nation having lost the internecine cultural war raging within Afrikanerdom.

This was a pivotal moment in South African history which unfortunately altered the trajectory of the nation toward legislated segregation, and eventual isolation. With Jan Smuts' exit, the influence of liberal Afrikaners waned and was replaced by their dogmatic, conservative brethren who held a far less forgiving vision for the future of the country.

The fundamentalist National Party now controlled all aspects of South African life. Yet, despite their political victory they never felt secure and the undisguised hostility they displayed toward others never ceased; whether it be liberal Afrikaners, the indigenous natives, or those of British stock. In fact the ruling party—these nationalistic Afrikaners'—would never come to accept white English speakers as their countrymen. So for decades a mutual hatred simmered below the surface as these two white clans, at the tip of Africa, indulged in a very personal cold war.

**

Lydia still sensed tension. And she knew its source. Afrikaners and English speakers mixed like oil and water—they didn't. And if she wanted more from Elsa, Lydia must get this issue out in the open. "Elsa, how old are you?" she asked.

"I've just turned twenty-three," said Elsa, showing none of the modesty of women who consider their age a state secret.

"It's 1976. What role should we modern women have in South Africa?"

Uncertain, Elsa tapped her foot nervously to an unknown beat. "Don't know. Never really thought about it," she replied.

"Well, how about politics? There's Helen Suzman, the lone Progressive Party member of Parliament. Despite all the guff she gets, harassed and ridiculed, she's still the only liberal voice sniping at the government. Now that's one gutsy lady!"

Elsa was annoyed. Surely Lydia understood Elsa's unswerving loyalty to the National Party that had swept her *volk*, her people, into power. And here Lydia was raving about this Helen Suzman, an English-speaking Jewish woman, who constantly embarrassed her government's leadership. Wishing to protest, Elsa felt it prudent to best hold her silence.

"And on the world stage there's India's prime minister, Indira Gandhi. It's a real shame about her guilt for political corruption. I don't know if they're related, but it's sad because she shares the same noble name as Mahatma Gandhi..."

Lydia continued. "Did you know Gandhi had a South African connection?" Elsa shook her head. "Well, he was a stretcher-bearer, and started an Indian ambulance service during our Anglo-Boer War."

Now she prodded deliberately at the raw wound. "Speaking about the Boer War, why do you Afrikaners resent us so much? You know us Europeans should really stick together."

Lydia got her response.

Cheeks flushed red with anger, Elsa said, "*Agh*, Lydia, you must be kidding me. You *rooineks* came down here uninvited and tried to take away our country!"

"Whoa, missy. Cut out that "rooinek" nonsense—I was born in this country. I'm not some pasty, pale British soldier who cremated the back of his neck in the boiling African sun some seventy-odd years ago. Personally, I'd like to end this feud."

A gesture of peace had been made, but would it be accepted?

Elsa clenched her fists, her fingernails carving half-moon indents into the palms of her hands. To her the Boer War still ran raw. Anguished, she said flatly in a voice of condemnation, "On my *oupa*'s knee I heard the horrors of the British "scorched earth policy"—it was so unfair. Our commandos lived off the land, shooting wild game for food, and yes, sometimes getting support from local farmers. But in payback the rooineks...sorry, the English, destroyed our farms, slaughtered cattle, poisoned wells, and forcefully removed our women and children into concentration camps. And did you know, in those camps, over twenty-seven thousand Boer women and children died!" Elsa sobbed pitiably. Her culture was so rich in survival; Elsa couldn't understand why the English didn't share the same sense of pride.

Lydia dabbed away the girl's tears with a napkin. Elsa didn't flinch. That's a hopeful sign, thought Lydia. The catharsis was necessary—we must speak of these things to resolve them. Then she offered Elsa a comforting cup of tea in a fine Wedgwood china teacup—an undeniable symbol of British imperialism.

For the first time, in the appearance of this lovely young woman, the Afrikaner's visceral hatred toward the English was understood by Lydia.

It saddened her that her side had played such a devastating role in this tragic saga. It didn't assuage her guilt to know that these concentration camps were intended as refugee camps only, and that those heartrending fatalities were not an intentional act of genocide. To the bereaved it did not matter how the victims perished, just that they were gone, forever.

Lydia felt shame. Rank incompetence had caused these fatalities: neglect, overcrowding, poor sanitation, and an alphabet of diseases including dysentery, measles, and typhoid. Shame, no wonder they hate us so. One would think that with this terrible history the Afrikaner would relate and be kinder to the local natives, mused Lydia.

An uncomfortable tension descended over the charming tea party. Leo sensed the shift in the wind, got up, stretched, circled a few times, glanced cautiously at the two women, and then settled back down at the same spot with an empathetic sigh.

◄►

CHAPTER **THREE**

LEO HEARD IT FIRST. His ears twitched. A millisecond later, the ether was shattered by a horrendous thud. A splintering, grinding din followed. Stunned by the suddenness of it, the two women leapt to their feet. Their ears were assaulted by the clangor of the car horn. Now anxious, they looked toward the source of the blaring racket—it was just beyond the driveway gates. Then all went eerily silent—the discordant decibels of the car horn had finally stopped.

The dog bounded toward the gate with that swift grace distinct to his breed. Lydia and Elsa chased after him across the plush lawn. They leapt over the immaculate flower beds lining the driveway and dashed through the granite pillar gateway. Lydia, hindered by her high-heeled designer pumps, slowed to kick them off. Elsa, shod with her rubber-soled tennis shoes, got there first.

Chaos greeted them. A pickup truck had fused itself to the rear end of a laundry delivery van parked at the side of the road. The chassis of both vehicles had buckled under the impact.

Debris littered the scene: shattered glass, crushed plastic, and crumpled metal. The pickup's radiator vented its last gasp with a hiss of steam. The cloying stench of scorched oil and brake fluid—or was it petrol—pervaded the scene.

"No skid marks, hey? The crazy *mampara* didn't even hit the brakes," said Elsa. She ran over to the parked delivery van and peered in.

"It's empty," Elsa called back to Lydia. "I'm gonna check out the *bakkie's* driver now. I hope the poor *oke's* okay?"

Lydia hung back, as the broken glass threatened her stocking feet. Elsa approached the crushed cab on the driver's side. "*Agh,* shame man!" she yelled.

▶◀▶◀

He struggled to get out. Blinded by blood flowing in his eyes, he desperately scrabbled at the door handle. But the door wouldn't budge. The vehicle's crushed frame had jammed it tight. Trapped, he attempted to cry for help. It was futile. Except for a gagged gurgle, no discernible sound sprung from his mouth.

Stanwell's bloodied hands were cramped in the rigor of panic. Having failed in their task to free him, they spasmodically flailed in and out of sight. It was an instinctual sign of life, a frantic signal for attention in a desperate quest for salvation.

Elsa noticed.

Her impulse was to aid the stricken stranger. Noting the lack of damage on the side away from the impact, Elsa chose her course of action well. She forced open the passenger-side door, leaned in, fumbled, then found the lap-seat buckle, decoupled it, grabbed the victim around the midriff, and then hauled with all her might, backing them both out.

"Lydia, help..." she gasped. Lydia cautiously reached over. Together they lowered the injured man to the grass verge.

Nevertheless, the distressed man was still in jeopardy. His head had taken the full brunt of the impact. Flesh and bone had bent the weathered steering wheel and shattered the windshield. Bloodied sputum from his broken nose and slashed tongue engorged the back of his throat. Despite his failing cognitive senses, Stanwell realized that he was drowning in his own bodily fluids and that there was absolutely nothing he could do about it.

With a simple act of common sense, Elsa saved Stanwell's life. She turned him on his side. The viscous gore, encrusted with shattered glass pellets, ebbed out of his mouth—to be replaced with lifesaving air.

The relief he sensed was immediate, and his gratitude was complete.

It was no wonder that when he witnessed his savior for the very first time, through blood-infused, heavy-lidded eyes, he appreciated it solely in transcendent terms; a presence was not bound by race, gender, color, or creed.

He peered up, curious, grateful. His head bobbed and weaved as his eyes attempted to focus, a task made more difficult by the halo of the midday sun gleaming behind the silhouetted figure.

Finally all came into focus. Every detail of her face was apparent to him. It was reassuring and friendly. Even with the worrying circumstances, remarkably there appeared to be a cheery gleam emanating from her almond-shaped eyes. Freckles danced across the bridge of her nose and gathered in amorphous clouds on her finely sculpted cheeks. Her lashes were lush and her brows generous, hinting at her apparent Dutch heritage. Smile lines in the corners of her mouth mirrored the luminescence in her eyes.

Radiating beyond her eyes were her ears—trim and taught. They lacked the fleshy lobes and obligatory chandelier earrings so in vogue with the affluent. Instead, two simple jade studs emphasized the hazel-green luster of her eyes.

Her mouth was full, wide, and generous. Her teeth displayed just enough imperfection in their alignment to assure they were genuine. Her nose was not the synthetic ski slope created by a plastic surgeon; rather, it was strong, and with the suggestion of a bump at the bridge, proudly noble.

Her warm honey-toned skin complemented her lustrous, shoulder-length golden tresses—both kissed by the African sun. All this was underscored with a perfectly inscribed jaw line. The only blemish was a fine scar on the cusp of her chin. Her pastel appearance was something most unfamiliar.

▶◀▶◀

"An ambulance, we need an ambulance." With Leo at her heels, Lydia rushed toward the house to make the emergency call. Elsa found herself alone. Not quite alone—an injured black man lay on the ground beside her. Her mind raced. Was she breaking the law?

Being raised under the strictures of apartheid, she had never prepared herself for such an eventuality—providing aid and comfort to a non-European—a black man.

▶◀▶◀

Elsa had no innate fear or loathing for persons of color. Her fondest memories were tumbling about her family's backyard with Thabo. Thabo was also five. He was a happy kid, with a sometimes-runny nose, who was intrigued with every form of insect life in their little kingdom.

Thabo's mom was Elsa's nanny. Her official job description, and so notated in her passbook, was "domestic servant." Nanny Rose was instinctively egalitarian—treating both her own brown child and white ward equally. She would summon them to meals with a hearty hail: "Come my *pikininis, kos is op die tafel*!" [Come, kids, food is on the table!].

At the kitchen table, Thabo would disgust and entertain Elsa with tales of discovery. The first seasonal rainfall had surfaced a wonderful host of *goggas*, bugs, and creepy-crawlies, and he enjoyed describing their body functions in fine detail.

He would regale Elsa with stories of a mythic twelve-inch *shongololo*—a millipede with one thousand legs he allegedly befriended. To her dismay, she would then discover a much smaller example of the creature, coiled up tightly around its exoskeleton and secreted under a lettuce leaf on her plate.

Elsa's response was invariably to feign terror, giving a shrill shriek to Thabo's giggling delight. Then they would bestow a name (and gender) on the insect. They'd feed it, observe it, keep it in a shoe box or glass jar, and if it survived a couple of days, restore it back to nature at Nanny Rose's insistence.

When Nanny Rose hand-washed the laundry, hanging the clothes and linens up on the clothing line to dry in the warm sun, Elsa would hold the little plastic pail of wooden pegs and hand them to her as needed.

All the while Elsa would enjoy listening to Rose's constant patter of wisdom, lore, and gossip—in a mélange of Zulu, Afrikaans, and English—punctuated with beautiful, full-throated songs learned at her Zion Christian Church.

The Marais family allowed this relationship to flourish within the confines of their home, and welcomed young Thabo as a playmate for their young daughter.

Nanny Rose was a woman of humble means—loving, maternal, and a dedicated servant to both the Marais family and her god. Elsa's dearest memories as a youngster were when Nanny Rose would bind her in a colorful plaid blanket and strap her tiny body firmly to her back as she went about her chores.

Swaddled and tightly bound, Elsa would turn her head and comfortably rest her ear against the starched uniform. With the slight pungency of bleach, Sunlight washing soap, and Vim scouring powder in her nostrils, she would listen to Nanny Rose's heartbeat. She would also hear the muffled tones of her jabbering with the other servants in the singsong pops and clicks of her native tongue.

Wrapped in a warm blanket, nestled against a warm body, a content Elsa would drift off to the hypnotic mantra of the work songs Nanny Rose sang to herself as she labored. In this way Elsa would assume in her dreams the rhythm of Africa.

She never felt more secure than when cocooned against the warm, nurturing body of her black nanny. In good time, Nanny Rose's influence would resonate with Elsa. No wonder Elsa treasured her so.

▶◀ ▶◀

Then something happened. Off to school at the age of six went Elsa, dressed in her little pale-blue checked-gingham uniform, a gymslip worn over a white blouse with matching knee socks, and a pint-sized Samsonite-type suitcase as a lunchbox. Thabo was whisked away to his school with a lot less—where he was destined to learn a lot less.

Youthful, unaware, and easily manipulated, Elsa did not realize that she and Thabo had entered the first stage of indoctrination—a grand plan designed to separate out individuals according to racial groupings.

It was the unapologetic mechanism of segregation whereby one group—the fair skinned minority—used power and the threat of force to categorize humans according to complexion and cultural heritage.

Privilege was bestowed based on skin shade rather than ability, with blacks at the bottom, whites at the top, and Indians and coloureds in between.

Despite the innocence of their relationship, Elsa and Thabo were never given the choice by this government, nor afforded the opportunity, to rekindle their childhood friendship again.

►◄►◄

Being a sensible girl, Elsa was not blind to the silly impractical lengths the apartheid regime would go to, to maintain the principle of "apartness." In her own home she and Nanny Rose comfortably shared the same space; they would cook together, sit around the kitchen table and snack, drink tea, and chat.

In the evening it was Nanny Rose who tucked her into bed and soothingly rubbed her back, singing the hauntingly beautiful Zulu lullaby "Tula Baba" until she fell asleep, coddled in the warmth of fresh bed linens. It was Nanny Rose who potty-trained her, weaning her off those cloth nappy diapers cinched in place with fearsomely sharp safety pins—and even wiping her bottom until Elsa was able.

But, once Elsa was an adult, if she and Nanny Rose needed to visit the post office together, Elsa had to "chauffeur" Nanny in the back seat. It was not acceptable to be seen seated together in the front seat of the car. The irony was lost on the apartheid regime: here was the "mistress" chauffeuring the servant. Elsewhere in the world, it would be downright peculiar.

When reaching the post office, they were met with two signs above two doorways, reading: *Net Blankes* (Whites Only), and

Nie Blankes (Non-Whites). They separated as they entered the respective designated portals, only to almost meet at the same long counter with now a metal railing dividing them. They would roll their eyes at each other, shake their heads, and mutter under their breaths something about "this stupid government!" They both knew it was nothing personal. They both understood it to be the government's will.

The net result was a kind of parallel universe where the indigenous native people were marginalized as aliens in their own land. However, the apartheid regime was not heartless. There was one relationship between the races they effusively fostered: that of master and servant.

Elsa's relationships with blacks could be considered kindly paternalistic. They in turn were deferential. With all her interracial relationships built solely on the basis of master and servant, it was inevitable that it would be so.

But it was nice to pretend—to pretend a sign of courtesy, respect, or even adoration from a second-class fellow citizen was deserved, rather than legislated by central command.

When an elderly black man doffed his cap, stepped aside, and let her enter a doorway ahead of him, she attributed it to good old-fashioned manners, to him giving preference to her fair gender (rather than her fair complexion). She would flash a charming smile of gratitude and enter ahead of the older gent without any consideration of guilt or shame. That's just the way things were meant to be.

Elsa was no racist. She never had to be; her government assumed that responsibility. But the role of the government did not necessarily absolve her, and this troubled her. She wrestled with the question of what defines someone as a racist.

She knew with certainty that at her very core, she had never felt corrosive hatred and visceral loathing for someone of another race. In her mind, to be racist was an overt personal decision: a willful, individual choice to harbor hateful thoughts against someone perceived to be different—and then to act maliciously on those vile thoughts.

Elsa was not naïve. She had no doubt that many of her Afrikaner brethren were racists, especially those isolated on *die plaas* (the farm). There some farmers believed they were the law unto themselves, that the blacks were menial labor, no better than working animals and only there to do their bidding.

The natives could be readily brutalized for minor transgressions, freely exploited for financial gain, and sorely abused for the farmers' perverse entertainment. And despite the depravity of their actions, the farmers were always secure in the knowledge that their crimes would be absolved by apartheid rule.

Then there were the institutional haters, those soulless and craven governmental bureaucrats.

**

Bureaucratic officials were highly qualified for their duties, if low self-esteem and high resentment of others unlike themselves were leading criteria for employment. Empowered with authority far beyond their competence, these uncivil servants relished their role as avengers for all transgressions—real or imagined—made against their own kind.

Simple tasks like changing a mailing address or purchasing a train ticket became hellish endeavors. Hat in hand like a supplicant groveling at the feet of his lord, a black man in need was compelled to place himself at the mercy of the lowest-ranked white official, certain in the knowledge that the price he would pay for his temerity would be absurd abuse.

Worthy principles such as "service," "responsibility," and "duty" were dispensed with as being superfluous and soft. To these functionaries, the purpose for holding the power of their office was to obstruct, bully, and victimize all those unlike themselves.

But the most awesome power of all, and the most abused, was the matter of "racial classification"—the power to designate the racial category of an individual or family. The consequence of a faceless bureaucrat's decision was devastating to so many. If white, you're privileged; if black, you're relegated to a lifetime of poverty, oppression, exploitation, and abuse—all by the stroke of a pen—solely at a bureaucrat's whim.

To people of this bigoted persuasion, a Bantu was treated as a primitive who belonged back in the bushveld. They adhered to the dehumanizing, callous philosophy that a native was best kept ignorant because a "dom" kaffir would have no need for ambition. And in this way they'd better know their place in the world. After all, their job was to fulfill the white man's aspirations, no matter how demeaning.

A future prime minister of South Africa and prime architect of the apartheid system, Hendrik Verwoed, succinctly expressed his view: "There is no place for the Bantu in the European community above the level of certain forms of labour...What is the use of teaching the Bantu child mathematics when it cannot use it in practice? That is quite absurd."

Apparently the quiet dignity of a people is most apparent when subjected to systemic humiliation at the hands of a bureaucrat; after being subjected to an abusive verbal tirade, the black man would not lash out, but would respectfully back away, then with full dignity mixed with a touch of sardonic self-deprecation he would muster up his courage, and in the tongue of his oppressor he would confess, "Ja, wit bass, ek is jammer. Ek is net a dom kaffir." [Yes, white boss, I am sorry. I am just a dumb nigger.]

**

The matter of apartheid had such heft to it that it weighed on Elsa's mind, so she had decided to discuss it with her father, Jannie Marais. Despite the diminutive *ie* at the end of his name, suggesting he was "little Johnny," Jannie Marais was an immense, burly bloke. A lock forward on his high school rugby team, with a bent nose and cauliflower ears from past skirmishes on the pitch, he was not physically afraid of anything. But matters concerning his faith and its role in justifying apartheid's policies troubled him.

Marais was a devoted lifetime member of the Dutch Reformed Church. Its Calvinist canons made him a conservative man, a moral man, and a decent man. Or so he hoped. He did not blaspheme. The notion of invoking the Lord's name in a cuss appalled him. He fastidiously obeyed the Sunday "blue laws." God rested on the seventh day and so did he. However, he did believe in the biblical commandment to "love thy neighbor as thyself," and therein lay his problem.

Elsa was worried. Her father was getting agitated. Usually a *dop* of peach brandy in his quiet home at the end of the day calmed him, but not tonight. She knew she was to blame. She

watched as he pried the grime from under his chipped fingernails. His prized pocketknife with its warthog-tusk handle men-
aced away as he whittled. She understood this was her father's
way of not having to look up at her. He was being evasive, but
the ferocity of his grooming habit was of immediate concern;
they may not agree on the topic of conversation, but surely
bloodshed was not in fact necessary.

Now that Elsa had her diploma, she was preparing for her
big move to the city. Possibly the thought of missing her had
more to do with his mood than their frank discussion, but her
query on the fairness of the apartheid doctrine had been taken
as a personal challenge, and it was too late to back down.

"Look here, it's only natural that folks would want to keep
with their own kind," rationalized Jannie Marais. "It only makes
sense that a people, especially a tribal people, would want to
remain with their own tribe."

"You mean like the English and us Afrikaners," Elsa replied.
"It's true, we seldom mix."

"*Ja*, that's right."

"But there's one big difference...Where are the laws separating us from the English?" said Elsa. "There are none! It's kind
of voluntary."

"But the problem is we'd be swamped by the blacks. There
are too many of them. They'd overwhelm us," Marais coun-
tered. "Surely we have the right to preserve our cultural identity
and our heritage, so tell me, what's all this fuss about?"

"You said it yourself. You said it's natural to be with your
own kind. If it's so natural, why do we then need to have these
strict laws, hey?"

"Because the Bible tells us it is so," stated Marais firmly,
glancing at the well-weathered book lying on the sideboard. "We

are told the Hebrew was forbidden from marrying others of a different faith. That is the law of God. Our laws have a similar purpose."

"First, the Bible is about faith, not race. Second, the Bible gives a remedy. A person of a different faith is able to convert, making the marriage possible—but there's nothing a black can do to turn white!" said Elsa in indignation. "It's jolly unfair!"

"Now young lady, don't get stroppy with me!"

"Well, our leaders always brag about everything being 'separate but equal,' but that's not true...you know it's not." Elsa had never spoken to her pa this way before; she knew she sounded petulant but couldn't help it. She took another sip of rooibos tea to calm her nerves.

"*Struesbob*—as true as God, I don't know what has come over you," said Marais.

"Pa, I know you're proud of me," said Elsa. "But I can't help thinking how different I would've been if I didn't have Nanny Rose in my life. She kinda raised me."

"This is the way you thank your ma and me...you insult us?"

"*Agh*, no. I'm not taking anything away from you two. With all my heart, you know I love you both. And I'm so thankful. *Dankie*," said Elsa sincerely.

"Then what's the problem then?"

"My problem...it is so unfair. Please listen now. Nanny Rose has been with us for over twenty years. In that time we've added rooms to our house, built a swimming pool, owned a variety of vehicles, gone away on holidays to Durbs, Cape Town, and the Kruger Park. You see our family has prospered, and I've had a good education. Life's been good to us.

"For Nanny Rose it's not been so wonderful, hey. She has the same job, but now she's just a heck of a lot older and frailer.

She lives in the same tiny room in the servants' quarters at the back of house. She doesn't even see her husband."

Now a little concerned, Elsa added, "While I'm a good girl with a good education, her Thabo has disappeared. He has no skills and is probably a gangster *tsotsi* somewhere. I know she's so worried about him.

"It's so sad. Her life has stood still all these years despite being a wonderful, devout person. She has no prospects, no true home or family—she's just our faithful *ousie*—just because of the color of her skin. When I see Nanny Rose, everything looks separate and *very unequal* to me..." Elsa's earnest voice trailed off in despair.

Marais felt exposed as if a charlatan. His conscience had been sheltered in the teachings of his church and the guidance of his government. Like so many South Africans, he had been able to objectify the black, conveniently remaining oblivious to their daily struggles, while taking comfort in his position of privilege.

He knew the white man enjoyed a disproportionate share of the wealth, claiming the choice bits of land for themselves and leaving the dregs to the indigenous majority. But Elsa had made it personal by shining a light on the plight of Nanny Rose, which was all the more damming because this individual lived under his roof, in his household, and he hadn't cared.

So much for loving thy neighbor as thyself!

▶◀▶◀

CHAPTER **FOUR**

"HOW COME DOING THE RIGHT THING feels so wrong?" muttered Elsa, frustrated by the conundrum. Reality had intruded on her uncomplicated life. It confronted her with a dilemma: obey the law or help the injured black man lying at her feet—it wasn't possible to do both.

Every day of her life, Elsa had conducted acts of racism as a consequence of the country's stringent apartheid laws. Never was this a personal decision—she simply obeyed, as was her duty as a good citizen. Now, with this helpless car crash victim, things were different. Decency demanded she help; the law insisted she shouldn't.

Her concern was justified. The government was ever omnipresent with laws that dictated every facet of a citizen's life. And the nature of that life was defined solely by skin tone. Where individuals stood on the color spectrum dictated where they lived, studied, and worked, whom they married, which door they used, and even where they shat.

Of course, there was an edict that explicitly outlawed intimate contact with a person of another race. Yet she'd already manhandled this black man out of the wrecked vehicle. With her bare hands she'd attended to his injuries. She was covered with *his* blood. Oh man, what could be more intimate than that?

However, Elsa didn't fail the test. A sense of human decency (and possibly the "Good Samaritan" parable from her pa's church) gave her strength to overcome her misgivings.

Her immediate concern was for his welfare. Using the hem of her dress, she began wiping the blood from the native-boy's face. Slowly she made progress, fastidiously dabbing the gashes and using the fabric to staunch the open wounds. Then she turned her attention to the glass splinters in his flesh. With her fingernails as tweezers, Elsa carefully plucked away, greeting each successful extraction with a cry of *"Eina!"* in empathy for her patient.

However, the tremble of her hands got progressively worse as she closed in on the cluster of shards imbedded about his eyes. Her anxious patient had become restless. And Elsa felt the pressure mount each time he moved. He began twisting back his head, panicked, attempting to expel blood from his eyes. Then his eyes fluttered and squinted as he tried to focus up at her.

"I hope he can see okay," Elsa whispered to herself. "We need a damn doctor..."

▶◀▶◀

Traffic swished by. No one stopped to assist the white woman administering to the black man lying on the grass verge. Strangers appeared unmoved by the evocative tableau. Or was it an emotional disconnection due to the incongruity of the scene that confronted them in stark black and white?

Elsa knew the truth: they didn't want to get involved. They didn't want any trouble.

Saddened by their detachment, Elsa became aware of her own. She'd regarded the poor man as a cipher; she'd made no attempt to know him.

"Hey! Are you okay? What's your name?" Elsa blurted in a reel of guilt.

"Thhssttaammell," he gasped, stifled by the blood pooled at the back of his throat.

"Samuel?"

"No." Frustrated, he hoisted himself on his elbow, spat out the detritus clogging his mouth and whispered, "Stanwell, Stanwell Marunda." Then, with a painful groan, he gingerly lowered himself flat on the ground.

▶◀▶◀

An amalgamation of sounds filled the air: the unremitting noise of the traffic; the suck, squeeze, bang, and blow of a neighborhood four-stroke lawnmower; the screech and howl of a cat-on-dog sneak attack; the irritated voice of a mother summoning her child; and the wheezing, rasping breaths of the injured man. Above the din they heard the welcome wail of a siren. Help was on the way.

Normally, the dissonant alarm and flashing lights of an onrushing ambulance would cause Elsa to cringe. Always as a child (and sometimes as an adult) she'd utter under her breath as she pantomimed the motions, "Touch my head, touch my toes, hope I'll never be in one of those." Not this time. This ambulance represented aid for Stanwell and a welcome resolution to her predicament.

The ululating lament of the speeding ambulance's siren grew louder as it neared the crash site. Elsa noticed Lydia hurrying back down the driveway with a bounding Leo in tow, as if enticed by the siren's call.

The ambulance came to a halt, the siren shutting down abruptly with a stifled squawk. The long vehicle was refrigerator white. An extended station wagon with opaque panels of glass on each side, it sported a single flashing red beacon light over the cab and Red Cross symbols on the doors.

It occurred to Elsa that if you painted the thing black, it would look like a damn hearse. She winced at the lack of subtlety. Nonetheless, she was grateful a competent rescue team had at last arrived.

Elsa glanced around for support and noticed Lydia paused, breathing heavily from her driveway dash, surveying the scene. Elsa would need her help in dealing with the medics.

Both ambulance driver and attendant leapt out of the vehicle. With a commendable display of urgency they grabbed a stretcher and the emergency response kit and headed straight for the blood-splattered European woman.

"Miss, where are you injured?" asked the driver. His deep-set eyes scanned the woman's body up and down. No doubt eager to champion an attractive woman's cause, Elsa considered. He was to be disappointed, she knew.

"Not me. Him..." She pointed to the black man lying on the ground.

"*Fok*! He's a *bladdy kaffir*!"

The slur—vile and bigoted—stung. Elsa sprung to Stanwell's defense. "*Hou jou bek*!" [Shut your trap!] she barked. Leo the Rhodesian ridgeback growled a warning of his own.

Cornered like a carrion jackal, the ambulance driver glared at his partner, seeking moral support. He was met with a shrug of muted disdain.

The quiet attendant quickly scanned the neighborhood; then tentatively he approached Elsa. She could see reflected in his worn face the past horrors he had witnessed. His dedication was apparent in the sallow tone of his brow and the looseness of his jowl—the price of too many nightshifts and sleep-deprived days on call.

She felt sorry for him, but her concern grew. She sensed his trepidation as he struggled to find the right words to explain the inexplicable.

"Ma'am, we can't take the Bantu," he said.

"What? You won't take him...Why?"

"It's a whites-only ambulance, and the victim is not a European. We aren't allowed to take him," the ambulance attendant bleated. "I'm so sorry."

"*Nooit*—no way, this is nonsense!" exclaimed Elsa, disgusted.

"*Asseblief*—please help us," pleaded Lydia.

"Take him to Baragwanath Hospital then. It's a nonwhite hospital close to Soweto," said the attendant. "But I warn you, it's overcrowded and understaffed, so he might not get the urgent care he needs."

Furtively the medic looked over his shoulder, as if certain that banishment to the desolate Kalahari Desert awaited him as a reward for the flagrant generosity and wasteful compassion he was about to show. He took from his emergency kit a roll of gauze bandage, some sterile pads, tape, and a small bottle of ruddy Mercurochrome antiseptic. He then cautiously handed the supplies to Elsa.

Without another word driver and attendant returned to their ambulance. With a cursory wave of disdain, they sped away. Elsa had a single distressing thought: neither of the medics had deigned to touch Stanwell—not even once.

Lydia realized they had only one option. "Let's get him back to my house," she suggested.

Carefully the two white women shifted Stanwell into a seated position. They wrapped his dark arms around their pale shoulders and gripped him firmly by the waist. After a brief struggle, they hoisted him up on unsteady legs and began the long trek toward the house. Though weak from loss of blood, Stanwell tried his best to carry his weight like a proud warrior, but in truth stumbled clumsily like a newly born karakul sheep. His head bobbled side to side, leaving in its wake droplets of blood on the gravel driveway below.

On entering the Duncan home, they headed for the guest bathroom. Among the traditional toiletries, the bathroom featured an enchanting bowl of scented candy-shaped soaps (as if one could resist the temptation to pocket a few), a tray of heavily starched *D* monogrammed linen guest towels (too formal for daily use), and for the injured guest the most welcome feature of all, a daybed.

However, Stanwell suddenly became agitated. In maneuvering him toward the bed, the ladies inadvertently positioned him between the makeup mirrors surrounding the bathroom sink. Seeing his ghastly image reflected again and again was too much—the room began to spin, and Stanwell slid to the floor like a discarded towel.

►◄ ►◄

He burrowed up to the light, leaving behind the blackout's murky darkness. Now painfully aware of his too-close proximity to the cold marble-tiled floor, Stanwell struggled to bring focus to the two shapes lurking over his prostrate body. As the haze dissipated, he was relieved to see the concerned faces of his two kindly benefactors; but with emerging awareness, his relief turned to embarrassment, as he realized he was lying at the feet of two white women. His first instinct now was the preservation of his masculine and ancestral pride.

▶◀▶◀

Due to tribal custom, Stanwell could not accept a state of subservience to any woman. Tribal tradition handed down through the ages had defined the respective roles of men and women through life's various stages. Men of the tribe were the warriors, the providers, the protectors, and responsible for meting out justice.

Women were their attendants, bearing their infants, foraging for food and water, pounding maize into flour, cooking, brewing, and weaving and beading. And these tribal women, for all their dedication, at the end owned absolutely nothing. The men were the sole proprietors of all the family wealth.

Yet a Bantu man demonstrated in the most tangible way the value he held for the woman he loved, in the form and magnitude of the *lobola*—a dowry-in-reverse he would pay to his bride-to-be's family for her hand in marriage. The more head of cattle he offered his prospective in-laws, the greater the esteem he held for his future wife.

Despite his injured state, this ingrained cultural reflex surfaced in the form of indignation. Stanwell in frustration grabbed the bloodied *lappie* cloth off his forehead and angrily hurled it across the room.

Here at their feet, a large black man, a stranger, and injured, had suddenly behaved aggressively—displaying unprovoked and deliberate hostility toward the two women.

Misinterpreting Stanwell's pitiable act of humiliation as unjustified violent behavior, Elsa and Lydia hastily backed away, their concern for him changing instantly to fear. The Duncans' guest bathroom may have been luxurious, but the tension in that intimate place took on the claustrophobic stench of a public lavatory.

Stanwell felt their fear. Though physically weak, he could still project power over his hosts, and he took pleasure in it. In his mind, the natural order of things had again been reestablished. But his glee was fleeting.

▶◀ ▶◀

He had lived long enough in their world to understand these two women deserved and expected gratitude. And in truth Stanwell was grateful. But they didn't understand: they didn't know the ways of his people, they didn't speak his language, and they had no appreciation of his culture. If they did, they'd know for a Bantu male showing gratitude was akin to displaying weakness; and weakness meant one thing—humiliation.

However, the three of them in that ornate bathroom now faced a unique circumstance, a situation so different that it required a break from the conventions they'd all adhered to in the past. Stanwell was the first to accept this strange reality. This wasn't a typical black and white matter—the situation in which he found himself was more nuanced.

In fact, these two women had extended themselves well beyond the prescribed roles decreed by society. Despite the women's ignorance regarding his ethnic values, Stanwell now regretted his behavior and truly appreciated the kindness they'd shown him.

He also appreciated how swiftly circumstances had changed from the perspective of his benefactors: one moment he was a victim of a traffic accident requiring their compassionate aid, and the next instant he'd become an ungrateful *muntu* thug displaying the predictable hostility of his race.

Stanwell realized he must act swiftly.

"Sorry, missus. I was in a bit of a *dwaal*—I couldn't focus. Look!" cried Stanwell, pointing to the opposite wall. "I've got blood on your nice house. I must clean it for you."

The Crabtree & Evelyn wallpaper with the bird and butterfly motif was smeared with blood from the soiled cloth Stanwell had hurled across the room. A singular bird embossed in the pastel-toned wallpaper pattern had borne the brunt of the strike. Stanwell was stunned by the image. A splotch of blood, his blood, coated the crop of the rendered bird. It was as if a bullet had pierced the creature's gullet and blood now drained from its chest.

The sight disturbed him. Stanwell's people read signs in nature—especially the *iSangoma.* Though a resident of a modern city, the role of the traditional tribal diviner still held sway over him. The bird wasn't real, but his blood was.

What does it signify, he wondered?

His eyes tracked the red-damp cloth lying against the floor molding. Dismayed, Stanwell hobbled across the room, got to his knees, and with the soiled cloth in his hand began to scrub at the blood trail issuing from the bird's chest. He achieved little, only smearing it into a gory mess.

Both ladies were horrified. Their fear now forgotten, they gently steered Stanwell back to the daybed. However, calm it was not to be.

In feverish guilt, Stanwell began to rant about "not letting down the Big Baas." He pleaded for the television sets in the back of the pickup truck to be rescued immediately.

In order to pacify him, Lydia instructed two of her domestic servants to carry them to the safety of the garage. Still not satisfied, Stanwell begged Lydia to telephone the "Big Baas." Unfamiliar with the sobriquet, Lydia asked for the man's real name. Stanwell replied enigmatically, "DGF." Lydia agreed to call him on condition that she could make two other calls, to the doctor and to her husband.

Lydia felt vital, useful. She had the inexorable desire to make decisions on her own—without deferring to her husband—and this emergency under her roof provided her with the opportunity to do so. She chose to make a single call, to the doctor.

Happily, Dr. Malcom Weitz was available. The good doctor still believed in making house calls, a practice he developed as a country doc where home telephones were scarce. Another habit gleaned from those backwoods days was his predilection to drop by unannounced, for a quick drink, on the pretext that he happened to be in the neighborhood.

To some it seemed peculiar that a man of medicine indulged in strong liquor, and they questioned his sobriety (and the state of his liver); but in truth he seldom quaffed it all back. Instead he'd toy with the tumbler, swirling the ice in the amber liquid, all the while gently prodding his surprised hosts about their state of health and mind.

Any wheeze, sneeze, or cough would be met with a stethoscope warmly rubbed to break the chill. And the eyes of young patients would light up with delight when he encouraged them to hear the lub-dub rhythms of their own hearts. If an ailment required further attention, he would act in a capable, kindly manner—without undue panic or alarm.

◄►

Dr. Weitz presented himself at the Duncans' front door within twenty minutes of receiving Lydia's call. Wearing his habitual black suit (more a uniform of competence than funereal) and clutching his battered bag, the doctor rang the bell. A relieved Lydia rushed to greet him.

To Lydia he resembled a crustier Clark Gable; the doctor's moustache was a fair simulation of the bristles underscoring the nose of the famed film star. In truth, a young Malcom Weitz adored the *Gone with the Wind* epic and subliminally assumed elements of the fictional Rhett Butler persona.

In fact, as homage to both the film and the medical profession, Dr. Weitz's favorite expression was, "Frankly, my dear, I *do* give a damn!" The irony was not lost on the good doctor, that as a Southern African he had modeled himself on a Southern gentleman considered to be the "black sheep" of his family.

Almost hyperventilating, Lydia poured out the tale of the past couple of hours: the accident outside their front gate; rescuing the battered driver, a native-boy; the shameful behavior of the ambulance crew; the decision to fend for themselves; and carrying the injured victim to the house. She then appealed to the doctor to be "the man of the hour" and rescue the situation.

Dr. Weitz didn't need an invitation. The moment he saw the wreck outside, he'd anticipated what was required of him. In one matter, however, he was surprised: he had assumed a Duncan family member was involved in the accident—the fact that the patient was a stranger, and what's more a non-European, was an intriguing twist.

►◄►◄

As an unflappable country doctor working in remote areas without electricity, running water, or state-of-the-art medical equipment, Dr. Weitz had learned to improvise. There were no ambulances, operating rooms, laboratories, or specialists to back him up. He understood that "in the sticks" he was the only recourse his patients had to achieve a satisfactory outcome.

There were other difficulties such as language and trust. Often he had to fend off the bitter rivalry of the *inyangas* and *sangomas.* The tossing of bones, the trance-inducing drumming, and the chanting of herbalists and faith healers didn't faze him—unless it cost a critical patient precious time.

But when these witch doctors tried to foist their foul *muti*—crude concoctions conjured from mysterious elements of suspect origin—on gullible and desperate patients, he was compelled to intervene. He didn't enjoy being a skeptic, but nothing could convince him to use iguana flesh to clear clotted arteries or monkeys' intestines to prevent miscarriages.

However, he had sutured many limbs damaged by wayward farming equipment and midwifed numerous needy babies. Neither race nor creed was a consideration; no patient was turned away, and no discriminatory signs hung over the door of his practice.

◄►◄►

"Lydia, you did very well," said Dr. Weitz. "Where's the patient?" He placed a reassuring hand on her arm as she led them to the guest bathroom.

The small room was filled with natural light that filtered through voile curtains covering the opened window. The delicate netting rustled in the breeze, projecting the shadow of the fabric's finely embroidered pattern on the opposite wall. Despite the gentle breeze, and a bowl of lavender potpourri, there was the stuffy air of anxiety in the room.

Doctor Weitz peered in. He saw a disheveled male figure lying on the narrow daybed, his injured head supported by a towel-covered pillow. So as to not encroach on the space of the suffering man, almost teetering off the edge of the bed, sat the trim form of a lovely young woman.

"Thank you, Lydia. You can leave this with me," said Doctor Weitz as he turned to shut the door. He was quietly stunned.

In all his years in medicine—nay, in all his years as a South African—he had never seen such an indelible gesture—so warm, and caring. It was all the more shocking because he found himself to be astounded. Unfortunately, even in this community—here in liberal Sandton—such a humane and genuine response would be considered outrageous.

What the doctor found to be both strange and unsettling was the image of a finely wrought, delicately manicured *white* hand in the firm grasp of a roughly hewed, labor-calloused *black* hand.

▶◀▶◀

Dr. Weitz entered the lounge with Elsa close behind. Lydia was leafing through the glossy pages of *Fairlady* magazine in a futile attempt to distract herself from the crisis occurring under her roof. She glanced up expectantly.

"Glad to say there's nothing life threatening," Dr. Weitz said, "but I sedated the patient to make him comfortable."

He turned to Elsa. "You were very helpful in there. Thank you." For a moment they remained silent, grateful the immediate crisis was behind them.

The doctor then asked, "By the way, what's the chap's name?"

"It's Stanwell," replied Elsa.

"Well I've cleaned Stanwell up as best I could, but we need to get him into surgery," the doctor continued. "Unfortunately I can't operate now. He's eaten too recently for me to give him an anesthetic."

"Then what would you suggest?" enquired Lydia.

"You may bring him to my rooms around seven this evening," the doctor said, glancing at his watch. "I'll have everything in my surgery prepared." Then, firmly gripping his trusted medical bag, he headed out the door.

The vigil began in earnest. Lydia and Elsa sat together on the couch, alone with their thoughts. Elsa discreetly took in her surroundings. Her eyes followed her ears—drawn by the perpetual ticking of the antique brass porthole clock on the adjoining wall, so appropriate for the nautical theme of the room.

Framed historical nautical charts covered the walls, with a map of the Cape of Good Hope route being the most conspicuous. Above the fireplace was an ominous collection of early to mid-nineteenth century whaler harpoons. Unlike the feminine guest bathroom, this clearly was a masculine domain. Elsa was growing more curious about Mr. Duncan.

After the onrush of adrenaline from the anxiety experienced due to the morning's unforeseen events, things had at last settled into a state of calm, and it was time to replenish. It was also an opportunity for Lydia to return to the reason why she had invited Elsa to her home.

"I'm famished," said Lydia. "Let's see what Dinah can conjure up for us." She rang a small brass bell and moments later the maid appeared. "Dinah, good, we're hungry. Please bring us a snack. I think the smoked *snoek* pâté, crisp melba toast, and some fresh fruit will do just fine, thanks."

She turned her attention to Elsa. "Despite what's happened, I'm sure you're curious why I invited you today. Since Stanwell's resting, if you don't mind, I'd like to continue..."

Elsa smiled and nodded in agreement.

"I'm fed up being a spoilt suburban housewife. I know our men don't like their women to work once married...They feel emasculated or something. Whatever. I'm really bored," said Lydia with conviction. "There's only so many times I can get my hair and nails done. And if I have to play another game of bridge, I'll go nuts! Do you know what I mean?"

Elsa didn't. This apparent indulgent lifestyle was way beyond her comprehension.

Lydia was just warming up. "Having to rely solely on my husband for all my needs is really a pain."

Elsa was surprised by this sophisticated lady's bluntness.

Lydia thought for a moment. "I need a challenge. We don't have any kids...except for Leo," she said with a wistful smile. "My only responsibility is our home, but I have servants to take care of the house, and the cooking, and the garden, et cetera. Heck, I even have a servant to take care of the servants!"

"Is it, hey? I must admit it doesn't sound too bad to me," said a perplexed Elsa.

**

Spoilt, pampered, and bored were the northern suburb ladies and Sandton socialites. These recent ersatz hippies now rolled in the wealth and privilege of their race. As a result, they all seemed to have gone bonkers in the go-go seventies. Playing musical-chair romances with ever-changing spouses was the vocation of the day. In an exclusive community so small, everyone knew one another—so much so that a kid's best friend's mother one week had a high probability of becoming his stepmother the next.

These shenanigans dominated the press and served as a distraction from the vital issues of the day. The back pages of the largest national newspaper, The Sunday Times, became tabloid heaven—a haven for gossip where she-said-he-did and he-said-she-wouldn't was the compelling topics for the vacuous.

In an obtuse trend, men endeavored to elevate themselves on the social ladder with boastful puffery.

Nothing was confidential. The larger the monthly alimony check paid to his ex, the greater was the divorced male's preeminence over his peers. Meanwhile the womenfolk counted their alimony checks and targeted their next marriage prospect.

The men had only themselves to blame. Conceit compelled them to insist their wives play only a decorative role, and not work. This was based on the flawed notion that a wife working implied one was an inadequate provider. And so these misguided men built servant-filled gilded palaces for their brides, and gave them absolutely nothing useful to do.

The sad thing was the great untapped capacity of so many well-educated European women. Considering white society was small enough, it made little sense marginalizing the members of the fairer sex, but that's what happened. Instead, left to their own devices these women created idle mischief—and as they fiddled, their world fell apart at the seams.

**

Lydia had been impressed by the manner in which Elsa had handled herself during the morning's crisis. Honestly, I don't know how I'd have coped without her, she reflected. What a *sucky* way to be interviewed for a job...shame!

She studied Elsa as she assembled her thoughts. Yes, this girl is a woman of substance, but would she agree? That lingering doubt compelled Lydia to validate herself further to this young Afrikaner woman.

"A little about me...I got my Bachelor of Commerce degree from Wits University here in Jo'burg. Despite my degree I couldn't compete with the men for a management position, so I then entered the work scene as a secretary in the typing pool.

"I'm telling you I filed, dialed, and smiled with the best of them. And, according to the script, found myself a husband. We got married. I stopped working. Now I am living the life of Riley. And voilà, here we are!"

"All right...So?"

"Do you have any idea why I invited you today?"

"No. Not a clue."

"At the stroke of midnight last New Year's Eve, I made a resolution to finally do something, to do something creative and exciting." Lydia cleared her throat, suddenly uncertain about articulating her dream out loud.

"Okay, this is it. I'm going to launch a fashion clothing line under my own brand...we still need to finalize the name...and distribute it nationwide throughout all the Denham stores," Lydia gushed, unreservedly.

"That's really *mooi*," said Elsa, now curious. In her sensible manner Elsa peppered Lydia with several questions.

Patiently Lydia responded, encouraged by Elsa's interested response.

Dinah appeared carrying a tray. She offered plates, napkins, and flatware to both women and bustled about arranging the smoked snoek (a distinctive fish found in the waters off Cape Town) and all its accoutrements on the table.

At the center she placed a fresh fruit salad in a large hand-spun alabaster bowl. Globes of *spanspek* cantaloupe and seedless watermelon were tossed with strips of mango and *naartjie* tangerine wedged between red grapes and orbs of fleshy lychees, all bathed in a tangy pool of *granadilla* passion fruit and orange juice. Slivers of Granny Smith apples were fanned over slices of cored pineapple, and crowning the presentation was a sprig of fresh mint (plucked from a plant thriving under the dripping garden tap).

"Yum, a really nice feast," Elsa said.

"Well deserved after our active morning," said Lydia. "Pity the poor native-boy can't eat. Just as well he's sleeping."

◄◄

The wait was gnawing at both women. They repeatedly looked over at the clock on the wall. Time stretched before them like a mirage in the Kalahari Desert, teasingly close, then reappearing once again at the farthest point on the horizon. Lydia said in answer to Elsa's last question, "You asked me about the launch. Well, we visited London last Christmas. Oh, by the way, have you ever gone overseas?"

Elsa gave a noncommittal shrug.

"Strange thing visiting London in December—after a nineteen-hour plane ride, the next thing your summer becomes the middle of winter!" Lydia continued. "And speaking of strange, you know South African Airways is banned from flying over Africa. Well, the route around the bulge takes much longer, so we needed to refuel. And the only place we could gas up was a fly-speck of an island in the middle of the Atlantic Ocean called Isla de Sal.

"The airport there was built by our government. So we had landing rights, but we couldn't, because the runway had been overrun by a large pack of feral dogs. It was quite bizarre, and rather scary.

"Imagine sitting in a big aircraft, running low on fuel, and unable to land because a pack of mangy flea-bitten dogs had the run of the place. Thank goodness some soldiers chased them away. I'm glad Leo is more considerate." Lydia rewarded the handsome ridgeback with a pat, which he reciprocated by squirming uninhibitedly onto his back.

"Back to London: it's magical though, with all the festive decorations and window displays in the great department stores like Selfridges and Harrods."

"It sounds wonderful," said Elsa, envious.

"Oh it is, but it was so cold I needed to buy more warm clothes. So I went shopping, it's then that the seed of a fashion line was planted."

"*Struesbob?*"

"Yep, it's true," said Lydia. "I want my fashion line to be trendy and youthful. These threads must be hip, but not too far-out...and meant to make the Africa vibe international by bringing it to the cosmopolitan world.

"Our signature will be strong animal prints and the hottest designs. This we can do because animal prints have no borders, so we can cut the fabric anyway we want to make our designs really vogue.

"Here are some sketches," said Lydia, handing over to Elsa a sketchpad she retrieved from beside the couch. "Tell me honestly, what do you think?"

The creative Lydia radiated enthusiasm. Elsa preferred this version of her new friend to the woman she'd debated earlier that morning. Elsa was swept up in the wonder of Lydia's vision as she leafed through the folio of fashion concepts. "They're terrific," said Elsa, clapping her hands with delight.

"You need to know I have a way to make this a big success. I have real clout you see," admitted Lydia. "My husband Sidney Duncan is the managing director of all the Denham department stores around the country."

Curiosity flooded Elsa's face. "That's where I work. What a coincidence..."

"Not really, in fact just the opposite. A while ago I went to meet my husband at the Rosebank branch and spotted you in the handbag department. I asked you directions to the store's restrooms. Don't you remember me?"

"Not really. I'm sorry."

"Don't be. When we spoke I noticed your identification badge. Now most ID photos look terrible, but your picture was gorgeous. You're so naturally photogenic."

"If you say so..."

"Are you ready to hear what I've got in mind for you?"

Elsa nodded in anticipation.

"Elsa, you have 'the look,' a natural freshness and modern beauty that's appealing. Tie that in with your authentic South African sensibility, and you're perfect for my plans. So, would you like to be our official model and the face of my new fashion line?" Lydia arched her brows as she posed the question.

Flabbergasted, Elsa found herself speechless. It had been a day of seismic ups and downs, from the turmoil of the traffic accident to this amazing job offer. Taking Elsa's silence as indecision, Lydia chose to be direct. "As this is a great career opportunity I expect you to work really hard, and even come up with some ideas of your own. Do you know what I mean?"

"Yes. Thank you so much."

"Alright then," said Lydia with a self-satisfied expression marked across her face. "And by the way, in addition to your wages, you get to borrow a company car, a brand new, bright-red Mini Cooper."

In gratitude Elsa hugged Lydia. In boredom Leo yawned.

◄►◄

CHAPTER **FIVE**

THE THUNDERSTORM roiled across the Highveld plateau like the marauding Zulu *impi* on the warpath. It was accompanied by a boom-bang of thunder, the pounding feet of forty thousand warriors in lockstep and countless *assegai* spears struck in unison against oxhide battle shields. Now and then the agitated air was shattered by lightning's vivid scar—a striking threat of the looming deluge.

This rain-swept inland plateau was massive, towering almost six thousand feet above sea level, and encompassed approximately a third of South Africa's landmass. It was the central hub for most of the nation's farming and business enterprises, and the magnet attracting the majority of a diverse population. The source of this attraction was always the gold. And after the gold was pulled from the earth, Johannesburg was left with legacy landmarks: the manmade mountains that surrounded the Rand (the reef), the mine dumps.

Dumps (such an unflattering name) began as digger's tailings in 1886 and grew to substantial flat-topped pyramids of fine yellow sand. These large mounds of soil, now lifeless due to the toxic cyanide and stripped nutrients induced by the gold-recovery process, had little use except as homes for the city's drive-ins—the Top Star being a motoring moviegoer's favorite, with a panoramic view of the city.

But when the winds blew, silica from the dumps coated everything in a fine powder—and irritated the lungs. But that was a concern for future generations; in 1976 children schussed down these sandy slopes on flattened cardboard boxes, oblivious to the chemicals they inhaled, their only concern was not to pee in their pants at the crazy thrill of it all. However, to those already allergic or fed up with the grime and dust, the rain was a blessing that washed the lousy crud away.

In this place of inequality, the rain was fastidiously egalitarian, pouring down equally on all the citizens of greater Johannesburg, from the townships to the suburbs. However, in the suburbs they remained dry in their mansions while the dispossessed soaked in their shacks. Yet no matter the circumstance, all people of the reef preferred the fertile bounty of a rainfall to the deprivations of a drought.

▶◀▶◀

Sidney Duncan's thoughts were elsewhere. He was stuck in his daily end-of-the-workday traffic jam. He glanced up at the Civic Theatre—the city's cultural bastion of the arts—and recalled a black-tie gala event featuring the American entertainer Liberace. Across the way, in striking contrast to the flamboyant pianist and his glittering candelabra, stood a powerful bronze statue: three gold miners—two black and one white—standing resolutely together for eternity, with their bronze-cast pneumatic drill piercing the sky. Sid gave a shiver; during winter these three stoic miners were sheathed in ice.

Rain added to the traffic delay. However, Sid felt comfortable and secure in these weather conditions. The previous year he'd treated himself to a 1975 Jaguar XJ6C sedan, with a British racing green outer coat and tan Connelly hide interior. He glared at the stalled traffic, shrugged, then reached for his luxury marque's high-fidelity stereo system.

Time for some music.

For Sid the compact cassette had been a revelation, and was a happy good-riddance to the funky eight-track system that preceded it. The cassette's rich stereophonic sound was a winner, and for Sid the interior of his Jaguar was now reminiscent of a concert hall.

He fed the Columbia-labeled music cassette into the trapdoor maw of the stereo, and the vehicle filled with the haunting strains of a single clarinet.

That evocative opening of George Gershwin's *Rhapsody in Blue* was, to Sid, sublime, and this was his favorite version of the piece—the Leonard Bernstein 1959 recording. What could be better, he thought. A master conductor and pianist conducting the masterpiece of another master conductor and pianist, and the similarities didn't end there: both were American born, of Ukrainian-Jewish parentage. Sid Duncan could not but appreciate this coincidence.

Beyond the splendid orchestration, this sixteen-minute recording meant a great deal more to Sid. It represented something novel, something both powerful and wonderful. *Rhapsody in Blue* was seminal. It melded disparate elements by merging two sounds into a single, eminently superior union, and in doing so shattered sonic barriers.

It was the first jazz concerto, fusing classical music with elements of jazz in a style that broke down the musical strictures created by the purists. Many critics condemned it, but what mattered most was the warm reception it received from the common man. In this positive blend of two musical disciplines, Sid saw a metaphor for his torn land, where an intermingling of the nation's people would create a unified South Africa. But for now such matters didn't weigh on Sid's mind; the music lifted his spirits and provided a prelude to what promised to be a delightful evening.

Fellow travelers were bemused to witness a refined patrician cocooned in the luxury Jaguar sedan stopped at the traffic light, soundlessly gesticulating as if a frenzied maestro brandishing an imaginary baton. Sid didn't care. Gershwin's masterpiece would carry him homeward. The light blinked green, and with a purr the big cat leaped forward.

⋈⋈

Duncan expected a delicious home-cooked supper. With Lydia providing the menu and Dinah cooking, he had an excellent team in the kitchen. Possibly the evening's treat would be the sole lorraine, a family favorite and a specialty of the executive chef from Die Landdrost Hotel.

Sid was most content.

Business was booming despite international sanctions. With the price of gold soaring, and South Africa being the leading supplier of the precious metal, in real terms the economy was thriving. But the nation's despised status in the world had become wearisome.

Being alienated and isolated by the world community had become costly with international demand for domestic products dropping precipitously. And any dealings, business or personal, with the rest of Africa were prohibited. To Sid, being persona non grata elsewhere in Africa was a disappointment, as there was much he felt he could personally contribute to the continent.

As he turned into the driveway in the gloom of dusk, the car's headlights reflected on fragments of shattered glass and twisted metal lying in the road. Sid frowned. He hoped nothing was wrong. He hadn't heard from Lydia throughout the day. In and of itself, that wasn't unusual, as she was quite independent and preferred not to be a nuisance. He tried to relax, but the first tentacle of anxiety reached under his skin.

▶◀▶◀

A key turned in the front door lock. Lydia looked up, an alarmed expression painting her face. "Crikey! I forgot to call Sid," she said. "He hasn't a darn clue about our situation."

"What situation?" asked Sid Duncan on entering the house. After seeing the debris outside, he was already alert, but his concern grew at the anxious tone in his wife's voice and the sight of a stranger sitting in his lounge.

Lydia greeted him with an effusive hug. "Thank God you're home. We must be at Doctor Weitz's in thirty minutes."

"We're not going anywhere 'til you tell me what on earth is going on!"

"There's been an accident and an injured native-boy is recuperating in our guest bathroom."

"What? And who is she?" He pointed accusingly at Elsa. "Is this her fault?"

Sid Duncan had left work at five forty-five, fought his way through rain and traffic, and expected a fine homemade meal waiting for him. Instead, he was prevented from parking the car in the dry shelter of his garage by a mysterious tower of large boxes blocking his way. Worse, the routine of the household was off-kilter. Frustrated at not having the end-of-day solace he expected, Sid found he wasn't hungry after all.

He allowed himself to be steered to his favorite chair by Lydia. After she introduced him to Elsa, they both brought him up to date. Periodically Sid nodded, visibly shaken, but chose not to interrupt their narrative. His regard for Elsa grew as his wife explained the role the girl had played in Stanwell's rescue—specifically her plucky confrontation with the ambulance driver. And he heartily endorsed his wife's decision to summon Doctor Weitz. Sid waved away Lydia's gratitude for his understanding, telling her he was glad he'd got home in time, as without his help they would've been unable to get Stanwell to the doctor's rooms by seven o'clock.

Duncan glanced at his watch. "I better look in on him. Let's hope he's awake. My car's right outside the front door." As he got to his feet, his wife had one more thing to add.

"The Bantu has been going on and on about someone called the Big Baas." Lydia had just remembered Stanwell's plea. "When I asked for more details, all he gave me were the initials DGF—all very mysterious, I must say..."

"That's not a problem, Lydia," Sidney Duncan replied. "I know DGF. We're board members together, and sometimes we play squash at the Wanderers Club. Just a fortnight ago we discussed carrying some of his products in our stores. I said I would look into it. Guess I owe him a call."

"Glad that mystery is solved. What do the initials stand for?"

"DGF is Daniel Gideon Firth. He's the Gallo Group's chief executive." Sid glanced again at his watch. "It's almost six thirty," said Sid. "Let's get whatchamacallit over to the doctor. I'll call Firth later."

With almost military-like precision, it showered every evening for a couple of hours on the Highveld. Then, in a disciplined about-turn, the daily precipitation swiftly retreated after wiping out the silica dust lingering in the air. With the tensions of the day cooled, the streets began to fill again with vehicles carrying passengers to dinner, a show, or a furtive rendezvous.

The Jaguar sliced through the northern suburbs and turned on Oxford Road heading toward Rosebank. The island verges separating the two wide lanes of traffic were foliage rich, interspersed with palm trees and flowering jacarandas. As the car slowed in tight bends, all came into sharp focus—the breathy, tubular jacaranda blossoms pop-pop-popped under the grind of the tires.

As the Jaguar surged forward again in a blur of vivid immediacy, impressionism merged into abstract expressionism. In the half-light of day, the jacaranda trees were a living canvas of mauve trumpeted blossoms and streaks of green pinnate leaflets, all rendered in a flurry of stippled brushstrokes—nature's reinterpretation of Claude Monet.

The purring car's rear wheels skidded on greasy blossoms jostled from the trees by the recent rain. Sid cursed under his breath, muttered a brief apology, and tightened his grip on the leathered wheel. At the left kink he veered right, now heading down Jellicoe Avenue. After another hundred yards he turned left on Cradock Avenue, and finally came to a halt under the discreet awning beside Dr. Weitz's medical practice.

▶◀▶◀

"Constant kindness can accomplish much. As the sun makes ice melt, kindness causes misunderstanding, mistrust, and hostility to evaporate." These were the words of the great missionary doctor, a man who knew Africa so well, the Nobel Laureate Albert Schweitzer; they were also Dr. Weitz's mantra. Though he and Schweitzer were of different faiths—Jewish and Lutheran, respectively—he saw common purpose in serving humanity through healing both the body and the spirit. But unlike his great idol, a classical music scholar, Dr. Weitz's zest for life was enriched by his enduring passion for the silver screen.

"*Oy gevalt!*" he exclaimed in Yiddish, a language he used in rhetorical surprise. Accustomed to chatting aloud to himself, the doctor continued, "I feel I'm in a mobster movie. Like some poor schmuck, usually it's a vet, forced at gun point to remove slugs from the bad guy, only to get a bullet in the brain for his efforts." The surreptitious nature of the surgery he was about to perform increasingly bemused him. "Let's hope for a more favorable outcome in this instance."

The procedure Weitz was about to perform was not the cliché creation of a screenwriter's fantasy; rather, it would be painfully real and would contravene a litany of apartheid's edicts. As a precaution, he'd deliberately scheduled the surgery after work hours to avoid prying eyes. And not wishing to implicate his nurse, he'd sent her away. Now he had to operate on the man lying on his treatment table unassisted.

Doctor Weitz was angry. His patient was a victim of a traffic accident—not a criminal. "What's criminal is forcing me to repair him in secret under threat of reprisal," muttered the disconsolate doctor.

Stanwell was sedated but not unconscious. Forced to do the surgery without an anesthetist to assist, Weitz alone couldn't monitor the breathing tubes. So he put his patient in a "twilight state." There were advantages: Stanwell needed to follow instructions during the procedure, then be easily awakened and quickly whisked away afterward—as Stanwell was a large man, the only hope of getting him into the Duncans' car would be under his own steam. Most important, however, was that Stanwell would not remember a thing.

Weitz peered at the lacerated facial tissue through surgical magnifying glasses and considered his options: better irrigate the mess with low-pressure sterile saline solution, so as to not drive the glass in deeper.

The process of extracting individual shards was painstakingly tedious. The transparent nature of glass made it very difficult to see, and an X-ray was of little use. So the doctor kept his eyes peeled for fragments glinting in the surgical lights. Tweezers and needles were the initial tools of choice. Then with the scalpel he tidied up the ragged lips of the many gashes. Finally, hundreds of sutures were applied with the dexterity of a fine seamstress.

His back and neck ached. His temples hurt and his eyesight had begun to blur; it was time to wrap it up. Weitz carefully closed the cutaneous wound on Stanwell's chin with a final square knot. The doctor then removed his surgical glasses, pressing his fatigued eyes into the crook of his arm. It was now imperative he inspected his handiwork and do an inventory of surgical implements. Fatigue was no excuse for leaving a needle or sponge in his patient's body.

Now that Doctor Weitz had cleaned Stanwell up, he could consider his patient for the first time. As was his habit, the doctor again spoke aloud to himself, "Stanwell here, with his shiny cranium, strong brow, high cheekbones, and the hint of the Orient in his eyes, reminds me of the actor Yul Brynner from *The King and I.*"

Doctor Weitz snapped out of his musings—extrapolating reality from the fantasy realm of motion pictures was a secret best kept from his patients or they'd doubt his reason—and went off to wash up. His patient's sedation would soon wear off.

▰◁▰▷

It was late. Outside, a glowing street lamp buzzed with moths. Above the awning, the night sky was obsidian black with countless random clusters of tiny bright crystals, with the Crux—the Southern Cross constellation—marking the south celestial pole.

The waiting room had grown stuffy. Earlier chatter had faded into a simple cannon cycle of yawns, with Mr. Duncan triggering the round, followed by Lydia and then a sheepish Elsa. Weitz entered the room. Three heads turned toward him. The drawn expressions on their faces were typical of those sitting in vigil—torn between sincere concern for the patient and a guilty desire to return to their normal lives.

Sid Duncan was the first to speak. "*Howzit*, Doc? How's the patient doing?"

"Quite remarkable, actually. I removed glass fragments from both eyelids. It's lucky he wasn't blinded. I sewed up both lacerations, which, mind you, was the most delicate work I've ever done."

"Not bad," Duncan said, in that typical English custom of understatement.

"I must warn you that the poor chap's face is a mess with all the stitches and bandages I applied," said the doctor calmly.

"Well, that's to be expected. I'm just grateful he's alive," added Lydia.

Weitz continued, "Stanwell's badly bruised and his nose is broken. Not a complicated fracture...just realigned the bone and packed his nostrils with gauze." Warming to his topic, he went on, "His chin got the brunt of the impact. The glass penetrated well below the dermis, and I've tried to remove it all—otherwise he'll have a glass jaw. Sorry, weak joke, but I'm a little punchy."

"Oh, cripes!" exclaimed Elsa.

"Yep. I'm not sure I got everything, but the human body's quite remarkable and will reject foreign objects if they're small enough. A pimple, when scratched away, may have a glass chip inside. So hopefully nature will take care of things."

"Anything else we should be concerned about?" asked Lydia.

"His tongue's swollen, making it difficult to eat. Thankfully he's a big strong chap, because solid foods will be out for a while. Oh, he may also have cracked a rib or two, so I've bound up his chest with a bandage."

Then, almost as an afterthought, the doctor added, "One more thing for you, young lady." He reached into his pocket as he approached Elsa. In his hand he held an inexpensive wrist-watch clotted with dried blood. "I'm sure Stanwell would appreciate it if you cleaned this for him. If you're patient, it'll clean up quite nicely."

"Sure, okay," said Elsa.

"Thanks very much, Doctor Weitz," said Mr. Duncan. "May I please use your phone? I must call Daniel Firth. Apparently, Stanwell works for him as a driver."

▶◁▶◁

CHAPTER **SIX**

THEY HAD A PROBLEM. Where to take Stanwell? He was still in need of care. A hospital was not an option. Doctor Weitz's able handiwork would raise suspicion, resulting in an inquiry, professional embarrassment, and a reprimand by the authorities.

They couldn't take Stanwell to his shantytown home. It was after curfew, not to mention dangerous, especially at night. There were other considerations: the absence of a telephone if an emergency arose, and the poor hygiene conditions—the place wasn't exactly salubrious, lacking power, running water, or modern ablution facilities. The risks to Stanwell of contracting secondary infections would be high in that wanting environment.

Sid Duncan squinted away from the high beams of the oncoming car. He rebuked the unseen driver with a mild insult. "Silly pillock!" he said.

In the rearview mirror, lit briefly by passing headlights, he saw the reflected images of the backseat occupants. Stanwell's head lay on Elsa's shoulder. Her hand rested protectively on his chest. How odd, he thought.

Sid glanced over at his wife. "What should we do now?" he asked, concerned.

"I've been thinking. We have no alternative but to take him back to our house," Lydia replied.

"That's impossible," said Sid, fervently shaking his head.

"What do *you* suggest then?"

Sid shrugged. He kept his eyes locked on the damp macadam road. A sense of unease enveloped him.

"Sid, I can see you're uncomfortable. What's specifically bugging you? C'mon, lay it out for me in that rational way of yours," Lydia asked.

"Normally I'd suggest the servant quarters behind the garage. Dinah could look after him there," Sid replied. "But now I'm worried."

"So...What's the problem?"

"Haven't you noticed the police raids have gotten more aggressive lately? Those intrusive bastards are determined to catch every poor bugger without a valid passbook."

"Okay, it's a risk, but what are the chances of our house getting raided?"

"Frankly I don't know, but remember that our neighbors were raided last week," said Sid. "To be honest, it really freaked me out. It felt like the gestapo...waking up to shrill whistles, barking dogs, and screams, and I wasn't even the victim.

"Shame, our neighbor Roger told me the cops were brutal and dragged away the nanny's husband from their servant's quarters, and bundled the poor blighter into the cop van.

"Just imagine being rousted from your bed in the middle of the night by a bellowing storm trooper sticking a flashlight in your face, demanding your identity papers while you're still half asleep. Un-fucking-believable!"

"Maybe we could put Stanwell up in the main house," suggested Lydia.

"I've considered that, but imagine the shock to the system our domestic servants will experience, finding a fellow Bantu sleeping upstairs in one of our guest rooms. It would surely freak 'em out!"

"To be honest, I've no idea how'd they react, either," said Lydia, taking a deep breath. "It could turn their whole world upside down. Will they tattletale on us? I agree we can't take the risk."

**

The capstone of the apartheid edifice was "influx control," which consolidated the National Party's ambition to separate the population according to race. It was the mainstay of the Group Areas Act of 1950 and used ruthlessly to enforce their Separate Development doctrine. A key component of this scheme were the Pass Laws. The goal was to prevent rural blacks from migrating to the cities in search of work. They feared this human surge would overwhelm the white cities, so these nonwhite peoples were systematically controlled. Robustly enforced, these laws severely restricted the free movement of black citizens within their own country.

Every black was forced to carry a passbook. These passes were domestic passports or identification papers that included a photograph, fingerprints, work permit, and residency and tax records, and which, if approved, permitted a black person to live and work in designated white areas. For example, domestic servants were registered to a specific home, and were restricted to that household; except for their long commute back to the township—a difficult task, as public transportation was not provided (deliberately to discourage blacks from visiting white neighborhoods). There were several consequences as a result of having an invalid passbook, they included jail time, hard labor, job loss, and banishment.

The SAP (South African Police) reveled in arresting those whose papers were invalid, and enjoyed intimidating the rest. Authority typically devolved to the lowest-ranking, cruelest, least judicious members of the police force. These thugs conducted house-to-house sweeps, set up neighborhood roadblocks, and cordoned off city blocks in search of fellow citizens with expired papers.

One would think that with the ardor of the pursuit, and the resources devoted to the chase, the cops were hunting down dangerous gangs on a bloody crime spree. Instead, they wasted their time on trivial pursuits dragging honest, hardworking black men and women from their beds and arrested them—just because their papers were not in order.

Terrorized by the heavy caged police vans and uniformed enforcers armed with pistols and nightsticks, many honest citizens were forced into the shadows— their families destroyed and livelihoods eviscerated. Some turned to crime to survive. Others, harassed and under the constant threat of surprise raids, "quarantined" themselves in the townships, countryside, or on subsistent farms—thereby limiting their access to big city opportunities—at the cost of future prosperity.

Many indigenous blacks wishing to remain close to their families—but prevented from doing so by the passbook police—stumbled upon an imperfect solution:

squatter camps. This was preferable to being restricted to ostensible "homelands" hundreds of miles away from their loved ones. These shantytowns would pop up near the central business districts of major cities. At the end of each workday, returning workers were seldom certain their homes would still be standing; frequently they'd find police had bulldozed their patchwork shelters flat. So, homeless, they'd drift on like ghosts, their only sin a missing stamp on an identity document.

A pass was difficult to obtain. And once owned, the onus to maintain it rested on the black employees— though they needed the white employer's cooperation. Whites, whether venal or apathetic, were irritated by the practice and would habitually ignore requests to update or endorse their employees' passbooks. As a result most passes were incomplete, leaving the holder in a state of constant peril, with a passbook in the pocket the per- petual instrument of fear.

Any black could be arrested for simply sleeping, walk- ing, or working in a white-designated area, despite it be- ing their own country. Understandably, they loathed the dreaded document, and rather benignly called it a "dompas"—a dumb pass.

** **

Elsa sat silently listening to the Duncans' debate. Her discom- fort grew as she heard the anxiety in their voices. Having Stanwell's shaved head pressed firmly against her cheek didn't help matters. She'd become acutely aware of the heat transferred between them at the point where their flesh touched.

Every time the Jaguar turned a tight bend or dipped into a pothole, she was painfully jolted by his mass. From time to time he would moan or involuntarily jerk his limbs. Elsa was worried the anesthesia was wearing off. And the further they travelled without a certain destination for him, the greater her concern grew. It was near midnight as the car closed in on the Duncans' home. A decision had to be made.

"I've an idea!" Lydia exclaimed, "How about our guesthouse?"

"Clever girl, that may work," Sid mused. "But we can't leave Stanwell alone. Would Dinah care for him there?"

"*Wag 'n bietjie*," [Wait a moment] Elsa pleaded. Startled by her sudden entreaty, the Duncans gave Elsa their full attention.

"Please, could you drive me to Hillbrow? I'm scared to take the bus on my own at night. Or, maybe I can just stay with you?" asked Elsa.

"To be honest it's very late and I don't feel like the drive," said Sid. "Lydia, is it okay if Elsa spends the night?"

"Sure," replied Lydia. Turning to Elsa, Lydia asked, "Would you mind keeping an eye on Stanwell tonight? I think it is best we don't get Dinah involved."

"*Ja*...sure thing."

"Thanks—*baie dankie*," said Lydia gratefully.

"Glad that's now settled," said Sid.

The strains of *Rhapsody in Blue* now accompanied them in the car's cabin—powered on by Sid, pleased by the decision.

In his semi-comatose state, Stanwell was aware of the music. It was most unfamiliar to him, nothing like the *kwela* or the *jive* music of the townships. He would learn the name of the composition later, but for now its ethereal quality soothed his fear and gave him much-welcomed calm. With a sigh he drifted back into darkness.

◄►◄►

The headlights swept over the debris from the wreck as Duncan turned into the driveway. Three of the car's occupants were alone with their thoughts; the fourth was totally oblivious.

They half-carried their sedated patient across the damp lawn, and then half-dragged him over the flagstones surrounding the pool. A pair of brass coach lamps illuminated the arbor and the French doors leading to the entrance of the guesthouse.

The overhead trellis bore a rich green vine that crept along wooden slats. The vine and its purple-blue fruit, juicy Catawba grapes, created a delicious protective canopy in the day from the heat of the African sun. These grapes had an unusual flavor with a hint of strawberry to them.

A famished Sid Duncan grabbed a handful of grapes and gulped them down, then awkwardly reached for another bunch for the women. Lydia ignored him—fussing with the keys in her rush to get inside. However, Elsa was grateful for the burst of sweet nectar. She self-consciously wiped away a squirt of juice in the corner of her mouth, before refocusing on getting Stanwell safely settled.

Her eyes swept the interior of the guesthouse. For both their sakes, Elsa needed to orientate herself to this new environment. She was surprised to see a spiral staircase leading downstairs in the corner of the living room. On the left was an alcove doorway leading through to the bedroom, with a bathroom en suite. Lydia rushed ahead, switching on the lights. With Stanwell supported between Sid and Elsa, the trio followed into the bedroom furnished with two queen-size beds.

It took all three of them to help get Stanwell comfortable. Shoes, belt, and the contents of his pockets were kept. His bloodied clothes were discarded. They debated removing his T-shirt, but the prospect of pulling it over his head was daunting and sure to be painful, so they left it on. With nurse-like efficiency the two women tucked him into bed, the sheets a groovy geometric pattern of brown, orange, and yellow. For warmth and a sense of security they added a comfortable waffle-weave blanket.

Then the three Europeans retired to the mod-white fiberglass table adjoining the kitchenette, for some tea to settle their nerves before bed. On the kitchen's Formica countertop sat an intercom to the main house.

For the first time since encountering the traffic accident, Elsa felt some sense of relief.

All was still, but not quiet. In the dark Elsa could hear the hum of the swimming pool filtration system, and the snort of the automated Kreepy Krauly's snorkel breaching the water surface as it blindly patrolled the pool floor on its quest to vacuum muck. But what Elsa found most unsettling were the intermittent gags and gasps from the dusky man no more than five feet from her in the dark.

Elsa was keenly aware of Stanwell's presence as she lay in bed, dressed only in panties and an old T-shirt emblazoned with "The Oyster Box Hotel, Umhlanga Rocks," which she'd found hanging behind the bathroom door.

She struggled to fall asleep.

▶◀▶◀

She awoke abruptly, alarmed. Disoriented by the unfamiliar surroundings, Elsa glanced around the room until she saw Stanwell sleeping peacefully in the other bed.

Relief. But then what had disturbed her?

"Help! Help! Help!"

Elsa heard the shrieks. They didn't seem human—but they were really close by.

"*Jislaaik*!" griped an alarmed Elsa. She leapt out of bed and headed for the intercom. A cheerful, tinny facsimile of Lydia's voice, wishing her a good morning, radiated from the gadget's speaker. Nervously Elsa told her tale.

"Silly girl! Those are neighborhood peacocks. They settle on fences between our homes and announce the sunrise. They're our wakeup call like roosters on a farm."

"Oh?" said Elsa, feeling foolish.

"Some find them annoying pests. Actually I enjoy the exotic flavor they bring. Don't worry, you'll soon get used to their cry. Tell you what I'll have Dinah bring us some *brekkie* on the patio. Say in fifteen minutes...okay? And don't worry I'll bring you a nice robe."

▶◀▶◀

Lydia appeared in a silk quilted cabbage-rose dressing gown with Leo loping at her side. Draped over her arm was the leopard-print robe she'd promised Elsa. A moment later Dinah appeared carrying a large tray with an assortment of breakfast delights: buttered whole-wheat toast lined up in a toast rack, a jug of fresh-squeezed orange juice topped with beaded netting to keep out flies, a split avocado pear dusted with sugar and a squeeze of lemon, two bowls of sliced bananas immersed in sweet and tart granadilla juice, and the obligatory love-it-or-hate-it jar of Marmite—the salty brackish tar-colored yeast extract used as a savory spread throughout the Colonies.

As Dinah set down the tray, Lydia apologized for the lack of conventional fare. The bacon and eggs would be served when the master of the house, Sid, awoke—but promised soon a fresh pot of brewed coffee.

After Dinah had gone, Lydia asked, "Now, tell me about our patient? Recovering well, I hope?"

"It was a really-really long night," said Elsa. "Last night can be summed up in one word—*worried*." She didn't wish to be plaintive, but fatigue has a way of stripping away pretense. So she described her anxiety-ridden night and the disquieting sounds of coughing, gagging, and wheezing that had emanated from the gloom of the other bed.

And that she lay in the dark being vigilant, unable to sleep—constantly on call, fearing a cough would become a choke and demand her immediate attention. Stanwell had been desperate to lie on his side, to clear his throat, but was unable to do so. So she moved across to his bed to elevate him, to enable him to breathe easier. In doing so she got stuck with this large man in her arms.

Oh dear!

Finally he fell asleep leaned up against her. But in the middle of the night he suddenly jerked awake in a frantic panic. She felt sorry for what the poor man was going through so she did for him, what Nanny Rose did for her all those years ago when she woke up from a nightmare. She caressed his shoulders and neck, and softly sang the "Tula Baba" lullaby. That worked. Eventually they both fell back to sleep.

Wonderful!

Before daybreak he'd awoken again, now desperately thirsty. So she'd fed him water in small sips, like a child, because of his badly swollen tongue. And she could tell he was grateful despite the discomfort and pain he was experiencing—and knowing she'd succeeded in making him feel more comfortable had touched her deeply.

That's most understandable.

And that's why, after a long night being on hair-trigger alert, the peacock's desperate cries had alarmed her, and please, would Lydia forgive the frantic early-morning intercom call. "I feel so

silly now," Elsa said sheepishly. "It looks like I was *skrik vir niks*"
[scared for nothing].

"No worries," said Lydia. "After such a torrid night, I understand. Hey look, there's one of your tormentors..." Lydia pointed
to a nearby flower bed. A peacock had poked his head in between
the floral plumage of a bird of paradise plant, and looked at
home nestling among the plant's crane-like blooms.

"That reminds me, do I have a good peacock story for you..."

"Oh, that's so?"

"Yup, when Leo was a pup, these birds drove him nuts. He
yelped, barked, and pranced about trying to intimidate them.
But they weren't particularly impressed. Until one day a mature
male peacock faced Leo. I thought there'd be a scrap.

"But the bird understood he was dealing with an immature
tike. He simply unfurled his splendid feathers, and began strut-
ting his stuff...no hissing or pecking whatsoever. And that's the
day Leo reached an accommodation with peacocks. So much for
my big brave lion hunter," snorted Lydia, giving a wry glance at
the dog curled up at their feet.

"That's cute," said Elsa with a laugh.

"Wait, there's more to the story," continued Lydia. "Just the
other day I saw Leo dashing around the guesthouse. Coming the
other way was a peahen with five chicks parading behind her. It
was a charming scene of maternal affection, until my son of a
bitch dog barreled into them.

"In a flurry of squawks and feathers, the mom and four of her
chicks skedaddled away. Unfortunately, a lone fifth chick scamp-
ered in the opposite direction. Leo chased after the solitary little
bird, and lots of desperate shrieks followed."

Elsa's brow furrowed, a concerned look darkened her face.
"You know, that's the basic tactic of the wild: first isolate the

weakest from the herd, then hunt it, kill it, and then eat it," said a troubled Elsa.

"I know. I'm freaking out now," Lydia said. "So I yell at Leo to stop. But he disobeys me!"

An apprehensive Elsa asked, "What happened next?"

"Leo had his own plan. He sprinted beyond the tiny bird, turned, and then herded it safely back to its mom," said a now very proud Lydia.

Elsa's face reflected her relief.

"Leo's my best! You should've seen the know-it-all expression he gave me after that."

Elsa chuckled sweetly.

"Now, to the matter at hand," said Lydia. "Last night we called Daniel Firth. Hopefully he got the message, because Sid wants his garage cleared." She noticed the melancholy expression on Elsa's face. "Look, this guy isn't our responsibility," said Lydia reasonably.

But Elsa wasn't ready to let go of the weird, unnerving attachment she felt for this black man, despite the uncomfortable emotions that now confronted her.

These feelings were so alien, so different, to that of her life's established path, but circumstances had compelled Stanwell to depend on her, and that was no fault of hers. And his appreciation had moved her in a meaningful way. What could be wrong with that, Elsa thought? Coming to a victim's aid was virtuous—and any gratitude shown by the victim was totally understandable—so why these misgivings?

At the moment, however, Elsa instinctively needed to sublimate her feelings, to numb them, so as to avoid facing the truth. She felt compelled to rationalize them: maybe it was nothing more than an act of compassion, the nurturing of something so helpless, like caring for an injured animal? Or, if she was being honest with herself, was it the thrill of having done something so foreign by touching him, a black man?

These were questions Elsa wasn't yet ready to answer. What Elsa did know was that she admired his stoicism, and for the most part the quiet dignity of his suffering. And that she was drawn to him when he was vulnerable, and she felt validated whenever he allowed her near to provide help and comfort.

For Elsa, this was a day into night she would never forget.

A cheerful Dinah served them coffee, unaware of the injured black man recuperating in the guesthouse nearby. Lydia and Elsa breakfasted together—the suburban socialite and the *boeremeisie* from Brakpan. The two white women discussed the extraordinary events that they'd so recently experienced together, and marveled at the new bond they had forged.

Both were amazed to realize not even twenty-four hours had elapsed since they'd first met.

►◄►◄

CHAPTER SEVEN

DGF WAS SEETHING. Despite the posh first-class accommodations and the efficient fussing of the Lufthansa flight crew, his frustration persisted. He'd traveled almost six thousand miles to attend a global managing directors' conference, and it had been a waste of time; not a damn thing had been accomplished.

He was now flying home to Johannesburg from Hamburg, Germany. The fact that the ticketing/boarding computer system at Flughafen Hamburg was on the fritz, resulting in uncharacteristic chaos at check-in, had not helped his mood.

The futile meeting at troubled music giant PolyGram NV had been held at one of the company's two headquarters. These "bifurcated headquarters" were symptomatic of what was ailing the company. Purportedly equal but separate, one HQ was based in Baarn (a Dutch city located in the Utrecht province), and the other in Hamburg (a German city on the River Elbe). Both were quaintly European, but neither could be considered hotbeds of the entertainment industry. David Gideon Firth, if given the reins, would relocate PolyGram's global headquarters to a neutral city—a hip city like London—where the music scene was far out, and where everyone who was anyone with a groove hung out.

The problem with PolyGram was its genesis as a post-World War II shotgun marriage between two mortal enemies—the Germans and the Dutch. Considering their recent history, it was inexplicable that German Siemens AG and Dutch Philips Electronics NV had merged their music interests—Polydor and Phonogram, respectively. The love child of this unhappy union was named PolyGram.

The Nazi jackboot had flattened Holland, which made the invasion not exactly sporting, as most of the Netherlands was already well below sea level; so it wasn't unexpected that the Dutch had trust issues. On the other hand, the Germans simply felt entitled. The lack of esteem each held for the other was not surprising. The "U-Boat Captains" were arrogant and the "Licorice Lickers" were stubborn. This created a corporate culture of absolutism, where issues were seen in stark terms of black or white, never shades of gray. With compromise verboten and common sense missing in action, the situation between the two suspicious partners became noxious.

PolyGram attempted to solve the problem their way. They implemented a global strategy and installed both Dutch and German representatives at every tier of management, in all forty-two countries. The result was both chaotic and inefficient. Whether a territory was large or small, it had two staffers doing the same job, operating under different terms of reference, and having separate reporting lines.

At top-level management, authority was divided equally among head office staff located in two separate countries. The result was internecine competition—Baarn butting heads with Hamburg—rather than competing side by side in the global marketplace. With nationalistic agendas superseding business fundamentals, PolyGram suffered huge losses due to ceaseless politicking, redundant personnel, bloated overhead, and muddled management directives. It was as if the two heads of Orthros, the mythological serpent-tailed dog, were devouring each other in an irrational clash of mutual self-destruction.

But DGF had a solution for tiny Trutone, the local Poly-Gram partner in South Africa. He noted that vinyl and tape sales in his territory had skyrocketed, yet staggering overhead costs had obliterated success. And the only way to quickly achieve profitability was to streamline the operation, and go for maximum efficiency, by eliminating redundant staff.

DGF proposed selecting the best staffers according to ability, rather than jingoistic allegiances, and he looked to Baarn and Hamburg for support in implementing this plan.

Both Dutch and German management summarily rejected DGF's proposal—ironically so, as this was the only instance they *did* agree on something. So Daniel simmered in his seat, twenty-eight thousand feet above the Atlantic Ocean, and considered his options. His inclination was to press forward with the scheme—doing nothing was an anathema to him. However, there'd be risks if they got wind of it: his head on the chopping block and the partnership destroyed.

On the other hand, his fate might already be sealed for his brash display of insolence. DGF didn't take the rejection lightly, and told them so. He equated PolyGram's Dutch/German feud to similar tribal-like behavior he'd witnessed among the natives back in Africa. He went on to "apologize for offending their First World sensibilities," but he could have saved himself the trip if he'd wanted to view up-close "primitive rivalries." With that, he stood and stalked out of the room.

"Such a load of bunk," DGF snorted aloud in derision. He doubted any of his copassengers had heard him above the din of the four powerful General Electric CF6-50-series engines keeping the huge Boeing 747-200C aloft.

Daniel Gideon Firth glanced at his watch, which still was set on European time. He calculated Stanwell would've already delivered the precious cargo to the homes of the influential lobbyists and bigwigs. He envisioned their excitement as they plugged in the gadget for the first time. Initially they'd be disappointed; for now only a South African Broadcasting Corporation (SABC) test card over an irritating whistle tone could be viewed, but in a fortnight the wait would be over with the first nationwide broadcast.

DGF pushed the button to summon the flight stewardess—it was time for a drink.

▶◀▶◀

Daniel Gideon Firth was born June 28, 1929, at the Florence Nightingale nursing home in Johannesburg. There was nothing auspicious about his birth other than that he was born in the month of June. This indicated the organized nature of his birth; June, July, and August being winter months in the southern hemisphere, disciplined women timed nature's urges to reach full term of their pregnancy during these cooler months.

And Daniel's mother, the always prepared Minnie, was delighted with the birth of their first child. His father Max, being very much older than Daniel's mother, had the expected enthusiasm of an out-of-touch Victorian disciplinarian—which is to say, very little.

Max never accepted anything easily. After escaping the annual pogrom rituals waged against those of the Jewish faith, Max fled the violence of Vilnius, the capital of Lithuania, and arrived in

South Africa. When he disembarked the ship in Cape Town, the only meaningful possession he owned was a camera, a Le Radieux "Shining Detective" twelve-plate automatic manufactured by Girard & Cie of Paris.

It was 1901, the Second Boer War was winding down, and gold fever had reached hyperpyrexia levels. Max's objectives were clear—to photograph the many fortune seekers and prospectors working the early Johannesburg diggings, and to get paid handsomely for immortalizing their likenesses. Always a shrewd opportunist, he optioned claims and purchased stands at a deep cash discount from down-on-their-luck miners. As Johannesburg grew, he grew with it, and Max became a well-heeled property owner.

▶◀▶◀

In the early twenties he met Minnie. There was an air of Russian aristocracy about her. She cited her slender wrists and refined ankles as proof of her pedigree, and firmly eschewed any reference to being of "peasant stock." Max never doubted her, as Minnie was a very literate woman, with a formal education superior to his. Despite their age difference, he found her to be alluring, and she found him to be a responsible adult. Love was not of paramount importance.

He remained an enigmatic character. What must have been an arduous journey to Africa, whether by horseback, train, ship, or shoe-leather, was never discussed. It was as if he erased every memory of family life back in Vilnius with each passing mile on his passage south. He never again referred to Lithuania as "home," unlike the British transplants who never could quite let go of Mother England's apron. He never mentioned his family in passing, or gave the "when I was a child" speech, or carried creased photographs of fading loved ones in his wallet.

To Max, his history was a blank (so un-Jewish and atypical of a people to whom tradition meant everything). He was content to exist on his terms. He didn't aspire to be an ideal husband or an admirable father figure, but in one regard Max did excel—he was the perfect refugee.

▶◀▶

With the birth of Daniel, they made their home in the emerging suburb for the wealthy, Houghton Estate. Every weekday Max would crank-start his green 1928 Austin-7 and drive to his office near the Rissik Street Post Office. As was his habit, he parked directly outside the front door.

Unfortunately, this was a no-parking zone. A battle of wills ensued between Max and the authorities. He held the belief that the owner of the building had the inalienable right to park smack-dab in front of his own building. Despite repeated citations and court summons, he stubbornly persisted.

In the spirit of self-interest, Max should have heeded the city's demands, because his beloved Austin paid the price. The car's black fabric roof was pockmarked with burn holes from cigarettes Max flicked out of his office's second-floor window. No one would dispute that Max Firth was a stubborn man. Fortunately, his son Daniel was nothing like him, being largely, and favorably, influenced by his mum.

In South Africa, the sting of the global Great Depression had quickly faded into the past, largely due to the growing demand for the gleaming bright-yellow metal nicked from the mines. With this economic boom, Max made increasingly lucrative real estate deals, and the family fortunes rose to new heights. Amid this wave of prosperity, Minnie presented Max with a second son, Aaron, and the future looked bright.

▶◀▶

Then tragedy struck. Aaron died on the operating table during a routine tonsillectomy. Though the child's unfortunate death was attributed to a monitoring failure while under general anesthesia, Max blamed Minnie for their loss. As a result he withdrew from both marriage and life, to only ghost between home and office in a morose cloud of reeking Russian cigarettes—his fingers stained filthy nicotine yellow.

In this haze of smoke Max faded away in Daniel's memory—as if his father was one of those aging washed-out sepia prints photographed in the early days of the gold fields. Many years later, when prompted, Daniel could only recall a remote, old-world character, perpetually dressed in dark three-piece suits. He'd then be amazed at remembering his last image of his father, still in that dark formal suit, lying under a kitchen sink, repairing plumbing fixtures in one of his buildings. Daniel was left wondering why his father always dressed as though every day would be his funeral.

▶◀▶◀

Daniel was brilliant. He had an extraordinary flair for numbers, being able to tabulate reams of figures in his head without the aid of scratch pad, pencil, or slide rule. And as a prodigy, he graduated from the Jeppe High School for Boys at fourteen. His school's motto, *Forti Nihili Difficulius* ("for the brave nothing is too difficult"), filled him with the piss and vinegar to take on the world.

The heraldic shield of his school depicted wavy horizontal lines of black and white, suggesting the peoples of Southern Africa, though they were in fact colors usurped from Trinity Hall, Cambridge. A golden bar, however, divided the lines and was a local tribute to the precious ore that gave life to the city of Johannesburg—a city Daniel intended to leave.

▶◀▶◀

He applied to Rhodes University, in Grahamstown, located a thousand miles away from Johannesburg, in the Eastern Cape Province. This was deliberate. Daniel felt a well-deserved respite from the palpable tensions at home would be a good idea. Or so he and his mum hoped.

►◄►◄

It was early 1945 and the end was in sight. World War II was almost over. Colonial soldiers from the North African, Italian, and Normandy campaigns had begun to demob. These troops under the command of Field Marshall Montgomery had succeeded in caging the Axis forces, and now began the adjustment back to their civilian lives in South Africa. Regretfully, success on the battlefield did not guarantee success back home. Job shortages and lack of qualifications stumped many in their effort to regain normalcy. A number of these returning heroes decided to continue their studies in order to compete, and many applied to Rhodes University.

Now only a fifteen-year-old boy, Daniel found he had classmates—these ex-soldiers—some ten years his senior. But the chasm between himself and his fellow students wasn't merely a matter of a decade's time; it was the insurmountable gap in life experiences. These *men* had lived the fearful horrors of the battlefield; they'd witnessed the capricious nature of violent death, the terrors of callous mutilations, and they grasped their personal role as the very instruments in the mayhem. It troubled them. And so they struggled to adapt to the peace.

They were damaged. These were weary men, their view of the world warped. As they struggled to find a role in the present, many were emotionally adrift, plagued with combat fatigue, survivor guilt, and sleep deprivation—and in some a misguided arrogance, aggression, and certain cruelty.

Daniel was underage and couldn't drink with them. He was too slight of frame to challenge them. He hadn't fought alongside them. Daniel didn't know victory in the campaign against the Italians under the gifted military strategist General Dan Pienaar at El Wak in Somaliland; nor had he suffered the siege at Tobruk at the hands of Lieutenant General Erwin Rommel. He'd even missed the seizure of Madagascar, a measure to prevent the Indian Ocean Island from falling into Japanese hands. To these veterans Daniel was just a wet-behind-the-ears kid, worth no more than quarry.

The ritualistic behavior known as institutional hazing put it too mildly; at times Daniel felt more like a battlefield enemy, constantly in fear that retribution was close at hand.

They'd roust him out of bed at three o'clock in the morning for a forced march through the dark college's corridors, with his toothbrush at his shoulder (in lieu of a rifle) until sunrise. That same toothbrush became an implement of revulsion when Daniel was forced, on hands and knees, to scrub the shower stalls and toilets with it.

►◄►◄

In the communal shower, a former "desert rat" who'd fought in the Western Desert spotted Daniel's circumcised dick. Enamored with the exploits of Oliver Cromwell's anti-monarchy Roundheads, who they'd been recently studying in History, the former Commonwealth soldier began a mocking chant, "Roundhead...Roundhead...Roundhead!" Other college mates took up cry.

If the incident had stopped there, Daniel would've greeted the joshing with an awkward laugh and riposted that they, the non-circumcised, had missed a certain irony; if he was a Roundhead, then surely they were Cavaliers, the royalists who failed to save King Charles I from the most drastic "circumcision" of all—having his head cut off with an executioner's axe.

But there wasn't time for a riposte.

Swiftly, a bunch of thugs surrounded him in the shower, and then *scragged* him to the slippery floor. Muzzled with a towel, Daniel tried to squirm away, but he was outnumbered. Then the chant changed; no longer Roundhead, but the slur "Jew-boy" echoed within the confined quarters of the shower stall. Terror turned to humiliation when they forcibly applied black shoe polish, with coarsely bristled brushes, to his genitals.

Despite the fetid stench of the Auschwitz ovens still lingering in the air, despite the mighty effort by the Allies to vanquish the evil forces of the Axis—it seemed inconceivable to Daniel that in this tolerant, liberal environment of higher learning, he would still be victimized because of his faith. In despair Daniel sobbed.

◄◄►

University life for Daniel was hellish for a couple of years. Anti-Semitism at school versus the unkind presence of his father at home left him in a quandary. Far easier to tolerate the unkindness of strangers than that of family, was his reasoned response, so he continued with his college education.

Though his father remained a remote figure in his life, Daniel treasured the memorable images of early gold miners captured through the lens of Max's camera. It was clear that Max really connected with his subjects. Their experiences were moments in time frozen for posterity: the heavily bearded men leaning on pickaxes and shovels with faces reflecting relief for the brief respite from heavy labor; the look of redemption in a gaunt, grimy face gazing down at a pan of washed gold; a down-on-his-luck gambler with a grim face of desperation; and then

the posh new arrival with the cocky strut, unknowingly projecting his naiveté to the all-knowing camera.

Daniel was puzzled by the contradiction. How could Max,
such a dispassionate man, display such warmth and artistry?
How could such an austere man prosper in those pell-mell days
of hardship and deprivation?

Of course, it was the camera! Seeing the world through the
viewfinder, hidden under a black hood, Max shielded himself
from the world. The camera was a mask, and his father's detachment enabled the old man to perfect his craft. More significantly,
it provided a way out of poverty and despair. Daniel decided to
adopt the same tool, but dispense with his father's detached
manner.

With camera in hand, Daniel needed a subject, rich in powerful imagery and with a compelling narrative. In the grand tradition of "every cloud has a silver lining," he found what he needed
in his classmates, the war veterans.

Daniel was fascinated by their wartime exploits. He found
their yarns to be heroic, harrowing, and often distressing. But for
the first time he and his battle-scarred, worldlier classmates began
to relate.

◄►◄►

Until now the Second World War had been a remote experience.
In truth the Firth family hadn't been decimated by the war,
remaining remarkably unscathed despite their Jewish roots. Or so
they hoped, as Max showed neither interest nor curiosity regarding the possible plight his relatives faced back in Lithuania.

However, there was one family loss Daniel was aware of: a
young doctor aspiring to become a heart surgeon who unfortunately tumbled out the back of a Bedford truck en route to a
friendly tennis game—in North Africa—and broke his neck.

Daniel's most vivid memories came at night, listening under the covers to the stately BBC broadcasts on shortwave radio. The *di...di...di...daa* of Beethoven's Fifth, the Morse code for the letter *V* (V for Victory), heralded a transmission of breaking news from the front. And though the plight of the Allies was often bleak, he would lie quietly in his bunk bed and listen, transfixed, to the stirring, lisp-laden oratory of the British Bulldog, Winston Churchill.

Hearing these words from afar through an invisible veil of crackling static, harmonic distortion, wobbly pitch, and fading squelch signals, created a sense of immediacy in the vivid imagination of young Daniel. And the grainy, black-and-white *Movie-Tone* and *Pathé* newsreels preceding the weekly cinema feature filled in more of the blanks.

Strangely, however, it was the fictional movie, *The Life and Death of Colonel Blimp*, which gave Daniel the grimmest insight into the realities of this modern mechanized war. By exposing the callous brutality of the Nazis' blitzkrieg, the film dispelled any similarities to the chivalric battles of the past.

►◄►◄

But one day the real war did intrude on Daniel's life, not far from his plush home in Houghton. Finally, young Daniel saw firsthand the horrors of war in all its crass blood-red and bandage-white reality.

It was at the Johannesburg Park Railway Station. A thirteen-year-old Daniel had dressed smartly in his school uniform for the formal send-off of vacationing relatives back to Cape Town, as he felt the responsibility of escorting his mother to the station most earnestly.

Amid billowing steam and clangor of carriages on the brake, a troop train halted at the platform across the way. All was briefly still, followed by a desperate surge of activity as a parade of wounded, bandaged soldiers disembarked. Daniel's senses were in overload. His eyes wrenched from one distressing image to another in a series of flashes; the limbless and near limbless on clumsy crutches, the sightless with blood-browned patches over eyes, too many heads bound in tarnished turbans, shrouds of drying bandages flapping hither and thither, and the phalanx of buzzing flies (too many of them) settling on yellowed putrid flesh; and in the midst of this chaos staggered stretcher-bearers, as stout nurses and medics flitted about establishing some semblance of order.

Triage doctors culled the weak from the strong as if applying the basest rule of the wild—survival of the fittest. There were moments of inspiration too—wounded men supporting others less able shoulder to shoulder—a brotherhood earned in solidarity shared, after facing so many terrible experiences together. And there were discordant moments as well—a military band pumping out victory marches in an unintended mocking salute to these sad, wretched, and wounded soldiers.

For too many it was their final journey, and they were laid at attention, side by side, in death. Their corpses were respectfully covered with coarse blankets as a feeble gesture against the morning chill, though the cold would bother them no more.

The most wretched memory that clung to Daniel's senses was the stench: the decaying, metallic, sickly sweet smell of so much spilled blood.

▶◀▶◀

As a civilian, Daniel was protected by military censorship and government restrictions from knowing the harsh reality of the conflict. But after the Johannesburg station visit, Daniel needed answers to a great many questions. Getting firsthand reportage from his veteran classmates was a gift, as it satisfied Daniel's curiosity, and lifted the veil off the secrets his university warriors were painfully carrying. The veterans were struck by Daniel's empathy, and lauded his mission to memorialize their exploits for posterity. For some former soldiers it was a cathartic journey, while others needed outside validation for all the sacrifices they had made; for all, it was a permanent record of their roles in the most significant event of the twentieth century.

Daniel's series of articles on the veterans, well photographed and keenly told, initially ran in the university press. Then, to his delight, *Grocott's Mail*, the well-respected newspaper serving the greater Grahamstown community, published the stories.

With each press edition, Daniel felt a growing change in his relationship with his warrior classmates—the ten-year age gap dwindled, and hostility transformed into kinship.

These hardened veterans grew protective of "their Daniel" and adopted him as one of their own, showering him with regimental patches, medals, and souvenirs from the battlefield. They affectionately nicknamed him "Cocoa," in reference to his thick mane of dark hair. The name stuck and became his photographer's pseudonym.

Finally, Daniel's days of harassment and abuse were over, and a life lesson learned: always strive to parlay a negative into something positive.

►◄►◄

Daniel's college career ended abruptly. His father died as Daniel was in the midst of writing his final mathematics exams. He never graduated. Instead, he immediately set home for Johannesburg to care for his mum.

His thousand-mile trip home was a near thing. Unaware of a recent rain shower, Daniel was speeding on his 490cc Norton

Model 16 motorbike when his front tire tracked into a rivulet coursing across the dirt road—and the machine jammed stuck.

This was an unpleasant surprise. His motorbike—the specially customized Colonial edition of the Norton—was specifically designed with higher ground clearance to better navigate inferior road conditions such as these, and driving incidents of the sort Daniel had just experienced wasn't meant to happen.

The handlebars were violently wrenched from his grasp. The now driverless olive-green machine skidded into a fire hydrant, snapped the cast iron structure from its footing, and unleashed a torrent of water into the air.

Daniel was pitched into a soft chicken wire fence guarding an adjoining property, dressed in the full World War II dispatch rider kit, including the rubber-proofed coat, khaki leather-patched wool breeches, tan leather boots, and a Mark 1 steel helmet with ear flaps, goggles, and British Afrika Corps patch (DR insignia with winged motorbike wheel).

Fortunately the sturdy uniform and slack wire fence saved him from certain death. Swearing off two-wheeled motorized vehicles for the rest of his life, Daniel continued his somber journey to Johannesburg—by bus.

►◄►◄

Thirty-one years had elapsed since V-E Day, and the "good guys" had won, but visiting his German colleagues in Hamburg inevitably caused DGF to reflect on the war. He could not help but wonder at the role his Teutonic business counterpart may have played in furthering the world-domination ambitions of the Axis powers.

As typical of many business relationships, to break the ice DGF had agreed to join his German host for drinks at the end of the day. Possibly it was the liquor, but this time curiosity got the better of Daniel and he probed.

The executive sitting across from him had a shock of silver hair, similar to their record label's brilliant maestro Herbert von Karajan, and always wore a black turtleneck sweater. Rumors inferred he was a submariner in Admiral Karl Dönitz's wolf pack, and that the sweater masked a dreadful scar from a lung lost while torpedoing a merchant ship.

Interested, Daniel asked, "Tell me, Hans. What did you do during the last war?"

Abruptly his garrulous companion clammed up. Evidently the topic was verboten.

▶◀▶◀

It was a machine that taught Daniel another important life lesson. Like many of his generation, he had personally refused to buy anything German, as a consequence for that nation's aggressor role in both world wars. But Daniel needed a new car, and he coveted a Mercedes.

When he took possession of the machine, he admired the superb craftsmanship and excellent service. It was then Daniel understood the principle that guided his purchase: based on *merit* as a criterion it was the best automobile. He then extrapolated further: maybe "merit" was the only true metric to judge *things*, or anything for that matter. It was then Daniel realized that by extension, merit should also be applied to *people*.

With this car purchase Daniel had stumbled upon the means to navigate South Africa's complicated societal structure with integrity. It was a truly colorblind solution, free of prejudice and oblivious to race, gender, and creed, wealth, status, and nationality. It offered dignity to anyone who chose to perform to the best of their ability—no matter their circumstances.

This principle of "meritocracy" would now guide all of Daniel's future human dealings.

However, in order to deal with any lingering guilt over his German acquisition, Daniel added a karmic countermeasure to the luxury vehicle; he mounted a silver St. Christopher medallion on the dashboard. After all, it couldn't do any harm, and over these hazardous African roads, every bit of protection from the unpredictable nature of the wilds helped.

▶◀▶◀

The chill of the Hamburg winter was now a distant memory. Through the plane's starboard window DGF saw the warm-yellow mine dumps ring the Golden City. From on high the homes were tiny, a patchwork of ochre, white, pink, and cream, their multi-colored roofs a free-form mosaic of intricate design. The land-scape below was dotted with kidney, oval, and rectangular sap-phire-blue swimming pools. The trees, clusters of olive-jeweled peridots, were bedded in a relief of lush emerald-green mowed lawns and palatial gardens.

This splendid panorama was tethered by two skyward-reaching scepters, a pair of gleaming towers named the Hillbrow and the Brixton. The aircraft skirted around the towers and then, with barely a shudder, the 747 jumbo jet touched down at Jan Smuts International Airport.

▶◀▶◀

As the massive wide-bodied aircraft made the trek to the airport terminal, Daniel recalled a tender moment he'd shared with his son several years before.

It had been a Sunday. As God had rested on the seventh day, so it was expected of every South African due to the strictures of the Dutch Reformed Church—everything was therefore closed, the airport a significant exception. So that's where Daniel took his boy, Jeremy, to see the planes take off and land.

The lad was fascinated with aircraft. Hanging from the blue-painted ceiling of his bedroom, suspended in space by translucent fishing line, were numerous model planes he had painstakingly built. The paraphernalia of model-building littered the flat topped surfaces of his room; paints, solvent, decals, tubes of glue, and hobby knife.

An unlikely mix of aircraft—military and civilian—from different eras and nations was suspended in a mock dogfight over his bed. Pride of place was a World War II Supermarine Spitfire locked in mortal combat with a De Havilland Comet. A puff of cotton wool ignited with a dash of orange-painted flame trailed from the portside jet engine of the larger craft. Jeremy knew each plane's specifications: the year it was built, its propulsion method, the airframe dimensions, paint scheme, and the weapons and munitions carried.

So a visit to the airport was a wonderful treat.

It happened to be a notable day in aviation history, and father and son were fortunate eyewitnesses. Boeing had selected Jan Smuts Airport, due to its six thousand-foot elevation, to conduct high-altitude take-off and landing tests for the 747 before its commercial introduction.

The massive wide-bodied plane was parked on the tarmac; Jeremy's mouth gaped, stunned by the sheer size of the aircraft. The lad convinced himself the tug tractors scuttling around the runway were too puny to tow such an enormous craft, and he expressed this concern to his father.

Daniel reassured Jeremy it wouldn't be a problem, especially here in South Africa, because of a secret weapon: the Boeing 747 would be towed by a herd of elephants—and that's why it was called a "Jumbo Jet"!

Jeremy had believed him. Now Daniel ruefully considered the state of his current relationship with his son. He was determined not to repeat the pattern he had experienced with his own father, but the one-on-one time they'd shared at the airport all those years ago had become far too infrequent in recent times—and he wasn't sure what to do about it.

▶◀▶◀

After surviving passport control and customs unmolested, Daniel entered the arrival lounge. A surprise: there stood Juliette waiting for him. As a former nightclub singer, Juliette never rose before 10:30 a.m. It was only six forty-five—just a tick after daybreak. Now Daniel was alarmed.

"Why're you here?" blurted Daniel. Seeing her disappointment, he explained, "Darling, I'm thrilled to see you, but something's wrong. You're up way too early."

"It's one of your drivers. He's hurt," said Juliette. "Last night Sid Duncan called, apparently it was a pretty bad wreck, and they've got him at their house."

"Damn! Do you know who it is?"

"I think he said Stan...Stan-something."

"Ah, Stanwell. Where's our driver with the car?"

"Steven's parked curbside in front of the terminal."

"Then we best get over to the Duncan's home immediately...before I collapse from exhaustion," said Daniel. "We mustn't inconvenience them any further."

He placed his arm protectively around Juliette, and together they strode through the exit.

▶◀▶◀

CHAPTER **EIGHT**

STANWELL WOKE. His eyelids were tender, painful, and under pressure. This puzzled him. His concern rose, and so he cracked them open only to see patchy traces of light. Disoriented, his fingers reached at his face and felt the alarming textures that covered it.

Stanwell would soon learn about the patchwork of bandages and sutures holding his face together. He would also understand what a near thing it was that he hadn't been blinded; just the gossamer thinness of skin, his eyelids, protected him from severe eye damage. With a reverential tone the doctor described removing the glass shards piercing both eyelids, and his wonder at discovering they'd failed to penetrate either eye—all the more remarkable considering the force of the accident and the velocity of the flying debris.

◄►◄►

"Hey, *howzit?* How're you feeling?" asked Elsa as she entered the guesthouse. It was daylight and the patient was awake.

"*Haw wena*, it is you?" asked Stanwell, astonished. He recognized the voice of the *ingelosi*—the selfless angel—that rescued him. Being only able to hear her, but not see her, Stanwell struggled to recall the likeness of his savior. His mind raced striving to remember their first encounter before everything faded to black.

It trickled back in a series of flashes, and then a form steadied: a girl's face silhouetted by the midday sun. She was watching him. Her hair, her mouth, and then her eyes came into focus. They were unlike any eyes he'd seen before—luminescent spheres of hazel flecked with amber. But it was the essence behind those eyes that reached deep within him, in how they reflected genuine concern for his welfare.

Then, Stanwell remembered her white skin.

The conditioning of a lifetime was difficult to disregard. With the mental image of a white woman, Stanwell mechanically reverted back to the accepted norm—a state of servility.

I'm sorry, madam. I don't know what I did. *Jussis,* it was a terrible thing!"

"Don't be silly," she reassured him. "Call me Elsa. I think your name is Stanwell, I will call you Stanwell, Okay?"

"*Ja*, okay."

"*Alles goed*—good, that's settled," Elsa said. "You must be hungry, and here's something to drink." She cheerfully prattled on about the pear juice, not too acidic to hurt his injured mouth, and the tasty ProNutro cereal, so nutritious he'd get his strength back really soon.

Elsa's effusive presentation was greeted with silence. Stanwell was visibly uncomfortable. Troubled, she asked him the matter. Squirming, Stanwell replied, "Like, madam, I need a toilet."

Elsa's muted girlie giggle erupted into a hog-like snort. She shyly peeked over at Stanwell and was happy to see his wide grin. Though his eyes were bandaged shut, Elsa intuitively knew they twinkled with amusement.

Now it was a matter of logistics. Elsa guided Stanwell to the adjoining bathroom and lined him up with the toilet seat. She told him the sink was to his left, and quickly exited. After the tinkle, the flush, the squeak-splash-squeak of the faucet, and the rustle of the hand towel as Stanwell dried off, Elsa reentered the bathroom. Firmly she gripped Stanwell's hand and dutifully steered him back to bed.

Elsa fed him as if he were a child. He depended on her simply because he couldn't see, and so she mothered him, spooning cereal into his mouth. Cued by his open mouth—heavily lopsided and swollen—Elsa fed him spoonful after spoonful. As he was famished, Stanwell licked away every last morsel. Elsa then leaned in closer, and with a serviette wiped away some crumbs at the corner of his mouth.

He was thirsty. It was time for a drink. In a moment of serendipity Elsa and Stanwell's hands linked around the beaded glass—a moist condensation caused by the chilled juice within and the warm atmosphere beyond—and a new tension, a stirring tension, entered the room with a wistful sigh. It was a fragile current that enveloped them, only apparent when hands fleetingly touched or the light breath of one brushed the cheek of the other. Elsa and Stanwell silently accepted these moments to be quietly incredible.

The question was who'd first acknowledge it.

To quench his thirst, Elsa raised the straw to Stanwell's lips. He drank his fill. Then with a slurp the drinking straw announced it had emptied the glass. Stanwell pulled away, stranding a drop of juice at the straw's tip. Due to the inevitability of gravity, the liquid languidly stretched, then split, falling as a fluid streak onto Stanwell's chin. Elsa leaned forward, and with a purr of her tongue swept it away. There she hovered in the uncertainty of the moment—then raised her lips to his full mouth.

There they lingered. The sweet nectar of the pear juice melded in their mouths as she brushed her lips on his. He winced. She retreated, momentarily. Then realizing the damaged tissue in his mouth was the cause, she returned gently to him with a light flitter of her tongue. Neither said a word. They were lost in that nascent moment of what was to become a forbidden love.

►◄►◄

Elsa knew the instant her feelings for Stanwell were more than mere compassion. Though until now, she had feared admitting it. When he'd panicked in the night, she'd propped him up against her. That physical proximity, heightened by the darkness, had elicited an unsolicited response.

Stanwell's warm powerful back pressed against her breasts was but one of many cues. Also keenly aware of his scent, Elsa had detected an enticing muskiness she found intoxicating—a mixture of topical liniment applied to his injuries and the smokiness of an open fire.

By then Elsa felt the compulsion to caress him, to soothe him. Her fingers traced the arch of Stanwell's collarbone, and, encouraged by his soft moans of contentment at her touch, her hands began kneading his shoulders and neck. And with each contact—overpowered by the sensuality of the moment—Elsa's feelings heightened until compassion became confused with lust. But then lust dissolved into panic (it felt so wrong!), and so Elsa was relieved when Stanwell's groans eventually subsided, and he slipped off to sleep.

In the dark, alone with her thoughts, Elsa struggled with a growing sense of yearning. No longer could she deny it. Her body had exposed her in the most brazen way: an unbidden, silky-slick moistness had seeped between her thighs. In that confused state of certainty and the irrational nature of dreams, an exhausted Elsa succumbed to exhaustion and drifted into a troubled slumber.

▶◀▶◀

Now, in the harsh reality of daylight, Elsa found her feelings in turmoil. She was unable to quietly accept the turbulent sensation roiling in her belly until one question was properly answered, "Were they both experiencing the same thing?"

There was much uncertainty within Elsa but one thing was clear, she had taken the initiative and this was of her making. After all, she was whole while he was injured; she was white, he black; she was the mistress, he the servant.

"Stanwell, let's get this bloody T-shirt off you," said Elsa as she tugged at the ripped collar. Initially the fabric gave way, but then stuck at the waist. Elsa was momentarily stumped; then Stanwell's powerful hands reached down and tore apart the recalcitrant seam. Gently Elsa removed the remnants, revealing Stanwell's bandaged torso.

White bandages to compress his fractured ribs were coiled around his ebony body. In the morning light the interplay of stripes, light and dark, were the striking rich coat of a zebra.

Elsa leaned over. Her lips anointed the bandage-free zones on Stanwell's body and face. Then her hands caressed him. Though aroused, Stanwell's pain compelled him to remain supine in the unaccustomed role of grateful recipient.

Carefully, gently, but most deliberately, Elsa straddled him. Cautiously she lowered herself to receive him. With gratifying moans, the pleasure in their union was mutually announced. Thereafter their rhythmic undulations, directed by her unhurried motions, heightened their ecstasy and diminished his pain.

▶◀▶◀

As they lay there, astounded by what had just happened between them, neither considered the penalty they'd pay for the barrier they had broken by the pure act of making love together. Though the loving couple had quickly grown comfortable with each other, the South African regime would never be comfortable with their forbidden union. The consequence of Elsa and Stanwell's action, if discovered, only promised them ostracism, humiliation, and the threat of imprisonment.

In the blissful afterglow of the moment Elsa hadn't considered the powerful forces that would soon confront her. This was horribly naïve. In the eyes of her people she had sullied herself, and by extension, them. As for Stanwell, he was oblivious of the steep precipice on which he'd placed himself.

They hadn't realized it yet, but in addition to their bodies the only thing Elsa and Stanwell now shared together was a dark— potentially destructive—secret.

**

The Immorality Act or Sexual Offences Act, of 1957, expressly prohibited sexual contact across the color barrier. This plank of apartheid legislation judged consensual intercourse between the races as "immoral and indecent acts." And the sanction for contravening the law was harsh: seven years imprisonment for both sinners.

However there was an alternative remedy. The white woman only had to make a claim, to be the victim of a rape—a conviction most likely as her "white-word" held more credence than that of a mere kaffir.

The penalty for the black man would undoubtedly be capital punishment because of the alleged "violence of the crime." So, if and when the white woman—his former lover—betrayed him, the native's destiny would be an unkind death by hanging.

And in sacrificing his life, the black man would go to his death knowing he had accomplished much by sparing the white woman from personal shame and the estrangement of her family. And by forfeiting his life, his lover would be saved from the anger of her church and the vengeance of a pernicious government.

As for the "saved" white woman, would she be secretly wracked with guilt, grateful for the selfless martyrdom of her deceased paramour? Or, relieved that fate had provided a way out; would she slip seamlessly back to her privileged side of the apartheid divide?

These were matters ignored or unknown to an interracial couple taking the first tentative steps on a path to an illegal romance.

**

PART **TWO**

ELEGY

"There is almost no country in Africa where it is not essential to know to which tribe, or which subgroup of which tribe, the president belongs. From this single piece of information you can trace the lines of patronage and allegiance that define the state."

Christopher Hitchens

≈

CHAPTER **NINE**

HE'D LEFT SO SUDDENLY they'd not had an opportunity for a proper goodbye. Since she last saw him, Elsa hadn't heard from Stanwell. Just silence... And she was troubled. DGF's morning arrival at the Duncans' had caught them by surprise. Panicked by Lydia's intercom summons to the main house, which erased any lingering pleasure from their earlier tryst, they'd quickly reached for their clothes.

The previous night, Mr. Duncan had kindly provided a somewhat formal shirt and twill trousers for Stanwell to wear, his bloodied clothes already in the scrap heap. Elsa began dressing until she noticed Stanwell's growing exasperation. Unable to be independent with his bandaged eyes, yet reluctant to ask for help, Stanwell had misbuttoned the fancy shirt.

The image of the stiff pinstriped shirt collar sitting askew on Stanwell's large frame, topped with his bandage-covered face, was fitting for a sad-sack clown. His futile efforts to fasten the buttoned fly of the twill trousers added to the comedy of errors.

Trying to suppress her laughter, Elsa had done her best to guide him, but his annoyance only grew.

Elsa remembered then reaching for Stanwell's hand and softly saying, "Hey, you are Simba the big strong lion, and I'm the tiny meerkat trying to pull a *wag-'n-bietje*–a wait-a-bit–thorn from your paw. Please, let me help you?"

Finally he'd understood and meekly allowed her to dress him. Once dressed, Elsa then led Stanwell from their private retreat into the outside world.

There, when last she saw him standing there in the Duncan's home, Stanwell had been awkward—even standoffish. Since circumstances demanded they feign nonchalance, which had dashed any hopes of a passionate farewell, Elsa had been unable to gauge Stanwell's feelings before he left.

▶◀▶◀

Elsa's first impression of Stanwell's employer was a surprise, a most pleasant one.

First, the *Big Baas* was not exactly big at all. Based on the esteem Stanwell held for the man, Elsa had imagined a giant of a gent, possibly a looming six-foot-six rugby prop forward. The reality was of quite a different stature.

A gentleman briskly entered the room, no taller than five foot seven in his leather crepe-soled shoes. Contributing to his dynamism was the fact that his heels never seemed to make contact with the ground. He bounced on his toes, moving with both energy and purpose.

Though South African by birth, he sounded properly English, speaking correctly as a devoted Anglophile. And when he spoke, he commanded attention.

Elsa felt compelled to address him as Mr. Firth. He wouldn't hear of it and insisted she call him Daniel or DGF if she preferred.

Intuitively she understood he would not tolerate being labeled either a Danny or a Dan.

Yes, Firth was most grateful to the Duncans, and Elsa, for all their help in aiding Stanwell. Without any hint of reproach, he asked Stanwell how he felt. Stanwell's sheepish response of self-admonishment was rewarded with a firm grasp of the shoulder, and the assurance, "The most important thing is that you weren't killed."

Once satisfied with Stanwell's condition, DGF quickly dispensed with the remaining matters. He was very pragmatic; his concerns regarding the wrecked vehicles were summed up with the crisp statement, "That's why one has motor insurance."

He assured the Duncans the company would reimburse them for all medical costs to date, as Stanwell was on company time when the accident occurred. And a company truck would be by later to rescue the television sets. As a way of thanks, DGF made Sid's day by presenting him with one of the advance TVs stranded in the garage.

▶◀▶◀

At DGF's side discreetly stood a lovely creature with alabaster skin. It was only her silence that intimated she was discreet; with her flowing strawberry-blond hair, colored from a bottle, and her va-va-voom figure sheathed in a coquettish polka-dotted dress, her appearance was anything but discreet. But she tried. Her eyes were hidden behind a pair of owlish Jackie Onassis-styled sunglasses, an umlaut punctuating the rounded vowel of her full scarlet lips.

Elsa thought she recognized her. "You are Juliette St. John, the singer, aren't you?" she asked.

"Yes, that's right," Juliette replied. The singer removed her sunglasses, and with them disappeared any veil of snootiness. "Sorry for hiding behind these." She continued in her husky tone, "I'm still a night creature from my nightclub years. This is way too early...Elsa, that's your name, right?"

Elsa nodded a little bashfully, as the Duncans, DGF, and Stanwell looked on.

With a disarming smile Juliette added, "You know you remind me of Jean Shrimpton, the supermodel. Just stunning! You should give modeling a go."

"Why, thanks," said Elsa, somewhat taken aback.

"The younger me tried the modeling racket," continued Juliette. "But I did something really dumb and realized I'd best quit."

Curious, Elsa pried for the gory details.

"Okay, but try not to laugh. To this day I feel like a right idiot," said Juliette, with the air of a woman who seldom knew embarrassment.

"Do your remember Twiggy from the sixties? She was a skinny waif-like thing and wore that oh so dramatic, yet naïve at the same-time look with big round eyes. So I got it into my head to crib her eye makeup technique," said Juliette.

Elsa leaned forward, intensely interested. The glamorous world of fashion had seemed very remote to a young girl in Brakpan, but Elsa's fascination was typical of her generation, as evidenced by pictures of movie stars and beautiful celebrities—torn from magazines—that she had taped to her bedroom wall.

"But to achieve perfection with each eyelash, especially the lower lids had to be individually separated. So I whip out a sewing needle, and with my face just inches from the mirror, I began digging between my mascara-clumped lashes. Next thing, I've stuck the blooming needle right into my eye!"

"Oh! Wow!" exclaimed Elsa.

"My eye's impaled on a bloody needle—it looked like a toothpick skewered into a pimento-stuffed olive—and I'm like fainting," said Juliette, relishing the queasy expressions on Elsa's face. "Telling you, it's really freaky tugging a sewing needle from your own eyeball. Glad it stuck in the white jelly stuff and not the iris of the eye...and that's the dramatic story about the end of my blossoming modeling career."

◄◄ ►►

Daniel glanced over at the two women and considered how fortunate he was. Thank goodness for second, and third, and fourth chances, he thought. With Juliette he was finally a winner in the romance department.

They'd met when he'd been excommunicated from his home during a messy divorce. It was never Daniel's intention to abandon his domestic responsibilities, but the former Mrs. Firth the third was manic, and for the sake of their collective sanity he'd been advised to vacate the premises. The lawyers termed it "constructive desertion," and with their assurance it wouldn't jeopardize an equitable divorce settlement, he packed and left. They were wrong. He was still paying dearly for it.

Daniel then found himself at the Balalaika Hotel, in Sandton. The hotel's faux Russian theme was happily toned down by the authentic countryside charm of the place. He booked himself into one of the pleasant two-bedroom thatched bungalows near the swimming pool. As the duration of his stay was unknown, he negotiated a special monthly residential rate.

In practical terms he found himself now to be homeless, wifeless, and childless—with his son Jeremy, from a previous marriage, away at boarding school—and it troubled him.

Specifically, Daniel hated eating alone.

One evening he found himself dining at the Balalaika Hotel's supper club. Juliette St. John was the sultry songstress performing that evening. Her wonderful concert complemented the fine food and excellent wine, and for the first time as a soon-to-be bachelor, he enjoyed a meal.

Thereafter, only on the evenings Juliette performed would Daniel make it his custom to dine there. For him the attraction was clear. The lush, honeyed tones of her voice, the lyrically exquisite dance of her hands, and the tantalizing promises in the swirl of her diaphanous gown mesmerized him. And there was the appeal of surreptitious stealth: she radiant in the glare of the spotlights as he sat anonymously in the shadowed corner at a table set for one.

Then anonymity morphed into desire, and he hoped she'd noticed him sitting there mysteriously in the dark. Apparently so—as fleeting moments of eye contact between them became more frequent, his spirits lifted. Then early one morning they woke up together in his rented bungalow, and they'd remained a pair ever since.

Though very successful at everything else in life, Daniel wasn't very good at being married. In fact he'd sworn to give up on the habit. So with the stakes lowered, he set aside his conventional protocols and didn't dig, delve, and conduct an in-depth inquiry into her past life. All he knew was Juliette St. John was her stage name, and her real name would remain a titillating mystery. Some cautioned Daniel in Juliette's interest in him: it was nothing more than a play to further her music career. Yet she never gave him cause to doubt her motive, or loyalty.

Frankly, after so many failed marriages allegedly based on true love, even if Juliette was an opportunist, this still made his relationship with her the most honest he'd ever had. Daniel was grateful the lady at his side was a genuinely loving, caring, and lusty companion. And furthermore it was mutual. Juliette had no interest in becoming his wife, or anyone else's for that matter, as she lacked the desire to be "owned" by someone. In fact, Juliette St. John was deliciously unconventional.

Elsa considered them to be a spectacular couple, DGF and the St. John woman. In their contrasting natures they actually complemented each other rather well. Her paleness set off wonderfully against his olive complexion. The dark thick mane crowning his large head, and the pair of long sideburns he sported (in the style of romantic balladeer Engelbert Humperdinck), juxtaposed rather nicely with the free-spirited wavy blond hair falling below her slender shoulders.

His no-nonsense businesslike demeanor sat comfortably with her boundless creativity. And they had an instinct for when the one should cede the spotlight to the other, with no clashing of egos. When he spoke she hung on every word, and when she took the stage he was mesmerized. True, they were opposites, but they were compatible and clearly cared for each other.

This gave Elsa a measure of hope when considering her unlikely suitor.

▶◀▶◀

CHAPTER **TEN**

STANWELL MARUNDA LIVED IN TWO WORLDS, yet he belonged in neither. Now he was chauffeured in a white man's car, wearing a white man's clothes, staying at a white man's hotel (admittedly in the staff quarters), and having recently slept with a white man's daughter.

He could not shake the memory of her. He had touched her. He had smelled her. He had tasted her. He had heard her. But he had not truly seen her. All he recalled were fragmented images of an apparition aiding him by the side of the road. Ever since, he'd wished for new data to fill in the gaps, but the protective layers of gauze that covered his eyes had stymied his ability to see her. In a land where color meant everything, all Stanwell could see was black.

Stanwell discovered the darkness from his bandaged eyes grew progressively more stifling as days went by. Understandably, the loss of independence distressed him; but far worse, the perpetual darkness forced him to relive nightmares from his life as an immigrant gold miner.

It was a long way from the mud hut of his birth in the village of Muzuzu, nestled in the outlying wooded, hilly region of northern Malawi. Farming, specifically the cultivation of tea, coffee, and rubber, was the main source of sustenance there—enough to provide a living for a few, but not for all.

Stanwell was born to the Angoni tribe. They were proud descendants of the Zulu and had the noble bearing, moral traits, and handsome features of those blood brothers living a thousand miles south, in the northeastern corner of South Africa. Unfortunately the Angoni were a minor tribe. Power rested with the Chewa people, the largest ethnic group in Malawi. Without power, there was no patronage; without patronage, there was no opportunity; and without opportunity, there were no jobs.

Stanwell, now a young man, had the responsibility of fending for his family. Like their Zulu relatives, the Angoni detested mining. They were first and foremost warriors and cattlemen. This made Stanwell's decision to migrate to Johannesburg, to work deep down in the bowels of the mines, all the more notable.

With his roots far north of the Republiek van Suid-Afrika, he was just another *uitlander*—a foreigner—one of many migrant workers hoping to reap great wealth in *eGoli,* in Johannesburg, the City of Gold.

▶◀▶◀

Tortured tales of raw native immigrants led astray in the City of Gold are legend, but Stanwell wasn't one of them. He never was inclined to sample the seedy underbelly of the city. Contrary by nature, Stanwell chose to zig while so many others zagged—only for them to succumb to temptation. Being bright, motivated, and willing helped, but Stanwell was cunning too, and quickly divined the managerial hierarchy at the gold mine.

By evidencing respect and initiative to the right pit boss, Stanwell rapidly distinguished himself from the toiling droves of indentured workers, and separated himself from the pack.

▶◀▶◀

Burrowing under the earth like an aardvark was not the natural state of man, according to Stanwell. At least nature equipped the anteater with the tools needed—its flat, shovel-shaped front claws. But a job was a job, even at depths beyond a mile below the earth's surface.

At the start of each shift, when Stanwell headed into the mineshaft, he found it best to forget the fresh morning air and the warm rays of the new dawn. The ear-popping descent into darkness was a daily test of his courage, and he was perpetually shaken by the lurching, unexpected halt of the rickety lift-cage as it terminated at the shaft base—the sensation eviscerating as it recoiled through the pit of his stomach.

For Stanwell it was only a brief respite as the platform steadied. Then there was the harsh clunk of the lift's gate opening, only for the worker to be disgorged in a tangle of tools, limbs, and lunch boxes as fresh fodder against the rock face.

Numbed with fear, Stanwell was swept along with a phalanx of nameless recruits toward the tightening cavern. Toward them, shuffling through a haze of drifting dust, were grime-caked, sweat-filthy men; the cheerful dance of their beaming lamps and jangle of their safety helmets belied their exhaustion. These were the relieved ones—the last shift, soon headed skyward. How Stanwell envied them.

Without the ability to witness the sun's path, time passing deep below became meaningless. Instead, Stanwell focused on his work, and despite the deprivations that became his salvation. He grudgingly accepted that he functioned in a netherworld of dust-plugged nostrils, sweat-stung eyes, and the constant clangor that assaulted his ears: spittle-filled curses, thudding jackhammers, wailing sirens, percussive rock blasts, the "all clear" yells, and then more cussing.

Bosses screamed instructions in *Fanagalo*—the pidgin language that was the lingua franca of the mines. While the babble of language didn't help, difficulties were compounded in the tight, claustrophobic confines of cold, highly compressed conglomerate rock. Communication, so vital, became a hit-or-miss endeavor with instructions frequently misunderstood. In this crucible, an uncomprehending, glazed expression on a worker's face was tantamount to treason to a pit boss.

As failure to perform could be deadly for all, confusion was quickly remedied with a raised fist and swift blow. If the crime didn't merit a physical cure, then rage by itself did magnificently in those confined quarters, as the recipient of the rebuke had nowhere to retreat. Then back to work, white and black working side by side and sharing the same fear: a cave-in—the collapse of tons of rock that crushed, killed, or worse, trapped.

▶◀▶◀

With tired limbs stumbling over miles of hissing hoses, Stanwell and his coworkers husbanded the sucking pumps and blowing ventilators that served as umbilical cords to the world above. The team labored under the stifling stench of diesel fuel, sweat, and fear. The chaos was unrelenting. Their Wellington boots sloshed through pools of water as their muscles strained to handle massive loads of steel, timber, and conglomerate. All this in support of faceless forearms bracing clattering drills against unforgiving rock.

Stanwell was not a student of World War I, nor obviously did he ever fight in the trenches of Verdun, but in an eerie sense he now lived it; experiencing a similar sense of battle fatigue when forced to dodge flashing, high-voltage sparks, detonating explosives, and ricocheting rock fragments.

◄►

Stanwell had had enough. With astute politicking, he got a new assignment and became a *cocopan* operator. No more digging, drilling, pumping, or pounding. Stanwell now drove little hoppers, carrying gold-bearing ore to the refinery on a small-gauge rail system networked throughout the mine. Though much time was still spent underground, the sense of motion as Stanwell traveled through the tunneled mazes hollowed under the reef alleviated his overwhelming claustrophobia.

On his subterranean travels Stanwell came across pods of miners laboring away. Frequently they'd break into a rousing rendition of *Shosholoza*—the song of the African miner—and he'd join them, sometimes taking the lead call as he swept by. Then he disappeared into another rock cavern, leaving in his wake the choral majesty of their voices reverberating off the unyielding granite, their spirits lifted in song like those of chanting manual laborers everywhere.

Finally, a siren called the shift. Wedged together in a caged basket, they soared upward toward the summit, feeling the onrush of fresh air on their faces. As they climbed Stanwell monitored the slithering creak of the steel cable falling away.

Then another abrupt gut-heaving halt, followed by further disorientation as the wire-meshed lift containing its humanoid chattel swung to and fro, suspended in space.

Gratefully Stanwell peered at the buttressed pithead frame that loomed over the shaft. He compulsively inspected the steel cable (the diameter of a man's arm) for imperfections as it looped over massive gears and pulleys. Then, with one final clang, the lift-gate opened. In a herd of automatons, just one of many faceless men caked in grime, Stanwell emerged onto the earth's crust.

He took a deep breath, coughed a throat-clearing honk, and then spat. The shift was finally over. It had been sixteen hours.

Yet though the sixteen-hour shift underground was hazardous, above ground things were far worse.

▶◀▶◀

Stanwell arrived in South Africa as a free man. He traded his labor in exchange for a fair wage. He never expected the shelter provided to be anything more or less than he deserved—just that it be comfortable, clean, private, and safe. But Stanwell was to be disappointed. Reality had simply reached in and quashed part of that dream.

The goldmine's accommodations were reminiscent of a prison camp. Set in a landscape of lifeless scrub and trash, the compound consisted of lines of single-storied buildings known as hostels; these were split into rooms holding eighteen occupants each.

Rather than finding the dignity of having one's own bed, Stanwell found himself and the other occupants stacked in tiered bunks like cords of wood. And he noted that when bunks were allocated, common sense didn't apply; invariably the arthritic sixty-year-old laborer drew the unreachable top bunk while a young lout lounged on the bottom shelf.

Hostel life was unnatural, as wives and children were unwelcome. These men-only quarters quickly destroyed family life, as the innocent among the men were exposed to sexual predators and other unseen risks.

With so many men packed into such confined living spaces, these buildings were a breeding ground for diseases like pneumonia and tuberculosis. And the infestation of mosquitoes, fleas, and rodents added to the miners' misery with every itch, scratch, and gnaw.

When Stanwell left his family and village for the minefields, he never anticipated a crowded all-male hostel as his future home. It was no substitute for his simple village of Muzuzu, surrounded by loved ones. But he had a mission: to provide an income for his family with as much dignity as he could muster.

Nonetheless, Stanwell quickly adapted and came to terms with the squalor. But nothing prepared him for the looting, bloodshed, and killings.

**

The atmosphere within the mine compound was rife with fear—fierce factional fighting was inevitably a hair-trigger away. An unlucky worker unfortunately housed in a hostel populated by members of a rival tribe made for an easy, unsympathetic target.

If robbed of his prized possessions, the laborer would consider himself fortunate. If he survived a beating, he'd have no alternative but be sanguine about it. But if killed, the man would have the satisfaction of knowing his death would trigger a reprisal in his honor by his clan—again completing the indeterminable cycle of vengeance. That was simply the tribal way.

The authorities were not unsympathetic to the problem—as they needed a healthy labor force—and consequently with the best of intentions they segregated the worker population according to tribal affiliation. Logically each tribe was allocated their own separate hostels within the larger compound area.

That addressed the rivalries between the local tribes, but the foreign workers had a gamut of problems of their own. Xenophobia was rampant because the local tribes resented foreign laborers encroaching on their jobs, and so the migrant workers were granted hostels of their own.

Now satisfied with these adjustments, the mine's management blithely assumed the possibility of future factional strife to be most unlikely.

**

Stanwell found himself lodged in a migrant-only hostel. Ethnically he was a minority, as only a few Malawian miners now worked in South Africa. A tragic plane crash two years prior, in 1974, had killed many of his countrymen, and as a cautious step the Malawi authorities had suspended its worker program with the gold mines.

With the majority of his bunkmates from neighboring Mozambique, and tensions rising, Stanwell prayed each night he'd not be slaughtered as he slept.

▶◀▶◀

It had been a difficult week. But now they were flush, their pay packets full. Friday night was a time to relax, and many were drinking to blunt the week's woes. Bantu beer glugged from quart-sized milk cartons were the most popular potion. No aluminum cans for this millet grain brew—only paperboard coated with paraffin wax would do. The traditionalists, however, drank a maize-brewed concoction called *Umqombothi* from glass jam jars. Its gritty texture and muddied brown complexion gave it the consistency of dirty river water. Stanwell thought it tasted cheap, thick, sour, and awful.

Instead he enjoyed a refreshing *cooldrink*, a pineapple-flavored soda, as he toiled away. He had collected the soda's bottle caps to use as wheels on a toy car he was making. In Stanwell's hands the VW Beetle's body had taken shape, pressed and rolled from a Havoline oil can. Now he was carefully crafting both the chassis frame and wheel axels with a twisted coathanger wire.

Stanwell pretended the toy model car was for a nephew in Malawi, but in truth he needed it for himself. He was frustrated by lack of control over his own life; he loathed his job, he hated his living quarters, he distrusted his colleagues, and his greatest fear of all was a mine shaft collapse. But with this simple toy, he was the one in charge. He didn't require the approval or opinion of anyone in its creation.

▶◀▶◀

Stanwell and his fellow celebrants sat on concrete steps leading up to their hostel. *Radio Bantu* blared from a transistor radio in the background, playing the latest *mbube* hit by the all-male a cappella choral group, Ladysmith Black Mambazo. All within hearing range moved to the rhythm instinctively—heads bobbed, fingers snapped, feet tapped.

The day's tales from the deep became the men's topic of conversation: the stupidity of Meneer Venter, who'd instructed the machine boy to drill in the wrong place. How the error compounded when the shot jammed into that hole failed to detonate. Then the "will-it-blast-or-not-blast" panic that ensued until Meneer Venter "bravely" sent the boss boy to disarm the unstable explosive.

They laughed now, but it had been a close call. They shook their heads at the gall of this foolish white man—a supervisor they'd entrusted with their lives. So many safety regulations had been ignored, and only luck averted a tragedy. "Hey, I've had a *gatvol* of that dumb *mampara*. I'm gonna *donner* him just now!" [I'm fed up with that dumb idiot. I'm going to beat him up soon!] boasted one of the team, but they all shared the sentiment. It was time the white man was taught a lesson.

The sun had set. The evening was pleasantly cool, and all was still except for the *oop-oop-oop* of African Hoopoe birds trilling in the distance. The topic of conversation shifted to their rumbling, alcohol-sodden stomachs and the need for food. For these tired men, *pap* and gravy was the consensus. Reminiscent of Native American grits, pap was both a staple and a comfort food.

The salted mielie-meal porridge was boiled to the consistency of mortar and best eaten by hand. The shaping of the mush was satisfyingly tactile; then it was dipped in fatty meat gravy and devoured with a flourish. These men were satisfied by their meal choice, and were gently prodding for a volunteer chef as they relished in the dish they'd soon share.

A whiff of petrol suffused with smoke failed to alert them. The shattered glass, the blast, and the wall of searing heat advancing toward them were another matter entirely. The firebomb had smashed to the ground within fifteen feet of the relaxed men, and a spool of flames now encroached on their position. Frantically the squad of foreign workers scrambled up the steps and retreated indoors.

Fate and poor judgment had served them unkindly. The migrant hostel was located between the rival Zulu and Xhosa tribes. The authorities had hoped the foreign workers would provide a buffer zone to keep the warring tribes apart. In fact, the migrant hostel was no more useful in preventing the looming Zulu attack than Belgian's Ardennes forest was in stopping Hitler's *Blitzkrieg* invasion of France.

The Zulus' calling card was the heel-strike of a thousand feet stomping the ground in unison, combined with bloodcurdling cries and the slapping of weapons against makeshift shields. Most enemies were cowered by this ostentatious show of force, but the Xhosas were immune. Fueled with too much *Skokiaan* moonshine, and false confidence due to their numeric advantage, they now advanced toward the Zulu tribesmen.

Both sides were well-armed with an arsenal of primitive weapons: *pangas*–the African cleaver-like weapon similar to the machete, *knobkieries*–a fighting cudgel masquerading as a walking stick, and *sjamboks*–a brutal whip made from animal hide. Many others brought mining implements to the fight: pickaxes, mallets, pitchforks, and shovels. Also grasped in the calloused hands of rival tribesmen were rocks, bricks, and fire-bombs of the Molotov cocktail variety. Surprisingly few men wore their miner's helmets for protection.

▶◀▶◀

An official investigation ascertained tribal jealousy was the root cause of the conflict.

With the exception of drilling at the rock face, which appealed to the warrior nature of the Zulu, the profession held little attraction for these tribesmen, and so they had a relatively small contingent in the compound. The Xhosas, however, were skilled miners and had proven themselves accomplished in a variety of skills, from shaft sinking to smelting operations. Because of their enthusiasm for the profession, the Xhosas enjoyed numerical superiority in the mine compound.

However, allowing a single ethnic group to dominate other tribes had been a fatal mistake by the mine's management. This deadly event was triggered by the promotion of a Zulu to shift boss, invoking the resentment of the Xhosas on the crew. Tragically, the European pit boss hadn't factored in cultural and tribal ethnicity in his consideration. As typical of a white man in

Africa, invariably myopic, he failed to recognize the schisms between local native tribes. As for the authoritarian style of management he applied to his black employees, it didn't allow for "such nonsense."

And the fate of the newly promoted Zulu shift boss, his terms of reference were short-lived. His Xhosa colleagues arranged an accident. They struck the butt of timber bracing an overhang as the Zulu passed under it, killing him in a crush of rock and lumber. He was one of 2,284 fatalities that year on South African minefields.

◄►◄►

The Zulus thirsted for revenge. Around the fire, at their elders' knees, they had learned about Shaka Zulu's military might. Now some modern Zulus yearned for the day when the Zulu *impi* would dominate the African continent once again. So the will to embody that warrior spirit–even for a brief, bloody, irrational moment–was difficult for them to ignore. For others, however, being high on *dagga* or weed would suffice.

Across the compound's scrubland, the opposing forces met. A ritual of taunts, feints, and mock charges ensued. These actions were uncannily similar to a belligerent elephant's: ears flapping wildly, body rocking side to side, trunk restlessly trumpeting, and front legs pawing the ground. These signs were either a precursor to a serious attack, or merely another mock charge—no one knew.

Standing on his bunk bed, Stanwell peered through the garret window. The battlefield lay before him. He was located on the halfway line, as if he had scored a prized seat at a Kaiser Chiefs soccer match. He wished. This was too close for comfort.

At his direction bunks and tables had been hauled up against the hostel's entryways. He knew it to be poor protection against a serious breach. Hopefully the stacked furniture blocking the doors would deter all but the most determined fighters. Perhaps the locals' bloodlust would be satisfied slaughtering one another and they'll leave us foreigners alone, Stanwell wished.

►◄►◄

The Zulus stamped their feet in a half-crouch, with knees bent. They brandished their weapons up high, then feigned sharp stabbing motions from shoulder to groin, all in a ritualistic battle dance. The Xhosa responded with jeers, crude gestures, and threatening charges of their own. They had their provocateur—a scrawny, cheeky, shameless little man. He faked courage with bold advances and flurries of lewd motions; then, when challenged, hastily he retreated behind his larger comrades. The frenzy built as the chanting of thousands neared a crescendo.

All that was needed was a flashpoint...

A terracotta brick arced in the night sky, in moments bridging the gap between the two forces, and struck the insolent provocateur on the temple. He staggered backward, clutching his head, then collapsed at the restless feet of his tribesmen. No one moved to aid him. Instead there was a furious call to action, and with weapons raised the Xhosas charged, trampling over the body of their fallen cheerleader.

The Zulus engaged. They instinctively deployed the "buffalo horns" tactic of their ancestors; some peeled off the left flank, and others went to the right, like encircling horns. The main force represented the "chest" of the buffalo and attacked from the center. That their opponents were coworkers, black miners like themselves that worked the same shifts and faced a common enemy—the white man—was never a consideration.

The Zulus ruthlessly proceeded with the slaughter.

More horrific by the glint of the moon than by the light of day, Stanwell witnessed the devastation wrought by the rampaging miners. With mutilating strikes, the *pangas* scythed through flesh and bone. And the hideous skull-crushing blows of the *knobkieries* unnerved Stanwell to the core. Those not killed had their flesh lacerated by the lightning slash of the *sjambok* whips, or worse, their eyes removed by slashing strips of leather.

But one dreadful moment haunted Stanwell most. He recognized one of the fighters: the courageous boss boy ordered that very day by Meneer Venter to disarm the misfired charge. It happened way too fast. A scarlet-stained *panga* gleamed in the moonlight as it swept down. In a futile attempt to protect his face, the desperate boss boy parried with his hands. The sharp blade separated both hands, midpalm, and ripped a gash from brow to cheek. Dark blood spewed from ruptured veins.

Stunned and headed into shock, the forlorn man gawked at his dismembered fingers resting in the gravel. Then he collapsed on top of them, as if protecting them one final time.

In the revulsion of the moment, Stanwell didn't consider whether the boss boy would live or die, only that he was permanently maimed, without fingers, he would never work again.

▰◁▷

The Zulus won this contest. After the police cleared the compound the following morning, among the battle debris littering the barren soil—smoldering embers, abandoned weapons, and looted possessions—the scarlet patches of the fallen could be seen. Disillusioned and frightened, Stanwell abandoned his mining career, and with a good reference applied for a job as a driver at the Gallo Group.

▰◁▷

CHAPTER **ELEVEN**

IT WAS A MOST UNEXPECTED SIGHT. He had lived in near darkness for a fourteen days. Finally the gauze bandages had been removed. And a well-groomed moustache was the first thing Stanwell saw. Attached to the moustache was the compassionate face of Dr. Malcom Weitz. Hovering nearby was DGF.

"Welcome, young chap, to a bright new world," boomed the doctor heartily. "You must give it a moment for your eyes to adjust to the light."

DGF chimed in. "Can you see okay? We were worried."

Stanwell nodded. He could see again. And now he had the ability to soon see *her* again.

Sensing his patient was restless, the doctor calmed him with a firm directive. "Now, now, my boy, there's more for us to do today. Let's remove those stitches." The most delicate maneuvers required absolute stillness and a steady hand, especially when removing tiny sutures from both of Stanwell's eyelids. Snip...snip...snip. Except for a disconcerting tugging sensation, all the sutures were removed with little pain. Some of the larger wounds, however, still required healing, and the doctor patched them with strips of adhesive tape.

Stanwell thanked the doctor for his care and meant it, and was even willing to see his repaired face in the mirror the doctor handed him. Evidently Dr. Malcom Weitz was proud of his handiwork.

But Stanwell was distracted. He needed to find Elsa. But how dare he do it without casting suspicion on their burgeoning relationship?

►◄►◄

It was the greatest of taboos, having sex across the racial divide. Man, had the *oke* freaked out because of the way we touched and kissed each other, thought Elsa? It had been two weeks since she last saw him. And she had no idea how to contact him. For sure he didn't have a phone in Soweto.

It was difficult enough for a white person to own a private telephone in Johannesburg. For such a modern metropolis it was surprising, but home phones were scarce because the supply was controlled by the government. Recently there'd been a suspicious increase of requests from doctors demanding emergency telephones for their patients, an apparent epidemic of high-risk pregnancies being the justification. Public works officials were investigating. However, Elsa was fortunate her roommate was a nurse; because of on-call demands from the hospital, they had a phone.

►◄►◄

That morning, when they were last together, was seared in Elsa's memory. She'd reexamined the intoxicating moments of their union, from first caress to postcoital kiss, and it had made her wince. Elsa keenly needed to justify the nature of the prohibited love that had stirred her in this unexpected way. Was it a matter of passion, something primal, like some feral she-cat in heat? Or was it the dark side of her nature rebelling against her conservative upbringing? Or was it nothing more than tried and true romance, and her treating it with suspicion was unfair? In fact her reaction to him may be no more complicated, or simpler for that matter, than the response to one of life's sweetest joys—that of serendipitous attraction. There were many unanswered questions. But one thing was certain: Stanwell shook her world.

Still Elsa's burden wasn't lightened by this guesswork; no matter how she parsed it, there was no escaping the fact that it was entirely her responsibility. After all, it was she who seduced him. Even if he desired her, he would never have tried. It was far too dangerous. Yes, he'd responded, passionately, and that pleased her. Nevertheless the onus was on her. But would they ever meet again? Just another question left unanswered...

▶◀▶◀

The mind has the habit of ignoring the most likely solution for the best possible outcome. This must be the trick of sprites, or misfiring synapses, intended to delight in confusion by meddling with (wo)mankind's sagacity.

When Dr. Weitz insisted Elsa clean Stanwell's bloodstained watch, she'd secretly resented it. It was a reversion to type: she was the mistress, and surely it wasn't her place to clean up after a native, especially his personal things. With a hint of a snit she'd stuffed the soiled watch into her bag and forgot about it.

"What a wise man!" exclaimed Elsa, recalling the doctor's sage counsel. Then she dug into the furthest reaches of her purse. As her fingers wrapped themselves around the inexpensive wristwatch with its blood-clotted expansion-metal band, Elsa was ecstatic. Hope was now possible.

All she needed was a plan.

▶◀▶◀

It couldn't have been more convenient; on the street level of her building was a jewelry store. A pretty, bejeweled blonde greeted Elsa pleasantly at the door. As Elsa stepped into the gleaming emporium with cabinets of pretty trifles promising enduring love and wistful fantasy, she was jolted by the reality of the bleak request she was about to ask of the jeweler. Apologetically, she laid the blood-spoiled cheap watch on a maroon velvet tray for the jeweler's inspection.

With gloved fingers he raised the timepiece to within an inch of his loupe, and then paused, nonplussed. Now flustered, in one breath a stream of chatter sprang from Elsa's lips. "The watch belongs to my...my boyfriend, and he...wrecked it...really good in a car accident...the other day. And he's in hospital. Whew!"

With a baleful squint from his magnified eye, the horologist announced from high, "Very well, ma'am. This watch will clean up quite nicely. Please allow us thirty minutes to do so."

With that, Elsa decided to visit the record store next door.

◄◄ ►►

With its fluorescent orange sign, Les Discotheque was a very inviting hangout. Its location slap-dab in the heart of Hillbrow made the trendy record bar a destination for both the hip and the misplaced. From time to time, when her roommate needed privacy or she just wanted a change of scene, Elsa made this sonic domain her oasis.

A self-claimed hi-fi geek with the somewhat contrived name Marcus managed the place. He'd no obligation to wear a uniform, and there was no doubt he wore fresh clothes, but his vision of hipness as a trendsetter in the record business was reduced to a dark brown, crushed velvet suit with bell-bottom trousers, and a vertical-striped Indian hemp shirt—inevitably unbuttoned midchest—that revealed a leather cord around his neck. From the cord hung a pewter lion's head the size of a door-knocker (strange, as in the realm of the zodiac Marcus was no Leo—when Elsa prodded further, he admitted to being a "moon child," as the Cancer thing freaked him out). In one regard Marcus was extreme: his hair was unruly, thick, and wild, as if each individual strand had a mind of its own.

But beneath those tresses, the dude totally knew his music, and nothing he dug more than turning customers on to the hippest grooves of the moment. Around him lay dog-eared copies of *Melody Maker* and *New Musical Express* magazines, in which he'd diligently scoured for musical intelligence and the next breakout hit.

Marcus and Elsa's first meeting had been rather odd. Bursting into the store, she had blurted out in her heavy, guttural Afrikaans accent, "I am a rock!" Marcus was stunned by this confession; his facial expression cycled between bewilderment and embarrassment. And there Elsa stood, confused by his strange reaction.

Then, at once, they both understood. "Rock" was a scornful word of derision used by many English speakers to describe their Afrikaner countrymen—insinuating they're thick, dumb, and inane. Seldom does a record shop offer moments of chivalry, but the girl was lovely, and Marcus now realized the true intent of her request. "I'm sure you meant the 45 single by Simon & Garfunkel." Of course he knew the song; it was the last track on the super duo's *Sounds of Silence* album.

Self-consciously Elsa tilted her head in acknowledgment. After a shared chuckle, they agreed everything was now copacetic. As recompense Elsa bought the seven-single—and they became firm buddies.

Elsa found Marcus stationed at his post behind the counter, like the captain on a ship's bridge. At his command four Garrard 401 turntables spun a stack of 33- and 45-rpm records. Marcus was in vigilance mode, monitoring the diamond-tipped styli tracking the undulating furrows of the grooved records. Elsa noted the joy in his eyes as they twinkled at the pleasure his ears were treated to.

Elsa had asked in the past why he didn't play an instrument himself, if he liked music so much. Marcus's response was either a cop-out or reflected a true understanding of his own limitations: he'd stated he'd no desire to add to the cacophony, especially as there were so many wonderfully gifted musicians already out there.

However, Marcus was dedicated to the process, and he reveled in his role as an acolyte helping the truly talented find their audience. Elsa understood and patiently humored him as he rambled on about "motion being converted into electrical impulses" via the Pickering cartridge pickups—and how these scratchy whispers were augmented by the powerful Marantz amplifiers racked behind him, which in turn drove the studio-grade Altec Lansing speakers to ear-splitting decibels that filled the store and sometimes irked the neighborhood.

But the island settee at the center of the store was his true domain, and where Marcus was the most assertive and territorial. It was an oval-seated monstrosity cloaked in shiny, black Naugahyde pleather. A column rose from the center, into which four headsets attached to spirals of black chord were jacked. It was here, only at Marcus's discretion, that someone could have the privilege of listening to some choice vinyl. Marcus handed across to Elsa a pair of headphones and invited her to sit down. He had something really rad to play her.

Seated next to Elsa was a pale waif of a girl; she'd bright red hair—closely cropped up top, with long strands covering the back of her neck—and a shocking blue-red thunderbolt painted across her right eye. Very much in her own world, the girl grooved to the music as she clutched the album cover as if her life depended on it. The jacket was *Aladdin Sane*, and it bore the likeness of David Bowie's androgynous alter ego, Ziggy Stardust.

Nodding at the girl, Elsa gave Marcus a quizzical look.

"Can you dig it? I don't," said Marcus. "She's never bought a thing, you know. But the poor chick seems lost. Maybe she's a poor Bowie fag hag, 'cause every single day she's trippin' on this record. It's really freaky-deaky, man!"

With a sigh, Marcus pulled an LP out of its sleeve and turned to his trusted turntables. After thoroughly inspecting it in the light, and giving a flick at wayward dust particles with a lint-free cloth, he placed the disc on the revolving platter. Leaning in close, he cautiously lowered the tone-arm until the needle met the groove. Satisfied, he stepped back and let the music spin after giving Elsa a thumbs-up to confirm the volume was cool.

Elsa listened. It was very novel to her. Nothing like the sappy pop and covered country tunes played on Springbok Radio. Nor reminiscent of the hick, traditional accordion *boeremusik* her pa liked. Elsa found it both disconcerting and compelling.

A solo male voice stood clearly over the array of musical instruments that supported him. This was deliberate. The singer had a message, and he needed it heard. Within catchy melodies—deliberately seductive—the lyrics were subversive, sometimes even crude and sardonic, but steadfast in their indictment of "the man" and "the system." The themes were universally antiestablishment—no more corruption, poverty, greed, or war—but there was empathy for other societal ills as a consequence of government neglect, such as joblessness, booze, and hookers. The music was profound, and into her ears poured the notion of a government's true responsibility to all its citizens—one of compassion, not suppression, overregulation, and abuse.

It's through the power and grace of music that unknowingly a thirty-year-old folk singer and part-time laborer from Detroit, Michigan, could create such a seismic shift in the attitude of a well-intentioned young woman half a world away. In the South African idiom, this was Elsa's *verligte* ("enlightened") moment. For the first time she resented the apartheid regime, its failings finally exposed. Also for the first time, she felt optimistic about her relationship with Stanwell.

Too soon the music ended with a sibilant hiss, as the stylus scratched to the end of the spiraled groove. The vigilant Marcus lifted it off the rotating disc. "Marcus, that was really heavy, really groovy. What was it?"

"Hey, I'm glad you're psyched by this record. It's called "Cold Fact" by some guy named Sixto Rodriguez. I'm telling you, he's gonna be bigger than Bob Dylan."

More than thirty minutes had elapsed. It was time Elsa fetched Stanwell's watch.

◄►◄

In a waft of recently sprayed VO5 hair lacquer, the beaming blond jeweler's assistant handed Elsa a polished Timex watch. After enquiring if Elsa was satisfied, she generously announced, "It's no charge. We all hope your boyfriend recovers soon."

With wristwatch in hand, a grateful Elsa now had an alibi to justify her actions when reaching out to Stanwell.

◄►◄

CHAPTER **TWELVE**

DANIEL FIRTH CALLED from the adjoining room, "Juliette darling, I need some advice!"

As DGF was most self-assured, Juliette was surprised by the request, though she was always flattered to serve as his sounding board. This time she was wrong. DGF was about to sail into uncharted waters and needed guidance.

"Darling, what's up?" she asked.

"I feel responsible for Stanwell's accident. He's a good man, and I want to make things right. So I have this idea—but it's kinda radical, and it's against the law."

"Now you have my attention..."

"For almost two years Stanwell has worked at our warehouse facility in Kempton Park, near Jan Smuts International Airport. He started on the "pick-and-pack" line, but the guy's a real go-getter and has amazing initiative. He's now indispensable in the smooth running of the whole place. So I'd like to promote him to senior management. But there's a problem; it's illegal in this complicated country of ours."

"That's just weird," said Juliette, perplexed.

DGF was surprised at her naiveté, but then realized that as a singer, Juliette would have little knowledge of the unique discriminatory regulations companies faced in South Africa, which prevented them from having access to the most able talent.

"Juliette, when you performed at the Balalaika Hotel, did you ever wonder why there were no black floor managers, black headwaiters, or even Bantu receptionists?"

Juliette shook her head, abashed.

"There's this Job Reservation law that literally legislates blacks out of the labor market. I guess some whites were scared of the competition, so they've kept all skilled jobs for themselves and left the dregs to the local natives."

"So there's no real opportunity for blacks to better themselves?" asked Juliette.

"Even if they'd the legal right to do so, the government has failed to provide them the skills, deliberately. God forbid an ambitious non-European with aspirations to be a typist, a receptionist, or become a manager; they'd be woefully unprepared. And of course, unskilled labor's cheap, so these poor blacks remain exploited and poor. At best it's very cynical.

"Setting aside the immorality of the issue, which in itself is unsustainable, I think this is about as dumb as it gets if a nation expects its citizens to be peaceful and content.

"No matter our complexion, we all desire the same stuff; a safe healthy home, nice car, clean clothes, full tummy, functioning utilities, and good schools. It's not surprising that those who lack these things, which are the majority in this country, could potentially become bomb-throwing anarchists.

"When I think of all the money wasted on this oppressive security apparatus to keep the black down, it's such a shame. If only we'd repurposed those resources to educate and empower them instead..." DGF's voice trailed off. He felt Juliette was lost by his lengthy polemic.

Quite the contrary—Juliette adored this man, but for the first time she appreciated his decency. She'd held to the cliché that by necessity a successful businessman had to be ruthless, heartless. But her Daniel Firth had proved to be more perceptive and "evolved" than she'd assumed.

She was bemused that his favorite adage was, "Whenever in doubt, think of it only in economic terms." This appeared very cold and calculating.

It had never occurred to her, until this moment, that there was a kind of purity to Daniel's economic calculus, wherein he understood capitalism to be colorblind to prejudice and driven only by productivity—which in the end is a win-win proposition for all—provided a heartless government removed laws that prevented anyone from participating.

"So, what's your scheme for Stanwell?" she asked.

"I'd like to officially appoint him as the general manager of our fifty-thousand-square-foot warehouse facility," Daniel said. "But the government won't tolerate a black man supervising white subordinates. And the unwelcomed attention from the authorities could be disastrous."

"Yes, but what's really holding you back?" Juliette asked.

"I've responsibilities to others, like our shareholders. I must consider the sanctions our company might face and the possible backlash in the state-controlled media. So that's my dilemma," said DGF. "What do you think?"

"Dear, dear Daniel, as a singer I'm always judged by others. And frequently it's unkind—the critics thrive on being mean spirited and as for the record label A&R executives, they're downright exploitive. But what always kept me strong was the fact that criticism was directed solely at my talent, my craft, which I always felt was within my power to improve.

"I can't even comprehend how much it would hurt if I'd been told the only reason they said no was the color of my skin. You see, unlike my talent, which I can polish, there's absolutely nothing I could do to change my skin...It would break me.

"So, for me, it's not even a close call." She nodded at Daniel. "Will you do it?"

▶◀ ▶◀

DGF never considered himself a rebel. Losing his father so young forced him toward responsibility, a role he quietly assumed with assured competence. There were trade-offs. He skipped the rites-of-passage buffoonery indulged by many of his peers. But DGF barely noticed, as he was set on the course of an earnest young man and seldom felt the need to deviate.

Affectionately his better friends joshed him, challenging him to "break out of his square." Their motives were kind as they lamented the lack of joie de vivre within him—and they teased the heck out of him, especially his self-imposed formality. His refusal to eat hamburgers with bare hands, even in the most primitive circumstances, had become legend. If no cutlery was available, DGF would resign himself to the beginning deprivations of a new fast.

However, in moments of crisis DGF was their go-to guy—the only "adult" their age they could trust—who would handle it; and it was at such moments his responsible ways were fully appreciated by his peers.

Though not a rebel himself, a rebellious streak did percolate in the family bloodstream. DGF's mother, Minnie, was a quiet rebel at heart.

▶◀▶◀

When Max suddenly died, Minnie discovered they were destitute. Emotional abandonment in their loveless marriage had been expected, but financial ruin was an unwelcome surprise— especially as it was such a premeditated, cruel one.

Max never lost a penny in business; instead he chose to lose it all on his deathbed. It was there that Max fixed a devious will for the express purpose: to torment his wife, Minnie, from the grave one final time.

Max's last will and testament demanded that at his death, his entire property empire was to be sold immediately, at fire-sale prices, no matter the market conditions. To ensure the willful nature of his demands were well understood, he carefully crafted a meager stipend for Minnie and their son Daniel. Then, in an act of irrational extravagance, especially for a man who loathed familial attachments, the assets from the forced sell-off were placed in a long-term trust for his grandchildren— grandchildren not yet born, and whom he'd never know.

A twist in the codicil stipulated these future grandchildren would forfeit their inheritance if Minnie ever remarried. So Minnie didn't remarry.

But she swiftly learned a marriage contract was not essential to enjoying the company of men, which raised many an eyebrow. This didn't deter her; to the contrary, she relished the reaction her rebellion received. In fact, dead old Max's spite empowered her, and nothing delighted Minnie more than knowing her consorting with other men irked the miserly fool from the grave.

After she lost the Houghton home, Minnie lived in a series of apartment buildings. She hated it, her superficial explanation being, "I loathed smelling everyone else's cooking as I tramped down to my flat." In fact Minnie detested eating alone, and when she did, she meticulously set a full-table ensemble, with placemats surrounded by fine silver flatware and her favorite cobalt-blue drinking glasses. It's as if she always wished to be prepared in the hope someone would drop by in search for a meal, unannounced.

◄►

So in keeping with her unconventional ways, Minnie took charge of her destiny and became the sole permanent resident at the luxurious Hyde Park Hotel. Here she was never alone, with the staff at her beck and call and a fresh buffet of new faces in the dining room. The constant churn of new guests at the hotel, from all over the world, provided her with stimulating grist for debate and fair-fought exchanges of ideas.

Evenings were stimulating too. The hotel was the hottest destination for the nightclub set, specifically at the Colony club. Behind the understated black awning covering the entrance, the nights took flight with the nonstop musical fanfare of Sam Sklair & His Orchestra. It was always dance time as couples went swinging on into daybreak.

But staying at the Hyde Park Hotel had a special reward for Minnie—it was run by family. Her favorite niece Beatrice owned the hotel with her husband Stanley, and the pair of them ran it superbly. They were the archetypical power couple, a true partnership—and as a team they complemented each other. She shaped the décor and menu, and he was the face at the front and manager behind the scenes. Daily Minnie noticed Bea's personal touches everywhere, from vases of fresh-cut roses to bowls of warmed cashews dipped in honey and sage. And Stanley's business savvy was apparent with the growing number of guests, who used the hotel as a way station en route to safari holidays. However, Beatrice and Stanley's greatest gift was the manner in which they treasured family—and Minnie was family, and always welcome.

**

The Dutch Reformed Church, or Nederduitse Gereformeerde Kerk (NGK), was the religious wing of the South African apartheid government. The National Party in power was effectively a closet theocracy. Church and state were one—and this union was imposed on everyone. Others were free to practice the faith of their choice, guided by priests, rabbis, and witch doctors; but everyone was legally bound to the social doctrines imposed by the government's officially sanctioned church.

Sundays had the feeling of a postapocalyptic event, with the streets deserted. No stores opened. No movie theaters, no concerts, no public festivities, no organized sporting events, no nothing. But church parking lots were full, and chorusing voices marched forth to the hymn "A Mighty Fortress is Our God" as the righteous sought succor beneath tall steeples.

Happily white citizens at home were generally left unmolested; a private gathering of friends, enjoying a braai—a barbeque—by the swimming pool was miraculously adjudged legal.

The suppression of fun did not stop there, however. Under the rubric of blaspheme, the volume of creative arts deemed unsuitable for the general population was extraordinary. The banning of books, music, movies, and theatre was oppressive. And, if there was any doubt as to the appropriateness of a work, the heavy hand of censorship snipped away any remaining vestiges of joy.

The censor's scissors were never subtle. There was never concern for artistic integrity. Many a leading lady was seen only in a film's opening credits; due only to her sumptuous cleavage, she was never to be seen again in the body of the picture, obliterated in a series of crude jump-cut edits. If not banned outright, pages were torn from magazines, lyrics were bleeped from songs, and the great performances that rocked the world were officially altered for local consumption.

But to the Afrikaner academics and their political apparatchiks, who midwifed the apartheid system, the Dutch Reformed Church provided much more than the suppression of personal pleasure—it provided the alibi, the moral justification for the tenets of government-sanctioned segregation.

**

Similar to Beatrice, Minnie had always worked—a rarity for a white woman of her generation. She started the Illovo Book Club, a private library for the well-heeled living in the northern suburbs. Illovo Books became the hub of social intercourse, with the literati constantly dropping in to explore the latest works of James Michener, Robert Ruark, William Manchester, John LeCarre, Irving Stone, Frederick Forsyth, Ken Follett, Herman Wouk, and Leon Uris.

Less highfalutin books, but writings of considerable gusto nonetheless, by Irving Wallace, Sidney Sheldon, Ian Fleming, Barbara Cartland, Alistar Maclean, Len Deighton, and Robert Ludlum were in hot demand.

As Minnie rubber-stamped the "due date" on her loaned out books, her members hovered about the little library, discussing the latest potboilers and exchanging tidbits of gossip. Minnie thrived on the tumult about her desk—unlike at the public library, silence was not a prerequisite here.

But Minnie had a secret—that rebellious streak once again—shared with only her favored, most trusted book club members. In the back stockroom, concealed behind by a beige curtain, she held a special shelf of at-risk books, books banned by the South African Publications Control Board.

**

Authors and their publishers feared the notorious and insidious Jakobsen's List. And local talent suffered greatly, as there was no special dispensation for South African writers—many demonstrated personal courage in their efforts to shine a light on the dark underbelly of apartheid, only to run afoul of the thought police. Works by Wilbur Smith, the playwright Athol Fugard, Nadine Gordimer, Andre Brink, and Alan Paton's powerful, "Cry, The Beloved Country" were all banished.

Books were banned for a host of reasons—sexually explicit, blasphemous, political, subversive, or promoting black consciousness—and too often for reasons that were irrational or stupid (due to the subjective prejudice of the individual adjudicator). For all these reasons, a roll call of some verboten works: Vladimir Nabokov's "Lolita"; Henry Miller's "Tropic of Cancer"; D. H. Lawrence's "Lady Chatterley's Lover"; Shirley Jackson's "The Lottery"; Jackie Collins's "The Stud"; Richard Wright's "Native Son"; Ralph Ellison's "Invisible Man"; Philip Roth's "Portnoy's Complaint";

Toni Morrison's "The Bluest Eye"; and Maya Angelou's
"I Know Why the Caged Bird Sings." Even Jack Kerou-
ac's "On the Road" was considered a threat and an af-
front to the volk's standards of decency.

However, the Publications Control Board really lost
the plot when they capriciously banned Anna Sewell's
charming children's story, "Black Beauty." They errone-
ously barred the book because some censorious idiot
was too lazy to read it, and assumed from the title that
it was about a gorgeous dusky woman, rather than a
touching tale about a black horse!

**

Minnie resolutely stocked volumes of all these forbidden works
on her secret shelf. Doing so was not a trivial act of rebellion, but
rather it represented a bellwether to her, a cautionary tale—as it
were the caged canary in the coalmine—because the apartheid
regime not only banned books, but it banned people, too.

At the broad discretion of the Minister of Justice, those persons banned had their physical movement restricted and their
voices stifled; it was a crime to publish the opinions and images
of these "nonpersons" in the media. Minnie feared the lessons of
recent history were already being ignored by the South African
regime—Nazi Germany had first burned books, but then graduated to burning people, too, in the death camps.

▶◀▶◀

Daniel thought about his mother. He'd always admired her
independent, willful spirit. He knew what she'd expect of him.

"All right," Daniel said, turning to Juliette. "I've reached a
decision."

"Yes?"

"I will offer Stanwell the executive position tomorrow."

▶◀▶◀

Stanwell Marunda—a black man, and now corporate executive—was the newly appointed (though illegally so) general manager of the Gallo Group's massive warehouse and shipping facility near Jan Smuts Airport. He would have a staff of one hundred seventy-five souls reporting to him, of which twenty-six were white—white men and women who were previously his masters.

His life was about to become considerably more complicated.

►◄►◄

CHAPTER **THIRTEEN**

ELSA MARAIS WAS USHERED into DGF's large office by his impeccably gracious executive assistant. The prospect of seeing Stanwell again made her edgy. A one-on-one meeting with this captain of industry unsettled her further.

Mr. Firth had readily accepted her explanation when she'd phoned about the now-cleaned wristwatch and her wish to return it to Stanwell. DGF suggested they should meet at Gallo's Newkirk Centre head office, at Kerk and Goud Streets, as he'd scheduled a meeting with Stanwell that very day—and it would be easier than having to schlep all the way out to Kempton Park.

DGF snatched a pair of owlish, heavy-framed square reading glasses from his face as he arose from his desk—more a table than a desk—and gave Elsa a welcoming smile.

"I'll let you in on a secret," he said in a conspiratorial tone. "I wear these heavy framed glasses for dramatic purposes only. On the rare occasion I need to reprimand an employee, well, I'm seldom that angry, so I put on these specs that make me look really mean...tell me, don't you agree?"

He plonked the glasses back on his nose and pulled a ghoul-ish face. Elsa giggled. She wasn't so nervous anymore.

"Please sit," he pointed to a chair. "Stanwell's downstairs with our human resources department at the moment. I sure gave that guy a big surprise today."

"Anything wrong?"

"No, quite the opposite. I've promoted him to an enormous job, running our entire warehouse facility. That's why I wore my ogre glasses; I've just fired Stanwell's predecessor. A lazy bloke, and I knew Stanwell had been covering for him all this time. Boy, was he livid, especially at the thought of being replaced by a black man. No matter. I've always believed merit should be rewarded."

"That's fantastic. Do you mind me asking, how'd you and Stanwell meet?"

"My driver Steven had a family emergency, so he returned to his Bantustan in the Transkei. Stanwell was working in our driver's pool and subbed for me in Steven's absence. On the long drives out to our record-pressing plant in Roodepoort, we'd have very interesting chats. Stanwell was very curious about our operation. Not typical of our average Bantu.

"I felt his potential was wasted as a chauffeur and found him a position at the warehouse. It didn't take long to notice the positive impact he had out there. Things began running a good deal smoother. Well, finally, today, he's being rewarded for a job well done."

As Daniel Firth spoke, Elsa looked around. She noticed a gadget: a varnished wooden box attached to large black and brass horn, clearly of old vintage, sitting on the credenza behind the desk. She'd soon learn it was an authentic 1905 Edison Cylinder Phonograph.

DGF delighted her by cranking the mechanism with a handle built into the machine's wooden base, then released the lever—the Blue Amberol cylinder began to spin. Emanating from the tubular horn Elsa heard in a distant, tinny melody the xylophone performance of a certain Charles Daab, now long-deceased, playing "Listen to the Mockingbird."

▶◀▶◀

Elsa's eyes lingered on the elegant cut-crystal bowl filled with mixed nuts and raisins on the desk. Possibly it was the nerves, but she felt hungry. DGF offered them to her and rang for the tea girl to bring refreshments.

"You were brave, the way you cared for Stanwell after his accident," said DGF pointedly.

"It was nothing," she replied.

"I'm not so sure. We're kind of in the same boat; we've both helped him recently."

"That's true." Elsa wanted to change the subject. "Your business looks so nice. How'd you get into it?"

"It's a dull story. I had no interest in the entertainment business, recording stars and all that glamor stuff—it was just about plastic.

"During World War II they used something called Bakelite for radios, pistol grips, telephones, steering wheels, and the like. This began my interest in ejection mold materials, so I wanted to get into the plastic business, but I couldn't find a plastics company to work for. As luck would have it, my mother's brother-in-law, Uncle Harrison, owned a small record company called Trutone with a tiny record pressing operation here in Jo'burg.

"Now, they never used plastic. Instead—it's way before your time—the 78-rpm gramophone records those days were made from shellac. It was so brittle. You just sneezed and the record shattered in your hands. No big surprise. It was made from a mixture of powdered slate and a special resin secreted from the innards of Indian bugs. Gross, hey?

"The sound quality was bloody awful—so scratchy—and it was a dusty mess to manufacture, but I didn't mind because it was a high-pressure molding process, which was a step closer to the real deal—plastic. But we eventually got rid of the messy shellac and replaced it with vinyl—first the seven-inch single, then the LP. Now I have a story to tell you about that. I must confess it's my most embarrassing moment in business ever..."

As impatient as Elsa was, curiosity got the best of her and she leaned in closer for the scoop.

"It was my duty to introduce vinyl 45-rpm singles to the national media. We held this big event at the SABC. I'm not exactly P.T. Barnum, but I grab a recent ten-inch shellac disk and drop it to the floor—the thing fragments in twenty different directions. Good. Now I've the press's attention, I then reveal this shiny, elegant seven-inch disc—give it a few whacks to show how robust it is, then hurl it like a Frisbee across the room.

"*Oy*, it must've been the way it hit the corner, but Sod's law, the damn thing shattered everywhere! Their silence, my shock, and then the press began to laugh. This doesn't make me happy. Admittedly it was more an act of desperation than cunning, but I grabbed the whole stack of vinyl discs and began tossing them Frisbee-like all over the room.

"The press were ducking and weaving to avoid the flying disks, and they were laughing their heads off, but not at me— they were having a jolly good time. And thankfully not one single disk broke despite the salvo of records scattered all about with reckless abandon.

"Whew, my mission was accomplished, and the 45's launch in the South African market became a sterling success.

"By the way, Elsa, you can just imagine how amused I was so many years later—I think it was around '67 or '68—when I saw the movie *The Graduate*. In one scene a wealthy executive type was giving an inexperienced younger man some sage career advice. He said something to the effect, 'I just want to say one word to you...Plastics!' Hmm, I sure chuckled thinking how I was into plastic manufacturing fifteen years earlier."

Daniel Gideon Firth's eyes lit up, he was plainly pleased by his foresight.

As she expected, Elsa found DGF to be a most interesting man. However, the need to see Stanwell again constantly gnawed at her. She restlessly recrossed her legs. Hoping Stanwell's interview with human resources would end soon, and stalling for time, Elsa asked one more question. "You began at Trutone, so how'd you end up at Gallo's?"

DGF enjoyed this part of the story. It was a tale of discrete familial revenge.

"I'm a bit of an engineer and have always been on the lookout for new technologies to improve sound fidelity and the quality of our pressings. It took some nudging, but I convinced Harrison to send me to British Decca in the UK. I'd learned they were using superior materials and systems over there.

"I eagerly rushed back and tried to convince Harrison to upgrade his plant. But Uncle Harrison was a bit of a fuddy-duddy— he didn't like been nudged by his nephew. He wouldn't budge. He went further—Harrison fired me."

"Then what happened?"

"Mr. Gallo called me out of the blue and gave me a job. Not much later, in 1962, we snatched Trutone away from my Uncle

Harrison—and not long afterwards I was appointed Trutone's newest managing director."

They were interrupted with a discreet knock on the open inner-office door, and the tentative greeting, "*Howzit,* hey?"

Elsa swiveled in her seat—there stood Stanwell.

⊲⊳⊲

DGF's voice boomed across the office. "Welcome, take a seat." Turning to Elsa, he added, "It's my pleasure to introduce you to the new general manager of our warehouse operations."

Seeing Stanwell again foiled Elsa's equilibrium. As she leapt to her feet to greet him, she left a fluster of nuts and raisins in her wake. Then reality set in; it was restraint that was most needed. We dare not show our emotions, not publicly, she reminded herself. Elsa feared Stanwell would give the game away. He had no idea I'd be here!

She had to take the initiative. She reached into her handbag for Stanwell's watch. "I had this cleaned like new for you," she said, holding it up for his inspection. "By the way, how are you feeling?"

"*Ja-wel-no-fine,*" he mumbled in confusion. "I guess I'm okay, thanks, and thanks for the watch." As he reached for it, their fingers touched momentarily, and warmth coursed through her being. Elsa was desperate for Stanwell to embrace her, to envelop her in his powerful arms. But she knew he couldn't, not with DGF present.

Elsa wondered whether he had grappled with the events from a fortnight ago, as she had. She'd grown more uncertain, fearing he'd come to regard her carnal embrace as a matter of sympathy, rather than true affection.

"If you don't mind, I have a favor to ask," said Elsa, looking at both men. "I need to put some things into storage. Would it be okay if Stanwell brought a bunch of cardboard boxes to my flat? I'm guessing you have some at the warehouse..."

"Of course, we'd be delighted," replied DGF. "Just let us know when and where."

"How about Wednesday then, at eleven," said Elsa as she scribbled her address on a nearby notepad. She tore it out and handed it to Stanwell. Deliberately her fingers touched his.

►◄►◄

Elsa's flatmate was on duty at the hospital. She and Stanwell would have the place to themselves. Better still, they wouldn't be restricted to her bedroom—and a good thing, too, as the living room was the most inviting room of the home. She fought her instincts and dispensed with the honey-trap frou-frou—no candles, burning incense, or muted lighting. She didn't wish to alienate him. She mustn't be the predator; it wasn't the tribal way. It was time he took the initiative as the man.

►◄►◄

Stanwell felt an uneasy mixture of anxiety and exultation. As the elevator ascended to her floor, he was burdened with bundled corrugated cardboard boxes tied together with jute twine. His mind was burdened too with thoughts that were both forbidding and enticing.

Everything about her was different from anything he'd experienced before: the form of her body and the color of her skin were obvious, but the way she behaved, also, was not akin to the womanly supplications of his people.

Stanwell wasn't in much pain now, and his tongue was no longer swollen. Finally, he could to speak to her and see her. But he was uncertain of the reception he'd receive.

►◄►◄

She closed the door behind him. She moved closer to inspect his wounds. Her fingers traced the raw scar on his chin, an angry pink tear in his rich brown skin. He smelled her perfume, her breath. The boxes tumbled to the floor. Then he furtively touched her cheek. She leaned against him in response. Both sighed, relieved.

He kissed her, powerfully. She pulled back—an anxious moment for him. But only briefly. Time for a little advice: "When giving someone a gift, you don't throw it at them. You gently hand it to them," she purred. Stanwell got the message, and now kissed her—gently, all over.

Others might light up a cig and flippantly chat, but these two lay quietly bound by their taboo love. Confidence grew with time, and they quietly began talking, though not much about the future. Elsa and Stanwell became keenly aware that their time together was dwindling with the oncoming dusk.

Their contentment turned to horror when they both heard a scream, then a thud, followed by deathly silence. The mood was lost and it was time to get dressed. A final embrace, with the desperate promise of a future rendezvous, and then it was time for Stanwell to go.

▶◀▶◀

Stanwell encountered a large unruly crowd as he exited the building. The crowd appeared belligerent and overhyped and he feared for his life, certain his actions upstairs were now public knowledge. As Stanwell shifted cautiously forward, the gawkers parted and revealed the still form of a girl. With what must have been a terrifying act of desperation, she had leapt off the roof of the building onto the concrete slab twenty-three floors below.

Someone had tried to shelter the suicide victim's body from the gaze of the crowd with a coat, but Stanwell could still see the shock of bright red hair and the blue-red thunderbolt drawn across the girl's face.

Despite the violence of the act, Stanwell was surprised at the tranquil expression on the waif-like face. Then a scarlet stain, spreading on the concrete ground beneath her head, drew his attention. He then remembered the wallpaper in the Duncans' bathroom, and the image of the bird with the bloodied crop. A sense of unease crept over him. Is this the *iSangoma* trying to warn me—again?

▶◀▶◀

Elsa and Stanwell began their life of subterfuge. Such was the tortured path they were forced to follow, that they nurtured their relationship by hiding it in deceit. They adopted the customary public role of a servant and his mistress. Disguised as a driver, grocery delivery boy, and handyman, Stanwell perpetuated the deception.

As the couple hid in the darkness, a great light switched on in homes throughout the land: the debut of South Africa's first television broadcast.

Cathode-ray tubes fired electron beams at the phosphor coating the inside of the nation's newfangled TV sets. The affluent watched in the comfort of their homes as the less fortunate clustered around electronic store windows. Everyone oohed and aahed as miraculous images of other worlds danced before their eyes.

▶◀▶◀

Lydia and Sid Duncan's new Decca television set had pride of place in their sitting room. They sat transfixed by the moving images while their servants hovered in the entrance hall, eager to take a peak. Eventually Lydia noticed Dinah's restless enthusiasm. In a curious moment of camaraderie, infrequently seen in South Africa, Lydia patted a spot on the sofa beside her and invited her maid to take a seat. Sid gave a satisfied grunt and shifted to make room. Lydia then beckoned the other domestic servants to join them.

This wasn't the 1969 lunar landing. Actually, the first evening's programming was cautiously bland, but TV was finally here and everyone wanted to enjoy the moment. Initially the servants hesitated at the invitation. Should they sit or stand? They'd never been invited to sit in their master's living room before. Some balanced themselves awkwardly on the arms of sofas and chairs, others stood respectfully behind—still conscious of the barrier between—but all leaned in close to peer at the radiant box.

Leo padded up to the TV and sniffed at the screen. He then carefully examined the cables behind the set box. Intrigued by the human voices and figures emanating from it, but confused by the lack of their scent, he gave a great shake of resignation and returned to lie at Lydia's feet.

**

The nation got their television, but the government got its way. Television was segregated to reflect apartheid's great vision, with programs broadcasted only in Afrikaans and English; though reportedly another channel, at a later date, would beam content suitable for the nation's blacks. As for programming meted out each Sunday? At the behest of the government's Dutch Reformed Church, all citizens were treated to a strict staple of religious programming.

The South African Broadcasting Corporation (SABC), the state-owned propaganda service, enthusiastically championed the goals of the regime by exploiting the new medium. One, considered of paramount im-

portance, was ensuring the survival of the Afrikaans language—the cornerstone of the volk's cultural identity.

The regime's authorities were dogged in their efforts to force-feed their language to the entire nation—even if it had little relevance beyond the borders of South Africa and was only naturally spoken by a small minority.

To the delight of the governing party and their adherents, but to the frustration of the rest, the news broadcast was manipulated, alternating daily between Afrikaans and English. Every other evening the majority of viewers struggled to understand the events of the day, or just switched off, more the happier to revel in their ignorance.

The charade was exposed when the most desirable programming, purchased in English from the UK and USA, was only made available exclusively in Afrikaans. These shows, at the expense of the taxpayer, were dubbed into Afrikaans, and the lip-synching was often comical; Afrikaans being such a guttural language, its hardened edges didn't blend with the smoother cues of English. So some watched, but many wouldn't.

However, a local soap opera named The Villagers, based on a set of scallywags on a gold mine, was embraced by the majority of the audience—despite its amateurish production—and the people of South Africa stopped their lives to watch.

So the conservatives felt they'd won the television debate—by conceding, they had gained the ultimate Trojan horse with a language instructor seductively incased within, reaching into more and more homes. Their gambit appeared foolproof. With the baited honey of *television came the sting-in-the-tail medicine: "One way or another, you will all bladdie well learn to speak the 'taal,' our nation's official language, or else..."*

But not for the first time the ruling party failed to understand human nature. Their compulsion to force their language down the throats of the majority of the population—mostly unwilling—would prove their undoing. Within five months, it would be the first step along the rocky road toward the end of Afrikaner rule.

**

The huge demand for television dispensed with any honeymoon period that the new executive may have wished for. Stanwell was confronted with an unprecedented task. The logistics of shipping expensive twenty-seven-inch television sets was significantly different to that of distributing twenty-five-count box loads of Quentin E. Klopjaeger's *Lazy Life* hit record.

At the facility Stanwell was responsible for the storage and fulfillment of thousands of items, large and small, from an individual gramophone needle to Farfisa electronic organs, from brick-sized nine-volt batteries to the chic Teppaz portable record player, from home kitchen appliances to the largest record catalog of singles, LPs, and music cassettes under one roof throughout Africa. The surge in demand for a complex machine like a TV, with special installation requirements, was no easy task. But Stanwell was more competent than the man he replaced, and as hiccups would be expected, he began with the confidence that no situation was insurmountable.

Stanwell settled into the corner office previously inhabited by his white predecessor and summoned his secretary, a holdover from the previous management. Melanie Coetzee, an attractive brunette, was initially rattled by her new boss, understandably so, as it was the first time a native was her superior. But Stanwell understood. He was considerate and patient. Initially he fetched his own tea and photocopied his own documents so as not to demean her.

Melanie in turn realized it was her duty to provide the administrative support for the warehouse's new general manager, and one morning brought him a steaming mug of tea with "The Boss" inscribed on the side. A team coalesced around that thoughtful gesture—now that the issue of color had been set aside—and they got down to business.

When word got out about a new black boss, the black staff members on the warehouse floor were curious. Seldom before did they volunteer to visit the executive suite; it normally meant trouble, a dressing-down for being a lazy-good-for-nothing, or whatever made the white boss feel important. But a parade of excuses took the steps up to the mezzanine above the shop floor. The black employees glanced through the glass wall as they walked by, and exclaimed a loud "Haw!" as they clapped their hands in disbelief, and then beetled back to their workstations.

The black man sitting in the corner office had unsettled them. It unnerved the white staffers as well.

▶◀▶◀

Elsa's first official day at her new job. She was one of five of them at Lydia's confab on the verandah. The new faces present were friendly, and introduced themselves by job description: head designer, production manager, and marketing manager. They knew her as "the model."

Lydia took command. "Welcome, gang. I've two major announcements: the launch date and name of our fashion line." Enthusiastic faces greeted this declaration. "From this moment we are Safari Èlan...a French-designed apparel line manufactured in South Africa."

"Why French, not locally designed?" asked the production manager.

"I'm not happy with the spin, but you know how our locals are such snobs. They're just weirdly prejudiced against domestic products. Look at our homegrown rock band, Rabbitt—they're the biggest thing around in years, yet they're damned with faint praise with a, "They're not bad for a local band; they're kinda okay, I guess." Well, at Safari Èlan we won't accept that kind of thing."

The designer piped in, "We've got the French part covered, then. My surname is Du Plessis. From authentic French Huguenot stock, I am, though I must admit the last time my people saw France was in 1692!" Her levity broke the ice.

Turning to Elsa, the designer stuck out her hand forthrightly and said, "Hi. Welcome on board. My name's Francine. You may call me Franny."

Lydia, impatient to continue, snapped her fingers to regain their attention. The customary Lydia "earnest-speak" fell away to the fluffy lingo of the fashion milieu. "We're taking cues from fab-Frenchy couture and their hip celebrities, like Serge Gainsbourg and Jane Birkin," she said. "They're really into a Lee Cooper vibe at the moment, wearing the brand's tank tops, hipsters, and bell-bottom flairs. Now, what's really rad and quite a coincidence, Lee Cooper have just added safari suits to their line—can't get more African than that.

"But we aren't rip-off artists. I'm not interested in making bell-bottoms so wide, which seems to be the trend at the moment, which could flip someone over feet first in a crosswind. And we can't all wear those mod baby-doll dresses forever.

"So we've decided to do a twist on something utilitarian. It's a really solid idea—a sexy designer jumpsuit inspired by the Israeli paratrooper uniform." Lydia, her enthusiasm unstoppable, plowed on. "I'm really truly stoked about it. There are cool pockets on the legs, chest, and the full-length zipper from tail to throat is slammin' hot."

"Will we include other items in the launch?" asked the marketing-manager.

"Damn straight. The miniskirt is still way cool, and minidresses, pantsuits, and the layered look will be our bread and butter. But we'll have some fun with hemlines on these threads. But...this is the hook, and it'll be truly stellar.

"It's how we intend to add our unique local flavor; so our signature stylin' will be the use of bone, Ndebele beadwork, and leather thongs as closures, instead of conventional buttons...and of course, animal prints."

"Awesome, don't you think?" said Franny Du Plessis, handing around renderings from her leather portfolio. The excited chatter that followed confirmed for the designer that she had the Safari Èlan team's approval.

"Now you see Safari Èlan isn't intended to be a curios line, covered in kitschy masks, to be sold to foreign tourists. Please remember that. What we're doing is a world-class fashion line—conceived to be wearable, stylish, youthful, and trendy—expressly for the active "me decade" woman."

Lydia's last comment was accepted with a bobbing line of agreeing heads. "Now the launch date...Early March it is." All heads suddenly stopped bobbing. Lydia sensed a hint of mutiny course through the team. "Okay, here's the scoop. The South African Formula One Grand Prix auto race is scheduled to take place early March.

"The whole world's heading to Kyalami—mindboggling considering the boycotts we're experiencing—and we must capitalize on this opportunity to get our products out there. Just imagine. All the jet-setters and the world press, on our doorstep here in South Africa. This auto race is *the* magnet for movie stars, international playboys, global business execs, and all those beautiful, chic birds clutching to the arms of those dashing racing drivers. They're coming here to see the fastest cars on the planet. And it's our job to make sure they see us!"

As the idea took root, the heads began bobbing once more. "It's a fantastic opportunity to showcase Safari Èlan to the world. And we have a secret weapon, the international debut of our star fashion model." Lydia looked directly at her latest recruit. "Our very own Elsa 'Kat' Marais."

Elsa raised her hand enthusiastically. She had an idea. She flapped her hand about seeking attention. With her hand raised, Elsa momentarily flashed back to Mevrou Carr's first grade classroom, back in Brakpan, when she was the know-it-all student eager to answer all the questions. Similar to her old teacher, Lydia briefly maintained the pretense of ignoring her, but then gladly gave Elsa center stage.

"Race day will be full of pretty girls dressed up in glamorous outfits, so I don't know what kind of impact I'll have, hey. But hear me out...I think this is a really *lekker* idea." Elsa was quickly growing comfortable expressing herself in English. "We must show our foreign guests something unique, like a real Zulu chief dressed in tribal clothes.

"You know the stuff: wild animal skins, leopard pelts, oxhide loincloth, beads, zebra-hide armbands, and feathered headdress, maybe even a battle shield. And here's the hook: he can escort me dressed in our glamor clothes during the event."

Elsa gave Lydia a pointed look. "And we know just the man to do it...Stanwell Marunda."

Lydia was intrigued. A powerful black warrior in traditional costume, protecting a gorgeous fashionable blonde dressed in contemporary flair, would be eye catching. It had an African twist on the universal theme of *Beauty and the Beast*—the juxtaposition of light and dark, slight and huge, primitive and modern. It would resonate just like the fairy tale, and the media would lap it up. Brilliant, Lydia thought. Would the authorities approve? Screw them. We'll deal with the consequences later, she decided.

Lydia was unaware of any ulterior motive, but Elsa had achieved the impossible. Finally, she and Stanwell would be seen together, in public, in the light of day, like lovers should.

►◄►◄

"Elsa, if you pull this off, we'll be getting a load of foreign business. If so, I promise you your first trip overseas," said a pleased Lydia.

But Elsa had a secret. She had travelled overseas before. It had been a difficult journey—a mission that broke her heart and caused her great shame.

Four years before meeting Stanwell, Elsa had stepped into another unknown, and tentatively explored social boundaries beyond that of her Afrikaner tribe. It was not a relationship she was seeking, but circumstances presented themselves in a charming, unrushed way. He was always attentive whenever she stopped in at the local general store. Eventually, he mustered the courage to ask her on a date. Elsa surprised herself when she agreed, and there began her earnest romance with a serious young man—a Jewish man.

Elsa considered him in her local idiom to be a "*correct oke,*" or, as she'd later learn in his Yiddish, a *mensch*—an appellation he considered to be of the highest order. His decency was a constant, and he endeavored to imbue her with the same, which was a difficult task in a society so torn and fraught with such convoluted layers of complexity.

Initially, Elsa hid their relationship from her family. After all, she was a devoted member of the Dutch Reformed Church, and her uncle was the *predikant*—the pastor of the church her family attended.

Eventually she plucked up the courage, and informally around the family dinner table, she just happened to raise the notion of Judaism. The response Elsa received was more positive than she'd anticipated. It wasn't exactly a glowing endorsement. Nor was there any great affection for the Jews expressed. But—and this allayed her guilt greatly—there were three very pragmatic, even constructive reasons not to alienate Jews.

One, as devout Dutch Reformed Church members, they'd always been haunted by the question, "What if Jews really are God's Chosen People? Dare we anger Him by hurting them?" Two, Jewry's reverence for academics was greatly admired by Afrikanerdom. The devout Afrikaner understood academic strength meant religious strength, and through the reading and comprehension of the Holy Scriptures the *volk* would prosper. And three, there's a great strategic affinity for the modern state of Israel, beyond that of biblical belief.

**

It's a small club of nations—with a shared sense of their mortality—and they've labelled themselves the Fifth World. South Africa, Israel, and Taiwan related to one another because they shared a similar predicament. These three nations live in close proximity to their mortal enemies. The pathologies are frighteningly similar: a sophisticated minority population, who having attained First World nation status, living alongside or amongst an overwhelming mass of Third World peoples that seek their destruction.

This common fear of extinction have bound these small nations together—both strategically and tactically—in their collective resolve to hold back the forces threatening to overwhelm them. Forced into a strange passive-aggressive role, these Fifth World leaders yearn for the day that the status quo (and their very existence) is accepted. And with the threat of belligerence set aside, they would far prefer devoting their efforts to the betterment of the plight of their larger, poorer neighbors by providing constructive contributions in the form of agriculture, technology, economic subsidies, and education.

Instead, locked in fear these three embattled nations devote their time collaborating on weapon development—by diverting scarce materials and resources to that singular pursuit—in order to punch above their individual weight, all in the name of survival.

**

With this implied blessing, Elsa encouraged the relationship with her Jewish suitor. He in turn charmed her, by good-naturedly accepting an old Boer custom called *opsitting*. Here a young man with romantic intentions was tested; he was permitted to "sit up" in the company of the young lady he desired, while the rest of the family retired to bed.

There was, however, a catch: a lit candle was left in the window, and when the flame flickered out, it was time for the smitten Romeo to leave. But for the young suitor there was always hope; a quick glance at the freshly lit candle would signify much—the longer the candle, the more confident he'd be he was liked.

Sadly, the relationship ended because she was seeking a husband, but all he wanted was a girlfriend, lover, and friend. He wasn't ready to commit; he felt he was too young and not accomplished enough to adequately provide. Or did his family object, or were they even aware she existed? Elsa never truly knew and pretended she never cared.

However, one thing was certain—she was pregnant. Quietly understanding the meaning of *mensch,* Elsa never told him, not wishing to burden him with any responsibility.

Abortions were illegal in the Republic, and horror stories of botched coat hanger jobs in the townships were rife. The only alternative was to undergo the surgical procedure overseas. Elsa barraged her parents with entreaties "to see the world." Soon they succumbed, because she was their *goed meisie*—their good girl, and she found herself on a Musgrove & Watson tour to Europe with twenty fellow travelers.

The itinerary was robust: visiting twenty-three cities, in eight countries, in only twenty-one days. Excursions to the Prado Museum in Madrid and the Sacré-Cœr Basilica in Paris were buried in a haze of anxiety, as were the Manneken-Pis in Brussels and the Anne Frank House in Amsterdam. Elsa kept to herself, not wishing to expose her secret and open herself to accusations of surliness. Even the tour director attempted to pry her from her shell, assuming her melancholy was a bout of homesickness.

Finally they reached London, a rare two-day stopover, and Elsa excused herself from the tour on the grounds she was meeting a relative. After a couple of difficult days, Elsa's spirits lifted the further the city of London receded in the luxury coach's rearview mirrors.

She then joined in all the activities and flirted with the boys, her reputation now ironically restored. And being woken on Christmas Day to the chiming bells in St. Mark's Square, Venice, freed of her burden, became a memory of a lifetime.

Yes, she had travelled overseas, but the experience had left an enduring scar.

▶◀▶◀

CHAPTER **FOURTEEN**

THE CHOPPER CAME TO A MOMENTARY STALL then slapped down sharply on the Grand Prix circuit's helipad. The hop from the Kyalami Ranch Hotel to the track had been quick, though flying in a helicopter wasn't Elsa's first choice. The notion of being suspended in space, in a clattering, vibrating facsimile of a deathtrap, held little appeal.

But the publicist had insisted their entrance be grand, and this was the way to go. The trip hadn't been exactly social either; the racket of the rotors had obliterated any hope of small talk with fellow VIP passengers, including the reigning Miss South Africa and her date, a famous record producer—most of whom appeared curious about herself and Stanwell, but then they were the novelty, being the only black and white couple in sight.

For Stanwell, the brief flight represented the extremes his life had taken, from scavenging deep below ground for gold to soaring high above the Rand's gold reef, in this *dinges*—this whirlybird contraption. As for his immediate dignity, any hope of preserving it had been buffeted away by the machine's turbulence updrafting under the skirts and pelts of his tribal regalia. But then again, the demand to keep flighty clothing items in check had helped distract Stanwell from the inevitable humiliation he'd suffer the moment the world's media captured him stepping out of the aircraft.

Stanwell understood he was the anomaly. His primitive animal skin costume set in contrast against the exotic hi-tech materials sheathing the Formula One cars was generally the point. Respectfully he'd been asked to accept the incongruity that his native dress, compared to the beautiful girl in the modern and sleek silver-blue jumpsuit, seated beside him, was specifically the point.

And the Safari Èlan marketing executive had made a compelling argument—that it was all about contrast—dramatic and eye-catching: "If the sheet of paper is black, we have to be the white dot to be noticed." Well, Stanwell would be a sport about it, and be the only black primitive in a sea of white sophisticates. At the very least, he and Elsa would be together.

Elsa reached for Stanwell's hand as she exited from the helicopter. Cameras clicked and flashes popped—they were certainly getting attention. Elsa had a mischievous smile painted across her face. It reflected her sheer delight at having such a private moment—grasping her man's hand—in such a public way.

Questions from reporters were drowned out by the banshee cry of speeding machines rocketing by in full song. The formation lap was underway. Soon the cars would line up in their grid positions, ready for the start. Quickly Elsa and Stanwell were escorted to the Denham Store's VIP tent in the paddock—a haven for clients, sponsors, team managers, public officials, and sundry beautiful people. There they found Lydia and Sid, and the rest of the Safari Èlan brain-trust waiting.

▶◀▶◀

Twenty-six clutch pedals released instantaneously in a smoking cloud of spinning tires, each wheel desperately fighting for traction—then the projectiles leaped forward. The air filled with the hornets' buzz of competing engines—the whine of the Ferrari Flat-12 rampaging against the throaty Ford-Cosworth DFV V8 in a discordant roar of relentless power. And the din was outrageous as it reached within the cranium of every spectator, despite earplug protection.

It was the McLaren M23 pilot, Englishman James Hunt, who owned the pole position, but it was Austrian Niki Lauda's Ferrari 312T that led first into Crowthorne Corner.

Seventy-seven more laps followed without any respite from the African heat. The contest's rhythm was broken by accidents, blown radiators, engine failures, and routine pit stops—but changing four tires and refueling highly flammable gasoline in a matter of seconds, within a pressure cooker, was all but routine.

The mile-high altitude of the Kyalami circuit sucked the strength from drivers and cars, the lack of oxygen crippling both man and machine. The extreme forces exerted by gravity in high-speed corners tweaked neck muscles, as weary heads bobbled under pressure from heavy crash helmets and the relentless loading of centrifugal force.

With each lap forearms fatigued, progressively, as drivers wrestled with increasingly unruly machines. The pilots had two enemies—their rivals and the fragility of their machines. And it cost them in wear and tear, with hands blistered raw with every manual gearshift, and liters of fluid lost from sweating within the protective swaddling of their layered fireproof racing suits.

**

Most Grand Prix drivers sublimated their fear. Yet they chose not to get too close, too friendly, with one another, as mortality rates were frightful, making friendship a painful indulgence they could not afford. But they made it their business to know the nature of the men they raced, wheel to wheel, at such close quarters—the risks taken by a daredevil hyped on speed were different from the caution of a tactician stirred by outthinking the competition. So each pilot categorized their grand prix rivals in one of two flavors: those considered "drivers"—strategic and cerebral; and the "racers"—the win-at-all-cost warriors bent on personal destruction. The crowd revered the former for their cunning, but adored the latter for their passion.

**

However, at the 1976 edition of the South African Grand Prix, all the pilots drove to the very edge. Ruthlessly they sucked themselves within the slipstream of the car ahead, then dared to catapult out front at the next bend. Down the main straight they maximized the limits of skill and equipment, until terminal velocity was reached after the Kink, then savagely killed-off speed and brakes before Barbeque Bend.

Getting both car and driver home safely depended on four small, sticky patches of Goodyear rubber—each the size of the palm of a hand—maintaining contact with the track. No matter the machine, the refinement of its paint job, or the pedigree of its marque—a basic question was asked, would the fragile racing machine cling to the track for the duration of the contest?

A drop of oil or a patch of white-painted striping, and all tire adhesion's lost, instantly. Without control, the pilot is but a passenger, with nothing to do but brace for the inevitable crash into the Armco barrier.

On this day the 1975 World Champion, the cunning, ferret-faced Niki Lauda, crossed the finish line first—just barely, as a tire had punctured. An Englishman named James came second, showing the drive of a future world champion that belied his "Hunt the Shunt" playboy reputation.

Homegrown hero Jody Scheckter, in his Tyrrell 007, finished a laudatory fourth to the joy of local fans and the patriotic SABC TV broadcasters. Unknown to him though his ambition was clear to see, this Jewish kid from the Eastern Cape was destined to become within three years the champion of the world for the legendary Scuderia Ferrari team.

The day had concluded without any loss of life and it was now time to celebrate.

►◄ ►◄

Chivalry sometimes has consequences, even if unintended. The return trip to the Kyalami Ranch Hotel had been uneventful, until Elsa snapped the heel off her shoe exiting the helicopter. Stanwell did the right thing and protectively rescued the equilibrium-challenged Elsa. But the broken heel was quickly forgotten, or not even noticed—dominated instead by the image of the beautiful white girl swept up in the arms of a proud black man.

In the bright eye of South Africa's new television service, the spontaneity of the moment sidestepped the rigors of censorship, and the indelible image of Stanwell and Elsa was instantly broadcast far and wide. It became a media hit, and Lydia couldn't have been happier—her Safari Èlan launch had become the buzz of the town.

Local authorities were aghast, but the proverbial horse had fled the stable, and little now could be done. But in the eyes of the foreign visitors—the press, the race drivers, their wives and girlfriends, corporate sponsors, and team principals—the moment was a very public sign of liberalization, which hopefully reflected a possible changing South Africa. So in the eyes of this international audience, Elsa and Stanwell were accepted as a couple, and invited to the post-Grand Prix festivities held under the thatched umbrellas surrounding the Kyalami Hotel's swimming pool.

◄►

The salivating smells of fresh grilled T-bone steaks, chops, *boerewors*—the traditional farmer's sausage, spiced shrimp, peri-peri chicken, and sliced pineapple on the *braaivleis* barbeque enticed the international guests as they surrounded the chefs preparing their feast.

The best racing drivers on the planet were now relaxed. Draped around these lean, driven men were a bevy of exotic, beautiful women; the "hotties" were out in full force. Many of the men smoked foul-smelling Gouloises cigarettes that stunk like the smoldering tire carcasses from their spent racecars.

Drink flowed freely in the spirit of international camaraderie. An assortment of expensive Scotch whiskeys, French champagnes, and the Italian aperitif, Cinzano, circulated alongside local beers—Castle and Carling Black Label. All were consumed with gusto.

Inevitably inhibitions collapsed, and with them, discipline. The swimming pool became the center of attention; newbie drivers were dunked in a sophomoric initiation rite, and soon girls in skimpy dresses followed—some delighted in the revelation of their bodies, while others modestly pleaded for the protection of towels. But when a senior team principal, fully clothed, was unceremoniously shoved into the water, a threshold was reached—his spluttering fury quickly doused further reckless fun. A media scrum witnessed the celebration, and some in the press questioned the drivers' childish behavior.

It took a veteran *AutoCourse* journalist to explain the sense of relief drivers felt at the end of a race weekend—only if they'd all survived, unscathed. These men made their living knowing Death could always be waiting around the next bend, and it wasn't mere hyperbole. The statistics were grim: one in fifteen drivers had an excellent chance of meeting his maker before the end of a given season.

However, one journalist appeared disinterested in foreign celebrities and the hazards of motorsports. He was the credentialed reporter for the *Citizen* newspaper. And as his paper had sponsored the Grand Prix, he was assured maximum access to all Grand Prix-related events.

Around his neck hung a robust Olympus OM-1 camera fitted with a telephoto lens. To the casual observer, it appeared the story he was pursuing had a distinct local angle, as he used his camera only when a South African citizen was in frame.

His telephoto lens zoomed on the black man with the scarred face. Then the lens settled on the lovely face of the girl standing alongside. A quick press of the shutter before the lens tracked down between their bodies and lingered on their hands. He lowered the camera and studied the body language of the pair. Troubling—the Bantu showed no signs of deference to the white girl.

He needed to learn more about them. Later, when he returned to his office, he'd begin an investigation. His office was located on the ninth floor of John Vorster Square, an ominous blue glass and concrete building in downtown Johannesburg. The building was named after the former minister of justice and present prime minister, Balthazar John Vorster.

It was the home of the Security Branch, the centralized apparatus that so doggedly enforced apartheid's restrictive policies. Within walking distance of his office, on the high-security floor above his head, the oppressed were detained without trial, interrogated, and brutally tortured.

CHAPTER **FIFTEEN**

IT HAD BEEN A GRAND DAY. And interest from prospective foreign distributors in the Safari Èlan line had exceeded Lydia's expectations, with much of the credit going to the couple seated quietly in the backseat of the Jaguar. Lydia looked ahead, thinking in terms of an accelerated business plan. Behind her Stanwell and Elsa didn't hold hands, but they'd kicked off their shoes, their toes acting as surrogates for their fingers.

"Dang, it's too late to drive you home," said Sid Duncan, "so I suggest you stay with us." The car's headlights swept across a road sign that read, "Speed like Lightning, Crash like Thunder." Sid instinctively lifted his foot off the throttle.

"What about those passbook raids?" asked Stanwell.

"Doubtful with all the foreign press in town, especially tonight," Sid continued. "Stanwell, you'll have to stay in the servants' quarters. Dinah will make a bed up for you. And Elsa, the guesthouse now seems to be your home away from home..."

▶◀▶◀

The servants' quarters were tucked behind the garage at the end of the property. A kitchen door provided the servants the most direct access to the Duncan home from the backyard, via the quadrangle between the main house and the servants' accommodations, where Dinah hung wet clothes and linens on an outdoor washing line to dry in the warm Witwatersrand sun.

The staff lodgings were drab and seemed, at best, an afterthought. The structure lacked any of the charm of the main house, the architect's creativity giving way to brash utility: the windows small, hallways narrow, and lighting poor. The large public room at the center functioned as both kitchen and living room, with a wood stove providing the only point of interest, as smoke poured from its seams. An enamel kettle sat on the stoveplate, surrounded with a coterie of mix-matched chipped mugs.

These modest surroundings greeted Stanwell. He was offered a glass of *amasi* to drink—unrefrigerated milk, deliberately left out for a day or two until soured and thick. It nauseated him, so he politely declined.

But the warmth of Dinah's welcome more than compensated—until he saw his bed. The narrow metal bed framed with wired springs was superior to his bed in Soweto, as was the coarse coir fiber mattress; but the bedframe stacked on tall piles of bricks perplexed him. For Stanwell, the bed was lofted uncomfortably high above the cold concrete floor.

As a citizen of Malawi, Stanwell was ignorant of many local native customs. He had never been taught about the evil-spirited *Tokoloshe*, the predatory dwarf no taller than an adult's knee. This creature of nightmares attacked when his victim was the most vulnerable, when asleep. His physical form was unlike other creatures of the dark. Having the body of a young child and the face of a grotesque old man was, of itself, unsettling, but this ebony hobgoblin also boasted the single buttock of a baboon and a penis the length of snake—so long that it slung over his shoulder. To the Zulu, the *Tokoloshe* represented the devilish incubus of the impotent male.

Being neither Zulu nor impotent, Stanwell would've preferred his bed nearer the floor, but not wishing to offend his hosts, he retired gamely to his strange cot.

▶◀▶◀

There was no possibility of sleep. And the *Tokoloshe* was not the culprit. Stanwell grew restless as did his desire for Elsa; she was so close, alone, and he needed to see her. He knew it was reckless, but nevertheless found himself at the guesthouse. He tapped lightly on the windowpane, and then slipped in. He called to her. No response. Cautiously he approached the bed, not wishing to startle her. She wasn't there. Stanwell grew concerned. Then he noticed the spiral staircase and made his way down below.

The room followed the shape of the swimming pool above. Avocado shag carpet led to a sunken conversation pit, curved-in tiers around it, and the base fitted with custom sofa seat pads. It faced a sweeping bar with two large underwater portholes eyeing the deep end of the pool. The swimming pool was illuminated from above, giving the underground hideaway an otherworldly electric-blue hue.

Elsa lay on sofa cushions with her hair fanned above her head. Her eyes were closed. Her skin was luminescent blue in the ionized glow of the pool's light—her freckles darker, more prominent. Stanwell noticed a richer darkness to his own skin. As he reached out to touch her, a diffuse aurora of blue-violet static danced across his forearm and met her cheek.

Elsa's eyes suddenly opened. They locked onto his face and bored into his soul. He stared straight back at her, by now indifferent to the convention of a black man averting his gaze when addressing a white woman. But this was neither insolence nor defiance—rather, it was the voiceless acknowledgment of their unconventional union.

Elsa was still dressed in the steel-blue jump suit. Stanwell grasped the zipper at her throat, then slowly, deliberately, drew it down the full length of her, exposing the golden fuzz of her *poes.* He had her consent.

In the ethereal pool's glow, the bold contrast of the two heightened the chiaroscuro composition of their intertwined limbs. As their bodies moved rhythmically, the interplay of light and shadow shifted in fused silhouettes against the far wall.

▶◀▶◀

The scent of her intoxicated him; it captured an extraordinary duality, being delicate and sumptuous, smoky and seductive, at the same time. This was not the cloying Estée Lauder "Youth Dew," so trendy, which was used by his secretary.

Stanwell was to learn it was a homemade creation. Elsa blended gardenia solifore with notes of wood, musk, and citron, then infused the essence in mineral oil. This potion had become part of Elsa's daily ritual—damp after a bath, she'd apply it to give herself a healthy sheen.

When they were apart, Elsa's fragrance haunted him. Now, plaintively, Stanwell mentioned this bewitching hold she had over him. In response she demanded he give her the shirt off his back. Stanwell looked on as the garment went on its "scentual" journey—behind her neck, between her breasts, traced across her abdomen, down to her navel—lingered for a moment—and then swished between her legs.

Elsa brought the fabric up to her nose, inhaled, gave Stanwell the most impertinent of looks, and then casually tossed it back to him.

"Now you'll remember me, my Simba," Elsa said. She knew it was primitive, feral, a gesture of the wild, where scent was the animal kingdom's bonding and mating force.

▶◀▶◀

The mood shifted like the seasons when the Berg winds blew down the escarpment to the Cape. "C'mon, Simba, time for a swim!" she challenged. A naked Elsa grasped a hesitant Simba by the hand, and together they rushed upstairs.

▶◀▶◀

Sid woke to the sound of giggles and splashing. He was annoyed. Damn those neighborhood kids, he thought. Why our pool, why tonight? He peered through the drapes. "Lydia," he whispered in a raspy voice. "You better come and see this."

"What's the matter?" asked a confused Lydia. "Okay, I'm coming..."

"Oh my word!" was her surprised response to the scene below. Lydia stood beside her husband, framed by their bedroom window. Gently she linked her arm in his and said, "There's something wonderfully pure about it. Let it be. Come to bed, darling. I love you."

In the shrubbery, beside the fence, another set of eyes watched. Beneath the binoculars affixed to his severe face, the watcher's lips were set in a tight grimace.

▶◀▶◀

CHAPTER **SIXTEEN**

THE SECURITY BRANCH MAN already had a *baie lekker*—a very nice—day. He'd just scared the living *kak* out of that English *pommie* bastard at the record company. Despite the protestations of the front office staff, Malan Zander had stormed into the record executive's office unannounced and plopped himself down in the man's chair. Zander's entrance had been dramatic by design, and it had produced the right response.

The startled music man yelped, "Whoa!" He looked up from the low turquoise settee where he'd been reviewing the week's hit releases. "Chill out, man!"

Quickly the music label executive would learn that the man seated in his chair had extraordinary powers, and that, as a zealous Security Branch agent, the official was chillingly frightening. As their "interview" unfolded, the jeopardy he faced became more apparent to the music man, as well as a sudden appreciation of the authority and discretion his inquisitor had over his life.

As way of greeting and unrestrained intimidation, Zander blitzed the *Engelsman* in Afrikaans. The pasty-faced chap bleated back, "*Ek kan nie goed Afrikaans praat nie*–I can't speak good Afrikaans. Sorry." The fear in his puny prey's eyes pleased Zander immensely.

▶◀▶◀

It hadn't taken much detective work to find the culprit. But Zander felt fortunate they'd stumbled upon this subversive activity in the first place. It had been hiding in plain sight, so much so that it had been dismissed as just another "record promotion." But Zander's instincts demanded he dug deeper.

When Malan Zander saw the "Big Black Sound" billboards posted alongside station platforms in the townships, he became alarmed. The graphics were provocative, as they actively promoted violence by the native population.

He sensed *Umkhonto we Sizwe* (translated as "Spear of the Nation"), the military wing of the ANC, was behind this shrewd propaganda plot. In the ten-by-six-foot posters Zander saw a raised, clenched black fist with red, gold, and green colors "bleeding" down the forearm. Clutched in the dark fist was an electric guitar. Plainly the guitar represented the *assegai*, the brutal stabbing spear of the Zulu, and the clenched fist was the ANC's militant call to arms.

Zander investigated. He sent teams in to monitor the major *shebeens*–the illicit speakeasies and dancehalls in Soweto. There he learned the "big black sound" was roots reggae, a new genre of music from Jamaica, and not a major conspiracy to overthrow the Afrikaner government. Disappointed by the truth, yet driven by spite to vindicate the false alarm he'd raised with his superiors, Zander was determined to destroy this subversive "reggae movement."

This turned out to be easier than expected, as a single record cover had all the incriminating evidence Zander needed.

Bob Marley's *Rastaman Vibration* album had become a legend in the townships, and one song in particular was now an anthem—referenced obliquely as "track nine"—stirred the disenfranchised masses. The song's actual name was "War," and its message was potent: it explicitly called for the complete destruction of the white South African regime.

Zander and his team scrutinized the *Rastaman Vibration* album-cover. What they found was damning. The picture of Bob Marley in green paramilitary fatigues, in the guise of Marxist revolutionary Che Guevara, was in itself prohibited. Their attention turned to the song "War" and an analysis of its lyrics. Zander was horrified by this subversive propaganda. Destructive words set to an innocuous calypso beat had already escaped into the minds of local blacks.

The Security Branch official then began to rationalize the mess; these were just the ganja-induced rants of a dreadlocked musician—no one would take it seriously. That was until one of his cohorts showed him the fine print: the lyrics of "War" were almost verbatim the grave words of one of Africa's leading statesmen—His Imperial Majesty, Conquering Lion of the Tribe of Judah, Elect of God, and Emperor of Ethiopia, Haile Selassie I—in a speech to the United Nations General Assembly.

Malan Zander had had enough. He needed to shut the thing down, immediately. The album cover of Bob Marley's record revealed one final secret—the distributor was a local record company named Trutone.

▶◀▶◀

Unimpressed by the framed gold-certified albums and SARI Award plaques on the walls, Zander went for the jugular. He threw the book at the music executive; he accused the man of sedition, of inciting unrest, and of being a communist.

"You're joking, right?"

"Insolent bugger," said Zander. "It's time you learned who's boss." He reminded the executive that he, Malan Zander, had sole discretion to lock him up for ninety days on suspicion of crimes against the State. That he could kiss his precious habeas corpus goodbye—there'd be no charges, no trial, no lawyer, and as a detainee, he'd just "disappear." Really enjoying himself, Malan provided the kicker: "Sure, I must release you after ninety days, but I'll just rearrest you the moment you step out the jail."

"That's heavy, man. Are you arresting me now?"

"*Nee*—but you better comply with my directives. This record is now officially banned. And before I leave, your entire inventory will be destroyed. Now I'm warning you, if I find one copy, anywhere, you'll suffer. I promise you."

▶◀▶◀

Zander climbed into the brown Chrysler Valiant at the expired parking meter. The undercover vehicle, though reinforced with performance shock absorbers, swamped under the weight of the Security Branch official.

"*Agh sies,* man!" Suddenly Zander wasn't having such a nice day. He'd intimidated the music *oke*, but failed to punish him. He hated all English speakers in *his* country—they were good-for-nothing imposters. "For *fok* sake already, they've lived here for hundred and fifty *bladdy* years and still call England home!" he ranted. "I should've grabbed that *rooinek* by his scrawny neck and shipped him off to Potchefstroom.

"Those army barbers would've shaved off the bugger's shaggy hair and shipped him to the border. Let him try fighting the

Cubans in Angola for a change...These *frikken poms* must learn their necks are also on the line. With or without him, we'll soon bloody *donner* those stroppy commies!"

Unfortunately that would not be the case. The next morning Malan Zander ripped his newspaper in abject fury. The *Cape Times* headlines read, "SA Troops Out by Tomorrow." Apparently, the Republic's botched incursion into Angola had ended in humiliation.

▶◀▶◀

The Security Branch officer took his job seriously. Malan Zander saw himself as a skilled intelligence operative, but his body belied the fact, showing him for the blunt instrument he was. He flattered himself brawny, but muscles earned years ago on the rugby field had turned to flab. His booze gut was topped with a bloated face crisscrossed with blotchy veins, the capillaries culminating as a purple mass at the end of his bulbous nose.

The wear and tear of Zander's body was symptomatic of sun and alcohol damage. He tried to be a discreet drunk, but that was more due to an unwillingness to share than pride, especially when he indulged in his favorite peach brandy, the hundred-proof *Hakkiesdraad Mampoer.*

The bloody hell of it, protecting the regime was Zander's destiny. With extraordinary foresight, or wishful thinking, his parents named him Malan after the dedicated supporter of Nazi Germany and hardline advocate for a "pure white South Africa," Dr. Daniel François Malan, South Africa's first official apartheid prime minister. As for his family's last name, Zander was a source of great pride, as it meant *protector.* Hence, in both name and fact, Malan Zander of the Security Branch believed he was destined to be the protector of a pure white South Africa.

Malan's fellow henchmen interpreted his Christian name somewhat differently. They found the methods he employed bordered on psychopathic, so they trimmed his first name to "Mal," which meant *crazy* in Afrikaans. The appellation stuck. After all, he was their "crazy," and he had his uses. Whatever— Malan "Crazy" Zander was proud of his prominence as a zealous government enforcer in the nation's largest city, Johannesburg. It was a far cry from the small town of Malmesbury, in the Western Cape, where he'd been born.

But recently Zander felt a gnawing uneasiness in his gut, a growing urgency over an awareness that the enemies of his people were closing in.

**

They were the declared enemy, the Communists. They came in two pernicious forms: First, the local Reds who disguised their true intentions in liberal, bleeding-heart black causes. In this way, every sympathetic liberal was unfairly labelled a Communist, and tragically many genuine humanitarian activities, such as building schools in Soweto, were considered acts of subversion. Second, there were the Communist Chinese. Like legions of army ants, these "yellow peril" propagators carved corridors of railway lines and highways down the length of the Dark Continent, headed straight for the heart of the Republic.

A more existential threat, however, was the "swart gevaar"—the black threat. This was every white South African's nightmare—that inevitable day of retribution, when the majority black population would rise as one and slit the throats of every white man, woman, and child as they slept.

This fear had some justification: South Africans had watched from afar the bloody demise of colonialism throughout Africa. Now the rot had relentlessly crept south with aid of Chinese and Soviet Union proxies, and every South African knew they'd be next domino to fall to the Red Scare.

It all made bitter sense; in the end, South Africa was the "crown jewel" of the continent, literally, with its extraordinary mineral wealth, thriving economy, and world-class infrastructure—and no doubt the "bad guys" wanted it for themselves.

The officials of the apartheid regime made no attempt to tamp down the paranoia that nothing would deter the dark forces from sweeping white South Africa into the ocean. They used it as propaganda to justify their coldhearted actions, and to keep allies more vehemently anti-Communist than repulsed by apartheid.

In 1966 a remarkable piece of propaganda presented itself and became required viewing by the Security establishment. It was the Italian shockumentary "Africa Addio." The film bleakly documented the dénouement of colonialism in savage hues of black, white, and red.

From senseless tribal wars to the murders of innocents, from Kenya's Mau Mau Uprising to grizzly massacres in Zanzibar, the unflinching lens captured it all.

The end product of all this raw bloodshed was masses of burned, mutilated, and decomposed bodies recorded in harsh Technicolor for all to see, "proving" the Nationalist Party's point—an apartheid South Africa was preferable to the uncivilized alternative.

**

Mal Zander was surprised by his personal reaction to the *Africa Addio* documentary—he was numbed by the brutal man-on-man atrocities. But footage of helicopter gunships gratuitously mowing down herds of elephants curiously dumbfounded him, as did images of white homesteads being desecrated. He couldn't fathom how things of such beauty, natural and manmade, could be so willfully, so savagely, destroyed.

Zander had assumed the dispossessed would feel entitled to these beautiful things, and keep them for themselves; instead he watched bulldozers senselessly tear up manicured green lawns, and hordes dump precious silver heirlooms—as though garbage—in the streets.

He had expected to be angered by the film, but the nihilistic wanton destruction by his neighbors to the north really frightened him. As far as he was concerned, the graphic, uncompromising reality of the film dispensed with any questions regarding its legitimacy. It was a vivid celluloid testament to the dangers of uprooting whites from African soil, as inevitably only a bloody mess would fill the void.

After Zander saw the documentary, he became more resolute in his mission—he would deal with any hint of subversion or unrest according to his rules. And the repercussions on the perpetrators would be *frikken* dire.

⫷⫸

Mal Zander's eyes were deeply shaded by his heavy brow and flaccid face. His sinister appearance was an asset in his job, but his looks also represented the true nature of the man, giving the Special Branch agent cover for a particular job perk—a perk he very much enjoyed. Zander had the license to be licentious, to be an official creep who could stalk his victims with impunity.

The other night, hidden by the shrubbery at the Duncans' house, he had spied on Miss Marais and become obsessed.

Through binoculars he saw the happy couple exit the swimming pool. Her exquisite body, wet, gleamed in the poolside lights. Sleek like a dancer, she arched her back, her long gamine legs on tiptoes as she reached for a bunch of grapes from the trellis above. In her state of nakedness, hair moist and plastered against her neck, with her arm outstretched to the vine, the devoted Security apparatchik and churchgoer saw a likeness to that of Eve reaching for the apple. That was it, the temptation—and the black man was the serpent in the garden.

Zander's tolerance was tested further.

Like a mischievous child, Elsa squeezed a blackish-blue Catawba grape between her thumb and forefinger. Under the pressure the grape slipped its skin and propelled itself over the opened distance, then splattered against Stanwell's chest. The game was on. Stanwell reached between the vine's heart-shaped leaves and curly tendrils for his supply of the succulent berries. Then he struck back.

A laughing Elsa, now sticky and drenched with juice, quickly called a truce. The couple advanced on each other under the fruit canopy, and embraced, fed grapes into each other's mouths as peace offerings—then washed each other down in the pool.

For Mal Zander, this wasn't about a breach of the Immorality Act—that he could handle as a professional police officer. This was now personal. "Crazy" Zander found himself impaled on the devil's trident of lust, betrayal, and vengeance.

►◄►◄

CHAPTER **SEVENTEEN**

"DANIEL, SID DUNCAN HERE...We need to have a talk, soon. It's urgent...No, not by phone...Good, I'll be at your office around ten thirty, then." Sid hung up the phone.

"Look, it's best we include him," he said to Lydia. "In a way we've both midwifed their relationship. We now have a duty to share responsibility." He gave her a telling look. "Let's pray Elsa doesn't fall pregnant—the humiliation would be devastating."

▶◀▶◀

The Gallo Group had turned fifty. To celebrate the anniversary, the foyer of the building housed a twenty-foot-tall statue of a golden rooster, the corporation's proud emblem. Rows upon rows of gold discs lined the reception area's walls, a testament to the vision of founder Eric Gallo and the management savvy of his chief executive, Daniel G. Firth.

Firth was briefly delayed, but with apologies Sid was invited into the inner sanctum of DGF's office and served fresh coffee. Alone in unfamiliar surroundings, Sid cast his eyes around the room and settled on an intriguing collection of contemporary

South African art. All the pictures, but one, were rendered in golden, earthy hues by artists he was familiar with.

The trio of paintings by Ben Macala initially caught his attention. On the surface the subject matter appeared benign, anything but controversial—merely three musicians with serene Madonna-like faces.

But Sid knew of the artist and the subtle rebellion of his work. It was all in the eyes; each musician's eyes were rendered in a lifeless, dull, solid black—an apparent oversight by a very talented painter. But Sid had great regard for Ben Macala's artistic choice. The artist had refused to paint in the eyes of his Madonna-like portraits so she wouldn't see the humiliation of his black people. Only when apartheid was abolished, Macala vowed, would his Madonnas finally get to see.

A great mentor to Ben Macala was Cecil Skotnes, so it was fitting that several colored woodcuts from Skotnes's "The Assassination of Shaka" folio hung nearby.

To the side rested a tranquil piece by Ernst De Jong. Two dozen horseshoe nails were collaged within a field of white, bordered with gold leaf and black trim—it was an abstract interpretation of the *kalimba*, the thumb-plucked piano so joyfully popular in sub-Sahara Africa.

Still, it was another work, so unlike the others in tone and theme, that drew Sid from his seat. It was a hyperdetailed rendering of the South African flag—probably airbrushed. The flag was monochromatic: black, gray, and white. Something else was odd; the flag hung upside down and back to front. The sky behind the flag was filled with a dark ominous blue, suggesting impending doom.

Inscribed in pencil by the artist's hand were the Afrikaans words, "*Uit die Blou van Onse Hemel*" (Out of the Blue of Our

Heavens). Every South African knew these words; they were the opening refrain of *Die Stem* (The Voice), the national anthem.

"Ah, Sid, very perceptive." DGF now stood beside Sid Duncan. "I see you've discovered the most subversive work in my collection."

"Hello, Daniel...Fascinating. Please tell me about it."

"Well, this is a Norman Catherine. Norman personally painted this for me. He intended it as a cautionary tale, a warning that us whites need to do the right thing before it's too late."

DGF glanced at his watch. "Sid, you mentioned you had something to discuss, something confidential, yes?"

"Suppose so," replied Sid, feeling uncomfortable. "In a way it's germane to that painting of yours. Some things can't be avoided. They best be dealt with head-on."

Duncan shared with Firth the mischief he and Lydia witnessed from their bedroom window that late Grand Prix night. Sid was concerned when he saw DGF's jaw tighten as the details mounted. But he was relieved when the tale once completed was greeted with a warm smile.

"My, our Stanwell has been a busy chap." DGF chuckled. "I've just appointed him general manager of our warehouse—which is illegal. Now you tell me he's found himself a beautiful white girl as a lover—and that's severely illegal. Sid, give me a day to think about it, okay? Meantime we'd better keep it under wraps."

◄►

"Oupa, please tell me again, how do bushmen catch monkeys?" pleaded a young Elsa.

Old man Marais's eyes twinkled. "You see, the monkey is sly...but the bushman is cunning," he began. "The bushman knows he's not agile or swift like a monkey. So it's hopeless chasing him." Oupa Marais enjoyed sharing this folktale with his granddaughter. "Remember now, the bushman doesn't want to hurt the monkey, so he can't use his bow and poisoned arrows to kill it. So Elsa, you tell me, what does a monkey-hunting Bushman do?"

The question was intentionally rhetorical. Elsa relished the ritual of eagerly raising her hand with the answer, only to be playfully ignored by her oupa.

"The bushman is a master of the natural world and the behavior of all God's creatures around him. He knows the monkey's weak spot: it's both curious and greedy. And he'll use this to capture the little *skelem.*

"First, the bushman finds a *calabash.* It has to be just the right size. Then, with great patience, he hollows out the gourd and dries it to a hard shell. Now these are the important parts: the bushman drills a hole into the side the width of the monkey's hand, places a bunch of shiny rocks inside, and then tethers the calabash to the ground. Then the hunter hides behind a bush and patiently waits."

Oupa's voice, now a crafty whisper, continued the narrative.

"Kwi! Kwi! Kwi! A nosey monkey rocks up. He sees the calabash...picks it up with a big shake...and it rattles!" Oupa paused, striking his briar wood pipe against his heel. Burning tobacco embers cascaded to the ground. "Haw! Now the little monkey's curious. He peers inside and what does he see...all those shiny pebbles? *Oweh*! He must have them!"

Elsa, in her mind's eye, can see the man versus primate scene unfold in the parched Kalahari Desert.

"You know what happens next. He reaches inside and grabs a handful of sparkly stones. Then he tries to pull his hand out—but it's stuck! Why, the monkey had no problem sticking his hand in the calabash hole in the first time! *Agh*, by grabbing the stones, the monkey's hand had formed into a tight fist. And his fist was now too large for the hole.

"You'd think the monkey would simply release the stones and scamper away, but no, he's too greedy. And so he tugs and pulls, struggling to escape, but he'll never ever let go. And as easy-peasy as that, the cunning bushman caught his monkey. Or did the silly monkey just trap himself? Those shiny stones were of no value—but the monkey lost his freedom by stubbornly clinging to them."

Oupa Marais delighted in telling his granddaughter this story, mostly because it illustrated the means by which the Afrikaner finally vanquished the *Engelsman*. Though conquered through force in the two bitter Anglo-Boer wars, his *volk* had finally prevailed through craft and guile. They'd exploited the Englishman's greed, and now the Afrikaner was the true ruler of all South Africa.

**

Unable to compete with the worldly, well-educated English in business, banking, mining, and academics, the Afrikaner chose to strategically relinquish those roles. The English were happy to oblige, and were further delighted when the Afrikaners seemed content to "accept their place" and do all those dull, second-tier jobs—unfit for the doyen of British imperialism—in the civil service.

But the English had underestimated the opposition. The Afrikaners had no interest in competing—at least not head-on. But they had the plan, and now the apparatus, to wrestle real power from their self-satisfied fingers of their fellow white citizens—the English speakers.

The Afrikaners moved forward with the certainty it was their God-given destiny to live in South Africa, and that to do so they must control their nation by fending off all "foreign elements," including English-speaking South Africans. So they formed a ruthless secret society, Die Broederbond (The Brotherhood), to implement their nationalistic Afrikaner-centric agenda. They based their mandate on their so called "laager mentality"—which was built on the idea of 'strength from inferiority' and a 'whole-world-is-against-us' martyr mindset.

Unaccountable to no one but itself, this group deliberately operated in the shadows, and in the process subverted any semblance of the democratic process; stealth, coercion, exclusion, self-promotion, influence peddling, and Calvinistic certainty were standard modus operandi of Die Broederbond. Its membership was never declared, yet every prime minister and president and powerbroker since the 1948 Nationalist Party victory happened to be a member.

Annually a mysterious caravan of dark sedans would disappear into the desert dust. It was Die Broederbond's "indaba," and from these secret meetings directives would flow forth—circumventing the nation's legislative, executive, and judicial process. In fact this shady super-committee held the true reins of power, controlling the actions of every elected official and appointed bureaucrat. And in its invisible grasp, the destiny of the nation was negatively predetermined.

As the English speakers crowned themselves upper-crust society's elite and potentates of the commercial sector, under the guidance of Die Broederbond the Afrikaner government built the largest civil service (per capita) in the world. This bureaucratic edifice became the source of Afrikanerdom's power, as they realized something the English didn't: everyone everywhere was dependent on public servants for everything.

In addition to conventional bureaucracies found in civil services elsewhere, the South African government created a unique bureaucracy of its own, with special enforcement powers—the massive infrastructure designed to regulate and implement apartheid. And the only people employed by this colossal enterprise were Afrikaners—no Englishmen were allowed.

Due to complacency and contempt for the Boer, the fate of the English speaker was sealed. As the English drank sifters of port in deep chairs at the exclusive Rand Club (founded in 1887 by grand explorer, mining magnate, and loyal British Empire flag-waver Cecil Rhodes), quoting Rudyard Kipling and discussing matters of the realm "back home," they were unwittingly ensnared by the crafty Afrikaner Nationalists whom now controlled the real levers of influence and power.

By the time they realized the baubles of wealth and status did not equate to supremacy, it was too late. In real terms, the English speakers became politically disenfranchised. Sure, they could vote, but the Nationalist Party—with its lockstep legions of bureaucrats, bible-thumping adherents, fervent anti-English minions, ever-

present security apparatus, and Die Broederbond's behind-the-scenes machinations—would not be dislodged.

**

Consequently Daniel Gideon Firth and Sid Duncan found themselves in a state of political impotence. They were powerless to change anything institutionally, but they made a pact: they'd do their utmost to provide help and support to two plucky individuals, Elsa and Stanwell.

▶◀▶◀

CHAPTER **EIGHTEEN**

THE NEW GENERAL MANAGER was troubled. Things had not gone well on his watch. Stanwell should've been celebrating; against all odds, he'd achieved the impossible, now a senior executive with a white woman as a lover. But the setbacks at work surprised him. For two years he'd successfully orchestrated the smooth running of the company's distribution unit—admittedly in an unofficial capacity, but everyone in the facility knew he was the decision maker. Surely the formal acknowledgment of his leadership role, with a title and executive office, didn't signify the mysterious disappearance of his competence.

Yet a plague of mishaps manifested themselves in shipments lost, delayed, damaged, and even stolen. Stanwell had anticipated pushback from the white staff—admittedly some were sullen, even insolent, but they'd remained professional. It was the muted mutiny of his black brethren, however, that frustrated him. So what was the black staff's problem? He needed to figure out a solution, quickly.

His affair with Elsa "Kat" Marais caused him a different set of problems. These couldn't be managed by a corporate restructuring or staff layoff, but by a fundamental shift in the social compact of the nation, and that was unlikely to happen.

Stanwell discovered love refused to thrive in the shadows; it demanded to grow in the reflected glow of witnesses. Love also demanded they be together, so his inability to be with her in the flesh was maddening, and all the more so because he was constantly reminded of her in the abstract. Wherever Safari Èlan fashions were featured, so was his girl.

Her presence was ubiquitous, her likeness splashed about town in a scale many times larger than life-size. Her beautiful face smiled at him—seemingly knowingly—from billboards at street intersections, placards pasted on double-decker busses, and from Denham store windows. It was weird having her image so publicly accessible, yet their relationship so secret.

Elsa had become a celebrity "face." A glamorous (and sexy) double-page spread in *Scope* magazine had made her an object of desire. Men—white, affluent men—had begun to pursue her. Stanwell wished Elsa all the success in the world, but resented the demands on her time. There always seemed to be another dress fitting, catalog shoot, or fashion show eroding the already-scarce time they had together. Elsa had assured him of her commitment to their relationship, and had pleaded for a little more patience.

Jealousy tore at him. He wanted to publicly claim her, announce their love to the world, but he dared not.

▶◀▶◀

Stanwell thought back to their last rendezvous. It had been a fiasco. Elsa's roommate, the nurse, had had her shift changed and was home. By necessity they'd resorted to the antics of teenagers, and a little red Mini Cooper became their haven, with the Inanda Polo Club (on the corner of 5th Avenue and Forrest Street in Sandton) being the venue.

The last chukka had concluded at 6:00 p.m. The fields were deserted and the sun had set. All was quiet, the ponies already fed and the grooms retired to their quarters for the night. With the tranquil setting all to themselves, Stanwell maneuvered the Mini next to an embankment sheltered behind a tall grass verge.

In the confined quarters of exemplary British automotive engineering, Stanwell and Elsa reclined the seats and attempted to get comfortable. Naked knees, elbows, and torsos made sharp contact with metallic levers and plastic knobs in a wave of titters, curses, and protestations. Finally, an accommodation was reached with the tiny car, and they'd settled into a position of mutual satisfaction.

An abrupt knock, then a flashlight penetrated the passion mist coating the windows. A demand they identify themselves, harshly barked, followed. Alarmed—it had to be the Security Branch—Stanwell flipped on the ignition, slammed the car in gear, and raced off into the dark, minus headlights.

Without warning the little car ground to a halt, its front wheels wedged in a drainage ditch. Stranded and out of alternatives, the compromised couple had no option but to then given themselves up.

The poor Bantu night watchman was horrified; caught in the glare of his flashlight were a black man and a white woman. That was traumatic enough, but the man was also seminude with trousers hovering around his shins, and the woman was frantically unfurling her skirt from its hoisted half-mast station. The night watchman dared not gloat. Instead he cast down his eyes and mumbled a warning, "You better *voetsek now-now*—go away before I call the police. You're trespassing."

Soon, however, the security guard became a willing collaborator when the evening proved financially lucrative, and the couple reassured him they'd tell no one if he'd promise to keep their secret. Gently bribed with a *bonsella* if he'd help extract the car from the ditch, the night watchman enthusiastically took the lead in heaving the little vehicle to safety. Then, knowing their ardor was now a distant memory, the guard watched the couple retreat into the night. He wouldn't know that Elsa and Stanwell went their separate ways—to Hillbrow and Soweto, respectively.

◄►◄

Stanwell's reverie snapped to the present, his secretary demanding his immediate attention.

"Mister...Mr. Marunda?" she asked, tentatively.

"Yes, Melanie," he replied, irritated.

"There's a gentleman to see you. Should I show him in?" Stanwell gave a curt nod.

A florid-complexioned man strode into the office. His heavyset jowls matched his large frame. His skull was thick with ratty thin strands on top and buzzed sandpaper-coarse hair on the sides. The only feature on an otherwise bland face was the limp caterpillar of a moustache meandering across the man's upper lip.

Stanwell noted the man willfully ignored his outstretched hand and sat down uninvited. From the broken nose, cauliflower ears, and dour attitude, Stanwell gathered he had a former rugby player and current Afrikaner in his chair. His guest's attitude didn't surprise him—but this was a prospective customer, so Stanwell kept calm.

"*Hallo! Hoe gaan dit met u?*"

Stanwell, in the Afrikaans greeting of "hello, how are you," deliberately used the pronoun *u* as a sign of respect, rather than the prosaic *jou.*

"*Goed, dankie...En jou?*" [Good, thanks...And you?] The respect not reciprocated.

Maybe I must put on the charm, thought Stanwell. He asked his secretary, Melanie, to fetch tea and biscuits for their uninvited guest.

"I see you have our white women doing whatever you want."

"What? Excuse me!" replied an astonished Stanwell.

"You don't know your place, you *fokken kaffir,*" snarled the stranger. "I know all about you and Miss Marais."

"Who the hell are you?" demanded Stanwell. He hoped indignation masked his fear.

"I'm the Security Branch, you idiot." Unfortunately Stanwell smiled; a reflexive nervous tic. This enraged the official further.

"I'm fed up with your nonsense!" the official ranted, as he sprang to his feet. "You think you're a smart aleck, hey? Well, I'm telling you, you're both in deep *kak* !" An apoplectic shower of spittle rained on the cringing Stanwell, as the tirade grew. "You see I've been watching you, real close, and I saw you two...*kaalgat* naked...together!

"Now listen here, I'm going to tell you this only once." To emphasize the point, the agent punctuated each word with a steely jab into Stanwell's chest. "You! Will! Not! Contact! Miss Marais! Again! Ever!" He paused. "Understand?"

Stanwell's response was a silent, insolent smirk. It was a look, simultaneously baleful and blank, that white men both detested and feared.

"Don't play dumb with me." Still no response, the frustrated security official continued, "Okay, I've warned you. I'll be having a conversation with Miss Marais in the presence of her father. We'll persuade her to file a criminal complaint against you for rape. Then, my friend, we'll stretch your *blerrie* neck 'til it snaps. So decide now-now; is that woman worth dying for?"

"No way, Elsa wouldn't do that to me," blurted Stanwell, visibly distraught.

"Think what you like, but I warn you I can be very persuasive. Just imagine your precious Elsa sitting in jail for seven years. She'll sell you out in a minute...I guarantee it!"

Doubt registered on Stanwell's face.

Zander tossed in the *coup de grâce.* "Even better idea—my John Vorster Square office is on the ninth floor. That's where the elevator stops—but give me the excuse to take Miss Marais up the stairwell, to our specially guarded tenth floor. Now that's where all the fun really happens. Hey, maybe I can soften her up a bit my way when we're alone up there," sneered the official. "Now will she betray her *volk*, disgrace her family, and offend her church, over you, a *bladdy kaffir*? I advise you ask yourself that."

Satisfied the message had been delivered, and received, the security officer stood to leave. Curiously, he extended his hand. Stanwell clasped it. The official leaned in close and hissed, "Remember me—Mal Zander. I'll be watching you. Such a pity about that pretty Elsa. I would've taken her for myself, but I wouldn't touch her now that she's been spoilt."

The words hurt, and Stanwell's anger was quickly brash. Suddenly that handshake became a battleground, with both men locked in hand-to-hand combat. Grips tightened.

The security official's cocky smirk telegraphed his misplaced confidence.

Stanwell glared defiantly back at Zander, determined to inflict pain on his tormentor. His powerful hand, hardened by years of manual labor, clamped tighter and tighter on Zander's large, pudgy paw. He noted the purpling fingers, and the agitated foot-to-foot hops as the man fought the pain. Stanwell ratcheted his vise-like grip further. He needed to see tears in the man's eyes.

Melanie Coetzee hovered at the office door. She sensed the intensity of the moment despite the absence of overt violence. Her boss had asserted physical dominance over the unpleasant guest—she'd never seen a white man cowered by a black man before. She had no understanding of the beef between the two men, but the hatred exchanged between them was palpable. But Stanwell and Zander understood; the intent was the other's destruction. Tears finally welled up in Mal Zander's shifty eyes, and reluctantly Stanwell Marunda released his grip.

▶◀▶

Stunned, Stanwell remained motionless at his desk. Something was fishy about his unwanted guest; this seemed a personal vendetta rather than an official investigation. Zander's behavior—no, he'd never forget that name—was questionable.

Stanwell couldn't cite chapter and verse of the Immorality Act, but he did know he and Elsa were willfully guilty of this supposed crime; simple sexual relations between whites and nonwhites. And yet he hadn't been formally accused, or arrested—just threatened. Was he in a *mano a mano* conflict with one crazy Boer, or was it a struggle against the entire South African regime? Stanwell needed more time to figure it out.

▶◀▶

Despite his bruised knuckles, Mal Zander was satisfied with the overall outcome of the "interview" he'd just conducted. He was confident the *kaffir* would do his bidding—typical of such a subservient race. It was crucial this matter was handled discreetly.

The subject, Elsa Marais, was a *boeremeisie*, a farmer's daughter, and one of his people. Her shame would be their collective shame. This needed to be stopped quickly, before, God forbid, they had a child.

▶◀▶◀

CHAPTER **NINETEEN**

THEY WERE IN HER HILLBROW FLAT. His deliveryman get-up made his visit once again uneventful. Maintaining the charade sometimes amused them, but tonight it was annoying. Both Stanwell and Elsa were exhausted by the demands of work, and they were beginning to feel the stress of their forbidden relationship.

Elsa remained unaware of the Special Branch's scrutiny, but the burden of deceit—especially from her family—wore at her. For Stanwell, the recent threats made for sleepless nights, and keeping it a secret from the woman he loved was all the more worrying. Normally Elsa prepared a meal for them. This evening she'd suggested they dine out. By this she meant take-out food, as dining together, in public, would be plainly illegal.

Elsa, still wary of cosmopolitan Hillbrow insisted Stanwell accompanies her to get the food. He wasn't happy about it. Not because he was lazy, but because it irritated him having to hover nearby, a few steps behind her as if they were strangers, rather than stroll down the street together hand in hand, like lovers did elsewhere.

However, he'd agreed. Good-naturedly, she had enticed him with salivating reports of fresh baked rolls and spicy rotisserie chicken from the nearby Fontana Café—and a promised picnic they'd soon be devouring in bed.

▶◀▶◀

They entered the elevator together, but as a precaution they separated—Elsa stood in one corner and Stanwell the other. With a chime the floors ticked by as the elevator descended. Then it stopped on the twelfth floor. The metal doors slid open, revealing two white men.

They were scruffy and large—the one squat and wide, the other tall and thick.

From a pair of bloodshot eyes nestled in crotch-red sun-burnt faces, the men squinted at the black man and white woman. Their heads sported institutional-grade cropped hair-cuts, and their tank tops—barely covering hairy, blotched shoulders—bore the green emblem of RAU, Rand Afrikaans University.

Thick remained on the landing and wedged one large hoof against the open lift door. The elevator pinged, attempting to close, but sensing the obstruction, sprung open again. Thick peered down at the man and woman trapped in the elevator. He thoughtfully wiped snot from his nose with the back of his hand, inspected it, and then nonchalantly tucked away the soiled hand in his trouser pocket.

His buddy, Squat, a creepy smirk revealing yellowed teeth, stepped into the elevator. "You bloody *kaffir-boetie*!" [nigger lover] he growled unexpectedly in Elsa's direction. His disgraceful indictment rang loud in the confined space. Then turning on

Stanwell, he shrieked, "You need to learn to leave our women alone, you *blerry kaffir*!"

Squat then forced himself toward Elsa.

Elsa realized it was hopeless to reason with her attackers; she could see the hatred in their bloodshot eyes, and the false courage, bolstered by *dagga* cannabis and beer. Fear gripped her. She instinctively knew the men's intent: a perverted application of justice was to be her fate. She'd betrayed her *volk* and had to suffer the consequences.

The lift doors tried to close, but sprang open yet again. They were trapped in a tin can, and their exit remained blocked. These thugs intended to rape her, then murder Stanwell. Elsa already knew their alibi—that they'd saved her from the savage native attacking her. Then they'd be hailed as heroes. Of course, she'd be expected to play her part in the cover-up for the greater good, unless...

"Help! Rape!" screamed Elsa. "This Afrikaner piece of shit's attacking me!"

Squat tried to muzzle her. "You're a *fokken* abomination!" he snarled. Elsa was screwing up their scheme.

"Get your filthy *rock-spider* hands off me!" Elsa yelled. "Don't touch me, you fuckin' *Dutchman,* low-life!"

With her desperate screams Elsa deliberately identified the race of her attackers, in the most scornful terms, as white Afrikaners. It was dinnertime, most tenants were home, and they would've heard the girl's cries. The police would learn the truth when they questioned the tenants. Now there was no way for Squat and Thick to fabricate the lie. They needed to contain the situation.

►◄►◄

Having never raised a fist to a white man, Stanwell had frozen. But Elsa's cries now released him. Stanwell struck just below Squat's sternum. The bundle of nerves constituting the solar plexus reacted violently under the sharp blow, causing the diaphragm to contract. Doubled over and breathless, Squat's face became the target. Stanwell drove a quick knee to the thug's jaw. The impact was devastating.

Of course, Squat had no idea about the nature of the damage he'd just suffered. Later, he would learn the details from the oral surgeon reviewing the X-rays of his fractured jaw: the blow had jacked up his yellowed teeth under the gum line, cracking the roots, and snapped the jawbone below both ears.

All Squat knew was that it hurt like heck. And that survival was an imperative. With his bloodied mouth agape, like a stringless marionette, Squat staggered back into his partner, dislodging Thick from his guard post. Finally unimpeded, the elevator doors automatically closed.

Shaken and huddled together, Elsa and Stanwell descended to the ground floor.

▶◀ ▶◀

"How...how did they know we were a couple?" asked Elsa quietly. "We weren't standing even close together, so how come he called me a *kaffir-boetie*?" Then cold reality compressed her chest in a python's grip. "*Agh*, they already knew, they were waiting for us..."

Stanwell nodded grimly.

"I can't believe my own people would do this. They tried to rape me—and who knows what would've happened to you?" said Elsa, distraught. "Oh my god, they're trying to destroy us...What should we do?"

Perplexed by his silence, Elsa considered Stanwell closely. She noticed the distant look in his eyes—strange, considering the violent confrontation they'd just experienced. On the surface there was an ominous calm, but she sensed there were titanic forces raging within him. She'd no notion of the secret he'd been hiding from her—to protect her. She was unaware Stanwell *knew* the identity—the face, the name, and place of employment—of the monster that orchestrated this attack. And Elsa would've been horrified to learn that in his silence, Stanwell had made a quiet vow of revenge.

Stanwell was transfixed by a vivid vision. In an arid wilderness he saw a mutilated carcass with its ribcage spread apart like blood-stained wings. In a flurry of feathers, a wake of vultures ripped at the victim's chest cavity in a feverish search for carrion, all the while peeing on their heated feet, to cool them and to sanitize them from the body's rot.

Stanwell saw himself beside the kill—he looked down at the corpse. Despite the gaping eye cavities and distended mouth, pecked clean by the carnivorous birds, there was no doubt about the victim's identity—it was Mal Zander.

Stanwell began to understand the earlier signs he'd received from the *iSangoma*: the blood streaming from the wallpaper bird in the Duncans' bathroom, and blood pooling on the concrete slab from the girl who tried to fly. There was the sense of inevitability to all these signs, leading to the vultures feeding off this bloodied corpse; and so Stanwell finally understood what the *iSangoma* had divined for him.

▶◀▶◀

Elsa was a traditional girl. Her pioneering Voortrekker forefathers had fled the Cape in the 1830s to free themselves from the grip of the British. As they headed north into the interior, their ox wagons were the mode of transport and the first line of defense. When attacked by rampaging Zulu tribesmen, these migrating *trekboer* farmers circled their wagons into a fortified *laager* and broke out their single-shot muskets. This became the basis of Voortrekker lore, and December 16, 1838, became a red-letter day for all of Afrikanerdom.

The Battle of Blood River had been a great victory, no doubt about it. Over three thousand Zulu warriors lost their lives on the battlefield that day. The Zulus' close-combat stabbing spear, the notorious *assegai*, was no match for the fusillade of musket fire, despite the numerical superiority of the Zulu *impi*. As for the Voortrekkers, they didn't suffer a single fatality.

It was indeed a miracle.

Every anniversary of the Blood River battle, Elsa and her family gave public thanks to God and private thanks to the muzzleloader. So guns were for Elsa a force for the good—and after the hateful elevator incident, it was time she got herself one.

▶◀▶◀

The Republic's authorities maintained a constant drumbeat of warnings against the inevitability of the *swart gevaar*, and strongly encouraged the white population to arm themselves. Black firebrands hyped the paranoia further with threats that payback time was imminent. And so a European could buy a weapon quite easily, despite the practical experience required at a shooting range to get a firearm license.

For Elsa it was an absurd situation. The first instance she needed a weapon to protect herself was not against vengeful blacks, as trumpeted by her government, but to protect herself from being personally assaulted by her own kind, the descendants of white Voortrekkers.

Elsa purchased a weapon ideal for her needs. It was a Smith & Wesson Model 39 semiautomatic pistol. Its warm walnut grip rested comfortably in her hands, and the business end looked ruthlessly efficient with its blue carbon steel and anodized aluminum frame.

Her need to feel safe was greater than her desire to know all the pistol's features, but that didn't deter the salesman from droning on about the "double-action trigger pull being heavier" and "the single-stack magazine holding eight nine-millimeter parabellum bullets."

But her interest perked when he suggested Elsa added her personal touch to the weapon; the firearm's front sights, to improve the accuracy of her aim, must be painted with her fluorescent orange-pink nail polish.

Elsa thanked the salesman for his help, then, as an afterthought, asked, "By the way, what would you do if attacked in an elevator?"

"Hmm...I'd drop down into a crouch and aim my weapon upward. If I had to fire, the bullet should safely exit through the lift's plastic-panel ceiling. Ma'am, you don't want to get hit by your own ricochet. A nine-millimeter bullet bouncing around four metal walls, in such a confined space—damn, it would be crazy, like a deadly pinball machine in there!"

With that, Elsa purchased a new fashion accessory: an ankle holster. If she didn't have her handbag handy, she'd conceal the pistol under her flared pantsuits or bell-bottomed jeans.

◄►◄

Mal Zander was spitting mad, literally. Two loutish yobs stood before him, quaking with fear as he soaked them down in a guttural tirade. He wanted answers. His trained stooges—two of them—failed to overpower a mere slip of a girl. It was so unlike them. Whenever random acts of violence had been required in the past, they'd performed admirably.

Zander never hid his disdain for English speakers from his henchmen. A leading Johannesburg learning institution, the University of Witwatersrand, infuriated him in particular. The basis for his vendetta against the college was triggered by an image on the front page of the *Wits Student* magazine in 1972. Notorious for lampooning the high and mighty on the local scene, the student magazine had had the cheek to ridicule the reigning prime minister.

The image was in artful black and white: a photo cartoon of a very young child, wearing only a diaper, peering into a toilet bowl. That of itself didn't offend. However, the speech bubble above the child's head, asking the question, "Excuse me, are you the prime minister?" did.

Balthazar Johannes Vorster was a hero to the *volk* and a member of good standing with Die Broederbond. One of his finest moments was the creation of the *Ossewa Brandwag* (Ox Wagon Guard) during WWII. The group's anti-British sentiment wasn't appreciated, and Vorster was arrested as a Nazi sympathizer bent on suborning the war effort. Now, in 1976, he was the leader of the right-wing National Party and South Africa's current prime minister.

As for Zander, it was a little more personal; the place he worked happened to be named after the very same B.J. Vorster. Such a great man shouldn't be trifled with, and as his acolyte, Malan Zander was determined to make those responsible pay.

He recruited Squat and Thick from RAU (Rand Afrikaans University)—the conservative polar opposite to Wits. The RAU campus was adjacent to the SABC (South African Broadcasting Corporation), the de facto propaganda machine of the apartheid regime. Naturally, as a learning institution RAU rejected free thought and expression and exemplified the Afrikaner philosophy of self-segregation; and as such served as the petri dish to cultivate future generations of myopic leaders.

Zander's first assignment for his student thugs was the hazed abduction of some Wits students. Their remit was sophomorically clear: "Grab a couple of longhaired hippies and shave their *fokken* heads bald 'til they bleed. And while you're about it, pelt the Witwatersrand campus with rotten eggs and stink bombs."

The typical Wits male student didn't stand a chance. A natural peacenik, he wore wide bell-bottom patched jeans, paisley see-through shirts (unbuttoned to the navel), and a zodiac sign pendant hanging from his neck. Add lavender-tinted glasses, and the Wits students were easy pickings for the RAU crew.

But a curious thing happened. Despite the bullying and forcibly shorn heads—and the rotten egg odor pervasive on the campus—the Wits students weren't intimidated, and began to protest en masse against apartheid policies, specifically as black students were being banned from the school.

Students held political rallies. They chanted antigovernment slogans and hung banners on the sidewalk of Jan Smuts Drive, near the university's main gates. Motorists driving by generally sounded off their car horns; most in solidarity and amusement while others noisily honked their frustration.

Invariably, however, the authorities weren't amused. In droves they bussed in the RAU students, with their buzz-cut haircuts, buttoned-down short-sleeved shirts, and khaki polyester trousers, and lined them in force across the road.

The police squawked obligatory warnings from their bullhorns, and then dispersed the crowd with water cannons and the odd truncheon charge. For some Wits students, this was rather fun, a happy break from their studies, though for many others it was a serious enterprise—the liberation of their fellow citizens wasn't a trivial problem—and so the protests continued unabated.

This resulted in numerous campus invasions by the police. It was no laughing matter when varsity students and staff were banned, exiled, and imprisoned. In a vindictive fit of pique, the ruling party cut off government funding to the University of Witwatersrand, and rewarded RAU with the funds instead as a kind of "loyalty bonus."

Not being students of note, Squat and Thick never troubled themselves with the realpolitik of the matter; rather, they reveled in the mayhem, especially as it had been officially sanctioned.

><|><|

Zander impatiently waited for a response from the sorry duo. No explanation was forthcoming. Squat, usually the designated spokesman was sorely handicapped by his wired jaw. Thick, being incapable of independent thought, had very little of use to offer, except to express his wonderment at his partner's new diet of liquefied baby food.

Exasperated, Zander dismissed them with a sweep of his hand. "*Pasop* you two, *jy moet jou vingerrr uit jou gat trrrek*!" [Watch out you two, you must pull your finger out your ass!] he yelled in the distinctive burr of his Malmesbury bray, which only tripped his tongue when he was drunk.

Then the Security Branch's favorite psychopath announced to the now empty room, "I think it's about time I made the Ma*rrr*ais/Ma*rrr*unda affair an official matter."

><|><|

215

CHAPTER **TWENTY**

STANWELL WAS AMAZED by the grandeur of his present surroundings. But the nature of the invitation surprised and concerned him. His fingers thrummed worriedly on the table-cloth as he awaited the arrival of his host.

Steven, DGF's driver, had arrived unexpectedly at his office. He'd presented Stanwell with a cherrywood suit hanger on which hung a single-breasted navy blue Jaeger blazer, a buttoned-down Oxford shirt, and a striped tie by the bespoke gentleman's tailor Gieves & Hawkes of London's Savile Row. The instructions were explicit: get dressed immediately. Steven would be chauffeuring Stanwell to meet with the Big Baas.

They drew up to the Twist Street entrance of the glistening Die Landdrost Hotel, the newest and most spectacular five-star hotel in the southern firmament. In its brief history Die Land-drost had become the swankiest boarding establishment for the wealthy and famed in the City of Gold. Its status was all the greater as its only competitor, the aging President Hotel, had recently been demoted to a paltry four stars.

Johannesburg's nouveau riche hobnobbed with glittering guests from around the world at Die Landdrost Hotel. The illustrious establishment still basked in the recent Elizabeth Taylor/Richard Burton visit, and claimed credit for the film stars' rekindled love and subsequent second marriage in nearby Botswana (a marriage rerun doomed to failure a mere eight months later).

Stanwell was flabbergasted by the courtesy displayed by the hotel's doorman, a white man, who opened his car door with a cheerful welcome and pointed him to the front entrance. Instinctively Stanwell searched the hotel's walls for apartheid signs to direct him to the nonwhite entrance.

He'd grown familiar with the cryptic "Europeans Only/Net Blankes" (quickly learning *blankes* meant white and that he was a *nie-blankes*, a nonwhite).

Depending on the establishment, however, Stanwell had found some signs to be quite direct in their intent: "NOTICE Delivery Boys, African Servants, Non-Europeans & Goods in Side Entrance Only," or the very specific and unsubtle, "FOR USE BY WHITE PERSONS ONLY These Public Premises And The Amenities Thereof Have Been Reserved For The Exclusive Use of White Persons, By Order Provincial Secretary."

But, on the façade of Die Landdrost Hotel, Stanwell found no such signs posted to enlighten him. It felt odd, disorienting, and nothing like the South Africa he'd become accustomed to.

Inside the reception area, the concierge, another white man, politely steered a nervous Stanwell to the hotel's celebrated restaurant, Ouma's Kitchen. As he headed down the hallway, Stanwell felt as if lured into a trap, expecting to be accosted midstride by a sentinel's cry—"Stop! Where do you think you're going, *kaffir*?"—but the command never came.

A relieved Stanwell was escorted to a corner table overlooking the entire restaurant. And there he waited, wondering. His eyes focused on his worrying hands—hoping his black presence in this white exclusive world wouldn't be noticed.

▶◀▶◀

"Nice tie," said DGF as he sat down. Self-consciously Stanwell reached for the knot at his throat. He'd never had a need for a tie, until now. His secretary, Ms. Coetzee, had come to his rescue on tiptoes. She'd whipped up the perfect full Windsor knot, tucked the rear blade into the keeper loop, buttoned down his collar, buttoned up his blazer, and sent him on his way with a humph of approval.

"Today you look like a businessman," the Big Baas said, studying his first Bantu executive. "These clothes are my gift to you. They make you look successful...but today they serve another purpose."

Stanwell gave his boss a quizzical look.

"Come on, look around. See that large table...surprised?"

Surprised? No, Stanwell was stunned. Seated at the table, apparently comfortable in these refined surroundings were other diners—as black as him.

"*Haw*, Baas! What happened to apartheid? Is it through?"

DGF shook his head, "Sadly not, but every rule has its exception. Our government must do business with foreigners, and often they're not the color of choice.

"Nowadays American companies really enjoy tweaking our South African noses, and deliberately send only black executives to negotiate deals."

"I see...very embarrassing, hey."

"Could've been...but Pretoria's shrewd. Visitors' race categories are conveniently changed. For example, we now do so much business with them, the Japanese are now considered "honorary whites" while the Chinese aren't so privileged. And the government has created these international zones where people of any race can stay and do business. So you see this five-star hotel is one of these special zones."

DGF anticipated Stanwell's next question. "You're wondering why local blacks don't come here, aren't you? Well it's too darn expensive for you guys, so there's no need for those rude "whites only" signs. Indeed, it's quite contemptuous."

"But Baas, I still feel most worried."

"Don't be. With those fancy clothes, you're an American executive or a diplomat. Heck, you're Malawian, so technically you are a foreign guest. Speaking of Malawi, your esteemed President for Life, Hastings Banda, stayed here."

A dark veil traversed Stanwell's face. President Banda was a tyrant, despite his diminutive frame, cherubic face, three-piece suits, and Anglo-American education. He presided over a police state designed to garner power and wealth for himself and members of his tribe. As for that signature fly whisk of his, Banda wielded it with the authority of a marshal's baton.

**

Banda's greed placed him in the pocket of the apartheid regime, and gave him the distinction of being the only African ruler to establish diplomatic relations with persona non grata South Africa. Malawians cringed at newspaper images of roly-poly Banda marching in step with the dour Prime Minister Vorster, inspecting honor guards in several Bantustans devised by the apartheid regime. These faux tribal homelands, somewhat akin to Native American reservations, were specifically designed to restrict indigenous native suffrage to less desirable regions of the nation—with the goal of eliminating the Bantustan inhabitants from having the privilege to vote in greater "white" South Africa.

Unashamedly Hastings Banda endorsed these artificial nations with the ardor of a man whose soul had been bought by and paid for by the gold-backed South African Rand. This made his public endorsement of the Bantustans—no more than a contrivance at artificial nation building, based on a policy of prejudice—a disgrace.

**

"Mr. Banda is not a friendly fellow to those who do not belong to his Chewa tribe," stated Stanwell. "Why do you think I left Malawi? There I'm a free black man, but I choose to work here in Jo'burg under apartheid. These are things us blacks never discuss because it shames us, but here I earn money, feed myself, and even send money back home. In Malawi I starved. And I'm punished because I am not a Chewa tribe member. It's a hard decision to live under apartheid, but at least here I know where I stand with these Afrikaners."

"Either get gored by a rhino or trampled underfoot by an elephant—that's quite some dilemma you have there. I guess freedom's overrated when you're starving," said DGF. "Being a free man in Malawi versus a fed man in South Africa must have been a tough choice for you. Shame man!"

Stanwell was ambivalent about the end of British rule in Malawi back in 1964, because the promised joy and rewards of liberation had failed to materialize. His country had merely replaced the benign government of Her Majesty Queen Elizabeth II with their very own maniacal homegrown ruler.

◄►◄►

Troubled by Stanwell's predicament, DGF quickly changed the subject. "Let's focus on the positives. At least it gave me the opportunity to hire you. Tell me, how are things going at the distribution facility?"

"Not too good, Baas."

"That's only to be expected. I thought the white staff may be a problem for you. Just try to be patient..."

"Some of the whites were shocked, one or two are trouble-makers, but most are professional and get the job done. No, the big surprise is the black staff...they're really-really giving me a hang of a hard time."

"That surprises me. I thought they'd be inspired. You get-ting the corner office and all...and replacing a white man," said DGF, now perplexed.

"Maybe I'm not the man for this job."

"Nonsense, you're a smart *chappie*. You've proved that to me over the past two years. Remember, nothing can take away the experiences and skills you've earned along the way. So all I ask is to please get the job done with a minimum of fuss."

"*Yebo, dankie*—yes, thank you, but how come the same workers who used to obey me when I worked the floor are now sabotaging me?"

DGF paused for a moment. In Stanwell's question possibly rested the answer to so many of the African continent's prob-lems. It was so obvious, but he, Daniel Firth, had failed to recognize the syndrome until this chat with his new native general manager.

"Stanwell, after listening to your tribal problems in Malawi, do you think the problem at our warehouse is your tribe? Are the black staffers disrupting things because you're not from a local tribe?"

"*Haw wena*, it could be that...but the problem's much bigger. Me being a foreigner is a small part of it. You know, the local tribes fight one another all the time." Stanwell then told DGF about his constant fear that was realized with the deadly tribal bloodbath at the gold mine hostel, and the bitter rivalries between the Xhosa and Zulu tribesmen underground.

"So let's see if I understand this," said an exasperated DGF. "The black staffers at our warehouse would prefer working under a white Afrikaner, their enemy and oppressor, to working for one of their own—just because of tribal differences?

"And they won't even consider you, Stanwell, though you've proven again and again to be capable, decent, and fair?" DGF answered rhetorically. "Apparently not. Not a member of our tribe? Then to hell with you! That's pathetic. No wonder Africa's such a basket case."

DGF shook his head, irritated. Until now the discussion had not consisted of a white man talking down to a black man. But the tone in DGF's voice had changed; it was now downright patronizing.

"Imagine if all your tribes had banded together. Apartheid would've been over in a day! There are over twenty-five million of you—we whites, maybe five million. Man, you must realize you people have got us whites badly outnumbered. The fact that tribal rivalries have prevented you natives from acting together, in a way that would mutually benefit you all, stuns me."

Stanwell didn't disagree.

▶◀▶◀

DGF sensed Stanwell's growing disquiet. The unfamiliar restaurant surroundings, the borrowed clothes, the disappointing work report, and the tribal debate were all contributing factors—but he knew of another matter taking its toll.

DGF was hesitant to raise the topic. Apparently Stanwell's discomfort had now become his.

"Will you tell me about you and Elsa Marais?" he asked.

Stanwell felt the earth collapsing about him—again he was back in that gold mine, underground, suffocated by dread. He gulped hard, stalling for time, as he struggled to concoct an evasive response. To his credit, Stanwell chose not to lie.

"Baas, how do you know this thing?"

"Sid Duncan told me," said DGF. "He and Mrs. Duncan saw both of you, together, the other night, splashing about in their swimming pool."

"Man, I'm sorry. We don't want to cause you nice people any trouble."

"Stanwell, relax. The Duncans and I are okay about it," DGF said gently. "In fact, we feel partially responsible. If you weren't delivering TVs for me, and Mrs. Duncan hadn't invited Elsa for tea, you two would've never met."

"So? What now?"

"Promise me you'll keep your head down. This government will come down on you hard if they find out. So *pasop* now—just watch out for one another."

"Baas, I promise..."

"Stanwell, one more thing." DGF reached into his jacket pocket and removed a heavy brass hotel key tag. "Remember I told you this hotel is an international safe zone. Well, I want you to phone that girl of yours, and invite her to join you for a night in one of the luxury suites upstairs—your room's already been reserved. And don't worry about the cost. It's a special treat on me. That's the least I can do."

▶◀▶◀

Luxury is a fleeting panacea; in its plush embrace the grittiness of reality fades—but only momentarily. Unlike the arid earth transformed into fertile soil with the first seasonal rains, luxury is always parched, and rarely changes anything of consequence. But a brief escape, a respite from life's harsh edge, is a wonderful thing. Such was their one-night stay at Die Landdrost Hotel.

Stanwell welcomed Elsa at the suite door. The surprised expression on her face met the incredulity on his. They never said a word. She draped herself languidly within the ardent embrace of his outstretched arms.

Elsa relished the lavish suite: courtesy fruit basket, luxury bath and body potions (furnished by Yardley of London), and crisp bed linens (woven by Frette of Italy). But the fact their forbidden love was now known, and accepted by their mentors, made her giddy with relief. The sneaking about, snatching at crumbs, had exhausted her. Finally she had time and space to get to know Stanwell better, in a manner that was delectably tranquil and comfortable.

Elsa studied his deep brown eyes, full lips, and radiant white, though not perfectly straight, teeth. She considered his powerful worker's hands, and sensitive, respectful demeanor, and realized it was this singular dichotomy that touched her. She felt safe when he was close. To her he was gentle, but he'd also proven an able protector, as evidenced by his forceful display against those hapless thugs in the elevator.

It was the stuff of childhood fantasy, the fluff of fairytales— but this was real life. He'd truly saved her. He was her champion. And now the night was theirs.

To Stanwell, Elsa "Kat" Marais had the feline grace that fit her name. Her natural beauty, sleek and tomboyish, was unlike that of other women he'd known. Elsa's bearing was proud, like Zulu royalty's, and her back strong, like those of native women carrying heavy loads of firewood and water on their heads.

Stanwell decided to test this theory. He coaxed a coy Elsa to balance the complimentary fruit basket on her head. The first attempt to walk like a native woman was nothing short of a calamity. Fresh fruit scattered everywhere. Her giggles met his laughter in shared delight.

Eventually Elsa succeeded. She did two laps of the suite with a wildlife-themed coffee book balanced demurely on her head. Stanwell applauded the triumph. Elsa admitted it was a useful technique to improve her posture for modeling, despite the fact it made her feel quite silly.

It was a night of revelation and exploration. He taught her some of his native ways: how the soft foliage of one tree served as perfect bush toilet paper, the leaves of another warded off evil spirits, and the succulent leaf of the aloe was a one-stop bush pharmacy—a remedy for sunburn, insect bites, and bruising, with the thorn itself a pre-threaded sewing needle.

She asked him how his teeth were so shiny and white. How she wished for a similar million-dollar smile. He showed her. Taking a twig from the floral arrangement on the dresser, he crushed the end of it with his teeth until the tip resembled the fibers of a brush. He then pantomimed the dipping of the crude toothbrush in charcoal ash, vigorously brushed, and then spat out the phantom granules (to her horror, as a lady never spits!).

She explored his face. Tenderly she peeled at the pimples breaking out on his skin, revealing glittering glass chips (from the car accident, as Dr. Weitz had predicted). With each discovery Elsa squealed with delight, as if she had found alluvial diamonds in fertile soil.

He in turn explored her face and noticed again the faint scar across her chin: the consequence of a horse-riding accident when a diagonal wire cable, which supported a telephone pole, swept her by the throat off the back of the horse. One foot had remained trapped in a stirrup, so Elsa was dragged on her chin—thankfully at a leisurely pace, as the errant mount had slowed to graze tufts of grass by the side of the road.

They reveled in the fact that scarred chins were something they had in common. That was until Stanwell told her the technique his people used to sew up chin wounds: the mandibles of decapitated fire ants were ideal sutures in the bush, with their clawed teeth used to pinch the gash together. Elsa was understandably skeptical.

Then she became pensive.

"Simba," she began. She insisted on calling him that because it meant *lion* in Swahili—despite his protestations that "Simba" was a popular brand of potato chips. "You do know I love you... don't you?"

"That's real *lekker*, as I do you..."

"Please say it."

"Elsa, I love you," he said simply, realizing there was nothing simple about it.

She drew them a long bath. Together they slipped into the warm water anointed with fragrant oils, veiled by foaming bubbles and rising steam. Unhurriedly she mounted him, swiveled as though on a spindle so her buttocks faced him, and then fell back into the reassuring embrace of his arms.

Deliberately she guided his fingers to those areas providing the richest rewards, and silently rewarded him in kind. Contented, they luxuriated in that bath as they shared a moment of weightlessness and renewed exhilaration.

In the stillness of the moment they listened to the music drifting in from the bedside radio. Both were aware it was possibly their life's soundtrack as they heard the soulful refrain of The Flames' "For Your Precious Love," and The Staccatos' plaintive ode, "Cry to Me."

Later, as Elsa slept, Stanwell watched her intently. She was so very lovely. He had taken her for himself, and now she was in danger.

▶◀▶◀

ZEBRA AFFAIRE!

White supermodel and black domestic servant in city sexcapade shocker

JOHANNESBURG, Saturday

The meteoric career of modeling sensation Elsa Marais may well be in free fall tonight after her sexual indiscretion with an unknown black man was revealed today.

The two were spotted this morning leaving Die Landdrost Hotel together. Her companion has not as yet been identified, but it is understood he works for her in a domestic capacity or serves as her Bantu driver. Prior to this morning, the two were last seen publicly together at Kyalami attending the Formula One Grand Prix, on 6 March, 1976.

It was at this event Miss Elsa Marais's stellar career took off. The memorable picture of a modern beautiful woman in the arms of a mysterious man dressed in traditional tribal costume captured the imagination of the nation. The result was the extraordinary successful launch of the Safari Èlan fashion line, and the introduction of a fresh new face to the modeling firmament.

ZEBRA AFFAIRE continued:

Authorities Comment

At this time it is unclear how the couple circumvented the staff at the downtown five-star hotel, but the authorities are making inquiries. An officer at John Vorster Square, when asked, said there will be an investigation and if a crime has been committed, there will be consequences.

When pressed further about whether the couple must be "caught in the act" to ensure a successful prosecution, the officer confidently replied, "Of course, these people are predictable—you know zebras cannot change their stripes."

Condemnation

Meneer W. P. Venter, the dominee of Miss Marais's NGK church, was outraged. He stated her conduct was reprehensible, that it was a crime against nature, and that she was a disgrace to her people, her church, and her family.

Miss Marais's shocked parents remain cloistered in their modest Brakpan home and refuse to speak to the press.

Publicity Stunt

Lydia Duncan, the founder of Safari Èlan, could not be reached at this time, but a staffer tells us they are reviewing their options. A comment was made that there is growing interest in their South African-made fashion line overseas, and this may just be the publicity needed.

It has been suggested in some quarters that this is nothing more than a publicity stunt. If so, it is shameless and reckless. The authorities will not take kindly to a scandalous affair that so blatantly flaunts the Immorality Act.

City crime reporter

►◄►◄

Mal Zander gloated. He slapped down the folded newspaper on an unsuspecting fly. The creature had the cheek to buzz around his treacly-sweet treat. With childlike satisfaction he inspected the doomed insect, dismissed it with a flick, and then licked the stained newspaper print off his gooey fingers. Eating sticky *koeksisters* (a deep-fried concoction of twisted dough dipped in syrup) and reading the newspaper simultaneously was proving a challenge.

Never mind—the newspaper's late edition was immensely gratifying. Usually Zander read the back pages first—the salacious gossip and tawdry pictures invigorated him—before the sports columns and front-page headlines. Tonight, however, all he needed was the back page. His prey had slept their way into his trap. And it was all there in black and white for the entire world to see.

The tell-tale photographs were damming. One showed an interracial couple exiting a downtown hotel. She wore dark glasses and a head scarf, and he, his tie askew, had his jacket covering their (apparently) clasped hands. The other image was from the Grand Prix, showing the same white woman carried in the arms of the same black man; this time, he wore indigenous clothing.

It had been so easy for Zander. Paparazzi always staked out the hotel in their quest to capture celebrities at play, and his shill at the paper was happy to oblige the Security Branch.

Regarding the need to catch the interracial couple in flagrante delicto? Well, that wouldn't be necessary. The soiled bed linens had already been retrieved by Squat, from a now very cooperative hotel housekeeper.

Zander had all the proof he needed; what once was a private vendetta was about to become a very public affair.

▶◀▶◀

CHAPTER **TWENTY-ONE**

TO BE IN LOVE WAS EASY, but to be together in love had proven to be far more difficult. Hastily arranged rendezvous at homes of sympathetic allies had become tawdry affairs. Lovemaking should be intimate, personal, a private thing.

It was humiliating skulking around expecting strangers to open up their homes with all the intrigue of a spy's honey-trap. And for their hosts it had become progressively more dangerous for them, having been subjected to heavy-handed threats for allegedly aiding and abetting known criminals. Eventually Elsa and Stanwell were turned away at every stop, the authorities having systematically eliminated all havens.

Lacking any other alternative, the loving pair retreated beyond the city limits to seek discrete shelter. In Elsa's tiny car they headed toward Rivonia. As they barreled down the road lined with grand Blue Gum eucalyptus trees, the morning sun projected between the trees and struck the couple's eyes with a discomforting strobe effect of alternating bright light and heavy shadow. This was an expression of the white-knuckle ride Elsa and Stanwell now endured since that notorious newspaper revelation—careening between light and dark, acceptance and rejection. They felt exposed.

►◄►◄

Despite the tension, Elsa and Stanwell grew comfortable with each other. Elsa tore away the systemic bigotry that haunted her and became proud of her guy, without reservation. No longer wishing their romance stifled within a shroud of secrecy, she stepped out of the shadows and publicly declared her love.

This took the apartheid nation by surprise. Courageously the mixed-race couple headed directly for the limelight. Some gawked and stared, shocked at what they saw to be unnatural and forbidden. Others spat, cursed, or rapidly crossed the street to avoid having any tenuous contact with them.

But there were amusing moments too, such as when, with a rubber-necked backward glance, a fellow walked into a parking meter with calamitous Keystone Cop results. Even the Marshall Street meter maid in her mauve uniform cracked a smile.

Stanwell and Elsa hoped the glare of publicity would provide a halo effect of protection. And at every red carpet event, the beautiful model and striking warrior were welcomed.

With their newfound celebrity status, they were no longer social outcasts, but rather thrived in the glare of high-intensity international media attention. Nonetheless, as grateful as they were for the safety of the bright lights, the flash also singed.

They craved normalcy, and so they found a haven in a suburban pizzeria. Mindful of the need to be cautious when roving beyond the media's protective glare, Elsa and Stanwell only travelled at night, and relied on their tried and true ruse to escape attention. Again he assumed his station as her chauffer, dressed in mufti under a peaked cap and jacket borrowed from DGF's driver, and she rode in splendor in the backseat as if she were the mistress dressed for a gala evening on the town.

The Tivoli was like a café somewhere in Europe, brimming with cosmopolitan zest. It was where, around delicious wagon wheels of pizza, ethnic differences (and foods) were embraced, and shared. Being comfortable with the other's culture and company—whether German, Jewish, Italian, Greek, Persian, Lebanese, Irish, or Armenian—freed these friends from the inhibition of offending tender sensibilities, and so they chided one another affectionately. No malice intended and no insult taken even if the joshing took on a distinct ethnic flavor.

All those who congregated at this suburban melting pot happily accepted Elsa and Stanwell as a most interesting couple. As for the mixed-race lovers, among this well-travelled group they didn't have to face judgmental stares. And so they sat at a large round table sharing a communal meal with special friends. A carafe of sangria—a refreshing mix of wine, a splash of brandy, diced fruit, honey, Schweppes lemonade, and ice cubes—was passed around. Tentatively Elsa sipped the concoction then declared her approval with the single word, "*lekker.*" But Stanwell didn't raise his glass to his lips—as the designated driver, he needed to avoid any trouble with the predatory authorities.

After the food came the entertainment. Beneath the spiral staircase there was only room for a single barstool. The troubadour appeared, and his friends affectionately showered him with derision. He smiled at their catcalls and whistles, enjoying the attention, then responded with a zinger of his own.

With faded Levis jeans, denim shirt, and a booted foot racked on the barstool, the troubadour sang with a twelve-string guitar wedded to his hip. He was known simply as the Armenian, as his real name was a lengthy tongue twister of too many syllables. He sang of joy and pain, the sins of the Turks, and the falling rain. He would sing of love too, in the poetic stylings of Georges Moustaki, Jacques Brel, Françoise Hardy, Paolo Conte, Charles Aznavour, and blind man Jose Feliciano.

But as the night grew long and the shadows on the singer's jowls darkened, his mood would shift, and he lifted the mood of the place in the spirit of his Greco-in-laws. A joyful tease of sing along songs appeared—a robust medley of Dean Martin's "Mambo Italiano," Andy Williams's "Music to Watch the Girls Go By," and any version of "Zorba the Greek"—and then the levity truly began.

Those same boots leapt over the diners into a crouch at the center of the restaurant table; then the boots began their rat-a-tat-a-tat cadence until the Armenian drew himself to his full height. He'd stamp his heels everywhere, scattering bread rolls, pasta, and sangria in reckless dashes, all the while leading the charge with exultations of, "O-pa! O-pa! O-pa!" and the patrons would clap and chant in happy unison—none brave enough to mount the table themselves, but all liberated by the swirl of energy from above.

The heavyset owner of the establishment would act out in protest, but never intervened, as he understood the need for revelry, and no customer had ever complained. It was within the Tivoli Pizzeria, near the OK Bazaars, that Elsa and Stanwell found acceptance among decent men and women: the bohemians, the ex-pats, the artists, and the continentals.

◄►

With the passage of time, Stanwell and Elsa believed they might succeed. It was true the authorities appeared to tire of the game and seemed content to allow the matter to slip off the front pages. But they were naïve. The government had other plans. Humiliated by the actions of one of their own—a pretty blonde with hazel eyes and fair skin—Pretoria's power-elite would resort to underhanded tricks, far away from the media spotlight to exact their revenge.

◄►►

CHAPTER **TWENTY-TWO**

SID DUNCAN FLIPPED the T-bone steaks slathered in monkey gland sauce on the *braai* barbeque. Flames flared up, fueled by drippings. Nonchalantly, Sid doused them with the Carling Black Label beer he was drinking—useful stuff, beer was: thirst quencher, flame suppressor, and beef marinade all at once.

"Lydia, Sid—thanks for having us over. Enjoying that TV of yours?" said Daniel, with Juliette beside him.

"It's *bledie lekker*, as our fellow countrymen would say," replied Sid. "Frankly we're addicted. I've changed my complete schedule to check out the trials and tribulations of *The Villagers*—it's so provincial, but damn we enjoy it. Thirsty anyone...?"

It being a warm day, DGF and Juliette chose to go teetotal. Sid treated them to refreshing cordials of Kola Tonic and ginger ale poured over ice in tall glasses, topped with fresh cucumbers, lemon, and a splash of Angostura bitters.

"Cheers!" announced Sid. "Daniel, I'm still amazed this government finally allowed television. How on earth did you get involved?"

"I was in New York," said Daniel. "Had business with CBS Records at their Black Rock building, but jetlag got me, so I popped out for a walk. A movie theater attracted me with air-conditioning. More to get out of the muggy Manhattan humidity, I went in. A film festival was on featuring an actor I wasn't familiar with. Sid, he's a namesake of yours, Sidney Poitier. Do you know of him?"

Duncan shook his head.

"Well, it turned out Sidney Poitier happens to be a black man," said DGF. "Let me tell you, I saw things I'd never seen before on screen, or in real life. In these two amazing films, *In the Heat of the Night* and *Guess Who's Coming to Dinner*, Poitier's acting was superb, and the cast, Rod Steiger, Kate Hepburn, and Spencer Tracy, were top class.

"Something else impressed me too—the courage. These movies were a bold poke in the eye for segregation. Sensibilities were still very raw when these pictures were first released—around 1967 I think—that's only a few years after America enacted their 1964 Civil Rights Act. And that's when I realized why all this time our government had outlawed television...

"They feared anyone seeing this image of an attractive, intelligent, erudite, and principled black man like Poitier would shatter their narrative. It's been critical to them to perpetuate the myth of blacks being no more than stupid natives.

"Regrettably both movies are banned here, but I now understood that television meant more than a business opportunity. It has the potential to become a catalyst for social change."

Sid, Lydia, and Juliette nodded in agreement.

Daniel had dominated the conversation enough. Time to switch topics. "Okay, so what do you think we should we do about our protégés?" he asked.

"Sid and I've discussed it," said Lydia. "We think it is best they stay here."

"That's decent of you. Won't the police bother you?"

"Possibly, but with all the publicity, the cops have kept a low profile."

"Let's hope it stays that way."

"How's Elsa coping?" asked Juliette

"I've become very fond of Elsa," replied Lydia. "Initially she was a pain with that Afrikaner chip on her shoulder, but she's come 'round, and her work for Safari Èlan has been fabulous. Now she's an absolute pleasure, radiating joy...I'm sure Stanwell's got something to do with that!"

"By the way, how have her parents reacted?"

"Her old man surprisingly understood—but her mother's a bummer. Seems the old girl is feeling quite a chump back in Brakpan. And her Sundays are now rough with glares from the pews and hell-and-damnation sermons from the pulpit. Shame really, but Elsa's her daughter and she should be supportive."

"And Stanwell?"

"Hanging in there, but having difficulties at work," replied Daniel.

"Because of Elsa?"

"Not at all. But it's an unexpected setback and I've no idea how to fix it." Daniel's eyes searched the sky, as if seeking an answer there.

A breeze snatched up a spiral of smoke wafting from the barbeque and whisked it into the southern sky—it seemed so unfettered in contrast to the gravity-bound issues back on terra firma.

Daniel's thoughts were equally ephemeral. This concerned him, as he was a prodigious problem solver, an expert at dealing with the tangible. But this was not a clear issue of black and white (he smiled at the irony); instead it was the fuzzy gray morass of human nature. Daniel considered whether it was possible to change mankind's very nature; regrettably he couldn't shake off a sense of futility at the notion.

The introduction of new voices stirred Daniel from his musings. Elsa and Stanwell had joined the pool party.

"My, you seemed distracted there." Juliette looked concerned.

"Just thinking," Daniel said, "about the complexities of the human condition. And for the record, I'm not referring to my three failed marriages." That raised a several knowing grins from his companions.

"I thought that was your favorite topic," Juliette said lightly. "Maybe you should tell us about it." Juliette knew Daniel had a well-rehearsed spiel on the subject of marriage, and a bit of levity could only be helpful.

He shrugged. "Oy, how on earth did I miss all those warning signs? The clues to my downfall were buried within the very words." Mischievously Daniel enumerated the coded warnings he failed to heed each time he tripped down the aisle. "Consider bride number one, she believed in marriage...that's *m-a-r-r-i-age*," he spelled, emphasizing the *age*. And dammit, she sure aged me. That woman stole my youth.

"Let's see, bride number two was all about matrimony. A little liberty with the spelling and you'll get my drift. Matrimony...hmm, *m-a-t-r-i-money*. That's right, folks, she's still costing me a small fortune—and every month when I cut that alimony check, I'm reminded how worthless it all was."

Daniel was enjoying the riff. "As for number three, she was all about commitment. She called it wedlock: *w-e-d-lock*! That gal had me locked up so tight, I felt like a sorrowful Italian inmate at the World War II internment camp in Sonderwater. Being able to finally bid her *arrivederci* has been well worth the price for my liberty."

The word "liberty"—uttered in flippant tomfoolery—wrested everyone's attention from the trivial to the consequential, due to the presence of the last two guests. Elsa and Stanwell's stark reality so unseemly and unkind, personified for all the sanctity of true liberty.

Sid Duncan took it upon himself to probe. "DGF tells us you're having challenges at work. What gives?" he asked Stanwell.

Stanwell locked his eyes on a banded garden spider weaving a wheeled web beneath a poolside chaise-lounge. "I don't know," he said, now uncomfortable.

Daniel gave Stanwell a nod, then offered the explanation. "This is beyond Stanwell's control. In short, his fellow blacks at our warehouse facility have mutinied against him."

"Why?"

"Because he's from a different tribe!"

Sid shook his head in disbelief. "That's nuts. How'd this happen?"

"Sid, as you know I promoted Stanwell to run our warehouse," said Daniel. "He's the first black in our organization to become a senior executive."

"You knew that's illegal, so what on earth did you expect!" exclaimed Sid Duncan.

"Okay, I'll admit I wanted to test one of the more screwy rules in this country. And I anticipated some kind of blowback. It was to be expected—maybe some officious bastard from the

Provincial Secretariat. But for the life of me, I never thought poor Stanwell would be done in by his own people..."

"It wouldn't have occurred to me either," said Lydia, as she traced her fingers on the handwoven grass placemat in front of her. "I guess tribalism has gotten a free pass. All those darling aboriginal people with bones through their noses, clicking away in exotic tongues, doing their beadwork and wood carvings; it's all so quaint. As for their naked breasts...just kidding! I've always accepted the façade, not realizing there's a darker side to it."

"So, what do we take from all this?" asked Juliette as she searched in her handbag for some chewing gum. Trying to quit smoking was proving to be an ordeal.

"Nothing good," replied Daniel. "Good capable people are being excluded simply because they belong to another tribe. Through no fault of their own, these minority tribesmen find themselves with no jobs or opportunities. And how can they when it's cronyism that wins the day and corruption is the norm. Worse, it's become deadly with the ethnic violence; more blood's spilled from factional strife than even apartheid's heavy-handed enforcement."

"And there's no easy remedy for the situation," added Sid. "It's not like in the next election cycle the minority tribe will regain power. If you're a small clan, that's it, kaput, because the largest tribe's always guaranteed a massive voter turnout. And what really sucks, once in power with their numerical advantage nothing can dislodge these tribal potentates, even if they're incompetent, corrupt boobs."

"Why's that?" asked Lydia.

"Voting in Africa's not about the most qualified person, or who has the best ideas. Sadly, that's irrelevant. Votes are only cast on the basis of tribal loyalty."

Daniel added, "As Sid just said, it's all about a tribe's numerical superiority. Sure there's a veneer of democracy. Ballots typically list political parties and catchy slogans.

"But peel it back and you'll find each political party is just another front for a tribe. And the results are predictable. I often wonder why we waste the time going through the sham of an election—because the chieftain or party leader of the largest tribe *always* wins."

"So there's no true democracy anywhere in Africa?" asked Lydia, disheartened.

"It's like this beautiful garden of yours, Lydia, where tough native plants have driven out your fancy imported flowers," said Daniel. "Likewise it appears democracy is unable to flourish wherever tribalism has taken root."

"Let's not ignore the truly sinister side," added Sid. "The strongmen of the largest tribes aren't complaining. Democracy's a gift the colonial powers gave them when they hastily exited the continent. The ballot box has given these thugs the appearance of legitimacy, when in fact it's a kind of tribal hegemony.

"Now with their hands on government purse strings and with billions stashed away in private Swiss bank accounts, these thugs are now so powerful.

"And if anyone objects—well, they can buy their own civil war—nothing like death squads, forced removals, or purges African-style with machetes and AK-47s. Just look at the poor Ugandans stuck with a jerk like Idi Amin and the horrors of his ethnic bloodshed."

Sid's diatribe was met with silence.

Finally Daniel said, "It's Rhodesia that troubles me. Ian Smith's UDI government won't last much longer. The civil war's tearing them apart and it's no fun being the world's pariah—heck, they don't even have the resources to produce their own toilet paper and light bulbs..."

The conversation had taken an intriguing turn. White South Africans commiserated with Rhodesia. They understood the end of white rule by their neighbor to the north was a significant stepping stone toward the end of white domination in the Republic.

"I'll make a prediction," continued Daniel. "There'll be a great deal of huffing and puffing by Whitehall's Foreign Office. Sitting comfortably in London, they'll insist on a democratic Rhodesia with free elections: one man, one vote. They'll then wash their hands of the whole damn business. Not for a moment will they pause to consider the fate of previously liberated ex-colonies—all failed states—using this so-called democratic formula. You'd think they'd have learned something by now..."

A restless Juliette reached for the leather-bound cigarette case on the coffee table. As the Peter Stuyvesant cigarette touched her lust-red lacquered lips, Daniel's gold DuPont lighter was at the ready. The lid flicked up with a distinctive ping. She leaned in toward the flame, inhaled, and in the essence of cool blew three perfect smoke rings. Noting the quiet admiration of her companions, Juliette turned to her partner and asked, "Now Daniel, where were we?"

"When they have the first one-man-one-vote elections in a future Rhodesia, I predict the winner will be Robert Mugabe and his ZANU party. Look, I'm not using a crystal ball here. The facts show that Mugabe is a Shona, and the Shona tribe represents over eighty-two percent of the population.

"As for the tribal plurality Mugabe enjoys, he's destined to become 'Herr President, el Paramount Chief and King for Life' even if he's a corrupt, syphilitic, murderous thug. They won't remove him unless someone from within his own tribe makes a power-grab. Once again it will be the perfect trifecta of incompetence: cronyism, corruption, and partisanship.

"Frankly, I wish we'd dispense with the charade of an election when the results are such a forgone conclusion. Personally, every time a tyrant comes to power via the legitimacy of the ballot box, I feel the institution of democracy dies a little."

"Is there a solution?" asked Lydia.

"This takes us back to Stanwell," replied Daniel. "For the sake of this argument, I'm accepting the antics in my warehouse are a microcosm of broader behavior in Africa. Let me explain. I understand the well-deserved anger directed at Europeans for the crass exploitation and brutality by the former Colonists. Not surprisingly, the natives rallied around an antiwhite nationalistic war cry and unceremoniously tossed us out. Fine, we deserved it.

"But what happened next is really telling. Removing the whites apparently solved little; in fact, things have got much worse. So getting rid of the whites wasn't the panacea they'd hoped for. Why?

"Let's get back to Stanwell's predicament. Everything at the warehouse ran smoothly because it was understood a white man was in charge—he sat in the corner office, sipped coffee, read the funny papers, and contributed little.

"In practical terms Stanwell ran the show, but with the white boss apparently supervising things, the black staff took direction from him. And why's that? Because the white man, though not popular, was seen to be a neutral and there was no tribal shame in being managed by this third-party outsider.

"Now, if I'd just kept that white guy in the corner office, all would've been fine, but I let him go. And that released all these tribal rivalries. And so we come back to our little parable. Accepting in our allegory the fired white manager represents the toppled colonial powers, then in both instances—a colonial freed nation and my fifty-thousand-square-foot warehouse—the removal of a nonaligned outsider not beholden to any local clan, had the unintended consequence of bringing to the surface tribal rivalries...with subsequently distressing outcomes."

⋈⋈

CHAPTER **TWENTY-THREE**

LYDIA WAS TROUBLED. She was in fact a moral absolutist—everything was either right or wrong, no middle ground, and her favorite word was "Never!" Whenever confusion and ambiguity appeared, she retreated, as she considered them a dangerous threat to her moral certainty. Long since she had concluded that all European colonials were evil and the indigenous natives were inevitably pure.

This new insight had been a bit of a shock, and she felt compelled to challenge it. "But...but the colonial powers behaved appallingly. Some things they did were shocking, like the Belgian's King Leopold II for instance during the 1880's, dismembering limbs of millions of natives in the Congo. So ghastly. At best they treated the locals like second-class citizens in their own lands. And they mercilessly exploited the resources in these little countries for their own ends. Then suddenly the colonists left, leaving pandemonium in their wake."

Sid, sensing things might become combative, intervened. "You're absolutely correct, my dear, many of the locals were badly exploited and sometimes ruthlessly treated by the Europeans—and that's unforgiveable. But there's another side to the coin, that to be fair, should be acknowledged.

"Under European stewardship, though not benign, it succeeded in keeping tribal rivalries and bloodshed at bay. Productivity increased dramatically, providing more jobs, new skills, and improved farming and manufacturing practices. Then there was a boom in infrastructure, roads, schools, and hospitals—which brought improved health, nutrition, and better education to the locals.

"Now, if these advances in native societies are compared to the life of privilege the colonials enjoyed, then it sucks and it's damned unfair. In truth it's one of those is-the-glass-half-full-or-half-empty situations that make this a really tough call—but looking back over the past twenty-five years or so since the Mau Mau rebellion in Kenya, I wonder whether the life of the everyday Kenyan has improved after their liberation.

"And more recently the new Republic of Zaire, which we once knew as the Belgian Congo—this new scheme of 'Zaïrisation' by Mobutu Sese Seko is driving out all foreign enterprise...It may play well as a populist rallying cry, but there goes another African economy into a death-spiral..."

And like in a relay race, Sid handed off the verbal baton back to Daniel.

"Now, what I'm about to say is bizarre, but accepting of an imperfect world and black Africa's inability to solve this tribal schism thing. One day when looking back through the rearview mirror of history, colonialism may well be seen as Africa's Golden Age. Heck, I hope that won't be the case. God forbid, I'm not interested in being an apologist for colonialism. But, unless this continent gets its act together and taps into the potential of all people—no matter their tribe—we may be stuck with the sad irony that those 'bad old days' may well be the high point of the African experience."

"But none of this rationalizes South Africa's unacceptable behavior," stated Sid.

"I agree, totally. Here things went way too far because the colonists stayed and became direct competitors with local tribes, using brute force and one-sided laws to impose their will on the majority."

"Is our government building fences with our black leaders?" asked Lydia.

Daniel shook his head. "Sadly not. They've adopted a cynical divide-and-conquer approach that deliberately exploits the various tribal fault lines. But what's worse, many of our tribes willingly collaborate—possibly it's 'the enemy of my enemy is my friend' thing. Whatever, I find that all troubling." With a pained expression on his face, Daniel continued, "You don't read about it much, but tribe-against-tribe violence is growing more ghastly every day. You should hear Stanwell's gruesome stories of the ethnic violence happening in our mines."

Grimly, Stanwell recounted the events of those terrible days above and below ground. A dark pall descended on the pool party. Elsa shivered. "Are you chilly, my dear?" asked Lydia. "Maybe it's time we went inside."

Daniel and Sid led the conversation; the others sat and listened. Once in a while Stanwell's opinion was sought, being the only apparent tribal member present. Elsa didn't feel compelled to represent the position of her people, the Afrikaners. Like others of her clan, she yearned for legitimacy on the continent—as the first true white tribe in Africa.

Daniel glanced at his watch. It was getting late, but he needed to get something off his chest. "Let's not stereotype things. Tribalism is not just a black African problem, nor is it exclusively the behavior of aboriginal peoples. Europe's history has been riven by clannish rivalries. Take Yugoslavia, for instance. A benevolent dictator he might be, but if it weren't for Marshal Tito, the Croats, Bosnians, Slovenes, and Serbs would be slaughtering each other. As for the 'troubles' in Northern Ireland, this endless schism between the Catholics and Protestants seems mighty tribal to me."

Juliette reached out and placed a reassuring hand on Daniel's arm. She was unaccustomed to seeing him this upset.

▶◀▶◀

The evening ended with all present accepting the fissure between tribes was a path to destruction. And that of all the isms—including racism, anti-Semitism, and colonialism—tribalism was the most pernicious.

They yearned for a time when tribalism only enriched, rather than divided. They hankered back to a time when all peoples joyously shared their heritage with the spirited generosity of children, without spite and the compulsion to proselytize and subjugate.

They wondered about that moment when all innocence was lost. When the narrative of a people—passed down through the generations from elder to toddler around communal fires—told in songs sung and stories spoken, or dances vibrant, or comical pantomimes that mimicked the animals and birds—became bleak and unkind to those of other peoples from other tribes.

Daniel and Juliette, Sid and Lydia, and Stanwell and Elsa went their separate ways, certain of a restless night. They all feared for Africa, as the continent seemed destined for darkness.

▶◀▶◀

CHAPTER **TWENTY-FOUR**

WEDNESDAY, 16 JUNE, 1976.

This was the day a language changed the course of history.

This was the day black youth disobeyed their elders.

This was the day black citizens marched on white citizens.

This was the day knowledge ended—for a generation.

This was the day old scores were settled.

This was the day language killed.

◄►◄

They dragged him from the Jabavu Youth Centre in Soweto, then hacked and bludgeoned him to death. He was the first white man killed that day. It was a revenge killing. Earlier the police had shot a twelve-year-old black boy, and a student mob in blood-mist rage slaughtered the man in retribution.

They savored this white man's brutal death with a vengeance that tasted sweet—their target condemned on the basis of the color of his skin. And in the most graphic terms, they used his pitiful remains to send a warning to the nation's rulers. A crude sign fastened around the victim's neck read, "Beware Afrikaners! Afrikaans is the most dangerous drug for our future."

Alas, this white man was not an Afrikaner, but an Orthodox Jew. If only the incensed mob had paused to weigh the worthiness of the individual, they may have learned of Dr. Melville Edelstein's philanthropic work with black and disabled youth, and of his stout advocacy on behalf of their community.

The late Dr. Edelstein had been an intellectual and in his work had demonstrated considerable foresight. He'd warned the authorities that Soweto was a powder keg, ready to explode. He had also provided the remedy: imploring that the authorities address the social inequities that confronted the township's youth. He insisted that only then disaster would be averted.

Tragically his warnings were ignored. And sadly the mob was oblivious to his decency.

▶◀▶◀

Early that day, two innocents had lost their lives, a twelve-year-old Bantu boy and a philanthropic white man; before the long-day-into-weeks was over, many others, of all colors, paid the ultimate price for the nation's self-inflicted aggression.

▶◀▶◀

They couldn't just let things be. They felt compelled to inflict their language on the nation's blacks. And so the Bantu Education Department had demanded that Afrikaans would be used as the main medium of instruction in Bantu schools. In addition, lessons given in English and native mother tongues would be severely reduced.

The old saw "sticks and stones may break my bones, but words will never hurt me" was disproved on Wednesday, June, 16, 1976—and a violent gag reflex resulted. Not surprisingly, the youth of Soweto resented the hated language of their oppressors being jammed down their collective throats.

They also had another demand: to be taught their history, their own Afrocentric history, and not just history from a white European perspective.

Steve Biko (a future martyr to the cause, brutally beaten until his brain hemorrhaged—then callously driven shackled and naked in the back of a police van to a prison hospital over seven hundred miles away—where he died) and his Black Consciousness Movement organized the protest.

In the chill of the Highveld winter, the students boycotted classes and faced both the elements and police in solidarity. These irate school pupils marched with placards that read "Down with Afrikaans!" and "Afrikaans will destroy our future." And at that moment, Soweto schools became the front lines of the antiapartheid movement.

> The *Argus* newspaper reported, "More than 10,000 angry Soweto school pupils rioted and stoned a large contingent of police at Phefeni Junior Secondary School in Orlando West early today. At least one pupil was shot as police fired hundreds of rounds into the air. Many of the 50 police cars that raced to the scene of the riot had their windscreens smashed by the rampaging students."

The Bantu students' rebellion was confronted with overwhelming force. Lines of blue-gray-shod paramilitary troopers faced stone-wielding pupils. Their screams were drowned out by the *whup-whup-whup* of helicopters overhead. Teargas canisters were dropped on the crowd below, obscuring battle lines in a cloud of confusion. Then it became deadly. A shot rang out. A spray of bright red blood vaporized in the air—a clean lung shot—and the death toll rose by the count of one.

Armored personnel carriers called "Hippos" then waded into the fray. Designed to protect soldiers from exploding mines, not for riot control, these behemoths lumbered about attempting to break up the crowd. But they were so slow that the rioters reformed their battle lines behind them as they passed—at great personal risk, as the soldiers safely secured inside the military vehicles peppered the rampaging students with rifle fire. More fatalities would be counted.

Then the Alsatians were unleashed. These attack dogs relished the hunt and pursued their prey with cold precision. Growls were followed by desperate shrieks. Torn, bloodied garments bore testament to the savagery of the attacks. Those driven to the ground were viciously shaken, like rag dolls—the schoolchildren no match for the large animals. And so the bloodbath continued...

▶◀▶◀

As the battle raged, just fourteen miles away the students at the all-white Rosebank Government School marched, in crocodile file, to the main hall for morning assembly—the girls in their sunshine-yellow frocks, and the boys in their blue uniforms. On the left breast of their school uniforms was a richly embroidered emblem, a Tudor rose with a large *R* at the center—a tribute to the British monarchy, and a vestige of a bygone era when South Africa was part of the British Commonwealth. The motto sewn underneath read, "Manners Makyth Man."

The daily ritual began with a recitation of the Lord's Prayer. In reference to the "troubles" in nearby Soweto, the headmaster emphasized the following verse: "Give us this day our daily bread, and forgive us our trespasses, as we forgive them that trespass against us. And lead us not into temptation, but deliver us from evil."

Quick announcements were then made: there'd be polio vaccinations for all, the seniors were cautioned to "play gently" with junior graders on the playground, and an appeal to respect the school's motto, especially in the classroom, was dutifully regurgitated.

The student body wrapped up the proceedings with a strident rendition of the hymn "Onward, Christian Soldiers," then marched back to their respective classrooms. There the white boys and girls sat, two by two at their wooden desks, listening to their teachers educate them all in English (the exception being their compulsory Afrikaans language instruction).

>◄►◄

Of course, crushing might prevail. In the resulting panic the mob splintered, running pell-mell between bleak shacks, carcasses of burnt cars, and destroyed "green mamba" buses. Other casualties of the conflict included many damaged schools, a vandalized library, and sixty-six beer halls and liquor stores plundered.

Then hunger set in. The township was under siege. Nothing could be replenished because Soweto's contact with the outside had been severed. No trains, buses, taxis, minivans, or delivery trucks dared enter that grim place.

The only thing left for the inhabitants to do was to wash down the blood-drenched pavements and bury the dead.

>◄►◄

This went on for a week, and was not confined solely to Soweto. The entire Reef was engulfed in black rage as the violence spread from township to township. In all directions, according to witnesses, pillars of dark smoke reached for the sky. No one felt safe. After all, from the northern suburbs Soweto was merely twenty-eight minutes away by car.

Whites clung to their cossetted neighborhoods in Johannesburg and the northern suburbs, surrounded, and waited for the long-threatened *swart gevaar.* This was the white European's African nightmare—a rampaging horde overwhelming all that is civil and secure. Was it about to be realized?

Not this time, though it had been a near thing. While the mob failed to reach the suburbs, through the unflinching eye of their brand new television sets, the suburbanites, sitting in their living rooms, felt the fear.

▶◀▶◀

To those of English pedigree, this was a wake-up call. They'd witnessed the blood-stained colonial rout from Nigeria (1960), Tanganyika (1961), Uganda (1962), and especially, with its ghastly Mau Mau uprising, Kenya (1963); not surprisingly, they'd little stomach for an encore performance. There was now a singular preoccupation for English speakers, asked in hushed tones at cocktail parties: "What's your exit strategy?"

▶◀▶◀

The Boer saw things differently. Proud of his immutable obstinacy, he drew the *laager* ox wagons into a tighter circle, to first defend, and then repel the hordes—aggressively. The Nationalist Party announced there'd be no compromise. Afrikaans would continue to be the language of instruction in Bantu schools. And all apartheid laws, petty or otherwise, would be strictly applied. No deviation would be tolerated, and all transgressors "better watch out!"

**

Unfortunately, the students of Soweto, the class of 1976 and beyond, never returned to school. "Liberation, then education" was the slogan that fed a child's natural inclination toward truancy. And becoming a revolutionary was far more seductive than being a student, as mass action was preached to be way cooler than having to study in the classroom.

As tribal beliefs and sloganeering cannot replace reading, writing, and a general education, this absence of schooling created future generations of stunted minds incapable of earning the freedoms of a good job, or of meeting the massive challenges of a South Africa destined for change.

So, for the first time, a generation of township children disobeyed the moderating influence of their elders—the same elders that wisely promoted education and knowledge as the true path to power. Instead the youngsters accused their mothers and fathers of being appeasers for the regime. Subsequently in this vacuum "comrades" replaced family, and "the struggle" replaced all else.

Regrettably, the nobility of the liberation struggle became subverted by the vandals and thieves drawn to the chaos—a pattern of arson, looting, wanton destruction, and ethnic violence followed. Students became vigilantes, and as they accosted tsotis and others looting the neighborhoods, more fatalities followed.

Then the inevitable spiral into despair destroyed the remaining remnants of a once noble cause, with the onetime militant protests descending into shameful thuggery. Bloodshed followed and opponents were destroyed. Traitors (operatives allegedly working for the government or just members of another tribe) were rooted from their midst and summarily executed. It was black-on-black payback time.

The more fortunate were "sent home" by relatively humane sharpened panga or ax, while the less fortunate were bludgeoned with rocks, bricks, and slabs of concrete.

But for special cases, Soweto's callous natives developed a novel execution technique guaranteed to inflict excruciating pain—the "necklace." It was cruelly easy to wedge a car tire around the wretched victim's neck, fill the casing with gasoline, set it alight, and then leave a writhing pyre to entertain the encircled pack of former schoolchildren.

**

CHAPTER **TWENTY-FIVE**

EARLY MORNINGS IN MID-JULY on the Highveld were gripped in the bracing chill of a Southern hemisphere winter. White frost dusted the parklands and lawns. These tiny ice crystals were destined to thaw as they faced a warming sun. However, in Pretoria's corridors of power, matters had heated up considerably. The nation's administrative capital was at full alert as a consequence of the Soweto upheaval. Though the mob violence had been contained, the threat still simmered.

The Soweto Riots had eroded the certainty of the ruling regime. They feared for their way of life. Despite their apparent insensitivity to the plight of other humans, the Afrikaners were great champions of wildlife conservation—and similar to the black rhino, a victim of senseless poaching, they too felt as if they were an endangered species.

An endangered animal is desperate. A cornered animal is dangerous. The ruling regime was both desperate and dangerous as they felt their grip over the nation loosening. The Soweto Riots invoked a regime dictate of zero tolerance. From on high, directives to the nation's security apparatus adopted an apocalyptic tone—the end of the *volk* was imminent, and all threats must be stopped, now. No deviation from the law by anyone would be tolerated.

The Security Branch considered Stanwell and Elsa's romantic entanglement a matter of national security; what was once considered a tawdry "domestic affair" became a public symbol of rebellion and had to be crushed. The couple had undermined a key principle of apartheid; the white minority's dominance could not be eroded by the intermingling of the races. Another outrage was Stanwell's status as a business executive. His authority over white employees signaled to the Bantu that they were the white man's equal, and that was unacceptable.

The Security Branch's first act in their campaign against the couple was plagiarism. They lifted the "Zebra Affaire" headline from the newspaper article that publicly exposed them, and made it the operation's code name.

Their second action was to classify Stanwell as an enemy of the state.

►◄►◄

Malan Zander was delighted. Finally he had his marching orders. The mixed-race couple was now fair game, and it was time they suffered the consequence of their actions. He felt the buzz of anticipation. Others chose to be doctors, teachers, or builders in order to heal, impart knowledge, or create. Zander never understood that mindset.

As a child he found it more gratifying to demolish things, and as an adult, annihilation was his guiding light. Fortune shone on him when he found an employer that regarded the destruction of people's lives a virtue.

For Zander restraint was an anathema; he'd much prefer bludgeoning the miscreants into submission. But his orders were clear: the Zebra Affaire must be handled subtly, as the world was watching. No killings, no public trial, no questionable disappearances—just make it go away. But for now just one problematic life required his immediate attention; he would deal with the girl later. As Stanwell's crimes against the State were twofold, in business and in the bedroom, Zander had fertile grounds to create mischief.

▶◀▶◀

Stanwell initially dismissed the disruptions, strange repeated hang-ups or silence on his telephone at work, as a nuisance. But paranoia grew when he heard mysterious clicks and echoes on the company phone. It could only be the State's Security Branch meddling in his business.

Then the threats started, and Stanwell's worst fears were confirmed. Vulgar in content and vicious in implication, faceless voices with rasping accents vowed public exposure. All Stanwell's claims of innocence to his invisible attacker were brushed aside with merciless laughter until he began to plead. At that point he was given a specific warning: Miss Elsa Marais would soon receive something in the mail. After that the calls stopped, but the pressure continued.

Two white men arrived unannounced at the warehouse facility. Their ill-fitting suits were a signal to Stanwell's staff that they were members of the Security Branch. The visitors were seen speaking with Stanwell through the executive office's glass wall. The three men leaned toward each other in a conspiratorial fashion. Their body language was clear—they wished not to be overheard.

After the men left, the warehouse swirled with rumors that Stanwell was a snitch working for the apartheid regime. In that cesspool of tribal mistrust, Stanwell's coworkers happily accepted the allegations as fact. This placed Stanwell's life in potential danger. A revenge killing by embittered colleagues was now a real threat.

Understandably, Stanwell was terrified.

◄►◄►

Elsa did receive a package in the mail. It was innocuous enough, but it injured the wrong target. It arrived at the Safari Èlan office addressed for her attention. They'd been expecting a package with a dozen T-shirts custom designed for a "Save Our Lions" charity event. The cause suited their brand perfectly, so inspiration had been a breeze for Francine Du Plessis, Safari Èlan's fashion designer. When Franny spotted the package at the reception, she couldn't resist opening it.

Franny sliced open the package. Then, needing privacy, she headed for the restroom. She stripped off her blouse, revealing a surprisingly conservative bra for such a trendy chick, and pulled a freshly silk-screened T-shirt over her head. Above the basin was a mirror. Time to inspect her creation, Franny took one stride—then screamed.

Her face, neck, torso, arms, and hands were stained a deep purple. Another shock awaited her. It began gradually; then a searing pain engulfed Franny's upper body. Wherever the T-shirt's fabric had touched the unfortunate woman's flesh, her skin had burned and blistered. Now hysterical Franny stripped off the garment, pulling it back over her head and face, and in doing so unhappily added to the damage. Fortunately, with the discarded shirt at her feet, the pain began to subside.

Investigators later established the clothes had been treated with a mixture of ninhydrin, a caustic agent expressly developed to irritate skin. It turns purple on contact with proteins in human flesh. The sophistication of the brew suggested this wasn't the action of an individual with an ax to grind against wildlife conservationists, but that of an operative with full access to the State's chemical-warfare resources.

The investigators discovered one other piece of evidence, tucked away at the bottom of the package. It was a brown envelope marked "Private & Confidential" and addressed to Mej. Elsa Marais.

A distraught Elsa, after learning about the bizarre assault on Franny, rushed to the Safari Èlan office. By then the document, addressed to her personally, had been opened. The lead investigator insisted Elsa wore gloves, then handed it to her with a telling look. She sensed him watching her closely as she began to read it.

Elsa turned her back on the room. Her hands trembled as she read the blatant threats and crude allegations. It had been meticulously typed on an IBM Selectric typewriter, that Elsa knew. She'd been fascinated by the state-of-the-art "golf ball" font element bouncing about in the machine of Lydia's office assistant. But this time, rather than generating a pedestrian business letter, a faceless monster using a similar machine—deliberately striking ribbon to the page—had spewed out filth.

Her stomach churned as she read "stop sleeping with that *fokken kaffir* or next time we'll permanently disfigure you...it would be such a waste, you *were* such a beautiful girl." Then the threat turned into a lecture. "The purple stain was to teach you a lesson...since you are not proud of your pure white race, you can appreciate life in another shade."

The communique concluded on a shattering note. "Your Stanwell's having an affair with his secretary because he gets off screwing white women...but he has another motive beyond sex. He needs the woman to do his bidding and cover up his crooked business dealings."

Elsa felt gutted. She struggled to fill the massive void enveloping her chest. She attempted to move, but her knees seemed disconnected from her feet. As her body froze, her mind did not. It raced backward in time, reimagining all the moments they'd shared together. Every nuance of their relationship was revisited, sifted, and then set aside.

The duality of the exercise pained Elsa; she was actively seeking signs of suspicion while hoping for none. In her head a debate raged. Should she confront him? But by doing so it showed mistrust. And what if it's a cruel hoax? Elsa decided she must attempt to find the answers before challenging him.

Unfortunately the many questions outweighed the few answers; the seeds of doubt had begun to sprout. Unless something was done quickly, it was likely Elsa and Stanwell would be torn apart by the South African government.

◄►

The temperate spring weather had enticed birds from the sanctuary of their nests, and the air was filled with enthusiastic squawks, twitters, chirps, and warbles. All this unbridled glee was lost on the young woman with a scowl on her lovely face. Elsa was both frightened and humiliated by the circumstances she found herself in, but she was desperate for sound advice. As the bellhop guided Elsa to the Firths' bungalow on the lavish grounds of the Balalaika Hotel, Elsa considered the enormity of the conversation she was about to have with DGF and Juliette.

Juliette greeted Elsa at the stable door with a flute of champagne. It was the weekend brunch, and Daniel had ordered a cornucopia of treats from room service. In a gracious flurry of hospitality, Elsa found herself seated with a napkin on her lap and a plate brimming with prosciutto-wrapped asparagus and triangle sandwiches topped with smoked salmon. A quick glance around the room revealed stacked suitcases in the corner, red for her and black for him.

A freshly shaved DGF bounced into the room, some shaving cream still clung to his sideburns. Juliette swept it away with a loving sweep of her thumb. The welcoming smile on DGF's face somewhat settled Elsa's fractured nerves. "Now, young lady, what can I do for you?" he asked.

"I think I need some advice," said Elsa. "Probably from both of you, hey." With that Elsa carefully unfolded the menacing message she'd received. As they read it, Elsa brought them up to speed on the chemical-laced T-shirts and her guilt over her colleague's misfortune.

Elsa noticed Juliette cover her mouth in horror as she digested the full implication of the warning, but DGF's face remained largely impassive. However, when he looked up, Elsa was struck by the flint mien in his slate-gray eyes.

DGF sighed as he leaned in closer to Elsa. "Listen to me carefully," he said earnestly. "I'm afraid I don't have all the answers, but on two facts I'm one hundred percent certain. One, there's no way on earth Stanwell's having an affair with Melanie Coetzee. I've known her family for decades. Her father worked for me at our Roodepoort factory, and Melanie joined us after she finished secretarial school. They are good people, but very conservative, very traditional and devout. What's more, Melanie is a married woman. Melanie having an affair with a white man would of itself be unlikely...but with Stanwell, being both black and her boss. No way, of this I'm certain.

"As for the second point, yes, Stanwell has struggled managing the warehouse. But we know the reason—the staff's tribal friction. There isn't a hint of any so-called 'crooked business' whatsoever. Believe me, a warehouse is a tempting target for dishonest employees, but on Stanwell's watch there's been less theft, what we call 'shrinkage' has actually reduced.

"So, on these two important facts I want you to rest easy. Promise me you will."

Silently Elsa nodded.

"Unfortunately I haven't an answer for your other problem. Not surprisingly, the two of you have made many enemies in this country. The only question in my mind is, is this the action of a vindictive individual, or something sanctioned by the state? If the latter..."

"Do you truly love him?" blurted out Juliette, unable to contain herself.

"*Ja*, I do," said Elsa.

"Good!" Juliette said, relieved by the young woman's conviction. "Look, I know love can be complicated. So I can't even imagine how difficult it must be to have the entire government gunning for you. But please, don't give in now to these silly rumors and innuendos, especially from such suspicious, unknown sources.

"Just think of the epic tale, if you succeed, you'll one day be able to tell your children and all your grandchildren. That you and Stanwell beat the might of apartheid South Africa...in the name of love."

Juliette reached for Daniel's hand. He gave it a reassuring squeeze.

DGF noticed Elsa hadn't touched her plate. "If you don't like the food, I'd be happy to get you something else to eat."

"No, fine thanks, I'm okay. But pardon me, may I please use your restroom?"

A pale Elsa returned. She had clearly been ill—though she'd valiantly attempted to cover for her failing. Juliette leapt up to provide assistance. "Is there anything we can do?" she asked.

"I don't think so," Elsa said. "I think I'm pregnant!"

►◄►◄

Nausea overwhelmed her. The first period missed she attributed to stress, but now the pattern was certain. She *was* pregnant. And Elsa was frightened, as she feared for the child's future. Interracial sex was a crime, and as a consequence, the baby produced from their union would be declared "illegitimate" by the State as it was unlawful for them to get married. As a consequence it devastated Elsa to contemplate their innocent child being forever branded as the white man's shame and the black man's outcast.

Elsa needed time. She'd implored Daniel and Juliette to keep her secret, and they'd vowed to do so. Now she must tell Stanwell. But she couldn't, at least not yet.

How the secrets piled up, and with each one, her guilt grew. Elsa hadn't told Stanwell about the T-shirt incident as she feared losing him, that he'd be driven away by a sense of responsibility to protect her from further harassment. However, having a child—a coloured baby—was a burden, and joy, they both must share.

But Elsa needed to be certain of her own fortitude before discussing parenthood with Stanwell. After all, she was still haunted by that harrowing event all those years ago, when she joined a guided tour through Europe and took a detour of her own to address some personal business.

◄►◄►

As they packed, Daniel glanced over at Juliette. He watched her struggle to close her red suitcase in her negligée, her shapely form revealing itself against the sheer fabric. She's definitely a keeper, he thought. Juliette had surprised him with her devotion. He'd expected bitter recriminations when he'd told her about the major job he had accepted overseas. Instead Juliette met the news with unbridled enthusiasm, seeing it as "a great adventure," and wholeheartedly committed herself to be by his side.

"Gee whiz," said Juliette. "I can't believe she's *preggy.*"

Stirred from his reverie, the best Daniel could do was grunt. The topic of pregnancy usually held little interest for him, though this pregnancy was very different—the social, political, and legal ramifications were potentially lethal. "I'm worried for their future," he eventually replied.

"It's really nuts when you think about it," Juliette said. "Judging someone's worth solely on skin color is insane...Elsa and Stanwell are a lovely couple."

"I agree. For me, seeing people only in terms of their willingness to contribute is the only fair way to go. I find it *uncomplicates* a very complicated world," said Daniel. "That's why I have you in my life," he added with a warm smile.

Juliette pretended to ignore the compliment, though hearing it delighted her. She needed to get something off her chest. "I've been thinking a lot about skin lately. At the end of the day, it's nothing more than a kind of sausage casing that keeps all the seamy gross stuff inside, and that's a benefit we *all* share, no matter our skin color. So I don't get why people are so hung up about it. Just look at Clifton beach in Cape Town. It's full of wealthy white people greasing themselves with baby oil to better cremate their skins a crispy tan, the darker the better...while our poor blacks try to lighten their skin with bleaches and other dangerous brews. It's all awfully sad and peculiar to me."

A bemused Daniel admitted he'd never considered flesh in such a utilitarian way before. He added everyone's skin could be cut, bleed, scab, and heal, no matter the color.

"That's my point," said Juliette. "Maybe in Elsa's tummy we have the solution—a lovely blending of colors. Then we can let skin go back to doing its true job—keeping all our innards in—rather than using it as a means of categorizing people."

Daniel ran his thumb across his mouth as he considered his response. "Again, you are correct. Juliette, I don't know whether you knew this, but I was raised an Orthodox Jew. Then, one day, sitting with my father in the big synagogue, I became keenly aware my mom couldn't join us but was seated separately from our family, alone, with the other women.

"This upset me, not because of any lack of appreciation of our faith, but because it felt very much like segregation to me—rather than Judaic tradition. I think it may have pricked at my white South African sensitivity that was beginning to emerge. As a result I quit the synagogue. You can imagine the rumpus it caused. It was the first time I'd rebelled against my father. And now I'm realizing it's time to quit again..."

"What do you mean by 'quit again'?" asked Juliette.

"I know this fantastic job offer was the catalyst for our move, but Elsa and Stanwell's dire predicament has really brought things into sharp focus for me. There's no doubt us whites are going to be stained by history for our role in this apartheid scheme. Now I'm grateful we've decided to quit this country. But it's just such a shame it took this crisis—so close to home—for us to wake up and finally do something about it."

**

The late seventies' exodus of South African Jewry was a flight unlike any other. They were not forced from their homes by a malignant government, zealous church, or rabid population; there was no Spanish Inquisition, Russian Pogrom, or Nazi "Final Solution" uprooting them with the threat of extinction. In fact, as a group they weren't persecuted at all by the South African government or general population.

Nevertheless, Jewish individuals did attract the wrath of the regime for their role in the freedom liberation movement. For instance, the actual genesis of the ANC's military wing, Umkhonto we Sizwe (The Spear of the Nation) occurred at Arthur Goldreich's home, Liliesleaf Farm, in Rivonia, an outlying rural suburb of Johannesburg.

Along with Nelson Mandela and other black leaders, Joe Slovo and Goldreich were inducted into the movement's military high command. The latter's practical experiences in the Israeli army made him a particularly valued asset.

The subsequent 1963 raid at Liliesleaf Farm by the nation's security apparatus resulted in the capture of Mandela and Goldreich, and fellow revolutionaries Denis Goldberg, Rusty Bernstein, Bob Hepple, Dr. Hilliard Festenstein, and later Harold Wolpe. The resourceful Goldreich and Wolpe succeeded in escaping from the police station that held them and found sanctuary in neighboring Botswana.

The less fortunate were prosecuted and imprisoned—some, notoriously, for life. Lesser actors were banned, placed under house arrest, and even exiled.

So why the sudden urge by the South African Jewish community to flee?

On the surface it made little sense. They lived comfortably and were generally accepted at most levels of society (the exception being some "proper" country clubs). And despite subversive activities of certain individuals, as a community South African Jewry were never under anti-Semitic threat.

In a word—guilt! In addition to flight, guilt is the other impulse akin to the Jewish experience. This sense of guilt stemmed from the collective realization that remaining in South Africa was tantamount to a tacit endorsement of apartheid.

As a group South African Jews realized they were on the wrong side of history, and liable to be judged in the future (in the same way they judged wartime Germans). This sudden awareness appalled them.

So the doctors and the dentists, the lawyers and the engineers, the industrialists and hoteliers, and even a few music executives headed for the exit with their families in tow. The "brain drain" had begun as the Jewish exodus from Southern Africa got underway.

**

CHAPTER **TWENTY-SIX**

STANWELL HAD HIS HANDS CLASPED as though in prayer, but in fact he was physically restraining himself from lashing out in frustration. Those words from the mouth of the beautiful girl with the pleading eyes had knocked him on his backside (almost literally). Unfortunately his face had shown its dismay. That he wished he could take back, but her stunning announcement of the happy tidings had him reeling because of a prescient sense of dread.

Stanwell couldn't shake off the now heightened sense of foreboding he felt once hearing her news. He saw the tears well up in those eyes—eyes that blinked between hope and despair as they scrutinized his. But a mask of concern still cloaked his face, and Stanwell saw Elsa's face crumple in anguish. Despairingly he reached out to her, but Elsa flinched, and then she stalked away. He felt like *kak*.

▶◀▶◀

In his faraway village of Muzuzu, the prospect of an heir, a welcomed sign of virility and fertility, was a family gift dearly treasured. A goat would be slaughtered in celebration, and his tribal kin would eat and drink, dance and jest until the next sunrise. But in this land such joy was not possible. It had to remain a secret. But a secret for only so long, as the certainty of time and nature would inevitably reveal the truth.

Stanwell realized that time was now working in cahoots with the Security Branch. He struggled for a solution, but their options were bleak. Stanwell wanted to protect Elsa from the government's tyranny. But the price expected of him was too high: possibly the sacrifice of their child and the destruction of their love. He needed advice. Hopefully the Big Baas, his mentor and friend, had the answer.

▸◂▸◂

Desolate. DGF's office was quite bare. Not a single item of furnishing remained. Unbleached rectangles, hidden for years from the sun by framed artwork, spotted the walls with only the odd hanging nail for company. A scattering of indentations marked the carpet where erstwhile tables, chairs, and settees once stood. The only evidence of the successful entrepreneur that had once inhabited the room was a lone telephone. It lay at the end of a twisted cord like a landed fish at the end of a line.

Though it was a Saturday, Stanwell had known DGF would most likely be at the office, as it was his custom to spend the quiet Saturday mornings recording memos on the Dictaphone in preparation for the new week. But finding neither the man nor the office furniture was a shocker. Stanwell gazed at the empty space and his emotions yawed into a void. Without the Big Baas, he felt rudderless.

▸◂▸◂

Thanks to the good graces of the Duncans the beleaguered couple had lived the past few weeks in the poolside guesthouse, quietly, unmolested by the ruling powers. But the tension in the Duncans' guesthouse had now stretched to its tensile limit. The warm bond that once fused together the black man and white woman was at this moment in time brittle, and verging on imminent failure. It was a sense of despair, rather than hostility that kept them apart. All the pleas, cajoling, and assurances fell fractured on the hard reality of the challenge that the now three of them faced. There was no escaping the pressurized atmosphere, so silence weighed down the mood in the room. But there was a glimmer of hope—despite the rupture, neither had said a single unkind word to the other.

The intercom squawked. It was Lydia's cheery voice. Please kindly join them on the main house verandah, as they had surprise guests.

The Great Escarpment supporting the Highveld had blessed Johannesburg with an agreeable and temperate climate. Though it was late afternoon, the sun still filtered through the arbor and brought a comfortable warmth to the shielded verandah. There, chatting with Sid and Lydia, sat DGF and Juliette.

The two men stood in welcoming Elsa, and both shook Stanwell's hand. DGF sensed a reticence in Stanwell's grasp and knew the man was troubled.

"I've some explaining to do," DGF began, "regarding our future plans." It was time to come clean. He'd no right to leave people, especially those dependent on him, in the dark.

Four pairs of eyes looked at him smartly, while Juliette hid behind her Jackie O sunglasses.

"On Monday there'll be an announcement to the Gallo staff and business press," DGF said. "Look, I'm sorry I couldn't tell you earlier, but things had to be kept hush-hush until we found my successor. Last night the new man signed the dotted line."

"You're quitting? Why?" asked Sid, never shy to pry.

"Apparently I'm no longer in the PolyGram doghouse. Several months ago I'd implemented a belt-tightening program at Trutone against the wishes of Baarn and Hamburg. Fortunately it's been a great success, and PolyGram has offered me the job to run their UK operation out of London. They want me to implement a similar program over there."

"Haw! That's a huge blow," said Stanwell, disconsolate.

After a brief glance at Juliette, DGF said, "We've not forgotten about you two. Once settled in, we'd like to send for you. I've already checked with PolyGram's legal staff to get you work permits. What do you think?"

An elegant solution was within their grasp. Leaving South Africa would miraculously mend the racial divide tearing them apart. Why then Stanwell's hesitancy?

Since the dust of Africa flowed in his veins, he was rooted in Africa. He felt the earth under his feet to be a living creature, and the idea of having to abandon her would be devastating.

He was sure Elsa had a similar connection to the land underfoot—why otherwise the Boers' bitter struggle to cling to this corner of the continent? Strange, in this regard he and his tormentors did have something in common, realized Stanwell.

And Stanwell had another concern. Wouldn't his small-town Elsa wither away in a faraway land, especially in the nation that had vanquished her forebears?

As Stanwell struggled for the right words to best respond to DGF's generous offer, Elsa found herself wrestling to reach a right and proper decision—possibly the most important decision she'd ever have to make. The offer was certainly tempting, she admitted to herself.

But, the prospect of their baby being born an Englishman felt to Elsa like a betrayal of her *oupa*. The bitterness in his voice over the years, as he condemned the English for the injustices of both Boer Wars had been intense, and was impossible to ignore.

Elsa also recalled his derision toward English speakers. He scornfully called them *soutpiels*, or "salt penis." Though the nickname made her squirm, its crude caricature of the Englishman with one foot firmly planted in England and the other in South Africa, while in the middle his pecker sagged in the salty waters of the Atlantic Ocean, was most fitting. Therefore she struggled at being similarly disloyal to her motherland.

Sensing their reticence, DGF got angry. "Tell me then, what other options do either of you have? You must leave this crazy country, if not for yourselves, then for the sake of your child."

Stanwell was shaken to learn others knew about their baby. But he pleaded for time. "Baas, this is a big decision. Elsa and me need to talk. But thank you...thank you very much."

"When will you be leaving?" asked Sid.

"In a couple of weeks."

"How come so quickly? Don't you have a house to sell and stuff to pack?"

"Fortunately not. We're just a pair of nomads living out of suitcases at the hotel. As for the house and furniture, well, the ex-wife has that. So we're all ready to go."

The gathering ended on a bittersweet note. As they said farewell to Daniel Gideon Firth and Juliette St. John in the driveway, the Duncans looked wistfully back at their beautiful home. They hated the idea of one day soon having to leave it.

◄►◄►

CHAPTER **TWENTY-SEVEN**

HE NEEDED TO MAKE IT RIGHT. Elsa had misunderstood him. She believed he'd rejected their child and made a mockery of their love. It upset Stanwell that she wouldn't accept his explanation that he was preoccupied by a cruel government stalking them. And that his immediate concern was for her safety, leaving him little room to truly grasp her good tidings.

So he returned to the way of his people, and prepared for Elsa a love letter—made from primitive colored beads.

Stanwell carefully harvested the beads from a family heirloom, a ceremonial loincloth of his mother's that she in turn had inherited from her *mayi*. His mother had thrust the rolled leather apron into his grasp as he set to leave Malawi for the City of Gold, and, with tears in her eyes, had wished him the blessings of his ancestors.

His message to Elsa would not be in words, but in colors. Stanwell patiently threaded tiny antique beads into a delicate necklace of such intricate design it belied his rugged, workman-like hands.

The beaded chain was predominantly yellow—the color of corn touched by the sun—and signified fertility and wealth. Hanging from the center was the rectangular "love letter"—a chevron of black and white beads trimmed with red and pink. The charcoal-black beads pledged marriage, the ivory white beads promised spiritual love, and the red beads—juicy-red like pomegranate seeds—vowed strong, physical love. But the single tier of pink beads, the color of Elsa's lips, was the most significant; these shiny little beads declared Stanwell's commitment to the birth of their child.

▶◀▶◀

Elsa accepted the uniquely crafted peace offering. She was touched by his handiwork, and the effort and thought he'd put into its creation. Happy tears rolled down her cheeks as Stanwell gently described the significance of each colored bead. At the moment he placed the necklace around her neck, Elsa's hand reached up for his, and then she turned to face him. Stanwell cupped her face in his hands—a bas-relief in ebony and alabaster—and held her close. No longer doubting his intent, Elsa raised her lips to his. Tenderly they kissed their sorrows away.

Impetuously Stanwell knelt at Elsa's feet. He placed his lips on her belly and kissed it. Then on his knees he began an earnest conversation with her tummy, whispering away in his mother tongue.

Elsa had never heard him speak the language of his people before. "What were you saying to our child?" she asked.

Stanwell first touched his fingers to his lips and then to hers. "Hush, I was speaking to our son," he said.

"A son! How do you know it's a boy?"

"I know," he said quietly.

Elsa saw the conviction in Stanwell's face; there was no doubt. She then knew it to be true. A trill of excitement coursed through her body. For the first time it was real; in her belly, created by their love, was their son. A boy destined to become a unique individual, a manifestation of the union of two great heritages, with skin a beautiful coffee hue. Such a child would be incapable of bigotry and tribalism.

"How could the white half of him hate his black half, or vice versa?" Elsa said softly to Stanwell. "He will be our wonderful gift to Africa."

As they gently affirmed their belief in each other, all was still except for music that filtered into the room from somewhere in the backyard. It was mesmerizing. The melody and rhythm remained steadfast, yet as the minutes passed, evocative layers of complexity were added. Both Elsa and Stanwell were fond of the recording, and knew it by the name "Mannenburg."

But the anguished cry of the saxophone soaring over the hypnotic strains of the keyboard meant something else, something hopeful for Elsa and Stanwell. This plaintive masterpiece by Dollar Brand was the birth of a wonderful new sound called Cape Jazz—a fusion of American jazz and local *Marabi* music from the District Six township—another unconventional, yet fruitful meld of two musical forms and cultural traditions.

◄►

It was dark—probably after midnight. Stanwell was already in motion. Something had alerted him, something rustling by the window. Then the barking started.

Elsa woke. "What is it?" she asked.

"It's Leo. He's barking outside our window."

"Ridgebacks don't really bark. Something must be wrong."

Stanwell, about to lunge through the door, stopped in his tracks. A fusillade of snarls and growls had replaced the barking; then a volley of frantic curses, "*Jy's 'n dood hond*! *Jy is 'n duiwel*!*" [You're a dead dog! You are the devil!], filled the night, followed by pounding footsteps and a thud as a body made hard contact with the fence, then he heard the desperate night caller scramble to safety.

Stanwell opened the door. A proud Leo—panting, salivating—stood with a trophy in his jaw. It was the ripped back pocket from a now tattered pair of jeans.

At daybreak, among the churn of muddied footprints they discovered an overstuffed man's wallet. Inside was the firearm license and driver's license of a certain Ulrich van Zyl. Elsa and Stanwell recognized the face; it was "Thick," one of the monsters who'd attempted to rape Elsa in the elevator.

Crass reality had forever invaded their discreet oasis. It was a chilling development. Stanwell hugged Elsa to his chest. Mal Zander's stooges were closing in. Yet still Stanwell couldn't bring himself to tell Elsa about his clash with the Security Branch operative. And he hoped he would never have to.

►◄ ►◄

Their spirits lifted with the monkey's wedding, the morning's sunshower, when nature indulged all creatures with the charming anomaly of simultaneous rain and bright sunshine. A shimmering rainbow bridged the Highveld sky from north to south in a prismatic display of colors. In this instance the rainbow did not belie leprechaun lore, as ample pots of gold undoubtedly filled the mine fields below. But for the workers underground, the sunshine was illusory, and the rain hampered their labors.

Elsa already missed Stanwell, and she hadn't even left yet. At the guesthouse door she lingered. They had grown accustomed to being a pair under the security of the Duncans' roof and Leo's watchful protection. Now separation promised to be painful.

Stanwell said he'd drive up to meet her on Saturday, at the end of his work week. And, with great certainty, pointing to the beaded necklace around Elsa's neck, he had reassured her he was always near. Then instinctively Elsa touched the "love letter" charm in warm response.

They both stepped outside, into the rain.

▶◀▶◀

Elsa paused for a moment, her attention caught by widening, then overlapping ripples from raindrops pitting the liquid surface of the swimming pool. Yes, change was constant, and she best put on a brave face. After all, it was her job tugging them apart. She was off on a safari shoot—no, not hunting game with big-bore rifles. This time she was the target. And photographer cameras were the weapon of choice.

Whipped up from one of Lydia's brainstorming sessions, it was decided a photo shoot at an exclusive safari lodge would emphasize both the uniqueness and authenticity of the Safari Èlan brand.

With ready access to South Africa's stunning, exotic wildlife, Elsa aside, the crew figured the animals would in effect become "celebrities." As an added bonus, wild animals never demanded appearance fees, royalties, or insisted on freshly cut arum lilies in their dressing rooms. Nor did these creatures need the pampering of makeup or require their hair blow-dried.

However, this didn't mean the animals behaved. It wouldn't do to have a glamorous model perfectly primped in picture frame, to only later discover two bristled, lump-faced warthogs rutting in the photograph's background. They were wild, after all.

Yet Lydia and her team decided to accept the risk, and set their sights on Indlovu Pan Lodge (Elephant Waterhole Lodge) in the Timbavati region on the western edge of the famous Kruger National Park. There were many splendid game reserves available to them, but only Timbavati offered something truly exceptional—the recently discovered white lions of Timbavati.

And the Safari Èlan creative team was on a quest to get a picture of a pair of these adorable white cubs nuzzling with Elsa. These beautiful creatures were not albino, for though their pelts were white, their eyes were naturally pigmented like their tawny cousins. It would be a stunning cover for a major international woman's magazine. To get that shot, and anticipating all other exigencies, Lydia had budgeted a full week for the shoot.

▶◀▶◀

Stanwell watched her go. He enjoyed watching her from behind. Her butt had a different strut from the familiar big-bottomed sway of local tribeswomen. Elsa glanced back at him fleetingly, swung her black duffel bag stuffed with pretty paraphernalia and intimates into the red Mini, then with a light toot of *adieu* on the horn, roared away.

With a sigh Stanwell climbed into his new company car, a silver Ford Cortina, waiting for him on the Duncans' driveway. It made little sense having the car when he lived in Soweto. It would've ended up a stripped skeleton. Since the riots, he'd never returned to his little corrugated shack. There had been no need. Whatever meager possessions he owned would've been looted in the aftermath of the insurrection.

No matter. He had a personal tribal schism to resolve at the warehouse and distribution center.

Stanwell had called a meeting of his black staff. If it was a neutral they wanted, well, he was their man, because he was a true outsider from Malawi with no allegiance to any local tribe—just like their former colonial masters and his predecessor, the Afrikaner in the corner office. If the color of his skin was the problem, Stanwell had one last gambit to play—humor. He intended to paint himself in whiteface and then insist his staff call him *Meneer van der Merwe*—all the while parodying the white man's stiff mannerisms—until his black colleagues realized their foolishness.

Stanwell hoped his plan would work. If he proved successful by solving the problem with logic and laughter, it would be a nice farewell gift for his departing mentor. Only then, with success at his back, would he make that solitary drive up to the Timbavati bush to meet Elsa. It would be a wonderful reward for both of them.

**

There is a truism in Africa: "Look to nature for life's lessons and answers." Despite our fractured human societies, we all share a sense of wonder, and joy, when we witness the improbable friendships struck between different breeds of creatures in the animal kingdom.

There are many instances of a variety of wild species forming symbiotic relationships in the African bush. As an example, the elegant zebra, the ugly wildebeest, and the ornery ostrich make an unlikely trio—one has poor eyesight, one bad hearing, and the other, a lousy sense of smell—but together as a team they constitute the perfect early alert system. They've learned that working together exponentially improves their chances of survival—as predators are repeatedly foiled.

Our trio set a wonderful example in allowing their shared instinct, the vital need to survive, to override their differences. When they set up their three-way alarm system, they didn't get hung up on clannish differences such as species, winged or four-legged, or the pattern on the other animal's hide. Only practical considerations shaped this life-saving interspecies relationship. Yet humans have failed miserably to achieve a similar level of common sense; despite our superior intellectual gifts. Somehow, as we got smarter common sense deserted us and we lost the base instinct to collaborate with others for the benefit of all. Instead we've become fixated on our differences, and as a result everyone has suffered.

As for the peoples of South Africa, despite their close proximity to nature's teachers, they've failed to heed the message. One wonders at the opportunities lost because the Boer, the Brit, and the Bantu—despite the fact their destinies were inexorably intertwined—were incapable of joining forces. Peculiarly, at some time in its past the Republic may have hoped for cooperation between its people, as the framers settled on the national motto "Ex Unitate Vires" ["Unity is Strength"].

So better we humans watch the zebra, wildebeest, and the ostrich. They have much to teach (and we have much to learn).

**

Elsa was just a child when she last visited the bush. She and Ma loaded into Pa's cream-colored Peugeot 404 for the long drive to Pretoriuskop Restcamp in the Kruger National Park. Her father loved that family sedan, despite its French pedigree. He often boasted it was the car that conquered Africa, with its simple, unbreakable four-cylinder engine and boxy exterior. He reminded everyone who'd listen that every traveling salesman worth his salt, selling wares from Cairo to Cape Town, drove a 404. Through her adult eyes, Elsa now realized that the car and her Pa were kindred spirits—the epitome of practical function over form, neither being particularly handsome but both surefooted, durable and a touch contrary.

That safari adventure so many years ago had been special. Elsa had pleaded to visit Pretoriuskop Restcamp, and her parents agreed once they understood the purpose. Most girls Elsa's age were infatuated with horses, and she had her dalliance with them, but her true love was dogs. One extraordinary dog in particular, Jock of the Bushveld, had captured Elsa's imagination. The trip was a pilgrimage to Jock's birthplace.

Jock had begun life as a feeble runt and was about to be drowned when future author Sir James Percy FitzPatrick saved him. Elsa was touched by the bond between the courageous Staffordshire bull terrier and his loyal master. And she was devastated by the unfair circumstances of Jock's untimely death. Yet, despite knowing the sad ending, Elsa insisted her parents retell Jock's story for her again and again. It was then that her parents realized their daughter had a heart for lost causes.

▸◂▸◂

Safari lodges come in a variety of flavors, from the five-star, air-conditioned variety so pampered that Le Majestic Grand Hotel in Cannes would've been considered primitive in comparison, to a crude tent furnished with a canvas cot and nothing else.

Happily, Indlovu Pan Lodge rested somewhere between. It offered the genuine experience with just a hint of danger. No fences, gates, or walls separated the lodge from the wild. In fact, the main sitting room and bar, with its high-thatched ceiling, safari chic décor, and massive wooden carvings, had one side permanently opened to the elements. This provided visitors with a comfortable viewing deck for the animal drinking hole no more than one hundred yards away.

A polite game-tracker boy guided Elsa to her thatched chalet. The queen-size bed stood on sisal-woven grass mats that covered part of the plain-sawn oak floor around the bed's base. The mattress itself was shrouded in fanciful netting draped from a ring in the ceiling. It appeared romantic, but Elsa knew it was foremost a critical barrier against the bloodsucking tsetse fly. Elsa had taken her mefloquine antimalaria tablets the week before, but she still intended to use the nets every night, at least to keep those pesky itchy *mozzies* away.

There was, however, an immediate mental adjustment Elsa needed to make. When she learned electricity use was limited, she hit crisis mode. It was silly, and maybe to others trivial, but as a model, not having a hair dryer was a problem. But she learned there was a camp generator used to refrigerate food and beverages, and she could plug into it in the main lodge.

Her chalet lighting, however, would be a naked flame in paraffin lanterns. Elsa then imagined the flickering glow across the walls at night, accompanied by the chuffing and yelps of strange creatures beyond, and she was both thrilled and fearful— and she wished Stanwell was by her side.

With the bed and power issues now settled, Elsa had one final concern—the bathroom. Please, anything but a crude hole-in-the-ground septic toilet and a poor excuse for a shower, with only one temperature—freezing.

Warily Elsa opened the bathroom door, and the first thing she saw was an ageless baobab tree. Beneath the magnificent tree was an alfresco shower, the stunning feature of a full bathroom en suite.

It was fair to say Elsa was over the moon about her surprisingly lavish safari bathroom, despite the absence of a 220-volt outlet for her hair dryer.

▶◀ ▶◀

The *boma* was a place of shelter and safety from both the elements and predators. A large fire crackled at the center of the reed-walled stockade as the stars overhead provided a ceiling of limitless possibilities.

The Safari Èlan crew had taken refuge from a brisk breeze within the circle of the boma; it had also been the venue for their outdoor dinner. Their bellies were now filled with delicious venison and apricot kabobs, or *sosaties*, braaied over open coals, a favorite Cape Malayan dish of curried minced meat slowly baked called *bobotie*, slices of pot bread, and the sweet custard pastry *melktert* for dessert.

It was a beaut night under the stars with the sparks from the fire flying into the sky, and a contented Elsa sipped at a small glass of KWV sherry. She had no interest in competing with the more robust drinkers in the group. One of the cameramen had already vowed "to get *vrot* on *donkie skop*" [get rotten on donkey kick] and had headed for the bar to get the *wit blitz*, or white lightning moonshine, with its distinctive bottle wrapped in coiled barbed wire.

Elsa was still inspired by the presentation given to the team earlier that evening. Lydia had made the obligatory welcoming speech, but it was the talented Francine Du Plessis who'd wowed them. She had pitched them the campaign's theme. It was pure, fresh, and easily captured in a single word: "blue."

The way Franny had presented it as a counterpoint to the gritty drab African scrub was brilliant, and she'd dazzled the creative and marketing team with images of azure skies and wildcat animal prints rendered in shades of denim.

From a nearby cassette player Franny provided the soundtrack for her vision, and as she spoke, Gershwin's *Rhapsody in Blue* teased at the senses. It was almost perfect, Elsa thought, until some drunken lout hidden in the shadows began singing the national anthem with a distinctive *gebreide* burr: "*Uit die blou van onse hemel...Uit die diepte van ons see...Ons sal lewe, ons sal sterrrwe...Ons virrr jou, Suid-Afrrrika!*" [From the blue of our heaven...From the depths of our sea...We will live, we will die...We for thee, South Africa!].

▶◀▶◀

The fifth day of the shoot had been exhausting. The lion cubs had been lovely, but Elsa was covered with scratches from their immature claws, and her hair was clotted with saliva from their affectionate chewing. Now it was a new day, but Elsa had already been up for hours. The wakeup call had been unseemly early. Apparently the sunrise was impatient, and the creative team had wanted the perfect picture. Having returned to camp, the camera crew was milling about waiting for brunch. Needing some solitude, Elsa parked herself at the wooden bench only thirty yards from the water pan. There she fell asleep.

Chomping, snorting grunts woke her. A family of warthogs grazed on grass tufts next to her, and she watched as they shuffled along on their front elbows with their tails straight high like radio antenna. Their tusks looked fearsome, razor-sharp, but curiously Elsa felt calm. She sensed they meant her no harm, and for the first time in months, she knew serenity.

Time filtered into midmorning and Elsa remained on that rustic wooden bench, a solitary figure. However, she was seldom alone, as many visitors were drawn to the water hole—mostly antelope and gazelle who flocked to the drink, reassured by the wind that no predators were about.

Nature's rich comedy put on a performance expressly for Elsa. She delighted in the lovely nip and dart of graceful impala, so plentiful they were regarded as "the fast food of the bush." She giggled at the *pronking* springbok as they bounded this way and that on their pogo-stick legs. Then the stately waterbuck drank its fill, only to leave a surprise when it turned, revealing a white ring resembling a toilet seat marked on its rump.

Soon a shy kudu took a bow, its magnificent spiraled horns almost inconsequential in comparison to its comically large ears. The kudu's wonderful hearing detected Elsa shuffling in her seat and the animal froze, momentarily threatened. Then its eyes found Elsa's, and for many seconds they stared at each other. When Elsa blinked first, the now reassured kudu began to cautiously drink.

Two zebra at that moment appeared, clearly a mating pair. Typical of the animal kingdom, it was he who was the most splendid. His stripes were jet black on a field of white, while hers faded to brown at the edges. However, the mare had a beguiling attribute of her own: her right ear perked straight up, whereas the left flopped to the side.

At first the stallion and mare faced each other, nostril to nostril, inhaling the other's breath. They then they twisted their necks about in a violent embrace. Eventually they calmed, moved forward a pace, and rested their muzzles on the other's back. They stood there, quietly contented, framed by the blue sky daubed with puffs of clouds.

Even the cackle of a predatory hyena in the near distance didn't daunt them.

Elsa sensed a presence behind her. Startled, she turned. Hovering so close that she could smell the stale alcohol on his breath, a burly man stood. He offered his hand. "Miss Ma*rrr*ais, I'm your g*rrrr*eatest fan," he said with a leer.

In the morning light Elsa barely could see his face under the heavy shadow of his brimmed hat—just a scrawny moustache and pig-like eyes floating above bloated jowls.

But the voice with its distinctive braying *r* Elsa recognized from that first evening in the boma. This was the drunken lout that sang *Die Stem* over Franny's presentation. Apparently alcohol unleashed both the man's speech flaw and his boorish behavior. Now a little afraid, Elsa felt it prudent to be polite. "Thank you, mister...Um, what's your name?" she asked.

"Malan Zander, but you must call me Mal."

"Do you work here?"

"*Ja*, security. You know, there are lots of poachers around," said Zander. "But don't worry, I'm keeping my eyes on you."

"Excuse me, hey, I'm really tired from this morning's early shoot. I need a nap." He's creepy, Elsa thought, giving an involuntary shudder as she turned to trek back to her chalet.

"Hold on," said Zander as he firmly gripped her elbow. "I can't let you go to bed without brunch, now can I?"

He then and there steered the protesting Elsa to the viewing deck adjoining the semi-outdoor dining area. Elsa tried to find Lydia, to please rescue her, but to no avail. She did see the camera crew, but they were clowning around too much—delighted by the early morning's work—that they missed her signal.

Other fellow travelers from as far as the United States, England, and Australia were enjoying some refreshments before the meal. Clearly they had no knowledge or interest in her plight, so Elsa didn't choose to impose.

They all stood in a semicircle around a man with hard-edged eyes and leathered skin creviced from the sun and the wind. It was their game ranger Dirk, and the throng was enraptured by his yarns from previous safari adventures.

Dirk was dressed head to toe in khaki, the sleeves of his shirt rolled up well above the crook of the elbows, and olive green epaulets on each shoulder. He didn't wear a watch but had an elephant-hair bracelet instead. The Sam Browne belt he wore, in the tradition of big game hunters, added to the aura of competence. But his grimed nails and dirt-smudged knees from tracking animal spoor showed his experience, as did the well-weathered *veldskoene* desert boots on his feet.

Elsa was struck by the contrast between Dirk and the poacher-security man. The latter had a farmer's tan showing through his too-tight shirt. And all his clothes seemed brand new; they still had the sheen and creases of a recent purchase. There was something fake about him. I need to keep my distance from that one, Elsa cautioned herself, though that was difficult to do as the oaf had attached himself to her like a limpet mine—hanging around, constantly at her side.

A middle-aged American, now talkative due to the generous lubrication of many beers, began to entertain the group with stories from the morning's daybreak game drive. "I don't mind admitting I was pissed off when I saw two youngsters would be joining us," he said. "I have no patience for whining brats. I say, better take them to Disneyland with its fake Jungle Cruise ride than this real wildlife adventure.

"But I must admit they did a good job. Sharp-eyed, too. On our drive this morning those kids spotted a massive Cape buffalo hiding in the brush right next to our Land Rover. Good thing, too. If they hadn't warned us, I would have had a heart attack when that monster lunged up at us."

An agreeable Australian bloke added, "At our coffee 'n cocoa break, well mate, it was my time for a wiz. What I found especially impressive about those two lads was the arc they made pissing at that termite mound. If only I could've splashed well beyond my boots today like they did." The amiable crowd, amused, chuckled at his expense.

Elsa had kept an ear trained on the many conversations about her, but a sudden bellow beside her instantly hushed the room. "*Jislaaik!* A *blerrie* tick bit me!" It was Mal Zander.

Now, Africa's full of strange things, like the dung beetle that rolls a large ball of crap to his beloved. But what Zander did was truly weird. He'd reached into his tight safari shorts and pulled out a handful of his scrotum—an ovoid mass of pale-veined flesh and matted hair—and began feverishly picking through his junk like a baboon scouring for fleas.

Elsa was stunned, as were those around her. She had the urge to do the girly thing and shriek in disgust. But instinct told her not to. Elsa doubted this public de-ticking was wise bushcraft. Instead she suspected Zander was attempting to intimidate and humiliate her. But why, she wondered.

But Zander had another surprise. He looked over Elsa's shoulder and yelled at a figure entering the room. "Around the back, boy! Where do you think you're going?" Then aloud to himself, "Lazy *kaffirs*...They're so *blerrie* stupid."

Elsa was appalled. The bond between game ranger and his partner, his game scout and tracker, is unlike any other black and white relationship in South Africa. It's forged by survival, shaped by skill, based on trust, and built on mutual respect—and countless hours of camaraderie in the bush.

Elsa turned to defend Dirk's game tracker from the insult.

A tall native-boy with a shining bald head and scarred face came toward her; it was Stanwell.

◄►

Seeing Elsa standing alongside Zander alarmed him. But Stanwell refused to panic, and by necessity a cool detachment enveloped him, as he knew any sign of fear would provoke the man. Zander was foremost a bully, and Stanwell refused to allow himself to be cast as a weakling. Calmly he approached the woman he loved and the man he hated. His purpose was to quietly extract Elsa from Zander's oppressive presence without creating a public incident.

Stanwell chose to improvise and for the second time in a week he was about to give a performance. His absurd caricature in whiteface had been a hit with the warehouse staff; but now the stakes were higher. Stanwell hoped for a similar outcome and so he slipped into the role of a servant.

The official gave him a long, suspicious look, then said, "What do you want, kaffir?"

Refusing to take the bait, Stanwell said, "*Verskoon my baas,*" [Excuse me boss] but I have a message for *juffrou* Elsa from madam Lydia."

"Then out with it, boy," sneered Zander.

Stanwell could see Elsa was visibly distraught by the abusive way he was been spoken to by the Boer. He looked reassuringly into her eyes. "Miss Elsa," he began.

"Yes, Stanwell."

"Madam Lydia instructed me to deliver some new clothes to you. I just brought them with me from Johannesburg." Confident he was more familiar with the fashion world than his nemesis, thanks to Elsa involvement, Stanwell continued. "She needs you to try them on now-now…she's worried they won't fit and may need to be altered before your next shoot."

"Okay, sure, where are these clothes?"

"They're being held for you at the lodge's front desk. Madam, please will you follow me."

▶◀▶◀

Initially they spoke of other things. He told her of his journey up from Johannesburg. About the kindly *toppie*–the old man who brought him tea in a chipped cup on the verandah steps of a whites-only café. About the wily creativity of black folks he passed on the road: wood carvings of birds and animals divined from the shape of the original tree bough, and a trio of musicians and their homemade instruments—the tea crate and broom handle stand-up bass with the strings made from twine and fishing line, the five-liter Castrol oil can township electric guitar, and a drum kit assembled from sundry boxes, plastic pails, and zinc buckets.

He told her about the ingenious modes of transport of the poor—a donkey cart hauled by two donkeys, but the cart itself being the cutoff rear-end of an old green Toyota pickup truck.

He then told her of his fatigue. How the bone-rattling drive across the washboard-ridged dirt road over the last five miles was the most difficult. And his relief when he saw the white-painted tires planted on either side of the driveway as he drove up to the lodge's entrance. And his absolute joy when he saw her. And his big fright when he saw her companion.

Only then did Stanwell tell Elsa about his past confrontations with the Security Branch official, the crazy "Mal" Zander.

▶◀▶◀

CHAPTER **TWENTY-EIGHT**

A HOT WIND SWEPT IN from the Kalahari Desert, making skin prickle with beads of sweat and parching nostrils dry. The midday sun added to the stifling heat. The animals, predator and prey alike, used their ebbing energy to seek refuge in the shadows of flat-crowned acacia trees and scrub vegetation. With animals hidden from view, sensible humans indulged their lethargic impulses at the game lodge, sipping refreshments by the pool or retiring to their chalets for a nap.

Both humans and animals had a shared desire: to wait for the onset of the cooling evening breeze. Only then would wildlife come out to drink—and to eat, the carnivores purposefully culling the weakest from the herds, with the rest hoping fate would allow them to eat grass, leaves, and insects in peace. And that's the time humans eager for the prowl, wearing khaki-olive safari vests stuffed with canisters of thirty-five millimeter film to feed their voracious cameras, gather at their resolute four-by-four Land Rovers.

Expectations for the night drive were high; a pride of lions had been spotted in the vicinity. The objective was clear: to track down Africa's Big Five—the elephant, leopard, Cape buffalo, black rhino, and of course, lion. The guests' excitement and anticipation elevated with the arrival of ranger Dirk and Mzila, his Shangaan tracker. It was the sight of his .375 Holland & Holland Magnum rifle, however, that briefly tamped down the mood. This was serious business and a real adventure; if a crisis presented itself, Dirk's weapon was the instrument of last resort. Quietly all hoped it had the capacity to take down the largest game.

▶◀▶◀

"*Sawubona, nkosi*" [I see you, chief]. Stanwell was surprised by the respectful greeting—that given to a superior—he received from Mzila the Shangaan. He felt it unearned. They were both Bantu and equals in the basement of the social order. In fact, out here in the veld, the game tracker was the master and he the student.

Mzila guided Stanwell to the rear of the four-wheel drive vehicle. Stanwell began to object, wanting to sit protectively by Elsa's side. But he appreciated his new friend's wisdom when Mzila pointed out Zander's malevolent glare—the man had insisted in inserting himself in the group—challenging them to do something foolish. So Elsa sat cosseted between Lydia and Franny for safety instead.

For Stanwell, his ride was a bracketed metal seat welded to the back of the Land Rover's tailgate. It was both uncomfortable and precarious, so Stanwell didn't protest when Mzila strapped him in place with a well-worn leather belt. But there was no brace for his feet, so they dangled in space.

The Shangaan joined Dirk up front. The game ranger and tracker communicated with monosyllabic clicks, grunts, and subtle gestures. With the itinerary settled, they were off in a cloud of diesel smoke—the dusk drive into night had begun.

Travelling backward was disorienting. Stanwell felt the dirt road's potholes, runnels, and ridges before he saw them disappear in a haze of dust. On the other hand, as the only person facing that direction, he was the last to see the turmeric to saffron hues of the setting sun. With the sun's departure, everyone felt a new chill in the air as the road disappeared into the twilight.

Stanwell heard the *bok-bok-kie* duet call of two *Bokmakieries*. In vain he searched the trees above in the hope of seeing their bold black throats and gray-green, bright yellow plumage. He appreciated them. He knew these bushrike partners were dedicated to each other for life.

Occasionally Mzila would spring from the vehicle to inspect game tracks invisible to all but him—the scat of a big cat, a tuft of fur on a thorn, a broken branch, a hoof print imbedded in the earth—and then he'd gesture to his partner. Dirk steered the Land Rover wherever the spoor led them, even off into the thick brush. The four-wheel drive vehicle went wherever Dirk aimed, scything down saplings and tall grass in the best tradition of what locals call "bundu-bashing."

Branches slapped and thorns scraped the sides of the vehicle before Stanwell saw them, sometimes forcing him to duck a whipped-back limb. And so they ploughed deeper into the undergrowth, Dirk determined to find a pair of bashful rhino— for some the earthly manifestation of the mystical unicorn— before they wandered into the unknown.

Unexpectedly the Land Rover lurched nose-first into a *donga*. It was a dry river bed. The rugged vehicle forged ahead and attempted to scurry up the steep-sided far bank. Dirk revved the engine but rocks, stones, and a shower of river sand gave way under the pair of spinning wheels. Traction was lost and they weren't going anywhere.

Stanwell found himself hanging face down, held in place only by the leather strap. He sensed rather than saw movement in a thicket of cattails. Then from out of the riparian undergrowth stepped a lioness. She stood there, the length of a single leap from him.

Their eyes locked and time slowed. Stanwell felt the surge of adrenaline course through his body. As for the big cat facing him, she appeared most curious. Stanwell knew this because she tilted her head inquisitively to the side as she watched him. He watched her too. Stanwell noticed the beard of whiskers under her mouth was lighter than the tawny tan of the rest of her coat, and this gave her a natural air of wisdom. He also saw the old fight scar below her right eye, and her sharp, retractable claws. Yet he remained unafraid because he understood it to be a gift, especially for him, as none of his fellow travelers had turned in their seats to look.

Dirk cursed, remembering the vehicle wasn't in four-wheel drive mode, then shifted the transfer gearbox and punched the throttle; the Land Rover comfortably crested the ridge and the moment was gone.

They came around a mopane thicket and found themselves in the midst of a Cape buffalo herd. Unpredictable and stubbornly fearless, these one-ton behemoths refused to give the tourists right of way. Two young males sparred close by; the massive boss of their horns an impenetrable shield as they twisted and thrust, the one seeking weakness in the other. There was none, and they soon retreated to their corners, panting.

Two old bulls, their noses heavily coated with mucous, edged closer to the off-road vehicle. Unhurriedly Dirk reached for his rifle. He confirmed a round was chambered and the weapon ready. A nervous tension rippled through the guests. Dirk raised his finger to his lips, giving a quiet hush.

Then Elsa did something quite extraordinary, or rather imprudent. It was a childish prank that hailed back to the times she'd spy a dairy cow from the backseat of the family sedan. Now in the Land Rover, surrounded by dozens of Africa's largest man-killing bovine, Elsa took a deep breath and bellowed "Mooooo!" Startled silence—then the earth shook as the herd of buffalo stampeded away.

The Aussie had the final word. "Young lady, thank goodness you didn't yell out the buffalo mating call!"

▸◂▸

The devastation was mindboggling. What was once a forest was now a tortured landscape of shattered limbs and uprooted tree trunks. It was as if a petulant colossus, in a fit of poor sportsmanship after a gigantic game of pick-up sticks, had tossed them back to earth and ground them underfoot. Only a solitary tree stood.

Dirk explained it was the handiwork of the *indlovu*—the elephant. And those trees were unfortunate because their bark was an elephant's favorite meal; sadly, by stripping the bark around the full circumference of a tree, the elephants killed it.

The uprooted trees were another matter. Sometimes they experienced catastrophic failure as elephant back scratchers. Often the rich green tasty foliage was too high to reach for the animals, so the trees were toppled as a price for nourishment. And then there were the indolent teenagers who tested their might with willful acts of destruction.

To the game ranger, the elephant was the "most human" of all the animals, with similar traits both good and bad. They were nurturing, loyal, intelligent, and rambunctious, and sometimes funny, but like humans, prone to anger, too. As if on cue, a herd of elephants arrived in an adjacent clearing. Their entrance had been surprising, despite their weighty bulk. As they walked, they appeared to be on their tippy toes; they were funny, and the crew in the Land Rover chuckled at what they saw.

Then something unremarkable, yet worth noting, occurred. It suggested a special symbiotic relationship between human and pachyderm—a bond wherein they watched us, understood us, and wished to please us.

The herd of elephants lined up (there were thirteen of them) and then turned to face the tourists. There they stood shoulder to shoulder, gently shifting from side to side. A matriarch irritably nudged a youngster in line with the whip of her trunk. An adolescent swayed sullenly with his trunk resting on a tusk. A baby stood protectively under its mother's belly. Then the patriarch flared his ears for dramatic effect.

Instantly flashes popped and cameras clicked. Then, with the family portrait taken, the herd turned and disappeared into the brush.

Elsa, Stanwell, and the others were now one hour into their trek—there were still two more hours to go.

They first heard the cries. They were ear-piercingly frantic. This unnerved the bush visitors, more so because of the darkness of the night. With only the Land Rover's headlights and a handheld spotlight to guide them, they tracked the distressed animal. They found her. It was Elsa's zebra mare. Elsa instantly recognized her distinctive ears—one ear up and the other down to the side.

The mare thrashed about in despair. She was bleating and pleading for the life of her mate. The terrified screeches of the zebra weren't like the nicker, neigh, or whinny of a horse; rather, they were similar to the "yip-yip" yelps of wild dogs. Though the zebra mare's desperate calls upset the visitors, it also whetted their appetite for the kill. Enthusiastically they challenged Dirk to find the missing stallion.

More cautiously now, they edged deeper into the densely thick underbrush.

The lack of light pollution from the big cities made the heavens pitch black, taking away the perspective of depth, and creating the illusion that space's vacuum was just overhead. Within this setting the brightly, luminous shower of stars known as the Milky Way appeared inches beyond a human's grasp, and the Southern Cross teased as if almost within reach. It was the perfect night sky for adventure and a journey of discovery.

At the critical moment of the hunt, the Land Rover's left rear tire burst, and in the safari group's imagination, visions ran rampant of being stranded overnight, surrounded by wild animals baying for their blood. In quiet desperation they all looked to Dirk for help. To their astonishment, the game ranger coolly announced a refreshment stop.

"Do I have some *bledie lekker grub* for you lot," Dirk said, and calmly unfolded a camping table. He began stocking it with beers and *cooldrinks*, chilled, some fine local wine, and a variety of snacks including cured, dried game *biltong*. As the party enjoyed their refreshments, especially Zander—he was engrossed guzzling the liquor—Mzila the tracker with Stanwell's help efficiently replaced the damaged tire without further fuss.

The distracted Security agent failed to notice Stanwell speaking in hushed tones to Mzila as they worked. If he had, he may have detected the state of intrigue between the two black men: the Shangaan had news for Stanwell. Before the game drive he'd overheard Zander reporting to a superior on the phone in the lodge's front office. The conversation was brief, and Mzila picked up only fragments of what was said, something about "the *kaffir* and his *kaffir-boetie* were both here...yes, they're together...no problem, it will be dealt with in the bush." Mzila cautioned Stanwell to be very careful. Stanwell then asked the Shangaan to be his eyes and ears, and please keep a close watch on the dangerous white man.

▶◀▶◀

Before they continued their adventure, Dirk suggested it was a good time to take a "potty break." Elsa accepted the invitation and hurried behind a discreet thicket, hitching up her skirt. Only then did it dawn on her that it could be hazardous, with countless creatures that stung or bite taking refuge under that very same bush, and for a moment the thought stalled her bladder. But when she finished, having survived the moment, Elsa found the moment thrilling—the notion of peeing on a spot where no human had ever peed before was to her very adventurous and strangely profound.

▶◀▶◀

Finally, they found the lion pride feeding off the missing zebra stallion. Content with their fresh kill, the lions ignored the Land Rover and its human passengers when it drew close.

Though two lionesses had made the kill, the male lion insisted on first dibs. With his dark mane framing his muzzle, he clamped his jaws around the throat of the hapless zebra and began dragging it behind a bush. A massive brawl ensued as the lionesses, with three cubs gamely clinging on, tugged in the opposite direction.

The dispute was settled in a cloud of churned dust accompanied with vicious growls, howls, and roars. With a low grumble the large lion disappeared with the bulk of the prey, the carcass's white ribs jutting starkly from its grisly entrails. Left in its wake stood a single lion cub. The cub had a self-satisfied expression on its face—clenched in its jaw was the black and white fetlock of the adult zebra.

The little critter's jowls were coated with gore, and its tawny coat, still bearing the spots of youth, was splattered with blood. From the exposed position of the open Land Rover, this dinnertime squabble had been a harrowing display of naked aggression.

For Elsa, she only felt revulsion. Only a few days before she'd playfully romped about for the cameras with some adorable lion cubs. After witnessing the savagery of these untamed creatures, she'd lost her desire for an encore performance with those maybe-not-so-cute cubs.

A stench drifted downwind as the big cats fought over the offal from the zebra's ruptured intestines. It stunk terribly, and some of the onlookers began to retch. It was time to leave.

There was now one hour to go before they returned to the safety of the lodge.

The drive back to camp was uneventful despite the heightened chill in the night air. Most of the safari adventurers were now happily exhausted after hours of constant vigilance. They'd seen plenty thanks to the teamwork and bushcraft of Dirk and Mzila. In whispered tones the sightseers revisited the evening's breathtaking encounters they'd witnessed together; some of them promised to exchange addresses and trade photographs. These shared experiences now bound onetime strangers into a bush-veld fellowship. Searching for warmth, they instinctively moved closer to one another, except for Stanwell, stranded and solitary, facing backward on his cold metal seat.

The headlights of the Land Rover picked out the eyeshine, the reflected glow, of countless wide-eyed creatures going about their nocturnal rounds. Then a single eye, shining bright, was spied by the tracker. Mzila swept over the animal with his spotlight; it was a male leopard, blinded in one eye as the result of a thwarted skirmish with a porcupine.

The animal was cagey and resisted Dirk's efforts to follow it to its lair. It had already made its kill and had no intention of revealing its larder. Dirk assumed the leopard had hidden the remains up in the crook of a tree nearby. But no matter—seeing the solitary leopard brought the game drive to a successful conclusion; it was the last item to be checked off everyone's Big Five game list.

Their hunt was finally over.

◄►◄►

CHAPTER **TWENTY-NINE**

ELSA NEEDED TO BATHE, considering that every pore on her lovely face had been powdered and grimed by the night's trek. She wasn't complaining. She loved the contrast—riding in a bumpy Land Rover one moment, then luxuriating in her chalet's splendid bathtub the next, was to her the essence of vitality. There was also a more dramatic consideration. It was the Safari Èlan crew's final evening, and Elsa, as the face of the fashion line, intended her entrance into the boma for the candlelit dinner to be spectacular.

Stanwell had already gone on ahead. He had a brief detour to make—the Lodge's staff quarters, to speak to his new friend, Mzila. Stanwell felt he owed the tracker a detailed explanation of the desperate situation he and Elsa faced due to Zander's treachery. Mzila had willingly volunteered to help, but Stanwell wanted to give the Shangaan an opportunity to back out, if with full knowledge he found the task too hazardous.

When the other guests gathered for drinks before dinner, Elsa excused herself to prepare for their last evening's revelry. As she entered her chalet, she failed to notice the dark figure lurking under the thatched eves of an adjoining bungalow.

As Elsa ran her bath, there was a knock on the bathroom door. Elsa smiled to herself. It was so typical of Stanwell's modesty—silly, really, considering he'd often seen her naked. "Come in!" she called cheerfully.

Another knock, more persistent this time.

Slightly irritated, Elsa drew her robe tighter and opened the door. Her irritation switched to terror in an instant. There stood Zander; his opened shirt exposed his bloated hirsute chest, more creature-like than human. But the man's fleshy face revealed much more—it was flooded with lust and rage.

Clearly drunk, Zander shoved Elsa. As she stumbled back, he raged, "We Af*rrrr*ikane*rrr*s have to stick togethe*rrr*!" Then, in spite, he ripped the beaded necklace from Elsa's throat. The beads fell with a *tik-tik-tik* as they hit the floor, and a rainbow of miniature globes scattered in all directions across the length and breadth of the lavish bathroom.

Elsa wept. Through the tears she saw the chaotic scattering of Stanwell's tender "love letter." It was a soul-searing loss, as if each bead embodied a feeling she shared with Stanwell. And as the beads disappeared into the shadows, Elsa felt her connection to Stanwell wither away, piece by piece.

But this was only Zander's first salvo. He gripped a handful of Elsa's hair and plunged her headfirst into the bathtub. Her scream choked off in a stream of bubbles the moment her face hit the hot water. Elsa struggled beneath the government agent's grip, frantic to once again fill her lungs with air.

Then Elsa felt the pressure relent, and he jerked her from the water's grasp. But this respite wasn't an act of compassion; Elsa was of no use to Zander drowned.

With the immense mass of his body, Zander forcefully pinned Elsa to the side of the tub as his hands tore at the tie holding her robe in place. His eyes bulged, his nostrils flared, and his lower lip drooped in palsied frenzy. In a choked voice Zander hissed, "Don't scream...or I'll *frikken* drown you."

Elsa needed a weapon. She scanned the room and spotted a trail of beads that had bumped up against a *shongololo*. Despite her dire predicament, or because of it, Elsa feared for the safety of the millipede and willed the *gogga* away from the scene of her desperate struggle.

As if sensing it was Elsa's last wish, the millipede unwound itself and began its inexorable march toward the nether regions under the bathroom vanity.

Now Elsa was ready to fight. She clawed at Zander's forearms, his face, and his eyes—determined to survive. Unable to check Elsa's counterattack, Zander cowardly flipped her over. Choking in bathwater and fear, Elsa thrashed about to right herself, her underwater screams a burble of froth. Instinctively her legs flailed in the air as her hands struggled to find secure purchase in the slippery bathtub.

Again Zander, with his pudgy hands firmly clamped around her throat, lifted Elsa out of the water, then dunked her deeper. He sadistically repeated the pattern, adding to Elsa's anguish—not knowing when or how it would it end.

But each time Elsa surfaced, she scrabbled for a weapon—something, anything. Soaps and shampoo bottles scattered about. As she surfaced for what could be the final time, Elsa reached down and felt the fringe of the bath mat. Firmly she grasped it.

Then, with the strength of her lioness namesake, Elsa "Kat" Marais sharply jerked the mat upward.

Instantly the pressure against her body eased as the thug staggered back against the wall. A spluttering Elsa regained her footing. Bruised and drenched, and terrified, Elsa took a deep breath, and then she pleaded—not for her own life, but for the life of her baby.

Hearing her utter those words eviscerated any carnal desire in the beast; it outraged him instead. In Zander's cold rage, his only urge now was Elsa's violent destruction.

His fist a cudgel, Mal Zander lashed out. From the force of the blow Elsa stumbled back and fell into the bathtub. With a sickening thud her head struck the faucet, leaving her body twisted, lying partially in the tub.

Mal Zander peered down at her still form as dark blood began to seep from beneath Elsa's hairline and drip into the tub's soapy water. Not for a moment did he feel remorse for the two innocent lives lost.

He saw himself only in heroic terms as the champion of his people. After all, he, Mal Zander, had saved the nation from major embarrassment. When his superiors learned of the coloured child in the girl's stomach, he'd be vindicated—and suitably rewarded. In his delusion Zander failed to realize how ludicrous he looked, standing over the lifeless woman, with trousers knotted around his ankles and his pale, flabby thighs exposed to the world.

Zander knew he was doomed the moment the bathroom door flung open. The Security Branch agent couldn't avoid Stanwell's lunge with his feet still trapped by his pants. Unable to flee the enraged black man in the confined quarters of the bathroom he was quickly cornered—it was no contest. Once again Zander felt Stanwell's iron grip, but this time it was clamped around his throat. Then he felt himself being lifted—almost effortlessly. As the Bantu named Stanwell had him suspended in air, by the neck, Zander became aware that his feet had lost contact with the ground, and that his shoes dangled pathetically at the end of his mismatched shorty socks.

Stanwell's eyes were blackened charcoal. He intended to destroy this vermin. There was nothing to be said, no last wishes or words—just revenge by crushing this *rock spider*'s larynx. As Stanwell squeezed tighter, he watched with great fascination as Zander's face turn darker shades of purple, and then the man's gob opened, revealing a gravely distended tongue.

It wasn't a quick death, giving Zander time for reflection, and what he considered didn't give him a smidgeon of relief: he was meant to be the master, yet his lasting legacy would be his death by the hand of a common *kaffir*.

Zander had now taken his last breath. His ears filled with the roar of blood as his starved lungs quivered with pain. His sight was the next to go. With his vision blurred, Zander noticed fluorescent-orange nail polish on the toes of a glorious pair of woman's legs dangling over the edge of the bathtub. For an instant he saw the toes on the woman's right foot move, and that would be the last cogent thought Malan "Mal" Zander would ever have. The Security Branch official's chest had pounded out its final beat.

There Stanwell stood, lost in his loss. In shock his body trembled. Yet his eyes remained dry. He couldn't shed a tear while that manifestation of dark hatred lay lifeless beside her. Stanwell had one final task. He must take Elsa from this evil place; only then would he weep for her, for him, and their lost baby.

Gently Stanwell reached for Elsa in the bathtub—she looked so uncomfortable there. But due to her deadweight and as a consequence of the mortal struggle he'd just endured, Stanwell found it a challenge to get to his feet. There he remained, crouched at her side, talking to her and speaking to himself. Finally he mustered up his strength, and with Elsa securely in his arms, Stanwell stepped over the slumped corpse of their tormenter and headed for the bedroom, leaving a trail of watery, bloodied soup from Elsa's soaked hair dripping behind him.

On entering the bedroom, Stanwell saw the beautiful bed shrouded in the mosquito netting. But being humble and unaccustomed to something so splendid, Stanwell couldn't spoil the bed with Elsa's blood, and so he laid her body on the plain-sawn oak floor. For a time he gazed at her, touching her robe carefully in place, and then silently he said his goodbye.

Now the tears came—and so did the guilt. He remembered the bleeding bird—the wallpaper in the Duncans' bathroom spoiled with his blood. He remembered the Bowie girl who thought she could fly—her blood spilled on the ground beneath the skyscraper from which she'd leapt. He remembered his vision—the wake of vultures pissing on their feet within the bloody entrails of the Boer's carcass.

And then Stanwell realized he'd been granted the power to change their destiny; therefore her death was his failing. But selfishly he'd ignored the prescient wisdom of his people, because the thought of losing Elsa had been too difficult to contemplate. He shuddered with remorse.

▶◀▶◀

CHAPTER **THIRTY**

STANWELL FELT HOLLOW, abandoned. Elsa was gone, and with her went their son. Numbed, Stanwell rummaged through Elsa's handbag and found what he was seeking. He fastidiously toggled off the safety catch, and used the Smith & Wesson double-action pistol for the first and last time.

The impact was sudden, shocking, and bloody bewildering. He should have anticipated it—after all, he'd pulled the trigger; but one doesn't gain much prior experience in regard to committing suicide.

Stanwell's senses were in overdrive. He desperately struggled to process the rank trauma inflicted upon his skull. This was an insurmountable task, as the more he struggled for clarity, the more his cognitive abilities inexorably ebbed away, as blood and extracellular brain fluid seeped out of the hair-matted gash ripped in his skull.

But Stanwell refused to concede; he persevered in trying to make sense of it all. Had he heard the percussion of the bullet as it exited the chamber? Had he smelled the acrid whiff of cordite expelled with the spent casing? Had he felt the violent torque of the firearm as it kicked in his hand? No, nothing. The more distant the event, the more atrophied his memory.

Some base cognitive sense within him recalled the bullet's impact (did it hurt?). But any latent awareness had been short-circuited by the blast, leaving him in a state of dwindling bewilderment, though he thought he dimly recollected his body hitting the floor.

The hardwood floor was scraped and timeworn. Miniature tumbleweeds of animal hair and lint dotted the floor-scape. All this he could see as his only functioning eye (the left) hovered an inch above the floorboards, supported by his flattened, bruising cheek.

With dying fascination he witnessed his blood navigate its way across the plain-sawn cut of the oak floor, tracking along the variegated grain patterns, growth rings, and knots. He was intrigued to see his blood meet, meld and pool in a shared puddle with blood from another source.

His single eye searched for the other source of blood, and finally he saw the blood seeping from beneath the girl's wet hair. Fascinated, he watched her blood track through the cracks and fissures of the hardwood floor toward him, to bind with his in a final liquescent embrace.

Yes, Stanwell Marunda's last taunting memory was the fact that his blood was the identical rich, red claret color as the girl's that lay beside him.

◄►

Far away under the New Moon, the *iSangoma*—the one with psychic gifts and diviner of futures—breathed into her worn leather pouch. The pouch held several items: dried chicken bones, semiprecious stones, and a couple of large seeds. With a stick the *iSangoma* scratched some hash marks into the dry earth. Then she tossed the contents of her bag over her scratchings. A dried chicken leg and the small bone from a chicken's foot fell outside the square; but the blood-red jasper stone fell within the hash marks. A moment later, a larger chicken leg and seed joined it.

The *iSangoma* screeched in despair. The first chicken leg represented the woman, and the chicken's tiny foot bone was the child. Both their futures were still in doubt. The red jasper predicted all that was evil, and the larger chicken leg was Stanwell, the man fated for death.

As for the seed...It spoke for the wisdom of the elders, and all their warnings that went unheeded.

▶◀▶◀

PART **THREE**

CODA

"In a tribal organization, even in time of peace, service to tribe or state predominates over all self-seeking; in war, service for the tribe or state becomes supreme, and personal liberty is suspended."

Sir Arthur Keith

≈

CHAPTER **THIRTY-ONE**

STANWELL'S FATAL SHOT saved Elsa's life. The loud report of the nine-millimeter bullet as it entered his brain brought everyone racing to the lodge. A housekeeper, the first person to enter the room, discovered the powerful black man ("He had the physique of a warrior," she later told the authorities) lying on the floor with his head near that of a stunning white woman—their hands lay just inches away, as if they had both attempted to reach the other for a final embrace.

What the housekeeper found most striking was the blood above their heads had merged together into a single crimson pool, looking "kinda like one of those speech bubbles in a comic book...just really-really red," in her words. She didn't pause to check Stanwell for signs of life—the nature of his self-inflicted wound being too awful—but headed directly for the beautiful girl with the serene face.

Except for the halo of blood beyond her hair, Elsa had no apparent sign of trauma. The housekeeper reached over and felt for the pulse on Elsa's throat. She was still alive.

Dirk was at the wheel of the Land Rover going way too fast. He didn't like this as he was violating a self-imposed curfew imposed after the last game drive, as poachers were now about, and he had little interest in a midnight firefight. However, the set of the game ranger's brow and the steeled look in his eyes showed his determination. He was prepared to break the limits of both speed and common sense on this emergency dash.

Time was vital. The injured girl was bleeding profusely from the head gash, despite Lydia's valiant efforts to stem the flow. She held Elsa's head on her lap, elevated, and did her best to maintain pressure on the wound, all the more difficult due to the incessant drubbing felt in the vehicle's cab as it lurched over the primitive road—more a trail or a path.

Without street lighting, road signs, reflective markers, or even white-painted rocks demarcating the road's edge, it was already a crapshoot, but the constant threat of an antelope or gazelle leaping into their pathway made it a perilous game of chance. After two nail-biting hours over rough, unlit terrain—swerving to avoid nocturnal creatures on their rounds—the Land Rover pulled up at the Nelspruit hospital's emergency entrance.

◄►◄

Lydia remained at Elsa's side throughout—except during surgery. Afterward the doctors filled her in on the details; Elsa had suffered a compound skull fracture, all the more complicated by broken skin around the opened gash.

Fortunately they were able to return the bone fragment to its original position with the help of some wire. As alarming as that sounded, the bone was expected to heal on its own. Any concerns of bacterial infection from the open wound would be dealt with by antibiotics.

Lydia was instructed to get some sleep in an adjoining empty ward, as Elsa was being closely monitored in the ICU, and it was best that Lydia was well-rested to help with her friend's hopeful recuperation. As Lydia headed down the red-striped passageway, the doctor caught up with her and said, "By the way, we've placed Elsa on a ventilator. We believe the oxygen-enriched air will help her—and the baby—quickly recover." At this news, tears streamed down Lydia's cheeks; despite Elsa's harrowing struggle for survival, her and Stanwell's baby was never harmed.

▶◀▶◀

Only later, a corpse with ludicrous pale legs, purple face, bulging eyes, and protruding tongue was found trapped behind the chalet's bathroom door. The authorities carted away the body with little ceremony.

▶◀▶◀

Mzila, the Shangaan, mourned in the way of his people for his new friend Stanwell Marunda, the man from faraway Malawi, a proud member of the Angoni tribe.

▶◀▶◀

Lydia dreaded the task. It fell on her to inform Elsa about Stanwell's death. And so she did. Despite Lydia's sincere efforts nothing could protect Elsa from the pain and sadness when she received the terrible news. So Lydia found herself to be nothing more than a useless bystander as she witnessed Elsa—feeling overwhelmed and isolated—mourn for Stanwell with gut-wrenching anguish.

Then the doctors summoned Lydia. They were concerned. Elsa's recovery was slower than anticipated, possibly jeopardizing both her and the baby's long term health, and nothing more could be done for her physically. The doctors were uncomfortable criticizing a patient's emotional state, but they felt Elsa's intense grief had hampered her recovery. They pleaded with Lydia for help.

A distraught Lydia walked slowly to Elsa's hospital ward. She needed a solution, or maybe an inspiration, to lift the burden the doctors' had placed on her shoulders. She thought of Elsa's life without Stanwell, and then she thought of Elsa's life *with* their baby.

Lydia balanced herself on the edge of the Elsa's hospital bed with its crisp, starched sheets and gently held the young woman's hand. With a voice so quiet and tender that it commanded Elsa's full attention, Lydia said, "Elsa sweetie, your life's still so precious because there is still a precious life inside your belly. And I know you're missing Stanwell terribly. But, when your child is born you will look at his adorable face, and in that cute face you will see Stanwell's—and he'll remain with you for the rest of your living days."

►◄►◄

Stanwell's mentor, boss, and friend, Daniel Gideon Firth, had one final duty before leaving South Africa forever. The disposition of Stanwell's remains had become a bureaucratic nightmare; there was no local family to contact, and Elsa's opinion was never sought.

As Stanwell's employer DGF had standing in the eyes of the authorities and claimed the body, not wishing his man's final resting place to be nothing more than an unkempt, nonwhite potter's field.

DGF recalled Stanwell's reluctance to leave South Africa despite the perils he faced. Stanwell had justified his decision to stand his ground and face his enemies head-on, because of the purity of his belief that the dust of Africa ran within his veins. This was a conviction DGF intended to honor—sadly, belatedly.

And so DGF respectfully had Stanwell's remains cremated. Daniel Firth didn't do this duty alone, and together with Elsa, Juliette, and the Duncans, they tossed Stanwell's ashes toward the heavens. Leo stood alongside Elsa with his tail still—showing none of his usual exuberance—as if he understood the gravity of the occasion. For a moment the mountain winds, always blowing seaward, lifted Stanwell's ashes toward the Indian Ocean; then, as in tribute to the warrior fallen, the winds subsided and returned his ashes back to earth's dust—the dust of Africa.

◄►◄►

On the twenty-eighth of February, 1977, Stanwell and Elsa's son was born. It was a *Blou Maandag*—a blue Monday. In South Africa every Monday was considered "blue," a chronic postweekend depression that plagued the nation. But for Elsa this particular Monday was a celebration.

Fittingly, Dr. Malcom Weitz presided over the delivery. A debate had raged over whether a coloured child, born to a white woman, should go to a maternity ward for whites or for blacks. Once again the good doctor came to the rescue and volunteered his medical office for the happy event—saving embarrassment to all by providing a neutral venue.

It was a swift affair, indicative of the little fellow's enthusiasm to get on with his life, and in the process he thoughtfully spared his mother countless hours of painful labor. At birth the child weighed in at a perfectly normal seven pounds, six ounces. His skin was slightly wrinkled, but had a radiant caramel hue. And despite being an infant, the boy already had more hair than his father.

Elsa and her son remained under the kind patronage of the Duncans. Annually the two of them received a generous bursary from the Firths, intended for the child's education and other needs. The birth of a grandchild does wonders. With Elsa's pa taking the initiative, the old folks had already reconciled with their daughter by the time their grandson was old enough to recognize them.

From his father's people in Malawi, there was silence; but no malice was attached to this, as all attempts to notify them of Stanwell's death had failed, so it was equally impossible to tell them of the birth of Stanwell's son.

At a quiet ceremony the baby was named Stanwell Daniel Sidney Marais. But it was considered too adult for such a small chap, as a result they now affectionately nicknamed him "Little Simba" instead. Nanny Rose attended the christening ceremony, and in time she became Little Simba's *Groot Tante Rose* [Great Aunt Rose].

In another exciting family development, Nanny Rose's prodigal son returned—a hero. Thabo became a favored uncle, and regaled the boy with vivid tales of his adventures as a freedom fighter in the armed struggle for liberation. With Elsa's blessing, Great Aunt Rose and Thabo instilled in young Stanwell many of the traditions of his African father.

▶◀▶◀

The media remained fearful of the regime and said little. In light of the unsavory conduct of one of its minions, the government found nothing instructive in perpetuating the story, which was fine with Elsa. As the pain was still raw, Elsa had no wish to relive it repeatedly in the gossip columns of the *Sunday Times*.

Now with a child to protect Elsa chose to avoid the spotlight and was content to return to the shadows. After all, it was prudent to remain invisible—as a white woman with a coloured child there was still no natural place for them in apartheid

South Africa. In this regard both Elsa and the authorities agreed, and so an accommodation was reached to the satisfaction of both parties: don't embarrass the regime and Elsa's family would be left alone. And fortunately an acquiescent press complied.

▶◀▶◀

The two intrinsic characteristics of the Jewish experience, both persecution and guilt, had been the *emet* ("truth") or the alpha and omega of the Firths' family history in South Africa. It began with Daniel's father's desperate flight from Lithuania to escape persecution in 1901, and it ended with Daniel's emigration from South Africa to alleviate his guilt in 1976.

For seventy-five years South Africa had been home to the Firth family. They had prospered and suffered, and prospered again. And now, with the Firths once again on the move, they and their descendants were again part of the great Jewish diaspora destined to be scattered to all four corners of the globe, though most trekked their way to distant lands such as Australia, the United States, England, and Israel.

▶◀▶◀

Daniel Gideon Firth surprised himself. He married Juliette despite his past failures in the matrimony department. Considering his suspect track record, Daniel was more surprised she accepted. For DGF the move to England had another happy incentive; he'd finally spend time with his two daughters from a previous marriage, who now lived there.

DGF held his tongue when offered the job to reorganize PolyGram in the UK, though the sting of ridicule still lingered from the harsh rejection he'd received earlier in the year. But in the end, only results mattered, and DGF began to replicate his strategy on the world's stage.

After a dramatic turnaround of the UK operation, he was appointed chief executive officer of the global PolyGram group—the first non-Hollander and non-German to head the company in its storied history. As his first act, DGF relocated PolyGram's global headquarters to neutral London, and once and for all eliminated the internecine rivalries and internal squabbling that had plagued the twin-headed Hamburg and Baarn HQs.

The new corporate head office was a few doors away from Clive of India's historical home in Berkeley Square. DGF adored the location, and swore that sometimes, above the hubbub of the busy metropolis, a nightingale could still be heard singing in the square—this a music man's tribute to Vera Lynn, the "Forces' Sweetheart" who selflessly inspired the Allied troops during the Second World War with her sweet song "A Nightingale Sang in Berkeley Square."

Under DGF's stewardship PolyGram NV became the largest record company on the planet, achieving annual sales of four billion dollars when he retired.

His sweetest year was 1989, when he took PolyGram public with an initial offering of thirty-five million shares valued at sixteen dollars each. DGF always felt the record industry had never been taken seriously, but when he rang the closing bell at the New York Stock Exchange after the successful offer, it confirmed the industry's legitimacy and a personal dream had come true.

In the same year—in a breathless talent sweep that extended across two continents and completed in only six weeks—DGF successfully acquired two iconic record labels, A&M and Island, for a combined seven hundred and thirty-two million dollars—a modest price to ensure PolyGram's future dominance in the global pop music markets.

In his later years Queen Beatrix of the Netherlands award-
ed Daniel Gideon Firth the *Order of Orange-Nassau* in recog-
nition and appreciation for the 'special merits he had earned
for society.'

So the timid boy from Johannesburg, shunned by his father,
harried at school, and outmaneuvered by his former wives, had
done just fine. Knowing his children were thriving, as were his
grandchildren, he and Juliette quietly retired to the tranquil village
of Shamley Green, Surrey. There they indulged in bracing strolls
through the hedgerows of the Surrey green belt, stopping at a
local pub for a ploughman's lunch or smoked salmon platter, as
their needs were now modest.

Music no longer played a role in either of their lives.

▶◀▶◀

By the time Little Simba turned eight years old, the edifice of
apartheid had begun to crack. In a gesture of goodwill (and in an
effort to buy time) then prime minister, P.W. Botha, and his
Nationalist Party government decided to repeal what they called
"petty apartheid" (though many felt there was nothing "petty"
about it) and in 1985 enacted the Immorality and Prohibition of
Mixed Marriages Amendment Act.

This neutered the provisions of the original punitive 1957 act
that had forbidden "unlawful racial intercourse" and "any immoral or indecent act" between a white person and a Bantu.
Though this did not affect the majority of the population,
symbolically it was a significant first step. And in an extraordinary breakthrough, any and all references that defined a human
being by color were specifically deleted from the new law.

It promised hope for the future and sent a clear signal that
institutional racism had begun to erode.

As for the dogged regime, it was the first tacit acknowledgment that it finally understood it had no right to stand between a woman and a man on the basis of color.

◄►◄►

They were nineteen and a half million strong. It took four days until the last person finally registered his vote. On 27 April, 1994, true freedom through democracy came to South Africa, and standing patiently in the long winding queue was Simba (he'd dropped the appellation "Little" as he was no longer *little* anymore, having just turned eighteen). His age and the nation's new circumstances permitted him to vote for the first time. This was a momentous occasion—a moment that most felt would never come in their lifetime.

A buzz of excitement rippled through the crowd as they sang and jived with joy.

Simba felt the reassuring squeeze of his hand—lovingly he looked across at the woman beside him and bristled with pride. Elsa, stately and beautiful as ever, gave him an encouraging smile. The passage of time had not aged his mother, just blessed her with the sagacity of experience, noted in the fine lines at the corners of her eyes.

Theirs was a tiny family of two, devoted to each other, and here they both stood on the threshold of history. Finally it was their turn. Stanwell Daniel Sidney "Simba" Marais placed his mark alongside the picture of Nelson Mandela and the black, green, and yellow colors of the ANC.

For the first time Simba's black heritage was as free as that of his white parentage.

Elsa cast her vote too. She paused a moment, as cultural tradition compelled her to select the current State President, F.W. de Klerk and his Nationalist Party. She looked about her and saw a parade of happy faces—one being her son—of all colors and stripes, and the spark of hope in their eyes for a new South Africa. With a sigh of release, Elsa added her mark alongside the image of Mr. Nelson Mandela.

**

Fourteen million blacks now had a voice in selecting their next government; and the whites were not disenfranchised, approximately three million of them participated in the electoral process as well.

Nelson Mandela received the clear majority of 62.6% for his African National Congress party. His predecessor, and now the newly elected second deputy president, F.W. de Klerk, earned 20.4% of the vote for the outgoing National Party, while Mangosuthu Buthelezi of the Zulu's Ikantha Freedom Party got 10.5%.

The devious hand of Die Broederbond was finally severed, and the shadowy manipulators of the past were nowhere to be seen.

The 1994 national election in the Republic of South Africa was deemed proper, and legally certified.

**

CHAPTER **THIRTY-TWO**

PRISONER NUMBER 46664, a Xhosa prince, became Africa's first *atribal* or nontribal black head of state. Mandela's Xhosa clan had expected that the winner would take all and salivated at the prospect—after all, this was the way tribal societies functioned—but they were to be disappointed.

Instead Nelson Mandela shunned the corrupting wisdom of typical African potentates, refusing to play the power game of exclusive patronage, promotion, and pandering to only those members of his tribe.

On 10 May 1994, at his inauguration as the first truly democratically elected leader of South Africa, Nelson Rolihlahla Mandela said this:

> *We have triumphed in the effort to implant hope in the breasts of the millions of our people. We enter into a covenant that we shall build the society in which all South Africans, both black and white, will be able to walk tall, without any fear in their hearts, assured of*

their inalienable rights to human dignity—a rainbow na-
tion at peace with itself and the world.

And he meant it. It became clear that Madiba would not coddle his own tribe at the expense of the nation. Mandela understood that to be president he must be more than the ANC's political hack, more than the Xhosa's paramount chief, more than a blacks-only leader—in short, he aspired to be a true statesman representing the needs of *all* South Africans.

But getting there had been difficult. After Mandela was released from prison and the prospect of overthrowing the whites neared, various tribes began jockeying for power, with the Zulu's IFP (Inkatha Freedom Party) being a prime mover. The threat of black-on-black civil war loomed.

With moral certainty, extraordinary grace, and well-honed humor—and the sharp mind of a litigator—Mandela settled these tribal fissures. But it didn't end there. Mandela hadn't forgotten Africa's only white tribe—the Afrikaner—and he wanted them to know they were still welcomed in their homeland.

Tata ("Father") understood that for South Africa to be truly free, the oppressed must be liberated, and the oppressors freed from their past. Thus began his personal crusade to face, not confront, those who'd torn apart his nation (and took away twenty-seven years of his freedom).

He visited the grave of Hendrik Verwoerd, an architect of apartheid, and met with the "Great Crocodile," the humorless P.W. Botha, South Africa's penultimate white head of state.

And then, in the green and gold colors of the Afrikaner's beloved Springboks, he famously attended his first rugby match. His presentation of the 1995 Rugby World Cup to the winning team's captain, the Boks' Francois Pienaar, healed the nation the moment the two men grasped hands in an emblematic hand-shake.

With these tangible gestures and more, Mandela set the world's newest democracy on the path of reconciliation. And after three hundred and forty years, white rule over the Dark Continent had finally ended, peacefully.

One wonders what would make a man, so tested, so forgiving. And what was it about the same man that made others so accepting of him? To most South Africans, he had been nothing more than a cypher, secreted away from the public eye—banned under the penalty of sedition. The mere mention of his message or the publication of his likeness resulted in imprisonment for the transgressor.

So for ten thousand days the man known as Nelson Mandela vanished from view, yet he was never forgotten, his name spoken in hushed tones in the townships. Overseas, however, his name was sung to the highest rooftops. On the occasion of Mandela's seventieth birthday, the 1988 Free Nelson Mandela concert at Wembley Stadium, London was a seminal moment. Eric Clapton, Sting, Dire Straits, Eurythmics, Bryan Adams, Whitney Houston, Stevie Wonder, and many others sang to Nelson Mandela's praises, as did some South African musicians, some in exile, including Mahlathini and the Mahotella Queens, Miriam Makeba, and Hugh Masakela. This was all wonderful, but would the jailed man be equal to the myth? It took two more years to find out.

In reflection, Mandela's forced removal from our midst onto that isolated Robben Island rock became a virtue. Why? Because he was a blank slate—we couldn't define or critique him by his daily deeds or his voting record, and so he came to us untainted when we celebrated his release on 11 February, 1990.

It was as if all those years hermetically sealed from the travails of daily life had a fortunate, though not intended (by his captors) consequence, because they had quarantined Mandela from tribal rivalries, corrupt business dealings, seedy politicking, the honey trap of women, and life's other temptations. The years away also sanitized his reputation—he entered prison as a "bad man, a terrorist, and a commie"—yet, when he was released twenty-seven years later he was regarded as a selfless martyr. None of this takes away from the remarkable grace, wisdom, fortitude, and generosity of spirit Nelson Mandela nurtured within himself during those difficult years of confinement. Those gifts were all of his making.

So an untarnished Mandela stepped out of Victor Verster Prison that day. Finally, he had arrived. Here was this hidden man, who from nowhere stepped into the light, and on whom we projected so much hope. And thankfully he delivered, becoming the gold standard for enlightened leadership in this modern age, in Africa and beyond.

><<

It must be acknowledged that Nelson Mandela was blessed with a courageous partner in South Africa's bloodless transition from white to black rule. For several decades Afrikanerdom had behaved badly, but in the person of their state president, F.W. de Klerk, Africa's last white leader, they found a measure of redemption.

De Klerk had at his disposal a potent army, an effective security apparatus, the means to lock Nelson Mandela away for life, and the committed *laager* mindset of his people as mechanisms to cling to power. Yet, at great personal risk, as many of his *volk* regarded him a traitor, he pragmatically negotiated himself and the Afrikaners out of power. This was an extraordinarily selfless and unlikely act from a true believer, unprecedented in the annals of modern governance, and unheard of in Africa's bloody past. As a statesman, though flawed, F.W. de Klerk proved to be truly "an enlightened one."

**

As I sit in my study writing these words the television is on in the background, keeping me company. It is December 5, 2013, a Thursday, a day I will now always remember: a news alert, immediately distressing but inevitable, as the reporter has just announced the death, at age ninety-five, of Nelson Mandela.

The confluence of circumstances and coincidences that led me to be writing about this exemplary human being, at this specific moment, is unfathomable. However, we all share in this great loss.

We are fortunate to have lived at a time when a person of such extraordinary wisdom, mercy, and humanity walked among us. Even today's youth treasure him—there's no so-called "generation gap" when it concerns Madiba; both my sons revere him and proudly wear T-shirts bearing his image (a gratifying counterpoint to all those years his likeness was banned).

On reflection, the only disappointment in Mandela's ascendancy to power was that it was so late in his life—he grasped the reins of responsibility at an age most men retire. This allowed us only a single-term presidency. Those five years were not enough to repair all the damage of the past; how we could all have benefited if a second term had indeed been possible.

But former prisoner Nelson Rolihlahla Mandela had no desire to become a sovereign: he relinquished the power voluntarily—so refreshing on a continent where provincial tyrants strive to rule forever.

But here I remain fearful (though I dearly hope to be proven wrong). Mandela was the nation's talisman—his very presence held the various peoples of South Africa on a rainbow path of dignity and equality, and by his noble example all tribal rivalries were set aside and all were welcomed at the table.

But now he's gone, I fear the quiet vow of loyalty to his vision of a united South Africa will be abrogated. With Mandela no longer living, lesser mortals will not feel bound by any allegiance to the "Father of the Nation"; instead, in a lust for power, they will once again unleash the tribal tensions that have forever plagued the continent. But a man is fragile, limited by the term of his life. His ideals, however, if merited deserve to remain in the consciousness of those left behind for all eternity. And Nelson Mandela's ideals were supreme. So as Tata takes his well-deserved rest with the ancients, it is hoped those who succeed him learn from his enlightened example, and avoid the pitfalls found on the dark path of the tribal divide.

However, for now we remain both hopeful and grateful. Nelson Mandela gave the nation he so revered one final gift. After forty years in the wilderness as a pariah among nations, South Africans now hold their heads up high due to the shining beacon of Tata's grace. We in turn are in his debt, and have a job to do to ensure his legacy lives on, by holding future leaders to the fine standards he set—to embrace all, and shun partisanship.

**

Now back to our story...

Alas, back in 1976, the prisoner #46664 was unable to reach out beyond his cell and protect Stanwell and Elsa within his rainbow embrace. However, Mandela's lasting legacy provides that a mixed-race love such as theirs will never again be subjected to official persecution.

In a nation where a prisoner became president, anything's possible; and through the virtue of Nelson Mandela's life, love across the color barrier will become accepted for what it is—simply love, to be neither judged nor condemned.

⋈⊲

CHAPTER **THIRTY-THREE**

WITH CRACKED, GRIMY NAILS he scratched the top of his head as he considered the best line of attack for the early morning raid. In the glow of the early sun, the glint of greed was reflected in his eyes, set close together and deep, overshadowed by his heavy brow. Tendrils of light began to wick between the branches and the leaves, and caught for a startling moment the dawn glow on dew-cloaked fruit.

It was daybreak and no one was about. The orange grove was still, the workers still asleep. The only evidence of any human presence was the stacked wooden crates stamped with the purple-inked "Outspan" logo. These oranges were destined for Europe, an exception to the antiapartheid trade embargo, as continentals yearned for out-of-season fresh fruit on their table.

The *bobbejaan* jutted out his prominent jaw with a twitch, then smelled the wind. In a fidget of doubt he scratched his backside; this was a solo venture, and it was his decision when to go. Momentarily the baboon closed his not-quite-human eyes—evaluating the risks versus the juicy rewards. Decision made. He reached for the lowest branch and swung himself up high.

He plucked an orange, momentarily inspected it, and then with startling malice plunged his razor-sharp canines into it. In the baboon's powerful jaws the citrus fruit disintegrated into crudely torn segments, leaving a sticky trail of juice trickling down his muzzle. Indifferently he wiped his chin with the back of his hand, licked it, and then reached for the next orange. This one the *bobbejaan* did not destroy, tucking it instead with his hairy right fist under his right armpit.

Now with his left hand, he grabbed another orange and secreted it in his left armpit. The baboon worked diligently, stealing one orange after another. Each orange he fastidiously tucked away, alternating between his left and right armpits. The primate swung feverishly from branch to branch, working at a breakneck pace until every last piece of fruit had been seized.

Then the *bobbejaan* paused. Irritated, he smacked his lips and sniffed the air. Then he snarled, showing his fighting fangs. He had heard the humans; the pickers were on the way. The yellow baboon scrambled down the denuded tree and dashed into the undergrowth, safe and satisfied.

The grove workers came to the tree; it was as if a giant had furiously shaken it bare. Just green foliage remained on its sparse trunk, and on the ground teemed hundreds of perfectly ripened oranges—not quite perfect. Many were split and needlessly bruised.

As for the all-conquering baboon and his loot, he had only two oranges remaining—one under each armpit. He'd refused to learn that as he reached for the next orange, the one already stowed within his armpit escaped. And each time he insatiably reached for more, the others dropped to the ground, until only two oranges remained.

In his greed the baboon had lost all reason, and as for the great effort he put into the endeavor, he had painfully little to show for it, except for the fruitless destruction and waste left in his wake.

As is said in Africa, "Look to nature for life's lessons and answers." And often these lessons learned are what *not* to do—otherwise we are condemned by our ignorance to repeat the same mistakes, again and again.

When Elsa first heard the *bobbejaan* tale she was a young girl balanced on her oupa's lap. She could still recall the old man sucking on the stem of his pipe, with the aroma of his buttered rum tobacco lingering in the air. Now it was her turn to share the story with Stanwell, her son.

Elsa was mindful that young should Stanwell truly understand the message behind the tale, for one day, beyond the future's horizon it would be Stanwell's turn to share Africa's wisdom with his own his children. As this was the manner of Africa—where life's most important lessons are not written down, but presented to future generations with the warmth of humanity's voice.

❈

AC**KNOW**LEDGMENTS

AT THE END it is all about family and friendship—the powerful bonds of blood and love that give life purpose.

My heartfelt gratitude to my sisters: resolute, brilliant, lovely, and talented women. It's due to them I was able to embody the female characters within this story with much empathy. All hail to the 'chief' Uncle Richard, who is the family's original storyteller and provided the impetus for me to tell mine. It's impractical to mention all my loving relatives, but for all the joy they bring to our family special kudos to one and all.

Their generosity of spirit is boundless, and I'm so grateful to Brett & Miranda Tollman for their care. Around their generous table we cherish and remember family: past, present, and future. To the brother I never had Philip Raphael Karakashian—thank you for your eternal friendship despite the great distance between us. And special thanks to Genevieve Karakashian for her thorough scrutiny of my penultimate draft. Your astute insights were invaluable, and I'm most grateful. As for my editor Savannah Vickers, and Malory S., thank you for the book's final polish.

My respect and thanks to Neil Farquharson, the most steadfast of friends and my guide for many of the safari scenes. For their unwavering support and friendship I'm glad to finally have an opportunity to acknowledge Chris Dunne, William Follett, The Gallo Family, Jon Leader, Monique Stephansen Adams, Norman Catherine, Joan Genender, Jeanne Mary Allen, The Healey's, Susan McRae, Keith Shaw, Julie & Wes Nichols, Jane & Raymond Wurwand, Mac Zlotnick, and Jeff Schechtman.

My loving gratitude to both my sons Nico and Derek for their patience—though never absent during writing I was at times distracted. It's my hope the two of you discover clues to your personal history—on a distant continent—among these pages. As for my "borrowed-daughter" McKenna, we are so fortunate to have found you. You've brought such joy to our lives.

Finally, this has been a solitary pursuit, but not a lonely one, thanks to my muse and most significant other, Erin Marshall. You have tirelessly proven my manuscript to be a cure for insomnia— and I love you for that, and so much more.

≈

FineWrites.blogspot.com

google.com/+MarkfineAuthor

facebook.com/mark.fine.writes

Twitter: @MarkFine_author

THE **END**

FINALE

"The demon of racialism, the aberrations of the Xhosa-Fingo feud, animosity that exists between the Zulus and Tongas, between the Basuthu and every other native must be buried and forgotten. We are one people, these divisions, these jealousies, are the cause of all our woes today."

Pixley ka Isaka Sem

≈

32799499R00212

Made in the USA
Lexington, KY
02 June 2014